It Ended with a Wedding

Book Three of
The Sea Glass Trilogy

Jane Ross Potter

ISBN: 9798371467096

Author photograph by Melissa Davidson
Cover design by Brandi Doane McCann at ebook-coverdesigns.com

Also by Jane Ross Potter

Fiction

Because It's There (2007 Indie Excellence Finalist)
Margaret's Mentor (Book One of *The Birsay Trilogy*)
Symbol Stones (Book Two of *The Birsay Trilogy*)
The Secret of Finlay Village (Book Three of *The Birsay Trilogy*)
Sharkbait
Seeking the Medicine Buddha
It Began with the Marbles (Book One of *The Sea Glass Trilogy*)
It Continued with the Cowries (Book Two of *The Sea Glass Trilogy*)
Frances vs. the Ice (short story)
A Year of Moments (short story)

Chapter 1

Attorney Diana Murray arrived at her Portland, Maine, law firm building at six o'clock in the morning on a late August weekday. She entered the locked front door using the keypad, hoping to get past the night guard without too long of a chat. She was on a mission; she disliked making the twenty-minute commute early in the morning, and wanted to be back in her car soon and heading home again.

The guard, a retired police officer, looked up from behind his desk at the back wall of the spacious, marble lobby. Only security lights were on this early and the space had a gloomy appearance, in contrast to the bright lights and mall-like feel it would have later, when the cafe and shops were open.

"First one in, Ms. Murray," he said, smiling and looking down to record her name on a pad of paper. He knew that law firm employees were tracked electronically each time they used their keycards to access a door, but he still kept to his old ways.

"Good morning, Bruce," Diana replied. She didn't see him often; she remembered that he preferred the first name for himself, but he'd declined to call her Diana, out of deference to her status as a senior attorney in the Martin & Sawyer firm. The firm at which her husband Hamish Murray was managing partner.

"Sorry, I can't stop today," she continued. "I have to get documents for a hearing this morning."

"I figured it was something important. You're not usually in this early."

"The kids, you know..." Diana muttered as she hurried past the guard and headed to a bank of elevators to the left of the desk. The documents she needed were in a file storage room in the basement and she debated going straight down, but instead she pressed the button for the fourth floor: she'd lock up her purse, get a cup of coffee, then tackle the file room.

1

In her mind, she was trying not to blame the file room clerks for her early morning trip to the office. She'd asked them two days earlier to find a folder of historic maps that had been used in one of her previous cases. As a member of the Environmental Law Group, Diana often handled disputes over land use and land ownership. But the night before, she'd received a text message that the file clerks couldn't fulfill her request: the maps were either missing or misfiled, and with thousands of folders in the basement, it could take days or weeks to go through each.

She exited the elevator and as she walked quietly through the deserted carpeted hallways, overhead lights came on automatically in succession. In her office, she locked her purse in her desk drawer: surely no one would steal it at this time of day, but the big office buildings of downtown Portland were sometimes being targeted by well-dressed thieves. They bypassed security by claiming to be clients or job applicants, and once inside, were rarely challenged. The firm employed a hundred and fifty people, so seeing a new face was not automatically a cause for concern.

Minutes later, armed with just a cup of coffee, she took the elevator back to the lobby level, then another elevator to the basement. That area was not all occupied by the law firm, hence the separate elevators. They prevented outsiders from getting to the law firm floors without at least being seen by the security guard during the night, or the receptionist during the day.

Most of the basement was taken up by a gym; as Diana passed the door, she felt her usual pang of guilt at being out of shape. One day, she vowed, she'd join the colleagues who managed to fit in a lunchtime workout. Mornings and evenings were out of the question, not with eight-year-old twins at home and a husband as busy as she was.

She accessed the file storage area with her keycard. She'd handled enough indoor air quality litigation to bring a mask with her: more than a few moments in the underground storage room would fill her lungs with paper dust, mold, and unwanted chemicals.

The door clicked shut behind her and locked automatically; overhead lights had come on as soon as she entered. Just inside the door, to the left, was a large worktable and a chair, over which was draped a denim jacket: one of the file clerks must have forgotten it, Diana figured.

Stacks of fresh accordion file folders sat on the table, all colors, waiting to be assigned to a particular case. Rolls of multicolored number and letter stickers sat next to the files. To the untrained eye they might look like something that belonged in a kindergarten, but Diana recognized them for what they were: building blocks for the complicated file coding system.

Each client was assigned a five-digit number, with the first two digits corresponding to the field of law (environmental, intellectual property, trusts and estates, etc.) and the remaining three digits were code for the client's name. These numbers were followed by a dash, followed in turn by another five-digit number unique to each case.

For most clients, the ten digits would cover all the information a file clerk or attorney needed to find a specific file. In a few fields, such as intellectual property, extra digits and letters added further details: a country code, or a number that linked one file to another. All these stickers were placed in order on a long tab that reached beyond the edge of the folder, making them easy to read on a shelf packed tight with files.

Knowing the code system wasn't enough for negotiating the filing system. Diana knew that the room was organized by area of law. Her area, environmental law, was near the door. The areas at the end of the alphabet, like Wills, were in shelving at the far end of the room.

Diana stood in the silent room and considered how to tackle her dilemma. She decided to start with the files where the maps should be, and she walked along the wide aisle leading from the door, looking at the labels on the ends of the wheeled mobile storage shelving to her right.

Just her luck, she realized, the shelf she needed to access was tight against both adjacent shelves, which meant struggling with the large black handles. They were the size of a car steering wheel, but with three arms and handholds at the end of each arm.

She stopped for a moment: the text from the file clerk had come in at seven o'clock the previous evening, at the end of his workday. If he'd been honest about searching for her maps, then that side aisle, between the rolling shelves, should be open. Unless someone had been down here during the night?

With most files stored electronically, the file room was mainly used now to house papers and items not amenable to scanning: large fold-out maps, estate documents with original signatures that had to be kept for posterity. And of course, the patent and trademark group, with their infringement cases that sometimes involved actual things: sneakers cut in half for the trademark litigation, and for patents, pieces of laboratory equipment or machinery that might be used as exhibits in the courtroom.

As she gathered her strength to tackle the handle and access the files she wanted to search, she remembered a partners' meeting when they'd debated installing manually-operated shelving, versus powered. In the end, the cost had been a determining factor. That, and the fact that the shelving would mainly be operated by the strong file clerks, not by multi-tasking lawyer-moms who rarely had time for the gym.

Her upper arms aching, she finally got the shelf to move a foot away from the adjoining one, but not enough for her to slip in between and search. She knew she should take the easier way out and walk further along the main aisle, then move the shelving units one at a time, but she'd seen the file clerks move five or six together as one rolling block, once inertia kicked in.

Flexing her hands a few times, she took hold of the handle again; imagining she was trying to loosen lug nuts to change a tire, she gave it all her strength. Suddenly the shelf deigned to cooperate, and in one quick move it traveled another two feet.

Diana wondered if a shelving unit down the row had been caught against something, like a box toppled from a high shelf; she'd check afterwards and put whatever it was on the work table for the file clerks to re-shelve. First, her maps. But even before that, she needed to adjust her mask, which had loosened during her fight with the shelf.

When she removed it, the next breath brought not just the familiar odor of the aging files: something else. Something unpleasant. Someone's abandoned take-out dinner, lingering in the air while the ventilation was on low during the night? She shook her head to dismiss the worry. That was not her problem. She quickly replaced the mask, found the maps she needed—why the file clerks hadn't found them, she couldn't imagine—and walked back from between the shelving.

She'd report the bad food smell to the night guard so he could instruct the office cleaning staff to deal with it first thing. But she had to at least retrieve whatever file box she'd crushed when the shelf suddenly moved. Leaving the maps on the worktable, she began walking along the sides of the shelving, moving each successive shelf to the right to close the gap.

By the fifth or sixth shelf, she was running out of patience and energy: all the aisles so far were empty, so where was the fallen file box? She turned one more handle to bring yet another aisle into view, then stared down. At first she couldn't make sense of the scene. Had a large box of clothing fallen over, was that it? But no, a person lay face down on the floor, motionless. A woman.

Chapter 2

Without her even being aware of it, Diana's brain immediately created a logical explanation for the sight. A busy young attorney, maybe finally at home and having a late dinner, receives a text that a partner needs a case reviewed for a client meeting the next morning. The file clerks are long gone, so the attorney comes in during the night, tired and annoyed; the file is on an upper shelf, and instead of searching around for a step-stool, she balances on the first shelf, stretches up with one arm while holding on with the other, loses her balance, and knocks herself out when she lands on the floor.

Instincts kicking in, Diana knelt quickly to try and rouse the woman. She knew not to move her, in case of a broken bone. But as she drew close, she realized something was wrong with that scenario. She felt the young woman's wrist, then her neck, but there was no pulse.

Now the full horror of what she'd done took over and she staggered backwards, away from what was really a body, no longer a young over-worked attorney. She automatically reached into her pocket for her cell phone, but it was in her purse, five floors up. She ran to the office phone mounted on the wall by the door, but a call to the front desk just rang out: Bruce must be getting coffee, or in the process of leaving if the day receptionist had arrived.

In tears now, she dialed an outside line and called her husband; he hadn't left home yet, not with the tasks of getting breakfast for their twins and making sure they had all their books and homework in their backpacks.

He picked up the phone on the fourth ring.

"Hello? Can I help you?"

"Hamish!" she cried, realizing the caller ID would only show the general office number. "It's me, Diana. Something terrible's happened! You have to come to the office!"

"Are you hurt?" he asked quickly.

She tried to explain the scene in the file room, fighting hard to control her panic. But even now, it didn't occur to her that the death could be anything that posed an ongoing threat.

"Diana, listen!" Hamish interrupted, his voice stern. "Get out of the file room *now*. Go to the lobby and tell the guard. I'll call for the police and an ambulance. The neighbors here are up, I saw them outside, so I'll take the twins over and I'll get to the office as soon as I can."

Diana mumbled her thanks. Breaking down into tears, she hung up. The stuffy room now seemed filled with the dead woman's presence, and the automatic lights suddenly switched off and plunged the room into darkness while she stood motionless by the phone. She took a step forward and triggered the lights to come on again.

With maps in one hand, she pulled the door open and took an elevator to the main floor. Bruce was back at his guard desk and she told him what she'd found. Not content to leave the emergency call to Hamish, Bruce also called the police.

Sick with dread, Diana sat on a bench by the lobby wall to catch her breath and wait. Had she *killed* someone, in her desperation to find a file? But now that she had a chance to process what she'd seen, and more importantly, what she'd felt, it dawned on her: the body had been cold, not just cooling. By forcing the shelves to move, Diana may have broken a bone or two, but she hadn't caused the death.

With that slight sense of relief, she focused on remembering the details: the police would arrive any minute and they'd have endless questions for her. After getting a piece of paper and a pen from Bruce, she took a few more deep breaths and began a list.

Before she'd left home that morning, she'd thrown on jeans and a sweatshirt, her hair tied back in a ponytail, and she'd not taken the time to apply any makeup. She'd expected to go home to shower, style her air, and put on a suit for the hearing; now she wished she'd done that before coming to the office.

Would the police take her seriously, dressed like she'd just woken up? Would they photograph her at the station, turning to the left and right while holding up a name and number card, horrible mug shots like in television crime dramas? Fighting her imagination, she tried to focus on the facts as she remembered them.

Item one on the list was the identity of the dead woman: Marnie Brent. Marnie, the young associate attorney who'd attended a holiday dinner at Diana's house not two years back; Marnie, whose hard work and enthusiasm marked her for early partnership. Diana felt her eyes fill with tears again.

How could that same young woman be lying *dead* in the law firm file room, her promising future already at an end? Ended, perhaps, because one of Diana's partners had been too disorganized to request the work from Marnie earlier in the day? That was a challenge for Hamish to handle, she decided.

She returned to her list. The odd smell, she made a note of that. And the fact that the night guard said Diana was the first one in: did that mean Marnie had been lying on the floor dead—dying—all night? Or had she arrived when the guard was on a quick break, making coffee?

Outwardly, the building security seemed good, but anyone with a keycard could watch through the front mezzanine windows, see the guard leave his post, then enter and be in an elevator before the guard returned. Not that Marnie would try to get in unnoticed, but it could have been unfortunate timing. If the guard had seen her arrive in the late evening or very early morning, surely he would have told Diana.

Then, she remembered, she was not factoring in the garage. Few attorneys who arrived at night would go to the bother of driving around the block to access the underground garage, with the effort of lowering and raising the car window to use the key reader, then taking an elevator to the lobby level, and another one to the office levels. Instead, they'd park outside on the nearby street and come in through the lobby.

But perhaps Marnie only planned to access the file room and had parked in the garage: if so, it's possible the guard had no idea she was there. Did he do rounds? Diana wondered. Maybe not these days, with security mainly based on the keycard system. She sighed, and, feeling selfish, wished that the lobby coffee shop would open soon.

Chapter 3

While Diana waited for Hamish and the police to arrive, another young associate who had attended Diana's dinner was three thousand miles away, across the Atlantic. That spring, Margaret Milford had traveled to Scotland to visit an ailing relative, but stayed on after the relative died, leaving her his house to clear.

Under the complex terms of the will, Margaret was entitled to keep the house, a beachfront cottage on the Fife coast, but only if she lived in it. Margaret had been able to put off the decision while she worked remotely and helped her boss, Hamish, to a successful and lucrative win for a major client.

That win had bought her a little more time in Scotland, and along the way she'd acquired a fiancé, Alistair Wright. He also lived in Portland and he worked as a private investigator there. But together and separately they'd found one thing after another to keep them on in Scotland.

With September looming and law firm work picking up after the usual summer hiatus, Margaret knew she and Alistair had to make a decision about where their careers, and their personal lives, were heading. But not right now: lunch first, then beachcombing. Dressed in jeans, a white cotton turtleneck, and a light blue cotton pullover, and with her thick red hair clipped back, she locked the door of her hotel room and walked down one flight of stairs to the dining room.

As a hotel guest, she had an assigned table next to a window with a view of a rocky shoreline, and beyond it, a channel of choppy gray water that separated two islands. The hotel was located on the island of Caraidsay, part of the Inner Hebridean group of islands on Scotland's west coast. The channel of water separated

Caraidsay from Caraidsay-Beag ("small Caraidsay"), but only at high tide; soon the tide would recede and reveal a tenuous rocky link between the two islands.

Margaret's schedule was governed by the tide, hence the late start to her day and the rare chance for a sit-down lunch, instead of wilted sandwiches on the other island. She glanced at the menu card that rested on a little wooden easel, but already knew what she would order: haddock and chips. That should keep her going for an afternoon of braving the weather, then tonight she'd sleep well and head to the ferry tomorrow.

After ordering her meal, she sipped a cup of tea and stared out at the view. The hotel, quite upscale she'd been surprised to find, was situated to take advantage of the location. Floor to ceiling windows on the south and west sides of the dining room gave views of the water and the nearby islands, weather permitting.

On the east-facing side of the building, the lounge/bar area had a large fireplace and looked out to the rocky interior landscape. In some Scottish Highland hotels and guest houses Margaret had visited, a room like that would have its share of mounted stag heads on the walls, lamps constructed from shed deer antlers, tartan fabric-covered sofas and chairs, and maybe even tartan carpeting.

In contrast, this hotel was allowing the scenery to speak for the Scottish location. Inside, apart from a few muted tartan blankets draped over sofa backs, it was all clean lines, light wood furniture, bamboo flooring, and decor and artwork by local artists. Margaret had examined the various paintings and collages on her first day at the hotel; the artwork was for sale, but she had so far resisted buying anything. She'd let her beachcombing finds be her souvenirs of this strange trip.

Three men strolled together across the grass outside the window where she sat. Oddly for the location, they were dressed in what she'd call business casual back home, not the hiking and outdoors look of most visitors to these remote

11

islands. One man was taller than the other two, and when he turned his head, Margaret had a moment of disorientation, for the face drew her back to Portland. No, she reminded herself, she wasn't on the Maine coast, so what was her fellow law firm associate Mark doing here?

She was tempted to go outside and say hello, but she didn't want to disturb what might be a business discussion. Instead, she refilled her teacup and thought about Mark. Their work didn't overlap at the office, with Mark mainly involved in environmental law cases. Yet, if her mother Jilly had had her way, Margaret would be dating Mark, or even better, engaged or married to him by now.

When Margaret began working at the law firm two years earlier, her mother had attended a meet and greet for the new lawyers and their families. Ever on the lookout for a match-making opportunity for her shy daughter, Jilly had singled out tall, handsome Mark for conversation. But unlike other associates who'd welcomed a chance to meet fellow new lawyers and the established partners at the firm, Margaret had hung back, her childhood stutter asserting itself in situations where she felt uneasy.

And so, to Jilly's disappointment, Margaret had declined to participate in her mother's casual chat with Mark, and the promising young man had wandered off to speak to other people.

Jilly didn't give up so easily. Three months later, Margaret had been invited to a holiday dinner at the home of the managing partner, Hamish Murray, and his wife Diana. Margaret hated the idea of a party, of being compared with four well-spoken, ambitious colleagues, but her mother had insisted.

In the end, Margaret had warmed up a little and found common ground with Hamish: both were afficionados of the English writer Dr. Samuel Johnson, although Dr. Johnson had been dead for more than two centuries. And just two weeks later, she'd found herself attending Christmas dinner at Hamish's house, this time the family dinner. Diana managed what Jilly had failed to do, match Margaret with someone to date.

That someone had been not Mark, but Henri, a charismatic young lawyer from France. Unfortunately, he decided to return to France the following year, leaving Margaret back where she'd started the previous year: shy, alone, and feeling like she didn't belong at the law firm.

She knew she'd changed since then: oddly enough, by spending the past few months in Scotland. Hamish and the partners had rewarded her with, to her, a huge bonus for her work on the major lawsuit. Bolstered by that external evidence of approval, of accomplishment, she'd learned to be more assertive, even offering personal advice to new friends she made in Scotland, and to top it off, she was engaged to Alistair.

With the sudden appearance of Mark, she imagined briefly what life would be like if Jilly's plan had worked and she was dating Mark, not Alistair. It took her only a moment to realize it would have been a mistake. Alistair's career as a private investigator was separate from Margaret's, with no real grounds for comparison. In contrast, the associates at the law firm were always comparing notes: who billed the most hours that month or year, who got bonuses, who was picked to work on high-profile cases, which partners invited you out to lunch or dinner.

Even though Margaret knew that, on paper anyway, she measured up when it came to hours and high-profile work, she knew she would always feel diminished in the presence of someone like Mark. She had a long way to go before she could match the confidence and outgoing personalities of her colleagues.

But, she realized, watching the three men head for the glass door into the dining room, now was as good a time as ever to start. The last time Mark had seen her in a social setting, if he even remembered, she'd been shy, stuttering,

13

mousy Margaret. She hated the thought of being returned, in his eyes, to that person, so she summoned her inner strength: just in time, for Mark was approaching her table, hand outstretched.

"Margaret! What a surprise, seeing you here!"

"I could say the same," she replied, standing up to shake his hand and be introduced to his two companions, one of whom was a junior lawyer at the firm. Then, using every ounce of courage, and not secretly hoping he'd decline, she added, "Would you like to join me for lunch?"

Chapter 4

Soon after Diana discovered the lifeless body of Marnie Brent in the basement file storage room, the towering mezzanine where she sat—the lobby below the office floors—had been transformed into a bustling scene. Police hurried about everywhere, inside and outside the front glass doors, with one officer specifically assigned to keep people out. To the left of the guard desk at the back of the lobby, police tape was drawn across the hallway leading to the elevators, barring access to the basement.

Dressed in jeans, a white shirt, and his navy law firm fleece jacket, his thick brown hair not as tidy as it usually was, Hamish sat next to Diana on a bench by the side wall. His arm was around her shoulders while he listened to her give a statement to a senior police officer; the officer had brought a chair from the guard's desk and she sat facing Diana.

Diana referred to the notes she'd hastily jotted while waiting for Hamish and the police to arrive, and she was trying to remember as many details as she could. She asked about going back to the file room to refresh her memory, but that was not possible.

"It's a, a *crime scene*?" she asked, almost in a whisper.

The officer tried to be reassuring.

"We don't know that yet. Until we rule it out, we have to avoid any additional contamination. But Diana, unless you're a really good actress and you'd actually been to the file room earlier than you said, your actions did not result in the death. Okay, maybe some extra physical damage, but even if you'd found her when you first went to the room just after six o'clock this morning, you couldn't have helped her. No one could have."

Diana smiled weakly, taking a little comfort in the officer's words.

"What do you think happened, officer?" Hamish asked. "As far as we knew, Marnie was in excellent health, so did she have a heart attack? Or an undiagnosed aneurism? But she's so young!"

The officer shook her head. "Honestly, we won't know until the autopsy is done and the medical examiner sees her medical records. We have her doctor's number from the emergency contacts in her wallet. That office isn't open yet but we've left messages."

"So," Diana ventured, "she could have been there for hours? I mean, overnight?"

"That's what it looks like," the officer replied. "The night guard said that no one came to the office building after eleven o'clock last night. A couple of people left, and they're at the top of our list to track down and question."

"You mean, in case someone in the firm attacked her? Oh, my God, is that what happened?" Diana turned to face Hamish. "Everyone's movements can be tracked, right, since the basement access and the file room are locked? Everyone needs their keycards to enter."

"Let's not get ahead of ourselves," the officer said. "As far as I understand, not everyone who goes to the basement is employed by your law firm. There's a gym and it's open until nine in the evening." She stopped and gestured around the lobby, with its imposing marble columns and photograph-lined walls. "The flower shop and the cafe both store supplies in the basement, so we need to speak to all those employees and managers."

"In case one of *them* killed Marnie?" Diana asked, incredulous.

Hamish took his arm from around Diana's shoulders and turned to face her. He adopted the tone he used for calming the twins when they were upset.

"Diana, dear, so far no one is suggesting she was murdered. I'm sure the police simply want to ask anyone who was in the basement if they saw anything. Maybe someone noticed Marnie there and could comment on her appearance. Maybe she didn't look well, or said something about not feeling well. Isn't that right, officer?"

The officer nodded, but didn't offer any further opinion about ruling out murder. If Diana noticed that, she didn't comment.

From where Hamish and Diana sat, it was easy to see what was happening outside on the sidewalk: people arriving for work and being turned away, worried looks on their faces, and the occasional person being allowed to enter. Now a door was opened by a uniformed officer and Hamish recognized the firm's head of personnel, Nancy Fields. She, like Diana, had dressed quickly and casually, in black pants, a dark green shirt, topped with a gray law firm logo fleece vest.

Hamish had great confidence in Nancy: despite being of retirement age, she chose to keep working, and her knowledge of the firm and its personnel and evolving policies stretched back decades.

First, Nancy asked if Diana was feeling all right; satisfied that Diana didn't need medical attention after the shock, she glanced around, looking for another chair. The officer who'd been questioning Diana relinquished hers and said she'd be back soon.

Nancy took her tablet from her shoulder bag and was poised to take notes. "Hamish," she began, "after you called me I sent out an eblast to all firm members and employees. I kept it simple, just that there was an incident and the office would be closed today and possibly longer. I spoke to one of the officers outside, and they said that if anyone absolutely needs access to documents, like for a court appearance today, they can come here and will be escorted to their own office or workroom. The police want to maintain the office space as much as it was last night as possible. I guess, to check for evidence of an intruder."

"Oh, no," Diana whispered, "so they really are thinking that Marnie was killed?"

Hamish stepped in again to reassure her. "Diana, think back to your law school criminal law training. All possible evidence has to be preserved to *rule out* foul play. If we wait until the autopsy is completed, and then learn Marnie was attacked, any evidence will be compromised if the firm is allowed to open today. You agree, right?"

Diana sighed deeply. "I guess. But what about the people who work in the cafe and the flower shop? And the gym? They won't get the eblast."

"It's fine," Nancy assured her. "I have the contact information for all their managers, in case something comes up that affects the whole building. And if any employees arrive early, they'll just have to be turned away at the entrance." She shook her head. "Although, not to be flippant, but it would be nice if the cafe could open at least. I left the house without having breakfast."

The police officer from earlier was back and overheard.

"It's not flippant, I've been thinking the same thing. I'd rather have the officers and staff be able to get coffee and food without leaving the premises. Can you, Ms. Fields, call the manager and say they can open up, as long as they don't need to access the basement? We'll talk to the employees when they arrive, and hopefully clear them from having been around here late last night."

"I expect you can," Hamish said. "The cafe normally closes at three in the afternoon, so I can't imagine any of them being here more than an hour or two after that."

They all looked up at the sound of the guard's voice; Diana felt sorry for him, having to stay on and answer questions when he would be more than ready to go home and sleep. Despite the fatigue, his voice carried through the mezzanine.

"Can everyone please move closer to the walls? The ambulance crew are on their way up."

To show respect, Hamish and Diana stood up, knowing full well what the request meant: Marnie's body was being moved. Diana was surprised for a moment; why not wheel the gurney to the garage and have the ambulance waiting there? But, perhaps, they were keeping the garage and the garage elevators sealed off to check for evidence.

The only other way out was through the mezzanine. Their backs to the nearest wall, they bowed their heads, Diana wanting to avoid any further reminder of the tragedy. The assembled officers and staff fell silent as someone released the tape barring entry to the elevator area, and soon two green-clad ambulance attendants came into view, one at each end of a rolling gurney, the body shrouded from view under thick black plastic.

After Marnie's body had been removed, the activity resumed. One of the crime scene technicians guided the police officer away from where Diana, Hamish, and Nancy stood. They all watched for an indication of relief on the officer's face, perhaps news that Marnie had died of natural causes.

But instead, the officer's face was grim when she returned to the group.

"The death is suspicious at this point. Diana, since you were the first on the scene, and your actions contributed to, well, to her current condition, we'll need you to give a full statement while it's fresh in your mind."

"Should... should I have a lawyer with me?" Diana asked. Her voice was weak and her face was so pale that Hamish took her back to the bench.

"Yes," he said gently, "not that you are guilty of anything, but I don't want you to face this alone. I'll make some calls." He looked up at the officer. "Can I be present for the questioning?"

"Sorry, sir, no. We'll need your wife to account for her movements last night and early this morning, and you may be questioned later to corroborate. You're free to go home, or if you want to stay here and deal with any issues that come up with employees gaining access to files, that's fine."

Hamish nodded, adding in his own mind the standard command in a crime investigation: *Don't leave town without letting us know.*

He watched in dismay as Diana followed the police officer to the front door and a waiting police cruiser. He just couldn't get his head around it: his own wife, needing a criminal lawyer?

Nancy touched his arm briefly. "It will be fine, Hamish. Surely you understand why they have to start with Diana. Look, there's the coffee shop manager arriving. Let's get some coffee and breakfast while we brainstorm. Worst case scenario, if Marnie *was* killed, we can discuss what cases she was working on for a start. And I can access the movements of people who used their keycards last night and early this morning."

She stopped to think for a moment, and Hamish felt grateful to her, admiring her take-charge approach and her focus on the practicalities, especially when his thoughts were focused on who would be the best lawyer to help Diana through this crisis.

Nancy continued, "The file room clerks work until seven in the evening, so I expect the death occurred after that. Otherwise, the idea that they went home knowing there was a body in the file room is too much to consider. Unless one of them is guilty? Oh, this is just horrible. They should be at the top of the list for questioning, but I'm sure the police will know that by now."

Hamish hesitated; would the police suspect gray-haired dependable Nancy, who he'd known for his whole career? Surely not. He nodded his head. "Yes, coffee, but first, I need to call someone to represent Diana during the questioning."

He took out his phone and made one of the most difficult phone calls of his life.

Chapter 5

Mark accepted Margaret's invitation to join her for lunch at the window table. The associate with him, Charlie Stevens, looked pleased to be included. The other man who'd been with them outside made his excuses and left them to enjoy their lunch.

Margaret had seen Charlie around the law firm and knew he was two years behind her, but so far they hadn't worked on any cases together. Charlie had worked at the firm during his law school summers, and simply continued on after graduation.

Although he was technically just starting his first year as a lawyer, he had some advantages over first-year associates who didn't have that familiarity. Margaret suddenly realized, *I'm now a third-year associate*, with the arrival of a new crop pushing her one more step up the ladder toward partnership. She felt almost giddy.

A waiter came by and took orders from Mark and Charlie, then Margaret sat back, sipping her tea and listening to the explanation of these Portland lawyers' presence in such a remote part of Scotland. She knew that Mark mainly worked with Hamish's wife Diana on environmental law cases and disputes, but surely he wouldn't be in Scotland in that capacity.

"It's to do with wind energy," Mark said. "Hamish has a client in Maine who's investing in wind energy projects, not just in the US, but in Europe. Charlie and I, we're here to assess the potential and advise on the investment."

Margaret felt a wave of annoyance: Hamish involved her in many of his cases, but this one was news to her. Was she being eased out, thanks to her extended stay in Scotland? Or maybe she was still riding the wave of the big win from earlier that summer. Not being included in this project, when she was already in Scotland, could be taken to mean either.

"Can you share any details?" she asked Mark. "Or is it all confidential at this stage?"

"I can share a little of it, but," he lowered his voice to a whisper and leaned forward in his chair, "later, not in the hotel."

Margaret saw Charlie nod his head in agreement, so she agreed to drop that topic for now and move to safer ground.

"Is this your first visit to Scotland, for both of you?" she asked.

"I've hiked up north," Mark said, "but this is Charlie's first visit. We flew to Glasgow, then a train to Oban, then a flight to this island, so he's only seen mainland Scotland through windows."

"The view from the air was great, when there was a break in the clouds, that is," Charlie added. "And I doubt I'll see much more on this trip. We're scheduled to fly back in two days." His eyes widened as he looked at Margaret. "But I'm so glad to have a chance to talk to you! I have to say, I envy what you've done from Scotland, I mean, helping get that victory for the plaintiffs in the workplace injury case during the summer."

Margaret smiled and thanked him. "It was interesting work. I didn't know much about the medical issues, but the case ended up being resolved on the basis of a conflict of interest. I was able to take a group of unrelated facts and put them together. It meant that Hamish had a strong case going into the mediation."

Charlie was still gazing at her, full of admiration. "You're kind of legendary among the first-years, to have a major win so soon out of law school. I hope I can work on a case with you. There's so much to learn that we don't get in school, all that dry caselaw reading. I know I'm new, but I'm already learning that some of the truth of these cases never gets into the decision, or anywhere in print. It's like we need a course on the practicalities."

"Charlie makes a good point," said Mark. "Margaret, maybe when you're back at the firm, you could present a lunchtime seminar and explain how you helped win that case."

Margaret smiled to herself: she couldn't reveal the truth to her fellow associates, no matter how much they wanted it. The "truth" was that she'd worked on the case from her temporary home in her inherited cottage on the coast of Fife. In her pj's some of the time. At first she didn't think she could work remotely from there, due to lack of internet access. But with Alistair's help, she'd managed to get online via a cable from an underground bunker.

With the settlement negotiation deadline looming, she'd hired three ambitious young people from the local town to weed through documents and do some creative research to try and discredit the medical experts that the opposing side had hired.

Separately, her then-boyfriend Alistair, using his PI skills, uncovered a document revealing a conflict of interest on the part of the defendant. But that document was a story about a Manhattan fund-raising event, published in a glossy fashion magazine: not a go-to source in a typical workplace injury case.

No, she couldn't share the details with the junior associates at the law firm; instead, she could put together a sanitized version that didn't mention untrained local Scots as research assistants, a secret wartime bunker, and a handsome PI, with all the legal work taking place in a remote Scottish seaside cottage. But being asked gave her ego a boost, and the idea, amazingly, did not fill her with dread as it would have a year before.

She looked up to see the waiter return with a tray of food, and soon conversation took second place to enjoying the meal while it was hot. She was glad to see that both Mark and Charlie were giving Scottish cuisine a try, each ordering a bowl of Cullen Skink, a rich fish soup that was more like a stew in this hotel's version. Now, if she could persuade them to try sticky toffee pudding for dessert, she'd have them hooked.

She enjoyed her fried haddock and chips, justifying the rich meal as providing the calories to spend the next few hours outdoors on the beach. So far, Mark and Charlie hadn't asked what she was doing on Caraidsay, so she was glad of the opportunity to think up a story that didn't focus on collecting cowrie shells, although that was in fact the main reason she was there.

Chapter 6

Before launching into her explanation of why she was on the island, Margaret decided to boost her own self-confidence and share a secret with her two colleagues. She took her phone out and scrolled through her photographs, then turned the phone so that they could see the screen.

"I've had kind of an exciting time in Scotland, on top of that big case with Hamish. This is a hoard of Pictish silver, from around seven hundred AD. It was hidden in the kitchen in the cottage I inherited. I took it all to a museum in Edinburgh and it's being evaluated. I don't know if you've heard the British term 'treasure trove' but that's what it is."

The two men stared at her, shocked. Mark finally recovered enough to ask, "Is that what you're doing out here on this island? Looking for more Pictish treasure?"

"No, I'm here on a project to help the prince, the man Hamish saved from drowning. It's an environmental coastal project." She stopped to see Charlie's eyes widen again in amazement.

"Royalty? *You* know someone in the royal family?"

She waved her hand in dismissal. "He's very down to earth. You haven't seen much of Scotland yet, but the prince's latest focus is on cleaning up the beaches. A lot of plastic is washed ashore, and there's litter from the increasing tourism up north especially. He's running a competition to reward people who pick up trash on the beaches. Some of the beaches are hard to get to, so as a bonus, he's also running a competition to find groatie buckies."

Watching the confusion on the two men's faces, she grinned. She retrieved a small plastic bag from her pack and placed it on the table; she carried a few for this very purpose—teaching. Mark picked up the bag and inspected the tiny shells inside.

"Wait, you mean cowries? I remember hiking on a beach on the east coast of Scotland, and one of the other people spent about an hour searching for them. She says that she tries to find one on every beach she visits."

"I'm not surprised," Margaret said. "Some people are obsessed with finding them. Not me," she added quickly, although that wasn't quite true.

She put the bag away. "Anyway, I got a hot tip from someone who'd vacationed here as a child. He claimed to have found thousands. Turns out he was right. I've collected a lot in the past two days, but now I'm focused on picking up trash. It's really disgusting how many little pieces of plastic and metal are mixed in with the small rocks and shale. Really, everywhere I've looked. The only way to remove it is by hand, one piece at a time. It will take decades to make these beaches pristine again."

Mark let out a groan. "Climate change will take care of that, right? From the little I've seen so far, some of these low-lying islands are basically doomed, or they'll at a minimum lose their beaches."

"And all that trash will be absorbed back in the sea, for the animals and fish to consume. It's so tragic." Charlie looked out to the sea, shaking his head.

The empty dishes had been cleared, and coffees and teas ordered, when a succession of pings reminded the three lawyers that the workday in Portland—five hours behind Scotland—was starting.

Margaret checked the time. "Look, I'm sorry but I have to get going soon. The small island over there, that's where I've been finding the shells and trash. You can see from the window that the tide is receding and I need to walk over and back while it's accessible. Maybe we can meet up for dinner..."

Mark and Charlie had their phones on the table and were reading the texts, alarmed looks on their faces, so Margaret fished hers out of her pack again. They all read, then looked up from the screens.

"What's going on?" Margaret glanced back and forth at her two companions. "The eblast says the office building is closed today, and perhaps tomorrow. I hope there isn't a fire!"

Mark was ahead of her, already placing a call to someone in Portland. He listened for a few moments, his face frozen in shock, then he sighed deeply and ended the call.

"I'm sorry to tell you both this, but Marnie Brent has died. That's all my friend knows so far."

"Oh my God! She must have died at work," Margaret cried. "If it was a car crash or something, they wouldn't close the office. Maybe, maybe she fell down a staircase? I don't think she was ill, was she?"

Mark shook his head. "She seemed perfectly healthy to me. But Margaret, if they're not letting people into the office, it must mean the death is suspicious, right?"

Margaret felt a shiver go through her body. "Well, there have been security problems lately, with outsiders trying to get in, the occasional theft of a wallet or cell phone or something. You think, um, you think maybe she saw someone stealing and they, I don't know, maybe knocked her over while they were trying to get away?"

"I'm sure that's it," said Charlie. "I can't bear the idea that she was intentionally killed, not by someone at the firm anyway."

They fell silent when Mark's phone pinged with a new text. He took his time reading through it. "It's from Hamish. He says that Diana won't be available today and maybe not tomorrow either, so I'll have to manage any urgent emails that come in for our cases. She's having all her emails forwarded to me."

Margaret gasped. "What does *Diana* have to do with it? I hope she isn't hurt! Maybe she's a witness? This is getting worse and worse."

She looked over to see the waiter approaching to take their dessert orders. Suddenly the idea of sticky toffee pudding seemed frivolous, and instead she asked for a selection of biscuits; she'd take them with her beachcombing. But that seemed frivolous too. Everything seemed frivolous in the face of poor Marnie's death.

Charlie asked quietly, "Did you both know her well? I didn't, since she was two years ahead of me. I didn't see her much during my summer clerkships."

Mark smiled sadly, thinking back. "She was among a sort of elite group when we were first-year associates. You'll learn this fall that Hamish, as managing partner, invites a small group of associates to his home before the holidays, and the associates have a festive dinner with Hamish and Diana and their children. The choice of associates is supposed to be random, but I suspect it has more to do with Hamish choosing people he'd like his kids to meet, and that he'd enjoy talking to. Him and Diana, I mean."

Margaret continued, "I was invited at the last minute when one of the chosen associates couldn't make it. I admit now, I was terrified. But the dinner turned out to be enjoyable."

"You and Hamish bonded over Samuel Johnson, as I remember," said Mark.

"Oh, don't remind me!" Margaret turned to Charlie. "I majored in English literature in college and I got a bit carried away studying Samuel Johnson. But I've moved on from that. Moved back a few centuries, that is. My new obsession is the Picts, after I found that silver in my kitchen."

Mark said he'd have to go back to his room and start checking for emails on Diana's cases. With a plan to gather for dinner that evening, Margaret left the table and headed up to her room to prepare for the afternoon.

Her enthusiasm for a few more hours of collecting shells and beach plastic had evaporated with the tragedy unfolding at her law firm in Portland, but she decided she'd do better to keep busy in the fresh air, than to hunker in her room, checking email every few minutes. There was nothing she could do to help alleviate whatever was going on three thousand miles away.

Chapter 7

Hamish and the personnel manager, Nancy, sat on high stools at the window counter in the lobby cafe. A police officer came in every so often accompanied by a law firm employee who'd requested access to a file or an exhibit in the office, and Hamish or Nancy would grant permission.

They both noticed that the employee would be told to don blue disposable gloves before being escorted up to the office-level floors. Although Hamish knew this was being done to avoid new fingerprints contaminating what could be a crime scene, the whole procedure made him uneasy.

In between interruptions, Hamish was chastising himself for the lapse in security, with Nancy seeking, unsuccessfully, to assure him that it was not his fault.

"But it *is* my fault, Nancy. Here I am, *managing partner* of the firm, ha ha, like I *managed* to do anything with the file room. Couldn't keep it safe from an intruder..."

"*If* that's what happened, Hamish," Nancy interrupted. "You can control a lot about the building security, but if someone is determined enough, they'll find a way. Plus, the hallway outside the file room is shared, and you can't control who's hired by the gym and the cafes and stores here, or when those people would be in the building."

"I know, what you say makes sense," Hamish conceded, "but I'm still responsible for what happens in law firm areas. The file room, I mean. Marnie should have been *safe* in there. My wife, oh God, what if she'd gone in there before Marnie, she could be the one going to the mor...the mor..."

Nancy placed a hand on his arm. "Yes, the morgue, but she isn't, right? She's safe. You must stop this self-blame, Hamish. Diana is fine, so don't let your imagination run wild, okay?"

He met Nancy's eyes. "I always thought of myself as a successful lawyer, a successful manager. Heck, I've been

29

reluctant to give up the position to someone else. I was arrogant enough to think no one could do a better job. That's me taught a lesson. A very *hard* lesson..."

He was distracted by a new text on his phone, from the criminal lawyer he'd contacted as soon as Diana had been taken away by the police. Relaxing his shoulders with relief, he read through the text, then gulped down the rest of his coffee.

"Kind of good news," he said to Nancy. "That was Norm Adler. He managed to persuade the police to question Diana at home instead of the station. He's asked me to meet him there. Are you okay here to handle things until I get back?"

"Sure, Hamish, take your time. It does sound like good news, if they aren't taking her into custody. I'm sure they'll find that she's done nothing wrong. I mean, nothing that made a difference in poor Marnie's, um, demise."

"Thanks, Nancy. I'll keep my phone on, so don't hesitate to call or text for anything."

With a quick word in the lobby to the officer in charge, Hamish left the building at a brisk walk, then broke into a run to his car parked across the street. For a normal workday he would have parked in the garage, but since access from the garage into the building was through the basement and the cordoned-off elevators, he'd had to leave it on the street, hoping not to get a ticket early in the day.

He reached his house in Falmouth Foreside twenty minutes later; a police cruiser was parked outside the house, and behind it, a brand new blue electric Mercedes. He just shook his head, thinking of the dual symbolism, wealth and environmental sensibility. It could only belong to his former classmate Norm, who had clearly done well for himself by specializing in criminal law. Some contrast to Mark's vegetable oil-powered car from two years earlier. But whatever happened, he knew he couldn't have chosen a better lawyer, for Diana's sake.

Hamish had been so focused on the flash car that he hadn't noticed Norm standing by the front door of the house, waiting for him. Despite the early start to his day, Norm was immaculately dressed in a navy suit, light blue shirt, and a navy and red striped tie. His face was tanned—all those hours on his yacht, Hamish knew—and his graying thick hair perfectly styled. *I guess*, Hamish thought, *when you drive a car like Norm's, you have to look the part.*

Hamish extended his hand in greeting as he walked along the front path, and the two men shook hands. Before Hamish could begin his expression of gratitude, Norm led him back along the path, away from the house.

Trying to temper his deep, booming courtroom voice, he said, "Hamish, I'm sorry but I can only help in a limited way. Since this is urgent, I'll sit in on Diana's interview with the police this morning. But if she is charged, God forbid, or if she gets called as a material witness, I'll have to step away."

Hamish looked at Norm in confusion. "I thought you told me earlier that you aren't very busy right now?"

"It's not that, Hamish. I ran a quick conflict check after you contacted me, and I'm afraid there was a hit on your firm. I could have represented Diana in her personal capacity, but since the incident, whatever it was, might involve others at your firm, there is potential for a conflict."

Hamish stared in disbelief. "I don't understand, Norm! I thought your firm only handled criminal cases. Who, or what, are you representing in a criminal matter involving my firm? As managing partner, what is it I don't know?"

Norm frowned and shook his head. "Sorry, Hamish, but you have to understand, that's all confidential. We'd better go in. I will do my best for Diana this morning, and if, after the police talk to her, she does need further counsel, I'm happy to recommend someone else."

"But Norm, I don't want second best," Hamish protested. They turned toward the front door. Hamish was deeply concerned about the idea of a criminal matter involving his firm, that he had not been told about, but for now, Diana had to be his entire focus.

Inside the house, the atmosphere was surprisingly relaxed, considering the circumstances. Three people were seated around the large wooden kitchen table: a uniformed police officer, a woman who Hamish guessed was a detective, and Diana.

She'd obviously been permitted to spend a few minutes preparing for the interview, with her hair styled, a dash of lipstick, and her gray pants suit that she normally reserved for court appearances. He knew she wore that suit when she needed the extra appearance of authority, and he was glad she was ready to assert herself, now that she was the one being questioned.

Then he felt his heart sink and he realized what was really going on: the police must have taken all the clothes Diana wore earlier, for forensics.

Norm handled the introductions, and asked that Hamish be allowed to sit in on the interview.

"Is that all right with you, Ms. Murray?" the detective asked Diana. From the introductions, Hamish now knew that she was a senior level officer named Clara Hibbard; her clothing mirrored Diana's, but instead of the pink shell blouse that Diana wore under her jacket, the detective wore a white high-neck shirt, with a turquoise pin at the throat. Her light brown hair was cut short, and she had a rather emotionless face, or perhaps that was from long practice at not showing her hand during witness interviews. But she had a ready smile, and seemed to want to put Diana at ease.

"Yes," Diana replied, "I'd like Hamish to be here."

Hamish and Norm helped themselves to coffee; Diana or someone had prepared a large pot, which sat warming on the stove. Once everyone was seated, the interview began. Hamish listened intently: he still didn't know in detail what Diana had experienced, what she'd seen, so he tried to stay calm and promised himself not to interject expressions of sympathy or reassurance.

Diana took a long sip of coffee, then leaned back and crossed her arms. Hamish knew it was a determined effort to maintain a level of control, of confidence. But it was also a front: how could she not be falling apart inside, having discovered the body of a young attorney she and Hamish had worked with for two years? A woman who, Hamish remembered with a physical pang, had attended a holiday dinner in the dining room next door, not even two years ago.

Before Diana had a chance to speak, Norm interjected, holding up a sheet of paper. "Ms. Murray prepared these notes immediately after the incident. Do you really need to make her relive what she saw? Can't you ask your questions based on her notes?"

Clara smiled; this seemed to be a scripted exchange for both parties. "I understand your concern, Norm, but Ms. Murray may remember details now that didn't seem important at the time."

"It's okay," Diana said. Now she leaned forward and placed her arms on the table, hands clasped. "I arrived at the office building at six o'clock this morning. Bruce was on duty, the night guard, and he knows me, although I'm rarely in so early. He said I was the first one in, which seemed reasonable to me. I took the elevator to the fourth floor. When the doors opened, the area was dark, but the lights came on automatically as I walked to my office. I locked my purse in my desk, then..."

Norm interrupted gently. "Diana, if you were the only one in, why did you feel the need to lock up your purse? Did something in the office make you nervous when you arrived, like maybe someone else was there?"

"No, it's habit. We've had occasional thefts, during the day I mean, by people who manage to get in posing as clients, so I automatically lock it up. Then I went to the coffee room on the same floor and made a cup of coffee. I went back down to the lobby and took a separate elevator to the basement.

33

That area was dark also but the lights came on automatically. I used my keycard to enter the file room. Same deal, lights came on automatically..."

Now Clara interrupted. "Ms. Murray, or maybe I should ask you, Mr. Murray, as managing partner, how long do the lights stay on after they've been triggered, I assume by movement?"

Diana looked to Hamish for an answer. "I don't know about the file room," he replied, "but in the office area, the hallway lights stay on for about half an hour. This is only during non-office hours. They're timed to go on for the day at eight o'clock in the morning, and off at seven o'clock at night."

"Okay," Clara said, "so assuming that the basement timing is similar, it means that no one had been in the basement or the file room for at least half an hour before Ms. Murray arrived?"

"That sounds correct," Hamish agreed.

"Also," Diana added, "remember, I said that according to Bruce, I was the first one in this morning, so it's possible no one had been there since the night before."

"Unless they stayed in the office all night," Clara countered.

Diana sighed. "I guess that's possible. Should I continue?"

Clara made notes in a small black notebook, then looked up and nodded.

After a few sips of coffee, Diana explained that she had been anxious—Norm wincing at that word—to find a set of maps that she needed for a mediation session that morning. A file clerk had texted her to say that the maps hadn't been located, so Diana had decided to double-check.

There was another diversion while Clara quizzed Diana and Hamish about the file clerks and their schedules, and took down their names for questioning. Diana's text from the clerk had come in just before seven the previous evening, which was consistent with the clerk keeping at the search until the end of his workday.

"So," Clara mused, "is it fair to say that you were not in a good mood when you entered the file room?"

"Wait, wait!" Norm cried, raising a hand, palm facing Clara. "Ms. Murray isn't a suspect at this point. I thought you were gathering facts, not trying to assess her frame of mind."

"It's fine, Norm," Diana assured him. "My mood did play into this, I admit it. I felt under pressure to find the maps. I'm supposed to be attending the mediation session I mentioned. It's between an elderly couple who want part of their property to be granted a conservation easement, permanent I mean, and their two adult children who expected to inherit the property as is, with rights to develop it in the future. The parents are in a care home and we had to make special arrangements for their comfort, and the children came up from Boston last night. So, yes, I was anxious! But anxious on behalf of the *family*. Anyway, I decided to have a look for the maps in the file folders where I thought they should be, in case the file clerks had searched in the wrong places."

She stopped to sip her coffee and try to calm down. Looking back and forth from the police officer to Clara, she asked, "Did either of you visit the file room this morning?"

Both shook their heads, so Diana asked Hamish to find a picture of the mobile shelving online and print copies. The group fell silent while Hamish did as Diana requested.

Chapter 8

Hamish soon returned to the kitchen and distributed copies of a photograph showing a row of ten shelving units, with the floor-level wheel track clearly visible. The end of each unit had the large three-prong handle for turning, to move the shelf unit. Of the ten units, four were tightly packed together with no space in between; there was a space between the fourth and fifth units, with a young man reaching up for a file, and the remaining units were also tightly packed together.

Using the picture, Diana explained about her difficulty in moving the shelving, and being too impatient to move the units one shelf at a time, instead using all her strength to roll four or five at once. She fought back tears, remembering her relief when the apparently stuck shelf down the row finally gave way, and her assumption that a file box had been on the floor between two of the units.

She stopped while Clara studied the picture, and waited for any questions. When none were forthcoming, Diana added, softly, "I never imagined that there would be a person between the shelving. Not with the lights off when I got to the file room, and believing I was the first one in the office this morning."

Now Clara re-read Diana's notes, making sure nothing had been omitted so far. "Your notes say you did find the maps, just where they should be. You placed them on the table by the door, then walked along the ends of the shelving to find and pick up whatever had obstructed the shelves earlier?"

"Yes, but I just remembered something. I was so focused before on explaining the mechanics of the shelving. I didn't mention that I usually wear a mask when I'm working around old files and papers, especially in an enclosed space like the file room. And the ventilation is turned down at night.

"Anyway, at one point, maybe just before I found the maps, I took my mask off to readjust it. I noticed something, I guess I would describe it as an unpleasant smell. I just assumed someone, probably a file clerk, had brought in a take-out meal, and maybe left food in the trash or sitting on a work surface. I made a mental note to pass on that information so that the day cleaners could track it down."

Clara nodded her head. "The officers who searched the file room found a container of congealed Thai noodles and chicken. That's been taken away for fingerprints and to determine when and where it was purchased."

"I guess that's some relief. Even if there was evidence of a recent meal, I really had no reason to suspect that anyone was lying on the floor between the shelf units."

She finished the story, explaining that when she wheeled aside the last shelving unit that she touched, she first thought it was a pile of clothes, then quickly realized it was a person, Marnie. But dressed in jeans and a tee shirt, like she'd either changed into casual clothes after work, or had gone home and come back.

Marnie had no pulse and was cold, so Diana withdrew, called the security guard from the basement but got no answer, called Hamish, then went up to the lobby.

"Is there a particular reason you didn't call the police from the file room?" Clara asked.

"If Marnie had been alive, then of course, I would have called an ambulance immediately. But since she wasn't, I decided to call the security guard. I assumed she'd fallen and hit her head while retrieving a file. But he didn't pick up, so I called Hamish."

"May I say something?" Hamish asked, and Clara told him to go ahead.

"When Diana called me, I was very concerned for her safety. With a body in the file room, and no explanation at that point, I had to imagine the worst, I mean, that Marnie had been attacked and the perpetrator might still be there. That's why I instructed Diana to get out of the file room immediately and go to the lobby, where the security guard was."

Clara took a deep breath, sighing a few times as she tapped her pen on the table. Finally, she said, "Yes, the security guard. He's being questioned now. Really, everyone has to be a suspect at this point, until we have more information about the cause of death."

Diana was having difficulty holding back tears, so Norm spoke up.

"I think Ms. Murray has told you all she can at this point, Clara. Once you know how poor Marnie died, maybe it will be material to learn exactly what kind of pressure might have been applied to the body by the shelving, and for how long. That should help the medical examiner distinguish damage that occurred before and after death."

Clara glanced at Diana, then addressed Norm. "I agree. If Ms. Brent, Marnie, died of natural causes, like a stroke or a burst aneurism or heart arrhythmia, or if she fell, maybe from climbing to reach an upper shelf, then post-death injuries will not need to be factored in."

The group stood up, and Clara thanked Diana for her cooperation. "I'll be in touch as soon as there's any new information. It probably won't be until after the autopsy. But until then, I'm sorry but the office will have to stay closed, with officers accompanying anyone who requires access."

When Clara and the officer were gone, Norm prepared to take his leave as well.

"I'm so glad you're here to represent me," Diana said, shaking his hand.

"I'm sure it will be resolved with the autopsy, an accidental death from falling while reaching for a file. It's tragic for the young woman, but from what you've described, Diana, you should feel confident that you had nothing to do with her death."

As Hamish closed the door behind Norm, he couldn't decide whether to tell Diana that Norm, in fact, could not represent her if the case went forward. But she seemed to take comfort from Norm's help so far, so he decided not to mention it. He hoped and prayed that poor Marnie had died of natural causes, or an accidental fall, and that Diana would not have to recreate the scene over and over for the police, or worse, in a witness box in court.

Chapter 9

In the kitchen, Hamish watched as Diana poured coffee from the still-warm pot into her travel mug.

"Are you taking that upstairs?" he asked. She often used the travel mug in her second-floor home office, to save frequent trips to the kitchen for refills.

"No." She pointed to the wall clock. "The hearing is in an hour. I want to get there in time to chat with the clients before it starts."

"Diana! You've had a traumatic morning. Please, let someone else handle the negotiations so you can rest."

She turned to face him. "I would, if you hadn't poached the only associate who's up to speed on the case."

Hamish felt his face redden. Diana was right, he had effectively "poached" Mark, the associate attorney who Diana had carefully mentored and trained in the intricacies of her environmental law cases. Hamish had taken advantage of that training and sent Mark to Scotland, with an assignment to assess the potential for a project to be financed by one of Hamish's clients.

Mark was only supposed to be gone for three days, and although Diana had approved of the short time away from the office, Hamish didn't remind her. No one could have foreseen the morning's tragedy.

In an effort to mitigate the problem he'd caused for Diana, he offered to handle the negotiations in her place.

"Really, Hamish? I know you're a great lawyer, but you can't talk with authority on conservancy easements, and you don't have the long history of getting to this point with skittish clients."

She softened her voice, smiling. "I appreciate the offer, don't get me wrong, but it will do me good to get out of the house and carry on with my day's schedule. I hate to be morbid, especially after this morning, but the property owners, the elderly couple, we've got to get the documents signed while they're both legally capable. Otherwise it will mean bringing in someone to represent their estate, get them to sign over power of attorney..."

Hamish held up his hands. "Okay, okay, you've convinced me, but on one condition. I drive you there, wait for you, and bring you home."

"All right." Diana finished filling her travel mug. "And as your reward, you can sit in on the negotiations. Who knows, maybe having a senior partner on my clients' side of the table will strengthen our position."

Hamish dashed upstairs to put on a suit and tie, then he met Diana at the front door.

"No good deed goes unpunished," he muttered to himself.

Diana laughed, despite the solemnity of the day. "I prefer to think of it as a positive aspect. I just realized you *have* to drive me. My car is still parked downtown and my purse is in my desk drawer. I only got into the house because my keys were in my pocket when I went down to the file room."

With Hamish promising to retrieve her car and purse later, they left the house. Given the strict daytime parking rules, he just hoped her car wouldn't be clamped or towed by then.

Hamish had parked his car beyond Norm's and was surprised to see Norm's car still there, with a tell-tale trail of smoke spiraling up from the driver's side window. Hamish handed Diana the car keys and asked her to wait for him in his car.

"You'd better not try to bum a cigarette off him," she said over her shoulder.

Hamish stopped by Norm's open window and made a show of batting away the smoke from the cigarette that dangled from Norm's hand, just inside the car.

"You should quit," Hamish told him. "I did, almost two years ago. Best thing I ever accomplished."

41

In deference to Hamish, Norm extinguished the half-finished cigarette in the ashtray, which Hamish noticed was full of butts. An incongruity, he thought—an electric car with an ashtray.

"If you had my clients," Norm explained, "you might feel otherwise. The smoking breaks during trials and hearings are where half the action takes place. But I can't stand there eavesdropping without smoking myself."

You're not at a hearing or trial now, Hamish almost said, but he held off, and instead asked, "Norm, pretend I have a cigarette too and drop a hint, please? Tell me if the criminal matter you alluded to at my firm involves a client or an employee. I need to know where to start."

Norm responded by pressing the ignition button, and soundlessly, the electric car came to life. His parting words as he began closing the tinted window on Hamish's face were, "Both, Hamish. Both."

Feeling like catastrophe loomed from every direction, Hamish watched the car glide away, silent as Norm's boat in the Portland marina. He continued on to where Diana was waiting for him in the car.

"Anything helpful?" she asked.

"No." Then he smiled at her, trying to lighten the mood. He held both hands open. "Not even a cigarette. With all that money, the guy's such a miser."

But, Hamish realized as he drove away, heading for the care home where Diana's elderly clients lived, Norm had thrown him a crumb. He began plotting how to solve this dilemma: a criminal matter involving both a client and an employee? Maybe the IT department could do some sophisticated cross-checking between the two.

However, until the cause of Marnie's death was known, Hamish had to let it rest and not contact anyone who might be implicated. Had Marnie died because of this mysterious criminal matter? Only time would tell.

Chapter 10

In her hotel room after lunch, Margaret prepared her pack and headed out for the afternoon trip to the tidal island. She was desperate to learn what had happened to Marnie, but at the same time, prayed that it had been quick and painless, like a stroke or heart attack so sudden that Marnie wouldn't have suffered. Marnie, a young woman of Margaret's age! All the more incentive to make the best of each day. Although, whether gathering groatie buckies and trash on a remote Scottish beach was the best use of a lawyer's day was open for debate, she knew.

But she took comfort in the knowledge that this was her last day of frivolity. Tomorrow, she'd take the afternoon ferry to Oban on the west coast of Scotland, spend one night at a B&B, then catch a train south to Glasgow and another northeast to St. Andrews, where Alistair would collect her by car that evening at the Leuchars train station. It meant a long day of train travel, but as long as the weather held, the views would be enjoyable.

Beyond the hotel, on the dining room side, a long series of steps had been cut into the cliff behind the beach. They led down to the shoreline, now exposed by the low tide. She was glad the weather had been dry recently, because the last few seaweed-covered steps could be slippery, either from waves or from rain.

As Margaret crossed the causeway, she remembered first learning about the tidal island from Richard Wilson, a retired police officer in the town of Kilvellie-by-the-Sea, just north of Dundee. He'd visited as a child and teenager, decades earlier, and he'd told her about spending up to eight hours out on the island.

Margaret wondered if he was remembering correctly. This was her third daily walk to the island, and from her observations, and consulting the "safe crossing" timetable in the hotel lobby, five hours seemed to be the maximum one could spend on the island, before water of the next high tide began covering the path again.

Maybe young Richard and his parents had taken a chance and crossed in ankle-deep water? But that seemed so risky, and he hadn't mentioned it. More likely, she thought, the reduced safe time on the island was thanks to climate change.

From halfway across the path, with gentle retreating waves lapping against both sides, she stopped to look back at the hotel. Set well above the reach of waves and rising sea level, the boxy, modern wooden structure faced west, with a mixed view of islands, water channels, and ocean far beyond. From this perspective, it was obvious that the dining room and upstairs rooms had been carefully angled for the views and to catch the sun setting over the nearby islands.

The hotel was built on sloping ground. The main floor was one level, with the dining room elevated above the land and supported by black metal poles. On arrival, she'd been assured of the safety, and was told that the design helped protect the building from the occasional high waves and surf generated by fierce winter storms. The hotel had lasted through two winters, so she assumed the architects knew what they were doing.

It was such a contrast to another hotel she knew well, the Templeton Grand Hotel in her temporary home of Finlay, in Fife. That hotel, much older, fronted a beach, and every year the waves and high tides damaged the retaining boulders and cement, necessitating annual repairs. Not to mention the constant battle with mold, from water seeping in through the edges of windows and in cracks in the outer wall. Here, the hotel's architects had made a seemingly smart decision to literally rise above the ocean's power.

Looking down at the shore below the hotel, she noticed for the first time a wooden rowboat beached on the rocks. A rope connected the prow to a rusted iron ring driven into the rock face, and another rope led away from the rocks and slipped below the water's surface. Unlike the hotel above, the weather had taken a toll on the little craft, its graying white paint peeling, and the name almost weathered away.

Margaret realized the boat must be an emergency rescue vessel for anyone who mis-timed their visit to the tidal island. She would look for the rope emerging from the water at the other side of the channel. Turning carefully on the slippery rocks underfoot, she resumed her walk and soon reached the tidal island.

On this, her third visit, she knew exactly where to find her quarry: a narrow section of west-facing beach nestled between two rock outcrops that reached into the water. On her first day, she'd worn Wellington boots and waded into the clear shallow water when the tide was at its lowest. Bending over and looking down, moving seaweed out of the way, she'd identified what she had learned was good groatie buckie environment.

She'd even seen a number of the little cowries moving around. Why so many of them died and washed ashore, leaving the shells for her to collect, was a mystery. For all she knew, these shells could have accumulated over many decades or longer.

But sadly, on close inspection, this seemingly pristine patch of shore also held decades of man-made detritus, in the form of soda and beer can pop-tops and other metal pieces, and plastic of all colors and sizes—disposable cigarette lighters were high on the list.

As she picked up her cowrie shells, Margaret was also gathering this material, partly to clean up the beach, and also to help document areas that needed targeted clean-up efforts in future. At least the lighters were brightly colored and easy to fish out from among the small rocks.

During her previous two beach visits, she'd deposited the trash in designated containers that would be picked up by boat, when the prince's beach clean-up competition ended a few weeks later. They were set far back from the high-tide line, in hopes that the trash wouldn't all wash away again before the next pick-up.

She chose a spot on the shoreline where she hadn't collected before, then extracted her supplies and equipment from her pack: a waterproof foam seat, several clear plastic sandwich bags, and a bucket to hold the trash. She sat down, took a few sips of tea, munched a biscuit from the dining room, noted the time to make sure she didn't get trapped by the waves, and got to work.

Chapter 11

Following the family mediation at the care home, Hamish and Diana headed home separately, within minutes of each other. Hamish had driven Diana to the office where she'd waited for him by her car, while he went into the still-restricted lobby area. Nancy and a police officer retrieved Diana's purse for Hamish, then he brought it to Diana.

Alone now in her own car, as Diana drove home she felt like the day had been one of the best of her life, professionally, but definitely the worst personally. It was impossible to reconcile the two and achieve a stable frame of mind. The mediation was a complete victory for her clients, and in the end, it seemed that their adult children had come around to the benefits of placing a conservation easement on the land adjoining the parents' home.

Diana had worried that a permanent rift would develop between the elderly parents and the ambitious siblings, their heads filled with visions of a towering condo building, but all seemed to be well. She was glad. Her twins, and Hamish's teenage children from his previous marriage, were all still young, and she hated the idea that, at some future time, she and Hamish might be forced to consult a mediator over a real estate disagreement with the children.

All thoughts flew from her mind as she turned into their street twenty minutes later: a police car sat outside their house. She felt a wave of nausea: *had* Marnie been murdered? Was Diana in trouble for disturbing a crime scene? Was she even a suspect, accused of lying about her arrival time at the office?

She'd been looking forward to opening a bottle of wine and having time to decompress with Hamish, but obviously that would have to wait. She parked her car nearby, waited until Hamish arrived and parked his car, then, hand in hand, they silently approached the house.

47

Hamish had arranged for the twins, the two children who lived at home with them, to be collected from school by a neighbor and sleep over there, to avoid witnessing any police activity in their own home. Let alone, their mother being arrested.

Soon the same group of people from the morning, minus Norm, the criminal lawyer, sat around the kitchen table. The detective, Clara, had offered to brew coffee or make tea while Hamish and Diana took a few minutes to change clothes, and Diana welcomed the chance to calm herself before facing whatever came next. She and Hamish soon joined the detective and police officer at the table, and gratefully accepted hot mugs of strong black tea.

They both listened while the detective read from her tablet. After a moment, Hamish exclaimed, struggling to comprehend the horror, "That's, that's just sickening. My God, poor Marnie. But at least it would have been sudden, right? She must have fallen against a shelf?"

Atlanto-occipital dislocation was the initial diagnosis, otherwise known as ligamentous separation of the spinal column from the skull base. Most cases were fatal, according to the medical examiner who was handling Marnie's death.

"*Is* that what happened?" Diana asked, picking up on Hamish's question. "She fell against a shelf?"

Clara took a deep breath and put her tablet to the side.

"Unfortunately, we know the *physical* cause of her death, but not the legal cause, the proximal cause. We're waiting on toxicology, in case she had something in her system that would have made her unsteady or disoriented. The medical examiner went to the file room himself and looked at the various possibilities. According to him, the blow to her neck is consistent with coming into contact with the edge of the metal shelving in the aisle where she was found. But he can't rule out someone using a piece of that same shelving to deliver the blow that killed her. I was there too, and I could see that there's unused shelving stacked against one wall."

48

"Yes," Hamish explained, "as more files are scanned and digitized, we've cut down on how much shelving the firm needs. I'm not surprised to hear that there's loose dismantled shelving in the area."

Diana sipped her tea, fighting down the panic of not knowing if she'd done something to ruin the crime scene, to prevent learning what had really happened. Now she wondered if she should have a lawyer with her after all, but Clara hadn't suggested that this was a formal interview.

"What's your conclusion?" she asked Clara. "I still can't believe it, but is there a chance she was killed, I mean, murdered?"

"As lawyers, you're going to hate this answer." Clara looked back and forth at Hamish and Diana. "The medical examiner said that if he was asked in court, he'd say there was a fifty percent chance she fell against the shelving, and by some horrendous piece of bad luck, the edge caught her upper spine just at the point where she probably wouldn't survive the injury. There's also a fifty percent chance that someone used a piece of shelving as a weapon and achieved the same result."

She stopped to let this news sink in: instead of giving them information they could use, she'd made the situation even more uncertain.

Hamish reacted first. "That doesn't make sense! What are the chances that some random person, I don't know, maybe a crazed killer who got into the file room, would hit her in that exact place?"

"That's really unanswerable at this point, I'm afraid," Clara replied. "I can imagine someone, most likely a thief who'd gotten in, grabbing a piece of shelving and hitting Marnie over the head, maybe to knock her out while they escaped. But to hit her with almost surgical precision?"

She sighed deeply. "I don't know, Hamish. We were really counting on the medical examiner for an answer, one way or another."

"So what next?" Hamish asked after sharing a glance with Diana. "I hate to be insensitive toward Marnie, but we need to get the office open again and let people return to work. Most can work remotely, but it would mean rescheduling meetings and client visits, or arranging for videocalls instead. Do you have *any* timeframe to give us?"

"I completely understand. Here's my dilemma. If there's a fifty percent chance Marnie was killed deliberately, then at this point we can't rule out anyone who works at your firm, or anyone who accesses the basement level. I saw the underground garage, Hamish. Do clients park there too?"

"Yes, they do. And they would pass the file room door to get the elevator to the lobby. So really, any member of the public could have done this, right?"

Clara shook her head. "I don't think so. The nature of the injury makes me think that someone knew what they were doing. Someone who's studied martial arts maybe, or someone with medical training, who knows how the spinal cord is put together, and the vulnerable regions. To me, that's inconsistent with a thief who Marnie happened to stumble on in the file room."

"So how *are* the police going to solve this?" Diana asked. "Am I in trouble for whatever the shelving unit did to her body, I mean, after her death?"

"No, Diana. At worst, by forcing the units along, you may have disturbed some evidence that a perpetrator could have left behind. I don't know, maybe Miss Marple's tell-tale button from a jacket. Sorry, I don't mean to be funny. As far as we know, no one entered the file room between the time you found Marnie and the time the police arrived. At least, that's what we know from the keycard access records from this morning. Any physical evidence, like a button or a shoe print, should be there from when she was attacked. If she was attacked."

They fell silent, until Hamish spoke up.

"Clara, what about the offices upstairs from the file room?"

"I'll get back to you later tonight so you'll know for the morning. I think you should be able to open tomorrow, as long as the file room is kept completely off-limits. If someone absolutely has to have a file from there, we'll have a police officer retrieve it."

"Clara, what are you going to do?" Diana asked next. "I mean, to figure out what side of the line. Which fifty percent to choose."

"This is another answer you won't like, but I don't know what more the police can do at the moment. We have to move from physical evidence to motive. What was Marnie doing in the file room around midnight, which is when she's likely to have died? What cases was she working on? Or was it personal? Does, or did, someone in the office have a grudge against her, or consider her a threat? Maybe a romantic entanglement gone wrong?"

Clara held up her hands and shrugged her shoulders. "The body can tell us none of this. Only people who knew her can provide clues. And as a detective just learning about your firm, I need your help in choosing where to start, who among your hundred and fifty employees to question. If it even was an employee who did this terrible deed. I mean, if it wasn't just a tragic fall. Anyway, my suggestion will be, once I clear it with the boss, to let you open the office again. We'll put out an appeal among all your employees for anyone to come forward with information that could help us. Completely confidential, of course."

"If it is work-related," Hamish suggested, "maybe it would help to know what file or files she was looking at when she died." He turned to Diana. "Did you happen to see what section she was in, like what area of law?"

"No, I was just shocked at seeing her lying there, and having that nightmare of thinking I'd hurt her. But if Clara could have someone take photographs of the files on both sides of the shelving where she was found, that might help. Photographs of the client numbers at the ends of the files, I mean. The files themselves don't have to be removed or touched."

"I understand," Clara said. "I noticed in the file room, you use multicolored number and letter tabs that stick out. Sure, I'll call after we're done here and get that started, then I'll have the photographs emailed to you both."

Clara placed her notebook in her jacket pocket, then asked if Hamish and Diana had any other questions.

"There are endless questions," Diana said as she stood up. "But no answers it seems. Sorry, Clara, I know you and your team are doing your best."

"I'll rely on both of you to talk it over and think about who in the firm might have had any reason at all to hurt Marnie. My gut, and I know that's not professional of me, but still, my gut tells me this wasn't a random attack or a panicked reaction by an intruder caught stealing."

"And there's nothing worth stealing in the file room!" Diana insisted. "The file clerks don't even have a computer down there. It's all centralized. When someone wants a file, a clerk will retrieve it from the shelf, scan it out with a hand-held device, and put it in a cart to bring upstairs in the next file run."

With that, Clara took her leave, and Diana and Hamish could finally sit together with wine and make a start on processing the day.

Hamish's mind couldn't let go of something Diana said, that there was nothing worth stealing in the file room.

In fact, there *was* plenty worth stealing, for the right recipient: information, trade secrets, intellectual property. He already had a sickening feeling, from Diana's description of where Marnie was found, that those nearby shelves were heavy with secrets of value to any number of individuals and companies, or even foreign governments. But most of those secrets were old, or were publicly available in patents and no longer secret. Why now? Why Marnie?

And with everyone at the firm a potential suspect, according to Clara, Hamish had no one to turn to: he and Diana would have to be each other's sounding board.

If only Alistair Wright, Hamish's trusty PI, was back from Scotland... despite the time difference, Hamish decided to call Alistair that evening. They could brainstorm across the three thousand miles of the Atlantic Ocean.

Chapter 12

Hamish's call was placed at seven o'clock in the evening in Portland, meaning that Alistair received it at midnight Scotland time. Margaret had texted Alistair earlier that there had been a death at the law firm, with no further details; she thought that Mark's information, identifying the deceased as Marnie, might not be ready for public disclosure, not that Alistair would broadcast it. Anyway, they only had one person's word: maybe Marnie was injured and not dead, or maybe it wasn't Marnie at all.

Diffuse moonlight reflected off the waves of the Firth of Forth. Alistair could see a slice of silvery water and the nearby beach from where he sat at the dining table in the Finlay cottage he shared with Margaret. Unbeknownst to Margaret, Alistair had taken on a research project as a favor to a police officer in the town of Kilvellie, an hour north of Finlay by car. His chair was surrounded by boxes, some open and some still to be opened, and in a way he was glad of the distraction of Hamish's call, even though he dreaded what he'd hear.

He hoped that Margaret hadn't been close with the person who'd died. He'd texted a reply to her, offering to drive west to the island she was on and bring her back instead of the long journey alone by ferry and trains. At least he could meet her off the ferry in Oban, the busy port town that served as a gateway to several western islands.

"Hamish, good to hear from you." Alistair moved to the sofa and made himself comfortable; with his free hand he poured whisky into a glass and sipped it.

"Is Margaret there? I'd prefer to speak to you away from her hearing, then you can decide how much to share with her."

"No," Alistair replied. "She may not have told you, but she's helping the prince with his beach clean-up initiative.

54

She's been going island to island on the west coast, and her last stop is Caraidsay. I expect her back the day after tomorrow."

Alistair didn't miss Hamish's sharp intake of breath. "*Really?*" Hamish asked. "That's such a coincidence. One of my clients is working on… oh, you don't need the details, but bottom line, two associate lawyers from the firm are on that same island, at my request. Depending on where Margaret is staying, maybe they'll have met up."

"I hope so, Hamish. Margaret had assured me that she'd be with a couple of other people on this trip, but they couldn't make it. I've fought the urge to go meet up with her, especially now that she has the awful news from the firm, but she hasn't asked so I've let her do her own thing."

"These associates will look out for her, not that I'm suggesting she needs looking after! We both know that. Anyway, one is Mark, who she knows as he's in her year, and the other is Charlie. He's more junior, so she may not have worked with him. Anyway, none of this has a bearing on why I called. I know it's late for you, but can you spare some time now to hear what's going on?"

"Of course, Hamish. I'm happy for you to bounce ideas and I'll give you any advice I can." He took a small sip of whisky, then readied a pad of paper and pen on the coffee table to take notes.

"I know you've had dealings with the police now and again," Hamish began. "Have you ever encountered a detective named Clara Hibbard?"

"I've met her, maybe at a police charity event or something. I haven't interacted with her for work though."

"That's fine. She's the main detective on the case, although I can't really call it a case, it only happened today. Well, almost yesterday by your time. Let me give you the outline and you can ask questions. Diana went to the office early this morning, arriving at about six o'clock. She was only there to look for some maps in the file room in the basement, that the file clerks claimed they couldn't find. You've seen that room. Well, this is so awful. She had kind of an epic struggle to shift several mobile file units at once. I know, you're thinking why not move them one at a time, but she was impatient as she had an important mediation this morning. You can probably guess what's coming. The units suddenly gave and moved about a foot or two along, then she could access the files she needed. After that, she moved the shelves back one by one, thinking she'd dented a box of files left on the floor, or that fell off a shelf. But tragically, she found Marnie's body between two rolling sections."

Alistair gasped, then sat forward on the sofa. "That's, that's horrible! Poor Diana. Poor Marnie. So when Diana forced the shelving along, did she, did she..." He faltered: surely Diana couldn't have killed the woman in that short a time?

"Diana managed to keep her focus. She checked for a pulse, but she already knew it was too late. She said Marnie's body was cold to the touch."

"So," Alistair began, poised to ask another question, then said, "sorry, I'll keep quiet, I'm sure you're about to answer anything I might think to ask."

"There's not a lot more to tell. We closed the office today. I still don't know if we can open tomorrow. I felt sure that the autopsy would indicate if she'd died from a heart attack, or an aneurism or something natural and sudden, or a fall, but the preliminary conclusion is that there was a hard blow to the back of her neck. The kind of blow that's more often than not fatal. They called it atlanto-occipital dislocation."

Hamish waited while Alistair wrote down the term.

"As for what did the damage," Hamish continued, "the medical examiner thinks it was the edge of the metal shelving. But there are pieces of shelving stored nearby, so, and I quote, Clara says it's a 'fifty-fifty' chance whether poor Marnie fell backwards and gave herself a one in a million hit in exactly the wrong place, or if someone hit her. And if someone did hit her in the neck with a piece of shelving..." His voice trailed off.

Alistair finished the thought. "A trained killer, I'd think. Or someone who knew exactly where to land the blow?"
Now both men fell silent.

Chapter 13

The concept that a young associate at Hamish's firm had been killed in the early morning, not by a street mugger or a home intruder, but in the relative security of the firm's file room, hung in the air. Alistair sipped his whisky while waiting for Hamish to respond.

At last, Hamish sighed. "*Thank you*, Alistair, for that confirmation. If she was intentionally killed, I can't imagine it was by a thief caught in the act. They'd maybe push her out of the way, or stun her over the head, but a targeted hit like that?"

"And," Alistair added, "if the injury was to the back of her neck, it's not a scenario where she walks in on a burglar or an intruder, and they look up and see her from the front. I'm so sorry, Hamish, for this loss. Did you know her well?"

"Ironically, she was one of five attorneys who attended a holiday dinner at my house, it will be two years ago this Christmas. Margaret was also there, and that's how we discovered our mutual interest in Samuel Johnson, which led to me being with her in Orkney and saving the prince's life. A long chain of what-ifs. But thinking back to that dinner, if you'd told me that Marnie would be dead within two years, at my law firm, under suspicious circumstances? I would have said, *no way.*"

That made up Alistair's mind: he would drive west and meet Margaret off the ferry. Or, he wondered, maybe he could get there in time to go over on the ferry and meet her on the island? If she'd been close to Marnie, she must be feeling terrible. He was about to end the call, now that Hamish had covered the preliminary facts as he knew them, but then Hamish spoke up again.

"Listen, Alistair, I'm not asking you to betray any client confidences, but I know you work for other attorneys at the firm on occasion. Have you been involved in any criminal matters for them?"

"No, I can assure you of that, even without breaking a confidence. Does this have something to do with Marnie?"

Alistair could hear Hamish sighing again, taking time to make up his mind before replying.

"It may, I just don't know yet. You're probably familiar with Norm Adler?"

Alistair groaned. "No-jail Norm? Sorry, that's what I've heard him called, for his talent in keeping perps on the street."

"I guess he deserves it. I went to law school with him. He's a brilliant lawyer, but I know what you mean, he does have that reputation. Although I'm sure it's all on this side of the law."

"*Just* this side," Alistair clarified.

"Good point. Anyway, I called Norm this morning when the police took Diana for questioning. Since it was urgent, Norm sat in on the interview. But he told me he couldn't represent Diana, if there is a case to answer, because of a conflict his firm has with my firm. And his firm only does criminal law."

Alistair thought back to cases he'd worked on for lawyers at Hamish's firm: mainly documenting workplace safety violations, checking peoples' backgrounds for employers, but nothing that he thought would involve Norm's firm. Then he remembered, the jewelry theft case he'd investigated for Hamish earlier that year.

"Hamish, what about the theft of jewelry you worked on, really as a favor for your neighbor? Maybe the neighbor or her aunt contacted Norm's firm if they were worried about being implicated?"

"Good idea," Hamish said, "but his firm wouldn't touch a small case of jewelry theft. No, it must be something bigger. And even worse, I asked him if it related to a client or an employee of my firm, and he answered 'both' then drove off in his fancy electric car before I could ask any more questions. Since he won't represent Diana, it could mean he has an ongoing criminal representation adverse to my firm, and involving at least one client and one employee. If it was a former client, I'd think he would offer to request a waiver from them, so he could help Diana."

"*If* she needs help from him, but it sounds like she's got nothing to do with Marnie's actual death, right?"

"I know that and you know that, Alistair, but at this point, everyone in the firm is a suspect. How can I quietly look into the criminal matter that Norm alluded to, without involving someone who could be responsible for what happened to Marnie?"

"Not *everyone* is a suspect, Hamish," Alistair pointed out. "Since she was killed, if she was killed, last night or early this morning your time, then anyone who's abroad is not a suspect. I mean, Margaret and the two lawyers you sent to Scotland. And me of course, not that I'm an employee, but I know your offices well enough to get around without being detected."

Hamish laughed. "I do know that, Alistair. I remember you pointing out potential security weaknesses when we first met. You recommended motion-detecting cameras in some areas."

"Like the basement and file room." The moment Alistair said that, he realized it was a low blow given Marnie's death. But Hamish didn't seem to be offended.

"Yes, and I can't tell you how much I regret not making that a priority with the building management, and instead, buying into their arguments about limited funds. Then they go and upgrade the lobby decor. It makes me so mad to think of it..."

Alistair interrupted before Hamish got into one of his rare tirades. "Listen, we were talking about how you have at least four people, I mean, me and your three lawyers in Scotland, who cannot be suspects in Marnie's death. Well, if they're involved remotely, you're looking at a conspiracy or..."

Now Hamish interrupted. "*No*, Alistair, I must believe that Charlie and Mark, and Margaret, have nothing to do with this. Anyway, I gave Charlie and Mark very little notice about their travel, so I can't imagine how they could have planned it all."

"Okay," Alistair said. "In that case, could you use us to trace what this criminal activity is that Norm told you about? Your records are mainly digital, so we wouldn't need physical access to files. Remember, Margaret's been able to work remotely for months now."

"I'm so glad I called you, Alistair. You always come up with something I hadn't considered. I'll need to narrow down what area of law to even look at. I'm thinking of asking the IT department to cross-check between our employees and our client list, see if there's a connection. New clients are supposed to provide any information that could cause a conflict of interest, and a family member working at the firm should be recorded in the client intake information..."

"Wait, Hamish. Do you mean, use *your* IT people to do that? I thought you said everyone at the firm is a suspect at this point."

"Yes," Hamish sighed, "I did say that. Do you want to take a whack at it? *Sorry*, that's so insensitive with Marnie being dead."

"I can try and help. This kind of project is what I'm missing, being over here."

"Great. I'll think about how to provide the information to you and we can be in touch tomorrow. Well, later today for you. I'm sorry to have kept you up so late."

They ended the call. Alistair finished his whisky, then realized he should get to sleep soon and be ready to help Hamish in the morning. He thought about his plan to drive over to Oban and meet Margaret. But if Margaret and her two colleagues were Hamish's hope for investigating, without involving anyone who could have killed Marnie, then surely all three attorneys should stay away from the office, maybe stay on in Scotland?

He called Hamish back. "Sorry, Hamish, but something occurred to me. I don't know how long those other two lawyers are scheduled to be in Scotland, but if you want them to help, shouldn't they stay here for now? It's a clean separation from people the police have to interview. Same for Margaret."

"Good point. I'll contact all three of them and ask them to remain in Scotland at least for a couple of days, not that I expected Margaret back so soon. I keep hoping the medical examiner will change his opinion and rule that the death was accidental after all, but Clara seemed to think he has his suspicions, as she does."

After the call, Alistair sent Margaret a quick text. He didn't know if her phone would ping and wake her up, or if it was on silent. Either way, the message was, *Stay where you are until we speak in the morning.* With that done, he had a quick search online, then finally went to bed.

But sleep was hopeless: he had looked up the medical term that Hamish used to describe Marnie's fatal injury. *Atlanto-occipital dislocation* was the literal description, but another was *internal decapitation.* He felt ill, imagining a sudden blow strong enough to destabilize the ligaments that attached the base of the skull to the first cervical vertebra. The injury wasn't always fatal. If Marnie had been found right away, could she have survived? It didn't matter, there was no point dwelling on it.

Instead, he thought about how his opinion of Margaret's law firm had shifted, had turned ominous. If the attack was random, it meant that Margaret could as easily have been the victim, or Hamish's wife Diana, if she'd gone to the file room in the late evening, instead of early the next morning. Leaving Hamish devastated, two young children without a mother, and two teenage girls without their confident and loving second mother.

He wondered now if Marnie was married. Children? He'd ask Hamish tomorrow. Marnie must have been Margaret's age, and Margaret was engaged and soon (he hoped) to be married, so most likely there was a significant other who would be mourning the tragic, senseless loss.

Internal decapitation he thought again, remembering back to the many workplace injury cases he'd investigated on behalf of clients. Yet somehow, even among complex machinery, dangerous construction sites, boatyards, and fish-processing plants, no one he'd investigated had managed to damage themselves in such a specific way. No, he realized, it could be murder. This was a serious matter for Hamish's firm. And if the person killed once, presumably to silence Marnie, would he or she kill again?

He sat up in bed and called Hamish yet again.

"Hamish, I've been thinking this through. Until you know why Marnie was killed, and yes, I'm pretty sure that this is murder, I think you should keep the office closed and have people work remotely. If Marnie was killed to silence her, after she discovered something about a client maybe, then who else might know?"

"You mean," Hamish replied in a near-whisper, "this might not be the end?"

Alistair wondered if Diana was nearby, listening, so he said, with emphasis, "Maybe this will help. If Margaret and I were in Portland now, *I* would not want *any* employees to go to the office until the murder, if it is a murder, was solved. That sounds bossy, but in this case I would insist on my way."

"Hear you loud and clear," Hamish whispered. "I'll send out a notification tonight, then we'll speak tomorrow. Goodnight, again."

Alistair lay down, but he suspected that sleep would be fleeting and disturbed.

Chapter 14

Hamish had barely enough time to put down his phone after speaking to Alistair and refill his wine glass, before the phone alerted him a new text. Alistair, Hamish assumed. He was more than ready to give his mind a rest, but he knew Alistair would only get in touch at night if it was important.

Not Alistair, though, the text was from the detective, Clara. Hamish read through it: she had new information and if he was going to be up for a while, she'd like to stop by. Anything new could only help, he figured, so he texted back and said it was fine. *See you in 15 m.* was her reply. He liked that, brief and to the point.

Diana had been upstairs relaxing in a bath while Hamish was on the call—calls, as it turned out—with Alistair in Scotland. He heard her footsteps on the stairs, so he got up to intercept her.

"I just got a text from Clara and she wants to come over."

"*Now?*" Diana was wearing her bathrobe and her hair was wrapped in a towel. "I'm so worn out, I can't answer more questions tonight."

"It's fine, darling." Hamish met her halfway up the staircase. He gently turned her around and together they walked up to the second floor.

"Stay in the bedroom, and I'll bring you up some food and more wine. I'm glad you arranged for the twins to have a sleepover at the neighbors."

Diana smiled sadly at the entrance to their bedroom. "I never thought that 'twins at a sleepover' would be the sweetest words I could hear, but after the day we've had..."

"I know." Hamish plumped up the pillows so she could lean back in bed and read. "Keep your phone nearby. I'll try not to bother you, but just in case Clara has a question when she's here." He waited until Diana was comfortable, then he draped their Hawaiian quilt over her.

She smiled, and he hoped the familiarity of their beloved honeymoon quilt and their shared memories would help push away the images from the early morning.

Back downstairs, Hamish put the wine bottle in the refrigerator and brewed a pot of decaf coffee. He set some homemade brownies and cookies on a plate while he waited for Clara to arrive. With the day she was having, he imagined her food intake was probably limited to take-out coffee and mysterious things in plastic wrap.

Soon he heard the doorbell, and he welcomed her in; this time she was alone, without the younger officer who'd been with her on previous visits.

Her face literally lit up as she entered the kitchen; she breathed in the aroma of the coffee and saw the brownies.

"I hope these are for us," she said. "I could eat six of them. Partly hunger, partly comfort."

Hamish offered to make her some proper food, but she said she was really joking, as she'd eaten a salad for dinner and was ready for dessert.

Once the coffee and brownies were served, Clara turned serious. She took out her phone to show Hamish a series of photographs.

"After you asked for photographs of the files located in the section where Marnie was found, I went back myself and took these. Before you look in detail, I'm hoping this one is helpful. Diana wouldn't have noticed this morning, but one file was under Marnie's body, when they removed her. We can't be sure she was actually holding it, given what happened when Diana..."

Hamish shook his head. "I know, when Diana forced the shelving against her."

"Exactly. But it may be a starting point, you think?"

Hamish looked carefully at the photograph of the file. It was a light blue accordion folder, but relatively thin, holding perhaps a hundred or two hundred sheets of paper. He jotted down the file number from the stickers affixed to the tab. To someone outside the firm, it would look like a jumble of letters and numbers, but to him, it represented a client number, a matter number, and a country number.

He looked up at Clara. "This is a patent file, I can tell from the sequence of numbers and letters, based on our filing system. But before you ask, I don't know the name of the client or what the file contains. I can access our matter numbers and tell you. It's easier to do on my laptop, so I'll get it from the other room. Meantime, help yourself to another brownie."

When he returned with his laptop and had it open to the list of files and file numbers, he cross-checked with the list of clients and their assigned numbers: one client per number, with separate unique numbers for each matter.

"I was right, it is a patent file, and I can identify who the client is." He picked up his phone. "I'll call the head of our patent practice, she'll be able to tell us more..."

Clara was about to sip from her mug of coffee, but she stopped and raised her other, brownie-wielding, hand. "Hamish, remember, everyone is a suspect until we know otherwise."

Hamish replaced the phone on the table. He closed the file list and opened the law firm website, then turned the screen so Clara could see. "This is who I want to call." He indicated the biography and photograph on the screen. Clara was wavering now, because the leader of the firm's patent practice was a petite elderly woman. Probably not someone who would assault, even kill, a much younger woman in the confines of a file storage room.

Clara sighed and turned the laptop back to face Hamish.

"Okay, I agree that she's a very unlikely candidate, but I can't pick and choose among people who had access last night. Is there no other way of learning about that file?"

Hamish thought back to his conversation with Alistair that evening. There were three lawyers in Scotland who were definitely in the clear, but none of them practiced patent law. Then, he felt a light go on in his head: someone else who did have a little patent experience, and hadn't set foot in the law firm for at least a year.

He felt a glimmer of hope. "Clara, a few of our attorneys are overseas just now. Two of them have been away from Portland for months, and the other two left a couple of days ago. If you're focusing on people with opportunity to kill Marnie, these four people are all off the hook. Can I use them as a resource for looking into the files?"

Clara thought for a few moments, munching on the brownie. Despite the gravity of the situation, Hamish had to stifle a smile. He remembered a story Margaret had told him about her parents unknowingly ingesting marijuana-laced brownies. They gave her a very stressful evening when, on a video call across the Atlantic, they looked like they had rapid-onset dementia.

He was pretty sure these brownies were in the clear; Diana had baked them the day before, and she wouldn't have anything in the house that the young twins shouldn't eat. Still, he amused himself with the image of police detective Clara dancing her way out the door after their meeting.

"One other thing," Hamish said to her. "I sometimes hire a local private investigator for, well, you can probably imagine, since we handle workers comp and workplace injury cases. He's known to other attorneys in the firm. Normally I'd want to ask for his help in this situation, with your permission of course, but he's also in Scotland right now. I don't know how much help he could be."

Her brownie consumed, Clara wiped her mouth with a paper napkin and drank more coffee. Her eyes lingered on the brownies for a moment, then she focused on Hamish's comment.

"If he's been in Scotland for more than a couple of days, then he seems to be in the clear as a possible suspect, or witness. I assume he has been in your office building, so depending on how far back that was, we might have to eliminate his fingerprints."

"He's been in Scotland for months. If his fingerprints are still in the office after all this time, I'll have to speak to the housekeeping crew. Sorry, didn't mean to joke. But he could be another resource for investigating whatever it is we need to investigate. All we have so far is this file that Marnie may have taken from the shelf."

"Right. It could have fallen, either when she went down, or when your wife..."

"Yes, poor Diana, she feels terrible about moving those shelves, not checking first if someone was there."

"Is she okay?" Clara asked. "I can arrange for counseling if that might help."

"Thanks, I'll tell her that, but I think she'll recover well. Our twins are staying at a neighbor's house, so she's relaxing upstairs and she won't have to get up early and prepare them for their school day."

Clara looked at her phone for the time. "I don't really have anything else to ask or tell you tonight, so I should probably..."

Hamish lifted the plate of brownies and offered another to her.

She pretended to waiver and then give in. "Oh, okay, one for the road. And when you mentioned the neighbor's house, that reminds me of something I wanted to tell you. We sent a few officers around the nearby houses earlier, and you and Diana are officially not suspects at this point."

He looked at her in surprise.

"What do you mean? Surely no one would have noticed either of us leaving the house between midnight and when Diana says she did leave, around five-thirty this morning?"

Clara smiled. "Not live witnesses, but you might be surprised at how many of your neighbors have front door cams and doorbell cams. I guess everyone's worried that their deliveries from Amazon and eBay and wherever will be stolen before they have a chance to take them in. We were able to patch together a seamless view of the street, and neither of your cars, or you getting a taxi or a ride, is recorded."

"I guess I should be grateful to my overly-cautious neighbors." Hamish turned serious again. "Earlier this evening, I spoke to that PI I mentioned. He reminded me that when he first visited my law firm building several years back, he didn't think the security was good enough. Then a couple of years ago, we asked the building owner about installing security cameras in the basement, around the garage door, the elevators, and the file room area. They claimed it was too expensive right now, but then they went and upgraded the lobby. You've seen it. All that marble."

"That's really sad," Clara agreed. "Although, if whoever killed Marnie was that determined, they'd have found a way to do it and avoid being seen or filmed. So it probably wouldn't have saved her, but I hope that after this, the building owner will make those changes right away. I don't know anything about Marnie's family yet, how litigious they are, I mean, but..."

Hamish just nodded his head: he'd already been thinking in that direction, about the building's liability for her death, and the law firm's liability. He decided he shouldn't keep acknowledging that he, as managing partner, had known the security could be better.

He got up to take a roll of aluminum foil from a drawer and hand it to Clara. "These brownies were made yesterday, so please have the rest of them."

"Are you sure? Won't Diana miss them?" But Clara was already tearing off a piece of foil and moving the brownies one by one.

"Since she'll be home for a few days at least, maybe baking will take her mind off things." He stopped and apologized. "I struggle to rid myself of gender stereotypes, but believe me, Clara, if I was capable of making decent brownies, I'd be doing that tomorrow too."

Clara stuffed the foil package into her pack, and put away her phone and notebook before standing up. "Your secret's safe with me. I can't cook to save my life. Thank goodness for ready-made meals. Anyway, I'll leave it to you to start investigating the files. If you get any leads on why Marnie might have selected the file that was found under her, please call me right away. I feel so uneasy, that someone in that big office building could be a killer, but until we can get around to questioning everyone about their relationship with Marnie, maybe unearth a hidden personal motive, the files are all we have to go on."

Hamish accompanied Clara to the door and watched while she walked down the path to her car: not a police car, he noted. Of course, he knew now that he didn't have to see her safely into her car, not with countless neighborly cameras watching silently from the lit entryways up and down his peaceful street.

Those cameras had absolved him and Diana of suspicion in Marnie's death, but then he realized the downside of the surveillance: he had no hope of privacy at his own front door. It was unsettling.

Chapter 15

Margaret was still awake when she received the text from Alistair: *Stay where you are until we speak in the morning.* She considered calling him back, but the text had been sent half an hour earlier, while she'd been soaking in the whirlpool bath in her suite, and maybe he'd be asleep by now. It was almost one in the morning.

She was only awake because she'd had a long dinner with Mark and Charlie, then still had to pack to leave on the afternoon ferry the next day. But now, she thought, looking at her careful packing and her groatie buckies secured in sealed plastic bags, perhaps he'd decided to come and collect her, maybe meet her in Oban?

Like Alistair, thinking of Marnie's death prevented her from sleeping soundly. She remembered helping Hamish with his lawsuit on behalf of several lawyers who'd become ill, perhaps permanently, from breathing construction fumes during an office renovation in another Portland building. At the time, she'd been plagued with the thought that it could have been her, and she began questioning whether she'd want to go back to the office full-time after her stay in Scotland.

Spending the evening with Mark and Charlie had been surprisingly enjoyable, under the circumstances. After sharing memories of Marnie—associate lunches, drinks after work when they'd compare notes about which partners to avoid—she'd begun to think she *would* like to go back to the office in Portland and put an end to her months of working alone at home, with collegial contact only by video.

But Marnie's death in that office brought back all Margaret's fears, even more now. If Marnie was dead from a random attack, it meant it could have been anyone. It could have been her. She wished she could get more information from Hamish or Diana, but they'd be in their own nightmare.

71

Margaret hadn't met Marnie's parents, who lived in California, but she knew it was a close-knit family, and the parents would be devastated. Would they vent their anger on Hamish as managing partner?

She felt more awake than she had an hour earlier, so she got up, wrapped herself in the thick hotel bathrobe, and made herself a cup of hot chocolate. Like all the food in this sleek hotel, the hot chocolate was gourmet, from a boutique chocolate company on a nearby island. She'd noticed early in her stay that the hotel had a preference for local products: from the delicate fresh greens in the salad, to the after-dinner mints. Even the wood furniture was locally made, and the artwork in the dining room featured local artists.

And she had to admit, as she opened her laptop and perused her email, the hot chocolate was excellent. Maybe she could buy some in the hotel shop... her breath caught: a new email had come in from Hamish, marked Urgent and Confidential. Finally, she thought, some news about Marnie.

She sipped the hot chocolate and read carefully through the email. No news about Marnie's death, but instead, Hamish wanted to schedule a video conference the following day with Margaret, Mark, Charlie, and Alistair, if he was free to call in. *Huh?* She couldn't imagine a topic that would include all three lawyers plus a PI.

Then she read further and felt a jolt in her chest: *Henri* would be on the call too. Henri, her first serious boyfriend since she'd left law school: Henri, who Hamish's wife Diana had set her up with. There had been several romance-filled months, then the bombshell when Henri announced he was moving back to France to pursue a career in immigration law. They'd had no contact since he left Portland.

Something niggled at her brain, trying to make a connection among these people. She, Marnie, Henri, and Mark had all attended the holiday dinner at Hamish and Diana's home almost two years earlier, but surely that couldn't be it. Then she realized something else: Margaret, Henri, Mark, and Charlie were all abroad when Marnie was killed. If she'd been killed. Was that the link? Were they the only current or former law firm employees who weren't possible suspects in her death?

With Portland being five hours behind, Hamish wanted to schedule the call for eight o'clock in the morning his time, which meant one o'clock in the afternoon for the small group on the island, and Alistair. What about Henri? She didn't know what time zone he was in. Was France an hour ahead of Scotland? Well, Hamish would have factored that in.

She typed a reply, saying she would be available for the call; she assumed that Mark and Charlie would respond on their own, either tonight, if they were still up this late, or first thing in the morning. She cc'd them all on her reply to Hamish, and was surprised when a new email came in moments later. Henri had seen her cc, and if she was going to be awake for longer, could he call her?

She stared at the email, stunned to hear from him after all this time. But curiosity won out and she replied with her cell phone number. No way was she having a video call with her ex-boyfriend in the middle of the night, in her bathrobe, but she was also not going to dress up to speak to the man who'd left her heartbroken.

Taking her hot chocolate, she went back to the bed, piled up her pillows, and placed her phone nearby, steeling herself to be heartbroken all over again at the first sound of his seductive voice. *Don't stutter!* she told herself, over and over, like a mantra.

She waited for several minutes and was poised to check her email again, in case Henri had changed his mind, but suddenly the phone jumped to life and she answered it quickly.

"Margaret, *Cherie*, I am so glad to speak to you again," Henri began, his French accent and slightly garbled English more pronounced than she remembered. "But I am sorry for the reason we are to being back in touch, from Hamish."

"It's good to speak to you again, too," Margaret lied. She wanted to forestall any personal reminiscing on Henri's part.

73

"Do you know why Hamish has scheduled the conference call tomorrow?"

"I know a leetle, which is why I call you. Marnie confided in me, since I had already left the firm."

Confided? Margaret hoped it wasn't a romantic entanglement with a married partner.

"Go on," she said cautiously, encouraging Henri to divulge more.

"You may remember, I worked in the patent group for a leetle while, almost a year. I thought it would be a good way to do international work, but I deedn't have the technical background. Marnie also had no technical background, but you probably know, she was taking evening classes in biology and chemistry."

Margaret thought back, and that did seem familiar—poor diligent Marnie was often torn between staying late to put in more billable hours, or hurrying to get across town in rush hour, to her evening classes at the university. Now, she regretted not knowing Marnie better; she blamed that on Henri, for leaving her just when she was gaining some self-assurance to socialize.

"Anyway," Henri continued, "she called me a couple of weeks ago. She'd received a strange email from a scientist in Europe. He was asking for details about some chemical structures. Marnie didn't really understand why he was asking, so she said she'd get back to him. And now she's dead."

Margaret tried to process this. "I assume you've told Hamish, and that's why he wants to talk to us, including you?"

"*Non,* I have not said anything to Hamish yet. Before I had a chance, he contacted me. Oh goodness, poor Diana!"

Margaret didn't know what exactly had happened to Diana. Maybe Henri would share with her, so she asked.

"Please don't tell anyone else," he replied, and this reminded her of his penchant for gossiping at the firm. She promised to keep it to herself.

74

"Diana found her body. I mean, Marnie's body. In the file room. But before Diana found Marnie, she, I mean, Diana, forced the heavy shelving units along the track, and, I don't know in English, she *squashed* Marnie?"

"*What?*" Margaret cried. "She killed her? I mean, *Diana killed Marnie?*"

"*Non, non,* not keeled. Marnie was already dead. But Diana has compromised crime scene, I think that's the problem."

"*Crime scene?*" Margaret was still trying to process the tragic scenario. "They've, I mean the police, they've concluded it was murder, that Marnie didn't fall over and hit her head or something like that?"

"Not officially, *non,* but Hamish says the detective he's working with, she has her suspicions. And that's probably why Hamish wants to speak to us, because we are not suspects since we're all overseas. The detective needs help to find a motive for someone to *keel* poor Marnie."

Surely Henri was exaggerating, Margaret thought. It was another of his less-attractive tendencies, along with his flamboyance. But he seemed to know more than she'd been told, or Mark and Charlie, judging from how little they knew earlier at dinner.

Could Henri be correct, that Hamish wanted to enlist four lawyers who had zero training in criminal law, except for a semester in law school, and somehow help solve Marnie's murder from three thousand miles away? Something didn't sound right. She sipped her hot chocolate, which had become lukewarm chocolate milk. Still delicious, though.

"Is there anything else you can share before the call with Hamish?" she asked Henri.

"Oh, Margaret, it eez so good to hear your voice. Sometimes I wish..."

"Henri," she interrupted. She didn't need another of his "full of regret" stories, she'd had enough of those before he left for France. "It's very late and I need to get to sleep. I'll see you tomorrow on the video call."

"I look forward to eet. *Bon nuit.*"

Margaret ended the call and realized she was completely over Henri: how could he be so insensitive to say he was looking forward to a call, the only purpose of which was to discuss the death of another lawyer, his friend?

Somehow, speaking to Henri after all this time helped put her mind at rest: there were none of the old feelings of *what if.* Alistair was her future, and she could truly tell him that Henri was in her past. Well, after whatever Hamish wanted them all to do. She just hoped that, during the call, Hamish wouldn't mention Margaret's former relationship with Henri, or her present relationship with Alistair. The idea of these two men being on a video call with her was just too bizarre to contemplate.

She finished her warm chocolate, and with one thing in her life finally settled—any lingering feelings for Henri were gone—she was able to sleep at last.

Chapter 16

Alistair had been asleep by the time Hamish emailed the request for a group video call, so it was the first email he read when he got up the following morning, bright and early with the sun. Late August sun, with sunrise moving forward by a few minutes each day.

As Alistair prepared coffee, he had a sense of this comfortable time in Margaret's Finlay cottage slipping away along with the summer. Soon the fall and winter weather would bring storms and pounding waves, and the wooden staircase that provided beach access from the cottage would once again be under siege.

No time for melancholy, he decided; still in his bathrobe, he carried a large mug of coffee to the dining table where his laptop was set up, and focused on Hamish's email. It requested a video call at one o'clock Scotland time, to be attended by Hamish in Portland, Alistair in Finlay on the east coast of Scotland, Margaret, Mark, and Charlie on a western island in Scotland, and, to Alistair's shock, a person called Henri, in France.

Alistair sipped his coffee and looked out of the window, watching the now-familiar shorebirds pecking in the gentle surf for their own breakfast, and the eiders further out, chattering away with their morning greetings. At least, Alistair liked to imagine that's what they were doing.

Surely there weren't two lawyers named Henri associated with Hamish's law firm, so this must be the Henri that Margaret had dated. She'd assured Alistair, months ago, that everything was over with Henri, even if he were to return to Portland. Alistair never dreamed he'd be face to face with the guy, even over a video call, and he wasn't pleased about it.

Would Henri attempt a reunion with Margaret? Not that Hamish was throwing them together again. That's what Margaret had told Alistair: the relationship with Henri began when Diana and Hamish did their matchmaking, meddling more like it in Alistair's mind.

But this call had to do with a tragic death of someone Margaret knew, so he would force himself not to be petty, and rise above any nascent jealousy. With cc's to the invited group, Alistair responded to Hamish's email, accepting the invitation to join the call at one o'clock.

He went back to the kitchen and prepared breakfast. So much for driving up to meet Margaret off the ferry, he realized. He'd have to be patient and see what plans emerged from the call.

As he ate his toast and blackberry jam, a new favorite from a nearby farm shop, he glanced around at the boxes on the floor, his research project for police officer Helen Griffen, in the town of Kilvellie. He'd be able to put in a few hours before the call, then either keep working or head up to Oban, depending on Hamish's plans.

Stopping often for a bite of toast and a sip of coffee, Alistair continued working through the papers in the box he'd opened the evening before. His goal was to find something that might not even be there: an explanation for a mystery that he and Helen had uncovered.

During World War Two, six young men had repeatedly attacked a well-established glassware factory that once sat above a coastal cliff just north of Kilvellie. Evidence strongly hinted that the young men had carried out the damage under duress: someone with power was behind it.

That someone might have been a senior town official, or perhaps a military officer at the soldiers' convalescent home where the young men worked and lived. They'd been evacuated from Glasgow for the duration of the war. The young men were all gone now, as far as Alistair knew, and the only surviving witness to the damage, a former wartime factory employee in his nineties, had just passed away.

But the convalescent home, now an upscale care home for the elderly, had held onto written records of its wartime history, in boxes tucked away and forgotten in the basement of the home. These boxes were now in the cottage where Alistair lived with Margaret. Alistair would have liked to know what he was looking for, but with no guidance, he had to check everything.

He finished his first mug of coffee and went to the kitchen for a refill. He considered getting dressed, but with Margaret away, and only rare visitors to the cottage, he decided to stay comfortable until he had to dress for the video call. Well, dress professionally from the waist up. He could get away with sweatpants, like the other participants might be doing as well.

It was getting on for nine o'clock and he decided it was late enough to call Margaret, but as he reached for his phone, a text came in from Helen. He called her first, best to get whatever it was out of the way before he called Margaret.

"How's the research coming along?" Helen asked.

"It's progressing, but so far I haven't answered our question, about who held some kind of power over those six boys, teenagers. But I'm only about halfway through so I'll keep my hopes up."

"Great, but actually I want to speak to you about something else. Remember Christy, the sea glass jeweler?"

Alistair remembered her well from his recent visits to Kilvellie: Christy's sister Justine had gone missing seven years earlier, when both were teenagers, and Alistair helped discover what had happened to her. Now Justine was a frequent topic of conversation since she was dating Alistair's good friend and fellow PI Adam, who lived further north, in Inverness.

"Of course, I know who you mean," he replied. "What's up?"

"Christy's thinking about helping to open a new sea glass and jewelry shop where you are, in Finlay. She'd like to spend a few days there, getting to know the place, but she doesn't want to be driving back and forth from Kilvellie, an hour each way. The hotel in Finlay is fully booked for the rest of the summer, so I wanted to ask you if she could stay with you and Margaret, in your upstairs guest room, well, suite."

Helen was familiar with the cottage, as she'd stayed overnight recently, mainly to discuss Alistair's new project. But Alistair suspected there had been a second motive: a meal at the popular new Indian restaurant at the hotel in the village.

"Normally I'd agree right away," he said, "but things are up in the air right now. Margaret was planning to get the ferry to Oban today, then stay overnight there and come back by train tomorrow."

"Oh, and do you think Margaret would mind?"

"No, that's not it." He hesitated, then told Helen about the death at Margaret's law firm in Portland.

"I should know more about our schedules after my one o'clock video call," he concluded. "I have no idea what Margaret's boss Hamish thinks we can do, I mean, in terms of trying to identify a suspect from among the law firm's employees, if it was a murder. But I'll call you later. Anyway, even if I go out to the island to meet Margaret, Christy is still welcome to stay here." He stopped and laughed. "Just don't tell her about the Pictish silver hidden in the kitchen counter!"

Helen laughed too. Alistair had taken her in on the secret that Margaret had found a hoard of Pictish silver in the kitchen; it came pouring down into a cabinet one day. More was still deep in the recess above the drawers, waiting for Alistair to dismantle the counter.

"I promise, your secret's safe with me. Although, I am curious about why it's still in there. Why don't you get the rest of it out and take it to the Edinburgh museum as treasure trove, like you did with the first batch?"

Alistair knew he had no good excuse. "I don't know, Helen, I guess things kept coming up, and I didn't want to start the work and not be able to put the kitchen back together quickly."

Helen said she'd let Christy know that she had a room at the cottage whenever she needed it. Before ending the call, she added, "Alistair, feel free, anytime, to discuss the death with me. I'm sure I can't help with figuring out what happened, but I can be a sounding board for ideas, like you've been for me recently. I do think that the detective you mentioned is correct. The medical examiner in Portland, like our coroners here, has to judge from the physical appearance of the body, so maybe it really is equally possible that she was murdered, or fell over and hit her head. But since the detective has asked Hamish about motives, and Hamish is asking his people who are in Europe, who aren't suspects, to help, they both must think there's something to be found."

"That's my instinct," Alistair agreed. "The way Hamish described the injury... I hate to say but it sounds like a professional hit. But the idea that any of Hamish's employees have that kind of background? I don't know..."

"It didn't have to be an employee," Helen pointed out. "Just an employee *who knows a guy*, as you Americans might put it in a gangster film."

"Maybe that's worse, Helen, the idea that Hamish's firm employs someone with friends like that. Anyway, I promise to call you later, and please tell Christy to contact me about staying here."

After the call with Helen, he tried Margaret's number, but it went to voice mail. He sent her a text and hoped she'd get in touch before the video call. It seemed ridiculous, but now that the mysterious Frenchman Henri was back in the picture, Alistair was worried that Margaret would find herself drawn to her ex-boyfriend.

After heating up his coffee in the microwave, Alistair spent a few minutes on the internet. By the time he'd finished his coffee, his mood had darkened considerably. He'd found Henri listed on the website for an immigration law firm based in Boston, with Henri employed as a European liaison, it seemed. Did that mean he was in Boston now and again?

81

Mark, one of the two attorneys with Margaret now, looked like a man Alistair could relate to. His law firm picture was not a studio headshot: instead, Mark was photographed in the act of capturing a snow-capped summit in some remote place, wearing reflective goggles, his face almost hidden behind a flapping prayer flag. Alistair had a photograph of himself near a snowy summit in Europe, but, unlike Mark, he'd reached it by a gondola.

At least Charlie didn't look like someone who might be competition for Margaret's attention. Alistair couldn't decide how best to describe him: a puppy, or a member of a high school cheerleading team. He had a sweet, slightly pudgy face, eyes open wide, as if being a newly-minted lawyer at a law firm in Portland was absolutely the best thing ever. He had thick floppy brown hair, and in his law firm photograph he looked as if he was dressing up in his father's suit.

Hamish was placing his trust in this puppy to help solve Marnie's murder? *Stop it,* Alistair said to himself. At least he should withhold judgment until the video call, when the young man would have a chance to prove himself.

Chapter 17

Hamish and Diana were up at seven o'clock the following morning. Their neighbors had promised to take the twins to school, along with their own children, then Hamish or Diana would collect them from school later. It left Diana and Hamish free to eat breakfast before Hamish's eight o'clock video call with the group in Scotland and France.

Still wearing their bathrobes and slippers, they sat together at the kitchen table and enjoyed a first welcome mug of coffee.

"You're kidding!" Diana cried when Hamish explained about the call. "You're having Henri and Margaret and Alistair on the *same* video call? Do Henri and Alistair know about each other?"

"Honestly, sweetheart, I was only thinking of Marnie. Margaret knows they're both on the call, so I'll leave it up to her whether to warn them ahead of time."

"Well," Diana relented, "maybe it will be okay. Just make sure you keep the conversation focused on Marnie and what you want them to help with. Seems a long shot."

"I know, but until we hear otherwise from Clara, investigating the file Marnie had under her seems our best hope. I've been in touch with all the partners and associates she works with, and none of them admit to asking her to fetch that file, or to read anything in it."

Diana shook her head. "*Admit* is the key word. Since everyone's a suspect, why would anyone reveal their involvement? Especially if it's the only reason she went to the file room late at night."

"Changing the subject," Hamish said, reaching for a small piece of white paper that lay on the kitchen table, "this was on the mat by the front door this morning when I got up. I assumed one of us dropped it, but I think it must have been put through the letterbox in the door."

He held it up for Diana to read. There were just two words, handwritten in block capital letters.

"Forsyth Industries," she read aloud. "What is that?"

"I don't know. I already checked our client list and there's nothing by that name, or anything close. And it has no website, I looked."

"You'd better tell Clara. Maybe they can have it tested for fingerprints."

"Even better, I can ask the neighbors across the street to check their front door cam. That should show who dropped it off. But it's too early to call them."

He placed the piece of paper aside.

"Have you learned anything about the file that was found under Marnie?" Diana asked.

"No, I wanted to call the head of the patent group last night, but Clara advised me not to. I can see who the client is from the number, but I can't tell anything about the contents. Well, there is a title for the matter but it's not much help. 'Modulating compounds' or something equally vague."

"Who's the client?"

"A local biotech company. They're in one of the industrial parks outside town. I think it's premature to ask them any questions. Marnie's not listed as a responsible attorney on their cases, so I don't need to contact them to give them assurance that their work won't be affected."

He finished his coffee and stood up. "I'd better put on something a bit more professional for the call. If you don't mind, I'd like to handle it myself. It's fine if you want to listen and not be on screen. Is that okay with you?"

"Definitely. I'd as soon spend the morning baking. I noticed the brownies I made are suspiciously missing."

Hamish laughed. "That's my fault! Clara ate three last night and I gave her the rest."

"Good, as long as *you* didn't eat them all. I'm glad you gave up smoking, but I don't want to have to wean you off sugar next." She poured herself another mug of coffee while Hamish went upstairs to prepare for the video conference.

Sitting at the table, she stared out of the front window, seeing the neighbors' cars as, one by one, they turned out of driveways and headed away to drop kids at school, or drive to an office or hospital.

But as safe as the neighborhood felt, Diana wished she could spirit herself away and join Mark, Charlie, and Margaret on a Scottish island, thousands of miles from her grim discovery of the previous day. She wasn't sure she could even bring herself to return to the office when it opened again, but she couldn't say that to Hamish.

Maybe they could downsize... move to a smaller house and live just on Hamish's income, and she could bake brownies and get more involved with the twins' school activities. Do some volunteer legal work from her home office...

To distract herself, she got up and pulled ingredients from the kitchen shelves, then assembled everything she needed for another batch of brownies. That detective, Clara, looked so thin and healthy, it was hard to picture her eating three brownies in one sitting, plus more in the car later.

But as stressful as things were for Diana, it must be more so for Clara, now responsible for finding out what had really transpired in that file room. Diana smiled to herself, taking out a second brownie pan: she'd make a batch just for Clara.

Chapter 18

If Diana had been able to spirit herself to the Scottish island where Margaret, Mark, and Charlie had gathered for lunch, she would have been comforted by their determination to find out what had happened. The three young lawyers sat at Margaret's table in the hotel dining room, sampling an assortment of local appetizers: artisan cheeses, rough oatcakes, chopped vegetables, haddock fritters, and to boost their mood, plenty of thin-cut French fries—chips on the menu—served with the hotel chef's selection of herbed vinegars.

Each had a notepad handy and they were scribbling ideas as they arose. Margaret was so focused that she jumped when the phone in her pocket beeped loudly with a new text; she'd turned up the volume after missing Alistair's text the previous evening, and had forgotten to turn it down in the restaurant.

"It's from Henri," she said to Mark. "I'll go outside and call him."

She left the dining room through the nearby glass door and stood in the sun while she listened to Henri. She'd been worried that he'd try to initiate a personal conversation, but instead he told her he wanted to share something with her, Mark, and Charlie before they spoke to Hamish.

"Hang on," she told him, and she went back to the table. Mark and Charlie both looked up at her.

"Henri wants to speak to the three of us before we talk to Hamish. Shall we finish lunch and then have a video call with Henri around twelve-thirty? That's half an hour before our call with Hamish."

The other two nodded, so Margaret conveyed the plan to Henri and ended the call. As they ate quickly, Margaret wondered if she should tell Charlie about her history with Henri. The handsome Frenchman seemed to be missing the professional decorum that she was used to in lawyers at her firm; perhaps, working on his own in France, he'd been free to be himself.

She turned to face Charlie. "Listen," she began, "this has no bearing on the case, but Henri and I used to date, when he still worked in Portland. Mark knows. So if Henri seems overly friendly to me, don't read anything into it. It's all in the past."

"I guess that makes it complicated, when a relationship is over but you still have to interact at work."

Margaret smiled at him. "Actually, the complicated bit is that I'm engaged to the other man joining the call, Hamish's private investigator Alistair."

She downed her tea and stood quickly, before Charlie could ask any questions. At least now it was out in the open, and she wouldn't have to get through the call with Charlie and Mark misinterpreting her interactions with the other participants. As for Henri and Alistair interacting, although in different countries? She'd have to wing it.

Before leaving the dining room, they discussed where to set up for the video calls. They'd already decided it made sense to be together, and not join separately from their own rooms. That way they could more easily exchange ideas and notes.

"The hotel has a conference room," Mark said. "We can each set up our laptop or tablet, whatever you two are using."

They walked together to the reception desk outside the dining room and learned that, yes, the conference room off the lobby was free for the afternoon. Tea and coffee could be provided as well, which they accepted with appreciation. After retrieving their laptops from the rooms, they got the meeting room set up, with three chairs arranged around the center table.

Floor to ceiling windows took up two sides of the room. Margaret considered drawing the semi-sheer curtains for privacy, but surely that wasn't needed: there was nothing confidential about the other three faces that would be on screen, Hamish, Alistair, and Henri. In fact, Hamish, sitting at home in Maine, would appreciate the view of the heather-covered Scottish hillside behind them.

They each spent a few moments plugging in the power cords, testing the microphones, and adjusting the speaker volumes. Hamish had sent an email with the connection link for the one o'clock call, and soon after that, Henri had sent a link for his call. They started with Henri's call, and suddenly Margaret found herself face-to-face with the man who had broken her heart.

Henri looked unchanged from the year before, although his face was more tanned than he could have accomplished in Portland. He wore his navy Martin & Sawyer logo fleece jacket over a white tee, although Margaret wondered how much use that winter jacket actually got in sunny France.

He raised a hand in greeting. "*Bonjour, mes amis*! And Charlie, very pleased to meet you. *Oui*, I have looked you up on the website so I recognize you. I am *Henri*." On-ree.

Margaret stifled a sigh. Ever the entertainer, she remembered.

"Hi Henri, good to see you too," Mark said. "Since we only have half an hour before the call with Hamish, can we get started on what you want to discuss with us?"

"Ah, *oui*, no time to waste, *c'est vrai*. I am so sorry about *petite* Marnie. She was a good friend to me when I was at your firm. And this is what I need to discuss, before we are speaking to Hamish."

He looked down for a moment, then held up a piece of paper. It took a while for him to get it in the right place for his camera, but soon a one-page email replaced Henri's face. He could still be heard while they read.

"Please, look at it carefully, *mes amis*. Zees is why I want to talk." He waited a few moments. "*Fini?*" he asked at last.

"Yes," Mark replied; he'd quickly snapped a picture of the paper using his phone. Margaret had hoped they could do a screen grab of the image, but Henri might have removed it while they tried. The phone camera was quicker.

Now Henri read the email aloud, to make sure the others understood. When he finished, he said, "That is the last I ever heard from *cher* Marnie. She told me that she received this email a week before, as you can see from the date. It was from someone at a place called Forsyth Laboratories. She told me, she had never heard of that place. The person who wrote the email, she'd never heard of him either. A Scottish name, I think, Margaret?"

Below the view of the laptop camera, Mark expanded the image of the email and scrolled up to the "From" line, then handed the phone to Margaret. The email appeared to have been sent by a Craig Sutherland, and the @ in his email address was, as Henri said, ForLab.co.uk. Short for Forsyth Laboratories, it seemed. She looked up again at the screen.

"Henri, it's not unusual for people at a law firm to get emails by mistake. Why did Marnie call you, and not simply let IT know so that they could re-route it to the correct person?"

"Ah, that is what I am needing to tell you, Margaret. You see, Marnie didn't know the person or the company, but she did recognize something in the email message. The sender, Craig, pasted a chemical structure into the email, as you could see. It's a very complex structure, and I have no understanding of it. I helped in the patent group at your firm for a year, but nothing with the chemistry. *Mon dieu*, that is complicated stuff."

"And what did she notice?" Mark asked. "Sorry, but I need to have a few minutes between this call and the call with Hamish."

Henri became agitated and spoke more quickly. "*Oui, oui,* I get to the point." He lifted up the email again and centered the chemical structure in front of his camera. He'd circled a small section of the structure. Mark again snapped a picture with his phone, and just in time because the image disappeared quickly.

"Okay, the point, *mes amis*. Marnie, she helped to write a patent application that has this chemical structure, and many many others. She remembered this one because, a couple of days after the patent application was filed at the patent office, one of the inventors, a scientist, called the partner at your law firm to say a mistake had been discovered in one chemical structure. It was a huge mistake for the client, because with the error, the chemical would not work as a drug. *Alors*, Marnie helped the partner to fix the chemical and file the patent application again, with the correction. They, what you say, they *abandoned* the first one, and that error should never have been known outside of a few people."

Margaret, Charlie, and Mark looked back and forth at each other. Big deal, Margaret thought, a typo had been fixed in a patent document; why all the secrecy and the call to France?

"Henri," she said, trying to hide her impatience, "we don't know a thing about patents. Can you explain what the real world problem is? Why did Marnie need to contact you?"

They all watched as he sighed dramatically and ran a hand through his hair.

"*Mes amis*, I am sorry I do not explain clearly. The patent application is what is called *provisional*. It is *secret*. It is confidential. It is unpublished. For a person with an email address in the United Kingdom to have the chemical structure with the *error*, then someone has revealed a client confidentiality, a trade secret, that's only in the very first patent application."

"Maybe the client is working with a lab or a company in Britain?" Mark suggested.

"*Non!*" Henri replied, quite vehemently. "They are working on a very new cancer treatment. Revolutionary. Nothing leaves their lab except to your law firm, to file their patents."

"So," Margaret ventured, "did Marnie think that someone at *our* law firm sent the information to a company in Britain, as a trade secret?"

"*Oui, c'est possible.* But Marnie didn't know who that could be. That's why she contacted me, to ask my opinion on what to do."

"And what did you tell her?" Mark asked. He kept glancing at his phone for the time, and Margaret knew they had to wrap things up and be ready to call Hamish.

"I suggested that she make a copy of the very first patent application, with the error. They are always kept as paper copies, not just electronic, to prove what the text was at the time of filing. Then she should present that and the email to Hamish, and turn the problem over to him."

"And?" Margaret persisted. "*Did* she tell Hamish?"

"I do not know!" Henri admitted. "That is why I am talking to you three, before the call with Hamish. Maybe he's the one. I mean, he goes to Scotland sometimes, maybe he has a connection there and is selling patent secrets?"

"Wait!" cried Mark, raising his voice. "You aren't suggesting that *Hamish* silenced Marnie because she discovered he was passing on secret cancer treatments to a Scottish pharma company, are you?"

Henri shrugged his shoulders and began taking off his fleece jacket. He seemed impatient to end the call. "*Je ne sais pas, mon ami.* I don't know. I just present you with facts. I have put everything in your hands, I feel better. Now I must change into more professional clothes for zee next call!"

And he was gone.

"Well," Margaret muttered to Charlie and Mark, "*he* may feel better but I sure feel worse. I wish he'd told us this with some lead time before we talk to Hamish. We could at least investigate this Forsyth company."

"How can we do that?" Charlie asked. "Google them?"

"No Charlie, I didn't mean *us* specifically. I mean our secret weapon, Alistair Wright. The PI on the next call. Mark, what do you think of me asking Alistair to see what he can find out about Forsyth? And he has a good friend, a Scottish PI in Inverness. Maybe together they could track down who this is?"

"Makes sense to me," Mark agreed. "What do you both think? Should we tell Hamish what we just learned from Henri?"

Charlie spoke first. "I know I'm the most junior of us three, but I'd suggest waiting to hear what Hamish has to say. He might have discovered similar information another way."

"I agree," Margaret said. "And Mark, can you forward me those pictures you took of the email? I won't share the chemical structure stuff with Alistair, but that way I'll have the correct email address and name to pass on to him."

Phone in hand, she jumped up, leaving the others to dial in for the conference with Hamish. "I'll be right back!" she called out as she left the room.

Chapter 19

Alistair had washed and styled his always neat black hair, and wore a denim band-collar shirt and summer weight tweed blazer for the video call with Hamish and the other lawyers. He had no idea how long the call would last, so he had an array of necessities around him on the dining table: a large mug of coffee, a bottle of water, pen and paper, tablet to check things online during the call, and cell phone in case someone called or texted him urgently while he was engaged on the other two devices. He was tempted to have some snacks nearby too, but he could hardly be seen munching biscuits while discussing a young lawyer's possible murder.

He sighed as he surveyed everything: life sure was complicated with so many communication devices. But at least there was a silver lining, a pleasant one. He was participating in this meeting while looking out the large picture window at the beach and the Firth of Forth. The kitchen door behind him was closed, so he was confident that the background was acceptable for the call.

Poised to click on the "join meeting" icon in Hamish's email, Alistair was momentarily annoyed when his cell phone rang, but it was Margaret, so he answered right away.

"I have to be quick." She sounded out of breath. "We just had an odd call with Henri, the French guy who'll be on the video conference with Hamish. He suspects that someone at the law firm is sending secret patent information to a company in Britain. Write these names down."

She waited while Alistair jotted down "Forsyth Laboratories" and "Craig Sutherland," making sure he had the spelling right. He also wrote down an email address that Margaret spelled out to him.

"Don't mention this at all to Hamish," she instructed. "I can't believe it, but Henri said we shouldn't rule out Hamish as being involved." Before Alistair could say another word, she finished with, "I'll call after the conference. Gotta go!"

Alistair replaced the phone on the table. This was too much to take in just before he had to face Hamish on screen. He was glad Margaret had warned him, but how could Henri, in France and far away from the law firm—no longer an employee, even—have that kind of information? Well, he'd just have to wait.

He pressed the connect icon on the screen, then while the little arrow went around in circles, he picked up his tablet and typed "Forsyth Laboratories" into a search engine, to make a start on learning what Henri thought he'd discovered. *Hamish giving away trade secrets*? If that was true, then nothing in Alistair's life was certain any more.

The connection finally cooperated and Alistair stared at the array of faces on his screen. Hamish seemed to be in the kitchen at home in Portland; there was Margaret at her hotel, and two other men, both of whom he now recognized from the law firm pictures. Finally, he groaned, there was the dashing Frenchman.

Henri was not dressed for a murder discussion at all, more like a lunchtime rendezvous on the Riviera. At least, a film version of it. Although only Henri's head and shoulders were visible, Alistair could tell he was wearing an elegant paisley silk shirt, collared, with what looked like a raw silk cream-colored tie.

Henri's face was deeply tanned, and his thick mane of blond hair also sun-blessed. No wonder Margaret fell for him, Alistair found himself thinking, but of course, if Henri had been in Maine for a year or two, that tan would have been long-gone. His thoughts were interrupted by Hamish, who was beginning the meeting with introductions. Hamish stopped now and again to sip from a blue and white law school logo mug, or to take a bite of what looked like a scone.

"Sorry for eating," Hamish mumbled as he chewed, "but I was on the phone early and just got off a call, so I didn't have time to finish breakfast." And on cue, Diana appeared behind Hamish's shoulder, topping up his mug from the coffee pot. She was in a pink terrycloth bathrobe!

Hamish motioned at the screen with his scone to indicate that he was already on his call; Diana whispered, "Sorry!" and quickly backed away from the scene.

With a final bite of scone, and rubbing his hands to indicate *that's out of the way*, Hamish focused on the reason for the call.

"You five people are the only individuals who are, or were, associated with the law firm, and are completely off the hook for being at the office at the time poor Marnie died. May she rest in peace. And before anyone asks, the police have also cleared me and Diana. Turns out many of our neighbors are security nuts, and the police were able to conclude that neither Diana nor I left the house that night or early morning, until the time Diana drove to the office at five-thirty."

He stopped and seemed to look directly at Alistair. "I know, as a PI, you could argue that there are ways around the surveillance, maybe sneak out the back door and dash from shrub to shrub, or leave by boat since we're near the bay, but for our purposes, assume Diana and I really are innocent."

Alistair nodded his agreement, although with Margaret's recent call and Henri's apparently inside information, was this all a bluff on Hamish's part? But at least the part about the neighborhood security systems was true: Alistair and people he knew had probably installed most of them.

Now Hamish held up a printed eight by ten color photograph. Leaning sideways so he could still be seen, he said, "This is an image of the file number for the file that Marnie was lying on when she was found. We now have more information about that. The file was grasped by her right arm, and her right index finger was wedged in between pages." He put the photograph down.

"The detective thinks that Marnie could have been looking at this file, or holding it open to mark a place, when she died. It seems very unlikely that she fell with it in that position by chance."

Alistair waited to see if Hamish would mention the post-death disruption of the scene, from when Diana shoved the file units together, but he didn't. Perhaps Diana was out of sight at the kitchen table, and Hamish didn't want to cause further distress to her.

Alistair also noted that when Hamish had first held up the photograph, Henri's eyes had widened: did he recognize the file number? But Henri kept silent.

Hamish continued, "The day of the incident, I met with the detective. A couple of times actually. I looked up the file records on our system and I know the client from the number, as well as the matter number, although the title of the matter is vague. I can tell you now, it's a patent application."

Margaret felt a pang of shock... was Henri right, Marnie *had* discovered that someone was disclosing patent secrets? But she also kept silent.

Everyone focused again on what Hamish was saying. "This morning I had a call with that client, well, with their president. Marnie's name doesn't appear in any of those client file records in our system. I mean, she's not recorded as being one of the responsible or working attorneys, but it turns out that the president, her name's Louise, she knew Marnie had done some work on their patent applications."

Hamish stopped to drink some coffee. Diana reappeared, walking across everyone's line of sight. She'd changed into jeans and a khaki shirt, Alistair was glad to see. Oh, there she goes again, now tying a floral apron at the back.

He wondered briefly why Hamish didn't move the laptop to somewhere more convenient, but the poor man had more on his mind than to think about Diana's cooking activities not being a suitable backdrop for a serious video conference.

With the muffled clanging of dishes and tins as off-screen accompaniment, now Hamish got to the point of the call.

"I truly wish that the detective could simply conclude that poor Marnie tripped on something and hit her head while retrieving a file, but after talking to Louise, that is probably not the case."

He sipped more coffee before continuing. "Now, Louise's company has been a client of the firm for over ten years. I've helped on a couple of financial matters, but the bulk of their work involves writing and filing patent applications, and doing all the legal and technical work to get patents issued. Not just here in the US, but worldwide."

He stopped when the coffee pot entered the field of view again and his mug was topped up by a disembodied hand. After another few sips, he continued.

"I am only repeating what Louise told me, but as far as I understand, when a patent application is first sent to the patent office, it is kept secret, confidential, for eighteen months. Only then can the public access it on the patent office website. Louise has been suspicious for a year or so that someone is leaking information about these patent applications when they're still supposed to be secret. The company is extremely cautious about this. They don't collaborate with any other companies, and they have no university ties. I have to say, that's unusual these days, especially in pharma work, but there's nothing wrong with her approach. She'd been suspecting that one of her employees might be selling information, but if we put together Marnie's suspicious death, and the fact that she was holding one of these secret files at death, I don't know, that's why I want to enlist your help, all of you..."

"Wait," Alistair broke in, "do you suspect the lawyer, I mean, Marnie, of being the one disclosing the secrets?"

Hamish frowned and shook his head. "No, I've thought about it and I really don't. I think she may have discovered something irregular about that patent file, or maybe she was going through them all and happened to have that one in her hand. She might have been doing her own research before presenting it to me, or to the head of the patent group. Maybe she didn't know who to trust in the firm."

"That's so sad," Margaret said. "Why didn't she come to Mark, or me, or another associate outside the patent group?"

Despite Margaret's subtle invitation to disclose that Marnie had contacted him, Henri continued to stay silent. She asked next, "Hamish, what can we do to help, practically I mean?"

"Thanks, Margaret, let's move on to that. I have a list of tasks, and between all of you, feel free to divide them up as you wish, or work together." He began reading from a list that he held in one hand, while holding his coffee mug in the other.

"First, I'm going to scan and email you copies of all the documents in the folder she was holding."

Alistair put up his hand. "Hamish, before you move on to the next topic, why are the patent files not all electronic these days? Just about every case I've worked on for your firm is only stored electronically."

Hamish looked embarrassed. "Good question," he began, before falling silent.

Now Henri raised his hand. "Hamish, I can explain that if I may. In patent work, it is very important to document exactly what information was in the patent application at the time it was filed. This is crucial for overcoming what they call prior art, meaning publications by other scientists. Also if there is infringement litigation. A digital file, it can always be altered, *n'est pas*, and it might take a lot of IT digging to prove that, which of course could be expensive and take time. In the patent group at your firm, every patent application is printed on durable paper, then each page is embossed, you know, like a notary would use. That way there's a permanent, unchangeable record of what the patent application contained on the day it was filed."

"I guess that makes sense," Hamish said. "The scanned copy I send over to you won't have the embossing, does that matter?"

"*Non,*" Henri replied, "as long as you use the true embossed copy as the starting document. I mean, don't print it from the electronic records."

"But we should have the electronic copy too, right?" Margaret asked. "Just, you know, to compare in case someone did change it in the system. For some reason."

"Good point," Hamish agreed. "I'm also going to have an outside IT consultant access all Marnie's emails for the past year. I'll figure out how best to get those to you. And before you ask, I'm not having our IT group do that because, as the detective said, everyone is still a suspect. Everyone on this side of the Atlantic anyway, and I can't risk the IT group doing anything to alter that record. Marnie's emails have already been secured from access by anyone in the firm. The police ordered that right away."

Now Mark raised his hand to speak. "That's all good Hamish, but what should we be looking for?"

Hamish smiled. "Honestly Mark, your guess is as good as mine. The detective told me to focus on motive, that is, unless the medical examiner can shed more light on how she actually died, I mean, accident or deliberate. *If* he can, that is."

He looked up suddenly at the sound of the doorbell, and Diana calling, "I'll get it."

Hamish was still looking up from the screen when someone walked into the kitchen; Alistair could hear heels on the wooden floor.

A woman's voice, not Diana's. "Good morning, Hamish. We may have a lead. The search team found a button lying near where the loose shelving is. Do you recognize it?"

Alastair couldn't believe that Hamish hadn't muted or ended the call, or at least told the detective, if that's who it was, to wait. Oh, it got worse: Hamish stretched his arm up and next thing Alistair saw, a clear evidence bag was in full view of the people on the call. Hamish examined something in it, something round and gold. Alistair started waving frantically at the screen to get Hamish's attention, but to no avail.

Hamish sighed deeply and shook his head. The item had clearly disturbed his thoughts. "I recognize it, Clara." Then, facing the screen, "Oh my God, I forgot all about our call. We'll have to pick this up again another time. I'll start getting the documents to you like we discussed. Bye." His hand reached forward to tap the screen and end the call.

Since Hamish was the host, his departure also disconnected Margaret's group, and Henri. Alistair stared at the blank screen. Whose button, and how could Hamish recognize it so quickly? Was it his, or Diana's? But if so, why did he look so worried? They both would have visited the file room: Diana the previous morning, and Hamish on other occasions. If one of *them* had lost a button, how did that relate to Marnie's death?

He decided that, after all, it probably didn't matter that the Europe-based group now knew there was a suspicious button. Unless Henri, Mark, or Charlie was in on whatever it was, but Alistair put that from his mind. Things were complicated enough without suspecting Hamish's special team.

It was a beautiful afternoon and Alistair yearned to be on the beach, as days like this would soon be a distant memory. Instead, he went to the kitchen, put some soup in a pan to heat for lunch, then went back to the tablet to see if his search for "Forsyth Laboratories" had any hits.

Chapter 20

Margaret, Mark, and Charlie looked at each other in confusion. It seemed the call had ended when they were just getting to the serious discussion.

There was a knock on the closed door. Margaret got up to open the door and see who it was. She hoped they weren't getting booted out, then remembered the room was free for the afternoon.

The hotel manager stood with a rolling trolley in front of him; Margaret was reminded of the tea service at an elegant care home she'd visited in Kilvellie. This was quite different, not the usual Scottish style with a big brown teapot hidden under a knitted tea-cozy, and old-fashioned cream cakes and treacle tarts. She almost salivated at the sight of the cakes and biscuits, tiny works of art. Or architecture, more like.

And three glass plunge-style cafetieres, a row of tea tins, and handmade ceramic mugs with the hotel's logo. She hated to think of what all this would cost, but surely Hamish would reimburse them.

"Come in." Margaret held the door open wide. "We just finished a call so this is good timing."

The manager thanked her. She realized he must be about her age. She didn't know much about him, except that he was the grandson of the wily old farmer who her Kilvellie friend Richard Wilson had known when he visited Caraidsay as a child.

"I don't normally do tea service duty," he said, "but most of the staff are in a meeting with our owner. Well, our chief investor. And before you worry about the cost, don't. As long as you don't mind being guinea pigs, that is. We'd love your feedback on these desserts."

Mark and Charlie also stood up and stretched their legs. The manager rolled the trolley to a credenza that sat against the wall at the far end of the table, next to the glass wall. As

101

he did, he passed Mark's laptop, still open. He glanced at the screen, and Margaret saw a look of surprise cross his face. She hoped Mark hadn't left anything confidential on the screen; in fact, by now his screensaver should have come on, although she had no idea what he used.

"What is it?" Mark asked the manager.

"Sorry, I really didn't mean to look, but I recognize someone in that picture."

Mark walked around the table and looked also. "Oh, my screensaver. It's a group from the firm that I took hiking a few months ago. Who do you recognize, or is it me?"

The manager took his hands off the cart handle and pointed to the screen. "That guy, he's the son of one of the investors."

Now Margaret also came around to look. "Who is it, Mark?" she asked.

"He's actually not a lawyer, he's a patent agent. Been at the firm for about five years, but most lawyers don't know him because he doesn't attend any attorney functions. Nice guy, our age. Keith Jones."

"*Really*?" The manager looked at Mark. "I guess I must be mistaken. He's the exact image of a man I know as Thompson Granger. Twins separated at birth? Anyway, I'll leave the trolley here. No rush, but please call the reception desk if you need more hot water or tea. There's a selection of herbal and regular."

He left the room, closing the door behind him. Margaret, Mark, and Charlie stared at the photo again, then Mark found the firm website bio for "Keith Jones" and they all read through it.

Margaret declared, "This is making my head hurt! Is it really possible that our firm hired someone who's using an alias? And if he's a registered patent agent, he has to have a license from the patent office, right?" She made herself a mug of tea, filled a small plate with architectural desserts, and waited for a reaction from her colleagues.

"You're right, Margaret," Mark said after a few moments. "The photo isn't that clear, and Keith, at least as we know him, is wearing a baseball cap. I think the manager must have him mixed up."

Chapter 21

Back in Portland, Hamish had changed his mind about recognizing the button. "I was distracted by the call," he explained to Clara. "Sorry to mislead you."

She had taken a seat at the table, momentarily distracted by the promising evidence of brownie-making.

"I thought maybe you recognized it as one of your buttons, Hamish, or from something of Diana's? I don't want to make light of this, but it's ironic, since we'd joked about finding a tell-tale button, like in a murder mystery."

"No, I don't recognize it." Hamish ignored Clara's attempt at humor; he got up and turned his back to her while he brewed more coffee. He knew, from his years of practice, that this action showed he was hiding something, shielding himself from Clara's perceptive eyes.

He came up with what he thought was a reasonable explanation, and turned to face her again. "I have a blazer with gold buttons, but they're smaller than that. I can fetch the blazer if you want." That was true, at least.

Clara shook her head. "Not now. Maybe the button's irrelevant. It would help to know how often the file room floor is vacuumed, and how thoroughly. I suppose the button could have lain under a shelf for weeks, or months, and was only found because of our careful search."

"Maybe," Hamish said. "That floor should be cleaned every night, or early morning. I'm not sure of the schedule. But you're right, they probably don't clean under shelving that often."

Soon the coffee pot was half full and Hamish grabbed it and poured two mugs, slipping it back under the dripping filter before he made too much of a mess. He handed a mug to Clara and sat across from her.

"Something kind of odd arrived early this morning." He'd put the piece of paper in his shirt pocket, and now he took it out and placed it in front of Clara.

"Forsyth Industries," she read aloud, then, using a clean spoon handle, turned the paper over to see if there was any other message. "What is it? A client?"

Hamish reached for the paper, but she was faster; she took an evidence bag from her satchel and, using the spoon again, slid the paper into it and sealed the bag. After asking Hamish how he got the paper, and the time, and who else had touched it, she filled out the label and placed the bag back in her satchel.

"You have no idea who left it?" she asked.

"No, it was on the floor just inside the front door when I got up. Other than me, I don't know who else has handled it. But there's no indication that this relates to Marnie, is there? It could have been put through my letterbox by mistake. I checked our list of clients and Forsyth isn't in it, or any similar spelling I could think of. It's also not in our database of companies that our clients are adverse to. We keep that up to date for conflicts checks."

Clara thanked him for the information. She gulped down her coffee and stood up. "Even if you can't identify the relevance of the company name, it seems too coincidental for it to arrive anonymously at your house, given what's just happened at your firm. Maybe someone's trying to hint at something, although what, I have no suggestions."

Diana had left them alone for the discussion, and now entered the kitchen. "Sorry for all the baking mess," she said to Clara, "but if you're in the area in, oh, three hours, I'll have more brownies cooling. You can take a tray of them to the station."

Clara laughed. "This is a terrible thing to say, Diana, but you're officially my new favorite non-suspect."

After the detective left, Hamish and Diana sat together in the kitchen and talked through the morning's events.

"I have a confession," Hamish began. "That button? I did recognize it. It's not one of mine. And it's not even a button. It's a badge from an elite high school in the Boston area. I only know because I, well, *we* know someone who went there. He always wears that badge on his lapel. It's partly so that other 'old boys' will notice it, and also to help his young hooligan clients. He tells them that he used to be like them, but he managed to go to a top school, then law school, next stop a brand new Merc. No idea if any of them buy into it, but he seems to enjoy telling the story."

Diana looked at him in shock. "You don't mean *Norm*? How did it end up in our file room? There must be others like it around."

"Who knows? If Clara thinks it's a button, I'm guessing the clasp on the back must have broken off. Otherwise she'd have said they found a pin, or a badge. Not a button."

"Hamish, you have to tell her! At this point you are officially hiding evidence, misleading the police in a murder inquiry." She picked up his cell phone and thrust it at him.

"Call her! *Now!*"

Hamish looked at her meekly. "Can I tell her when she comes over for the brownies, and she'll be in a good mood?"

"NOW!" And with that, Diana stormed out of the kitchen. Hamish heard her go up the staircase; she probably would have stomped her feet for emphasis if she hadn't been wearing her huge fluffy slippers.

He waited until she was out of hearing to make his call, but not to Clara.

"Hi Hamish," Alistair answered right away. "Are you calling to follow up from the video conference?"

"I will want to do that, yes, but for now I have an urgent request. Diana's just accused me of misleading the police and I need your advice. Do you have time?"

"Of course. Anyway, anything I'm doing takes a back seat to what you're going through. I wish I was in Portland and could help you from there."

"That's why I'm calling, hoping you can rope in a colleague to help. Actually, I have two things I need help with. One is this. Early this morning, a small piece of paper was slipped through the letterbox in our front door. It had two words on it, Forsyth Industries..."

"Wait, Hamish, spell it for me."

Hamish spelled out the words. "I was ready to disregard it, maybe it had been meant for another house, but Clara took it away in an evidence bag. I told her it doesn't correspond to any of our clients, or anyone in the conflicts database, so I don't..."

"Hamish," Alistair interrupted. "Clara may be correct. I know even less than you at this point, and I'm waiting for Margaret to call me. But right before our conference call earlier, she told me to write down three things. One was 'Forsyth Laboratories,' another was the name 'Craig Sutherland,' and the third was an email address that ends in 'ForLab.co.uk.' I can't believe your anonymous note would be a coincidence."

Hamish had written the words as Alistair read them out. "Is the name Sutherland a surname, or could it be Craig *in* Sutherland? It's a large area in Scotland."

"I think it's the surname. I didn't read you the whole email address, but his name is part of it."

"Why did Margaret give you those names?" Hamish asked next. "And where did *she* get them?"

"No idea, Hamish, sorry. That's why I'm anxious to hear back from her. I'll let you know when I have more information. What's the other issue you wanted to discuss?"

Hamish described the item that Clara thought was a button, whereas it looked to Hamish like a badge, or pin, that Norm was proud of wearing.

"Not No-jail Norm again? His name's come up twice in two days. This is too much."

"I agree. The problem is that Clara says the item was found in the file room, near where spare shelves are piled up."

"That's crazy, Hamish. There must be more of those pins. Someone else could have dropped it. Or maybe it fell out of a storage box? Your intellectual property people store all kinds of samples and exhibits."

Hamish sighed. "I suppose. The bigger problem is, I told Clara I didn't recognize it. After I first said I did. I truly don't know what came over me, denying it like that. Diana's furious. She tried to stomp out of the room but her slippers were too quiet."

Alistair laughed. "That is kind of funny, Hamish, but it sounds like she's right. Do *you* think Norm could have attacked Marnie? It seems very unlikely, but with his hint that someone in your firm is involved in a criminal matter, it seems all bets are off."

"I agree," Hamish said. "I can't believe it either. And if he is involved, he's even more of a snake than I thought, because he sat in on the detective's initial interview with Diana, after telling me he had a conflict and couldn't actually represent her..."

"Hamish!" Alistair interrupted again. "Why did you include him, when he'd said he had a conflict? If he is involved somehow, he's now privy to the police's preliminary findings and Diana's explanation of what happened. He could use that if he needs to defend himself."

Hamish turned quickly—Diana was coming down the staircase. "I'd better go," he told Alistair. "I have a call to make. Let me know when you've spoken to Margaret, please?"

"Of course. Bye Hamish."

Diana sat down at the table, arms crossed over her chest, and glared at Hamish. "That can't have been Clara, if you're waiting for someone to talk to Margaret. Have you called her yet?"

"No, but I'm about to. Let's have some lunch after I speak to her. I'll probably need a whisky with it."

Diana stood up and rummaged in the refrigerator for something to throw together for lunch.

Hamish took the phone to his office and closed the door. With shaking hands, he selected a name from his contact list.

"Norm? It's Hamish. We need to talk."

Chapter 22

In the meeting room at the hotel where Margaret, Mark, and Charlie were conferring, Margaret's call to Alistair soon grew into an argument. She reacted when Alistair told her he'd shared the Forsyth, Sutherland, and email address information with Hamish.

"*Why* did you tell him?" she asked, trying to control her temper. "Henri gave me those details in confidence."

"Sorry, Margaret, I only mentioned those names because Hamish said someone put an anonymous note with the words 'Forsyth Industries' through his letterbox at home. So the company name wasn't news to him."

Margaret sighed and calmed down. She looked over to see Mark and Charlie watching with interest.

"Alistair," she said, "I'm still in the meeting room with the others. Can we have another video call now and talk this through?"

Alistair agreed, and the three lawyers assembled themselves at their laptop screens again. Soon they were connected, with Alistair looking like he hadn't moved from his place at the table in the Finlay cottage.

"Is there anything new you can tell us from Hamish?" Margaret asked first.

She watched as Alistair considered this: obviously, Hamish had told him something, but she couldn't tell if Alistair was ready to share.

"Okay," he began, "but the usual caveats. Don't pass any of it on, right? Not to Henri either. He's not employed by the firm any more, and we can't be sure how he fits into all this."

He stopped while Margaret and her two colleagues looked at each other, all nodding in agreement.

"Two developments in Portland, that I know of anyway. Hamish told me that when he got up this morning, early, there was a small piece of paper on the floor by the front door, that looked like it had been dropped through the letterbox. It had two words, Forsyth Industries. At the time, he thought it was probably delivered to the wrong house. He checked against databases for the firm, you know, clients and adverse parties, and there were no hits on the name."

Margaret added, "And we, I mean, me, Charlie, and Mark, heard from Henri that Marnie received an email with a Forsyth name on it. What's the other development?"

"The detective, Clara, showed up at Hamish's house with a gold button in an evidence bag. It was found in the file room. Hamish's immediate reaction was, he told her he recognized it, then he retracted that soon after. Remember, that's how our call with him ended."

"But not the retraction part," Mark said. "Did Hamish tell you why he did that? Is he protecting someone?"

"Possibly." Alistair looked away from the screen for a moment, his resolve wavering. "Look Margaret, and Charlie and Mark, I'm beginning to feel like we're pawns in some bigger picture. I'm not even sure I should tell you who he thinks the button belongs to..."

"Alistair," Mark broke in, "if someone in our law firm is a murderer, we need to know who Hamish suspects. Perhaps one of us knows something that could shed light on all this."

Margaret agreed. "Come on Alistair, who did Hamish say the button could belong to? It must be quite distinctive, right?"

"It's not actually a button. He said it's a pin, or badge, from an elite high school that a criminal lawyer called Norm Adler attended. Hamish knows him from law school, and probably from Bar functions too. The guy apparently still wears it on his jacket lapel."

Mark was working away on his tablet, and he held up the screen to the camera.

"Is this him?" he asked Alistair. "He's nicknamed No-jail Norm?"

Alistair nodded his head.

"Hamish thinks *this* guy could have killed Marnie?" Mark put the tablet down again. "Wow, we're into godfather territory now. Well, Portland's version anyway. And is Hamish reluctant to disclose the connection? Wait, isn't Norm the lawyer who sat in on Diana's questioning by the police, right after she found Marnie? Diana said something like that in one of her emails to me."

Alistair nodded in agreement. "Exactly. Is he playing both sides?"

Mark exhaled loudly. "Whew, I guess I'm glad we're investigating from this remote island. What did Marnie get herself involved in?"

"Hold on." Alistair held up his hand. "Hamish only *thinks* the pin or whatever could have come from Norm's jacket."

"But he's going to tell the police, right?" Charlie asked, his first question for the call. "I mean, he has to, otherwise he's obstructing justice. A lawyer can't do that, let alone a *managing partner.*" He pronounced the title with a reverence usually reserved for royalty.

Mark and Margaret both looked at Charlie: the poor young man seemed to droop, his high regard for Hamish and his enthusiasm for the law firm being worn away by the enormity of what was happening.

"I *hope* he'll tell the detective," was all Alistair could offer. "But back to the mystery note dropped at Hamish's front door. Remember, he mentioned that his neighbors have cameras that pretty much cover the whole street. Hamish didn't suggest asking the neighbors what they've got recorded for the time the note would have been left, so I want to run this by you three. As Margaret knows, I have colleagues in Portland. I'm sure I could have one of them pose as a delivery driver, maybe say a neighbor complained that their package had been lifted from their front door, and ask to see anything recorded in that time frame?"

112

"Sounds like a good idea," Margaret said, "but couldn't the police do that?"

"If they were investigating a theft, then yes, but I doubt they'd commit the resources if they knew it was really to check on a piece of paper that may have nothing to do with any crime."

"Do it," Mark urged, "before it's recorded over or however those cameras work. Or maybe it's stored digitally forever. Sorry to be insistent, but the sooner we get answers, the better for everyone. I'll commit to pay your colleague whatever it costs, and I'll make sure to get repaid by the firm."

Margaret thought Alistair looked both surprised and pleased at Mark taking charge of the situation. She knew Alistair preferred action to long discussions and dithering. He'd be impatient to get off the call and start making the arrangements with a colleague in Portland.

"Thanks, both of you, for thinking of that," she said to Alistair and Mark.

Looking away from the screen, she glanced back and forth at Mark and Charlie. "I don't know about you two, but I could use some fresh air and walk off all the desserts."

"Desserts?" Alistair asked, eyebrows raised, poised to end the call.

"I promise to bring some back to Finlay," Margaret said, grinning. "Bye for now!"

The windows in the meeting room faced away from the water, but Margaret knew from the tide schedule that there was no chance to get over to the tidal island that afternoon, not before sunset anyway. She thought about how to spend the rest of the day, and decided she'd like to be alone and think things through. She hoped Mark, or Mark and Charlie, wouldn't expect to continue on with the endless discussions and what-ifs.

"I really need a break," she told them. "I'll probably be ready for dinner around seven tonight, but don't feel you should keep me company. I'm sure you have things to discuss for your own project."

"I can't speak for Mark," Charlie said, "but I'd sure like the chance to eat with you. We can talk about something other than Hamish's dilemma. And poor Marnie."

"Count me in!" Mark agreed, and with the plan in place to meet for dinner, Margaret wrapped a couple of the remaining desserts in a paper napkin and headed for her room, but stopped first at the reception desk.

"I was supposed to check out today and now I'm not sure how much longer I need to stay here," she said to the manager, who seemed to be multitasking.

He checked the hotel computer for the upcoming reservation schedule.

"As of right now, you're fine for a few more days. If need be I'll juggle a few guests around. But since you're a guest of the prince, you have priority."

Margaret felt herself blush. Sure, the prince was covering what should have been four nights at the hotel, for all her help with his beach clean-up project, but she couldn't expect him to cover her staying on to help with Hamish's crisis back in Portland. She was not thrilled at paying the room rate herself, several hundred pounds a night, but she also resisted the idea of moving to a small B&B room in another part of the island, away from Mark and Charlie.

She assumed Hamish would cover Mark and Charlie's prolonged stay, since presumably they couldn't justify charging the client, but that was their business. Neither had made any mention of moving to other accommodations.

Not knowing how long she'd have the luxury of the whirlpool tub in her room, she decided to treat herself to a long soak and a couple of hours of relaxation before dinner.

Chapter 23

In his home office, behind the closed door, Hamish willed Norm to answer the phone. If Hamish had to leave a message, he knew he'd have to put off calling the detective, Clara, and confess to knowing who the button, the pin, might belong to.

"Hamish?" came the loud voice, and Hamish breathed a long sigh of relief.

"You shouldn't be calling me," Norm complained. "I told you, I can't represent Diana."

"It's not that," Hamish assured him. "This a courtesy call, but I won't insult you by saying you mustn't reveal to anyone that I spoke to you."

"Okaaay," Norm said cautiously, "where are we going with this?"

"Just a yes or no answer, first," Hamish began. "That Boston school pin you always wear on your lapel, do you know where it is now?"

"Sure, but I don't know why you're asking. It's on the jacket I wore to a meeting with some local teenagers a few days ago, part of a neighborhood crime prevention program. A friend of mine runs it."

"Humor me," Hamish continued. "Is the pin on the jacket right now?"

Norm was silent, but Hamish could hear him taking deep breaths. Not a good sign at all. "I'll be right back," Norm muttered.

Hamish almost didn't want to know the answer. He'd done what he'd set out to do, put Norm on notice, but he couldn't hang up on the guy. Maybe Norm *did* still have the pin, and the presence of a similar one on the file room floor was a false lead.

"That's a shame." Norm returned to the call but didn't admit that the pin wasn't where it should have been. "I sure liked it. I hope I can order another one from the school. I wonder where it got to?"

Hamish groaned inwardly. Surely Norm wasn't going to play innocent?

He spoke quietly. "Norm, the police have it. They found it in the file room. They searched every inch of the place after they took Marnie's body out."

Now Hamish wished he'd made the call on video, because he'd love to see Norm's face, how the man was processing this information.

"Norm, can you tell me, assure me I mean, that you didn't harm Marnie?"

"I did not harm Marnie, I'd swear to it in court," Norm declared. "And in case you ask next, I was not present at her time of death."

Hamish was taken aback: *he* didn't even know Marnie's exact time of death. Maybe Norm had a source in the police station? Wouldn't surprise him.

"We don't know the time of death, to my knowledge," Hamish argued.

"Well..." Norm seemed to falter. "Whatever the time of death was, I have an alibi."

This was too much, and Hamish raised his voice. "Norm, there's a promising young associate lying stone cold in the morgue. I have to meet with her grieving and angry parents. Does practicing criminal law make you *that* insensitive?"

Hamish glanced around his office, wishing now for a cigarette: he hadn't smoked for ages, but if he started again it would be Norm's doing. Maybe he could find one stuck in a drawer?

Before he began rummaging, he was distracted by Norm's more contrite denial. "Sorry Hamish, but no, I don't have the luxury of your *genteel* practice. To be more delicate, I was not in the file room when poor Marnie passed away, whenever it took place. And whatever caused it."

"But you *were* in the file room recently, I'm assuming, if you say you had the pin on your jacket just a few days ago?"

Now a deep sigh came through the line. Hamish had a sickening feeling he knew what had happened, so he answered for the man.

"Norm, I can't claim the high moral ground, since I started dating Diana before my divorce came through. If you're having a fling, serious or not, with someone at my firm, now you have a heads up that the police have your pin. I was caught off-guard when Clara showed it to me today in an evidence bag. I was busy on a conference call and I automatically said it looked familiar, but then I basically retracted it. Diana heard both of those statements and she's not even talking to me right now. Insists I tell the detective, Clara. And I have to, don't you see, even if it involves your private life?"

Norm was quiet for a few moments, too long, Hamish thought.

"Of course you do, Hamish. Just tell Clara you've seen me wearing one like it. Don't repeat our conversation. Let them do the work of fingerprints and all, if they can even get prints off that tiny thing."

Ah, thought Hamish, No-jail Norm re-emerging: "Let the police do the work" without any help from someone who actually knows the truth.

"And remember, Hamish, by protecting my privacy, you're protecting someone who works at your firm, don't *you* see that?"

Another Norm-ism, use one's own words to come back with an argument. Well, he'd done his bit to alert Norm. Maybe he'd broken a few ethical rules, but a fling between adults, or even something more serious, was not murder.

He ended the call quickly. Now to get the really hard part over with. He called Clara's cell phone number, deciding to go on the offensive and not give her a chance to berate him. He summoned his courtroom closing argument strategy.

"Clara," he said when she answered, "it's Hamish. I remembered about that button, you know, from the file room. Sorry about earlier, but I was distracted with my conference call, I didn't get a good look at it. Do you want to come by? I can tell by the smell from the kitchen, the brownies must be just perfect. Now, do you want regular or decaf with them?"

He ended the call feeling slightly sick, but now at least Diana might quit stomping around the place and be nice to him again. How could he fault Norm for one or two evening liaisons in a secluded file room when he and Diana were just as guilty? He did wonder for a moment who at the firm Norm was seeing, but decided he *really* didn't want to know.

Chapter 24

Alistair had no success with asking a colleague to find out if any of the security cameras near Hamish's house had recorded someone putting the piece of paper through Hamish's front door letterbox. The colleague reported back that both neighbors across the street from Hamish claimed their systems were down, and hadn't recorded in the relevant time frame.

"*Both*?" Alistair had asked. It seemed too coincidental, unless there had been a neighborhood-wide disruption in power or internet connection. Plus, the cameras were working fine when the police checked on the movements of Hamish and Diana in the hours prior to when Marnie's body was found.

Alistair was taking a quick tea break after the call, before turning his attention to the mysterious Craig Sutherland and the Forsyth Industries/Laboratories question, when an email came in from... *Henri*? No one else seemed to be cc'd on it, unless they were bcc'd Alistair thought, so he'd have to tread carefully.

Henri's email left Alistair speechless. The guy had, amazingly, booked a plane ticket from France and would arrive in Edinburgh at some point, more details to follow. He was asking Alistair where he should go from there: to the island where Margaret and the other lawyers were staying, or to Margaret's home, where Alistair was, if she was returning soon.

Alistair wanted to email right back and tell him to cancel the ticket: what was Henri thinking? But instead, he made a pot of tea and gave himself a chance to think things through. Henri, Margaret, and Mark (plus Charlie, but he seemed to be tagging along and not part of the decision-making) were tasked by Hamish to find a motive in Marnie's death, a motive that might have links in Scotland. If Henri's patent

119

background was integral to the investigation, maybe it would help to have him around in person?

He returned to the laptop and stared at the email. He was trying not to let his personal worries get in the way. Margaret had assured him that Henri was only in her past. But if Henri showed up on the island, would Margaret be drawn back by his obvious charms?

Leaving that aside, at some point Margaret had to come home to the cottage, in the next day or two Alistair hoped. Should he invite Henri to stay in the upstairs guest suite? *No* was his immediate answer.

Helen Griffen had told Alistair that the Finlay hotel was booked for the rest of the summer. Alistair considered investigating other hotels, but decided that Henri could do that, or maybe he had an assistant who handled the travel logistics.

Never dreaming that he'd be writing to Margaret's ex-boyfriend, he typed a quick reply. He said that the nearest hotel was full, but there would be others nearby, some of which catered to golfers, that might have a room. He wondered if he should offer to meet Henri at Edinburgh Airport when he arrived, but the guy could rent a car. He just hoped Margaret wouldn't be furious, and that, instead, she'd be glad that he'd put any potential jealousy aside for the sake of the investigation.

Next task: speak to Margaret and get all she knew about Forsyth.

She sounded relaxed when she answered the phone. "Do you have time to talk now?" Alistair asked. He had just realized it was six in the evening, and she might be heading to the dining room for dinner. Or ordering room service.

"Yes, I've tried your cell a couple of times but I figured maybe you've been on the phone with Hamish. Is there any news from Portland?"

"Not yet. Can you explain to me about the Forsyth name and that email address you asked me to write down just before our conference call with Hamish?"

"Yes, Henri had a phone conference with me and the others, I mean, Mark and Charlie. A few days ago, Marnie contacted Henri and sent him a copy of an email from that UK address I gave you. The sender asked Marnie for clarification about a chemical structure pasted into the email. It's convoluted, but she told Henri that the structure had a crucial error in it. And the sender in the UK could only have known about it by having access to a patent application with the same error. The error was correctly quickly."

"Patent applications eventually get published, right?" Alistair asked. "I'm no expert, but I did get a Patents 101 lecture when the patent I'm on was filed."

"True, but again, according to what Marnie told Henri, this chemical structure is top secret, an important discovery. And from a follow-up email Henri sent me, no one in the UK should have had it, because the US patent office hadn't granted an export license yet." She stopped to let Alistair take it all in.

"I know," she continued, "too much detail. But the bottom line is, Marnie did seem to have evidence of theft of a trade secret, or industrial espionage. And the source could be the law firm."

"Or the company, the client I mean," Alistair countered.

"Good point. To get back to Hamish's involvement, Marnie contacted Henri because she didn't know who she could trust at the firm. Anyone, theoretically, have gone to the file room, then photocopied or photographed the important chemical information and emailed it to the UK. Henri suggested she tell Hamish about it."

"And did she?" Alistair asked.

"Henri doesn't know. She was dead soon after. So Henri is concerned that Marnie did go to Hamish, but I can't believe Hamish is involved. He has a great life and he wouldn't risk it, would he? He loves Diana, he's got a nice house, and the four kids..."

"Margaret, I'm sorry to burst your bubble, but those things could all be argued the other way. Maybe Hamish is struggling to afford his lifestyle, and he gave in to temptation to sell a trade secret."

"No, Alistair! You'll never convince me of that possibility. I say we share with him what Marnie told Henri. I mean, *Henri* should call him. Right away."

Alistair stopped and took a sip of tea. He had to tell her eventually...

"Margaret, Henri's, well, he's..."

"He's what? In meetings all day?"

"No. Don't be mad, but he's coming to Scotland."

"*What?* Why on earth..."

"It was his idea, Margaret, and he did make a good point about the five of us working together to help Hamish through this. At least not be spread out in two countries and a remote island."

"He's not staying at the cottage, is he? Please tell me you didn't invite him!"

"Of course not! It's your cottage, I would never do that without asking you. He'll get a hotel room somewhere. But since we're on that subject, Helen Griffen, remember, the police officer in Kilvellie, she wondered if Christy the sea glass jeweler could stay in the cottage for a couple of nights while she talks to people here about opening a shop."

"*She* can stay. When is this?"

"I don't know. I told Helen I'd get back to her after I talked to you. I guess it could be as early as tomorrow."

"Should I come back?" Margaret asked. "I don't want you to have all the work of taking care of a guest."

"It's up to you. Do you think you can help Hamish more effectively if you're in the same place as the other two lawyers? I suppose they could come to Finlay as well, but the hotel seems to be booked up."

Margaret groaned. "Ugh, this is such a dilemma. I want to come home, but I absolutely do not want to see Henri, or have him expect to eat meals with us. And I guess, I can probably work more effectively with Mark and Charlie on the island. Anyway, I really hope this will all be cleared up in a day or two, and Mark and Charlie can head back to Portland."

"I do miss you, Margaret. I'd love to leave right now and get the morning ferry from Oban, but with Henri arriving soon... I guess I should stay."

"It's fine," she assured him. "What are you going to do next, for helping Hamish?"

"I'll start investigating the Forsyth information, hopefully find out who Craig Sutherland is and why he emailed Marnie with information he shouldn't have possession of. I wonder... do you think I could involve Adam? He's far more familiar with Scotland and its industries. Maybe he'll know without me spending a lot of time."

"I don't see why not. But who's going to pay for his time? I think Hamish is too distracted to realize what having three non-billing attorneys is doing to the bottom line, not to mention our stats. I'm not in a position to say that the firm would reimburse Adam for his time and costs."

"Don't worry about that now. Adam and I are used to doing favors back and forth, and he always likes a new challenge."

Margaret glanced at the time. "I'd better get going. They start serving dinner soon, and after our day I need some comfort food. Talk to you later?"

"Definitely! Say hi to the guys from me."

She laughed. "*Don't* say hi to Henri from me."

They ended the call. So, Alistair thought, Margaret was not happy about Henri showing up in Scotland. Knowing that was the highlight of his day.

123

Chapter 25

The following morning, with the twins off to school thanks to a neighbor offering to drive them again, Hamish and Diana sat together at the kitchen table, both with laptops open and catching up on emails. Although Diana had an "out of office" message on hers, she was still keeping up with news and questions from clients, and from the junior associates she worked with.

Thank goodness for Mark, she was thinking: his carefully worded replies to numerous inquiries did him credit. She glanced up when Hamish emitted a loud, "*What the heck*?"

He shook his head, then looked at Diana. "You won't *believe* this. Henri is off to Scotland, to the village where Alistair and Margaret are living. Margaret's still on the island with Mark and Charlie, so why would Henri do that?"

Diana smiled. "He probably regrets breaking up with her and maybe he's gone to Finlay to check out his competition, I mean, your handsome PI Alistair?"

"Fat chance," Hamish replied, laughing. "Not with Margaret engaged now."

Diana smiled again and shook her head. "Hamish, you pursued me when I was *married*, so anything's possible for Henri. But really, why has he gone to Scotland? Certainly not for the food."

"Ha ha. It's not all haggis and neeps these days. Seriously though, we're still trying to find a motive, *if* Marnie was murdered, and the patent file is our best lead for now. Among the four non-suspect attorneys, I mean the ones who were overseas at the time, Henri is the only one who knows something about patents."

"You have a point," Diana conceded. "But back to Henri and Margaret. You've said yourself, Margaret is not the same shy young attorney from two years ago. Maybe Henri got a shock when he saw her on your video call and wants to see if he still has a chance."

"But why, Diana? Henri made a choice to go home to France and practice from there. Margaret will be back in Portland soon..."

"Are you *sure* about that?" Diana interrupted.

Hamish stared at her. "Do you know something I don't?"

"No, but she must be done clearing out her uncle's cottage by now, then she finished that big case with you, which by the way the partners are still talking about, and some of them are ready to pounce on Margaret when she's back in the office. Not literally, of course." She gasped. "Oh, that's so insensitive. Maybe that's what happened to Marnie—was she fending off an unwanted advance in the file room?"

"Oh my God," Hamish blurted out, his eyes widening in shock. "The thought never crossed my mind. Maybe I should tell Clara..." His voice drifted off.

"What, Hamish? You're mumbling. What are you thinking about?"

He stood up to make a new pot of coffee while he thought through the scenario. He was pretty sure of two things: first, Norm, the criminal lawyer who claimed to have a "conflict" with Hamish's firm, had been in the file room at some point in the past few days, just prior to Marnie's death. Second, Norm had most likely been there for a personal liaison with someone who worked at the law firm. Could *Marnie* have been involved with Norm?

He felt himself physically cringe at the unwanted image. But, he forced himself to think, that could tie all the evidence together, and better still, it would rule out involvement by any other employees of the firm.

When the coffee had finished brewing, he refilled their mugs, sat down again, and shared his suspicions with Diana.

"Yuck!" was her initial response. "Really? You think Marnie, a junior associate, was carrying on with Norm? He's, he's…"

"He's my age, yes," Hamish said. "Not that the age difference would rule it out, but they seem like such different people. Marnie was working full time and going to science classes at night so she could qualify for the patent attorney exam, or whatever it is. If nothing else, she had no time for an affair."

"Careful, Hamish. Norm is divorced and Marnie was single, so it would have been a relationship, not an affair. If there is anything, *was* anything, going on between them."

"This is really upsetting. I need a break." Hamish closed his laptop and stood up. "Talking about Henri and Margaret was much more pleasant."

His phone pinged with a text message, so he sat at the table again and scrolled through it.

"So much for my theory," he told Diana. "It's a message from the detective, Clara. Someone from the law firm arrived at the police station this morning, ready to confess."

"To *killing* Marnie?" Diana whispered.

"I don't know what they're confessing to. Clara wants to stop by soon and show us something. No slouching around in our bathrobes all day."

Hand in hand, they went upstairs, Hamish dreading what Clara would tell him. He couldn't imagine any employee capable of murder, so he prepared himself to be shocked, whoever it was. But, he realized, it didn't clear up his nightmare thoughts of Norm and Marnie together. If that scenario were true, he could never look the guy in the eyes again without being tempted to punch him. Or knock the hood emblem off the shiny new Merc.

Chapter 26

While Diana and Hamish prepared to meet with Clara and learn what had really happened to Marnie, as related by whatever law firm employee had confessed, Margaret, Charlie, and Mark were finishing lunch in the hotel dining room on Caraidsay Island.

Margaret planned to visit the tidal island for another trash-collecting session: at this rate, she thought, she might single-handedly win the award for the most trash from one beach. But until they heard more from Alistair and Henri, with information about the Forsyth companies and the puzzling email to Marnie, there wasn't anything they could do to help Hamish.

She could tell that Charlie and Mark were impatient, basically stranded on Caraidsay, their client work there finished. She was ready to get back to Finlay and be with Alistair, but it felt rude to leave the two others alone here. And Henri arriving in Finlay just complicated things. Would he say something to Alistair that could damage their relationship? She hoped not.

As she stood up to leave, she told the others that she was walking over to the tidal island for the afternoon. They stood up also, and all three looked out of the window as she pointed at the rocky path.

"You're welcome to join me," she added, "but you can see, the footing is pretty challenging."

"I have hiking boots with me," Mark said. "I'll like to see the island while I'm here."

Charlie also offered to go, but then Margaret looked down at his brown loafers. "You need some better footwear. You'll risk falling in those. Hamish would not forgive me if you got stuck here with broken bones."

With a deep sigh, Charlie reluctantly agreed. "Too bad the hotel doesn't have anything like that in their gift shop. Oh well, see you both for dinner."

Margaret and Mark arranged to meet outside in ten minutes, and they each went to their rooms to change into suitable clothing for an afternoon on the windy coast. Upstairs, Margaret checked her phone for emails; it was still early in Portland, and there was no news from Hamish. Alistair had texted that Christy was arriving soon to stay at the cottage. Too much, she thought, too much going on at once.

The day had begun cloudy, but the wind had picked up and the sun was breaking through. Margaret led Mark down the uneven stone steps that provided access to the shore below the hotel. It would only take a few minutes to cross the now-exposed tidal path, but they took their time, Mark stopping now and again to pick up a small rock or shell.

At the tidal island side, the land rose slightly; Mark went first and extended a hand back to help Margaret up. She'd done this alone and was momentarily annoyed at his assumption she'd need help, but Alistair did the same thing long before they were a couple, so she accepted it without comment.

However, when they reached level ground, Mark kept hold of her hand. She could hardly yank her hand out of his grasp, so she said, lightly, "I'm fine now, Mark. No more help needed!"

But instead of letting go, he turned to face her.

"Margaret, I don't know why we didn't get to know each other better over the past two years. I'd like to make up for that lost time."

"We're friends now," she replied, trying to project confidence but already sensing that something was wrong.

"I meant, more than friends. I wish I'd asked you out after Hamish's Christmas dinner, but before I had a chance, Henri was dating you."

You could have asked me out when Henri left for France, she felt like saying, but kept quiet.

"I'm engaged to Alistair now," she reminded him.

Mark let go of her hand but stayed close, still facing her.

"But Margaret, he's so different from us. Does he really understand the work you do, the pressures of getting ahead at the law firm? Maybe he won't be sympathetic to the long hours, the travel, all that."

Margaret almost laughed. *Long hours? Travel?* If those words didn't encapsulate Alistair's career, then nothing did. But Mark didn't seem ready to be persuaded by logic.

"Look," she said, "I only have a couple of hours on the island before the tide turns and the path gets submerged again. I want to get to my trash collecting area and accomplish something this afternoon. You're welcome to help or go explore the island, although there's not much to see."

Despite her effort at assertiveness, Margaret was actually ready to go right back to the hotel, hunker in her room, and forget this whole awkward exchange. What was the matter with the guy?

Now he was looking out to sea. He'd moved a couple of feet away from her.

"I'm *really* sorry, Margaret. I misread signals. I thought maybe you wanted to be alone with me over here, on the tidal island, and that's why you discouraged Charlie from coming along too."

She turned and looked up at him; he was standing on a slight rise in the land, so he seemed even taller.

"Mark, I only discouraged him because he has no appropriate boots or hiking shoes with him! He's obviously in awe of you, a third-year, and he wants to impress you. I'm sure he'd be over here, not missing out on anything, if he'd thought to bring hiking boots." *Or if you'd suggested it in Portland,* she felt like saying. Poor Charlie: unlike Mark, he was obviously not an experienced traveler, but he also hadn't done his homework and learned about the terrain of the place they were visiting.

129

Mark had placed his backpack on the ground, and he lifted it and hoisted it on his shoulders again.

"Okay, Margaret, can you forget we had this conversation? Totally my bad. Do you want me to go back right away? Or, please, let me make it up to you and help collect whatever it is you're after."

Margaret shouldered her pack as well, at the same time feeling the emotional weight of the past few tense minutes evaporate. She decided to give Mark the benefit of the doubt; they might have to work together for years. "This way." She led him toward the break between the rocks that she'd focused on in her past few visits.

She pointed out the trash containers above the high tide line and gave Mark a couple of the trash bags stowed nearby, out of the wind. Soon they were each sitting on a patch of the rocky shore, diligently collecting small pieces of plastic and metal.

Margaret was smiling to herself. She wondered if she should tell her mother Jilly about this development: Jilly had mentally selected Mark from among the first year associates, hoping Margaret and he could develop a relationship. Would Jilly think that by turning Mark down now, two years later, she was making a mistake? Or would Jilly applaud Margaret's resistance to Mark's charms, instead staying with Alistair?

Either way, it would make for an enjoyable exchange one of these days. She let herself relax into the sunny afternoon. Maybe it would be her last on this island, at least until a future trip to Scotland. She glanced over at Mark, who was taking a break and standing to look around.

She stood also. "Would you like to explore the island while we're over here? If we keep an eye on the time, we can have a walk and still cross the causeway while it's safe."

He smiled. "Yes, and I want to get your opinion on this project. I mean, the wind power that Charlie and I are here to investigate."

After securing their collected trash in the large container, they headed along a rough trail at the edge of the island, away from the path back to the causeway.

Chapter 27

Now dressed in comfortable clothes—jeans, shirts, and their law firm fleece vests—Hamish and Diana returned to the kitchen to wait for Clara's arrival.

"Should we meet with her in your office?" Diana asked. "It seems so casual in here, having coffee while discussing Marnie's death."

"No." Hamish filled the kettle. He'd offer Clara a choice of tea or coffee, he decided. "If she wants a formal meeting, she'd ask us to go to the station. I'm fine in here, but would you prefer another part of the house?"

She smiled. "Kitchen is best for me too."

Clara arrived a few minutes later, looking more relaxed than on her previous visits. She accepted a mug of hot tea and produced a half-eaten scone from her purse. Diana handed her a plate, and Clara began breaking off pieces of the scone, apologizing.

"I was halfway through breakfast at home when the station called and said someone had shown up, offering information about Marnie's death. When I arrived, we began talking, but right away the person, well, he confessed."

"To *murder*?" Hamish had been preparing a mug of coffee for himself at the counter and he turned quickly to look at Clara, then at Diana, who was already seated at the table.

"No, not murder," Clara explained. "To accidental death. To, um, I hate to say this, but a romantic meeting gone wrong."

"You don't mean, he tried to..." Diana didn't finish the sentence.

"I don't know." From her facial expression, Hamish thought Clara seemed unconvinced by the confession. "It's just his word unfortunately. Although, Marnie's body had no signs at all of, well, you know what I'm getting at. And none of what we'd call defensive wounds. Nothing under her fingernails even, fibers, skin, like she'd clawed at someone."

She waited until Hamish was also seated, across from Diana, then continued.

"The man, he admitted to meeting Marnie in the file room to look at a file. He claims that they decided to take advantage of being alone, and at some stage, she lost her footing and fell backwards against the piled-up shelving. It's consistent with the medical examiner's report, that a hard fall like that, with the shelving at the right—well—*wrong* angle, could cause the sudden death."

"Who confessed?" Diana demanded. "Was it an attorney or one of the legal assistants? A file clerk?"

"Actually, none of the above. It was your patent agent, Keith Jones."

"*What?*" Hamish's eyes widened as he looked at Clara. "That meek English guy? He's been with us about five years. Can't believe he'd do something like that."

"Why didn't he report Marnie's injury right away?" Diana asked next. "Maybe Marnie could have survived if she had medical attention!"

"That's all to be discussed," Clara assured her.

"I don't know Keith," Diana said, shaking her head. "Since he's not an associate and he's not on partner track, he basically does his work then goes home. Not much professional socializing. Are you saying that Marnie was dating him or interested in him? I guess that's possible."

"Better than my scenario," Hamish muttered.

Clara stared at him intently. "What scenario was that, Hamish?"

He waved his hand dismissively. "When I realized it was Norm's pin you found in the file room, I had this sickening thought that he and Marnie..."

"Please, no need to finish that thought. For now, at least we can be confident that we have the right person. We've released no details about Marnie's injury to the public or to your employees, and I'm assuming neither of you told anyone else?"

Hamish looked at her, feeling chagrined. "Maybe I made a mistake. I told my PI in Scotland, Alistair Wright. But I'm sure he wouldn't share that information. Especially not with any law firm employees."

Clara sipped her tea and thought this through.

I hope not," she said. "Anyway, even if Alistair had made a slip in a conversation, would that have a bearing on someone confessing to having been there?"

"Maybe to cover up for someone else?" Hamish suggested. He still couldn't get the image out of his head, that Norm might have been with Marnie. "Clara, what about the button you found, the pin? The one belonging to Norm?"

"I'm getting to that, Hamish. Again, we need to go through Keith's story in detail, verify the timing and his movements, but he claims that he panicked when Marnie fell. I'm sorry to upset you more, but he said she had no pulse, and from the angle of her head, there was just no way she had survived."

Diana started tearing up and she dabbed her eyes with a tissue.

"My God, poor Marnie! But if she fell against shelving on the floor, or against the wall, how did she end up between the rolling shelf units where I found her?"

"This is where it gets really ugly, I'm afraid, and your pal Norm enters the scene. Literally. Keith called him..."

"Norm's *not* my pal," Hamish interrupted. "Please, I'm not sure how much more of this I want to hear."

Clara took him at his word. "I can go, Hamish. I thought you'd like to know what happened, but if it's too..."

"Sorry, Clara, my head's reeling..."

"Wait!" Diana interrupted and put up her hand. "Why would Keith call *Norm*? Why didn't he call the police, or at least get the security guard involved?"

"I don't know yet," Clara admitted. "All I know is, he contacted Norm and let him into the garage level of your building, then into the file room. That was all done out of sight of your security guard, sitting at his desk in the lobby. Together they moved Marnie's body and put what they said was a random file in her hands, making it look like she'd fallen."

Diana spoke up again. "Will my actions, I mean, pushing her body between the shelves, will that affect what you do going forward?"

"No. As you say, poor Marnie, all the damage was done long before you arrived. And it sounds like there was no relevance to the file after all, so I'm sorry I sent you on that wild goose chase, Hamish."

Hamish stared into his coffee mug, trying to unravel what he thought he understood about the scene, about what had happened. Could Clara be right, that the file really wasn't important, that Henri's email from Marnie wasn't part of the story after all?

Clara pulled a thin file folder from her briefcase and took out a color photograph. "Keith had this on his phone. We've had enlargements printed. He says it's evidence that he and Marnie were in a relationship. At least, it's what he could show us at the station. I don't know if he has other photographs at home, maybe on a camera."

Hamish took the photograph and studied it, then handed it to Diana. "This group photo by the Portland Head Light was taken during a summer associate hike," he explained to Clara. "Mark, one of our associates, was the leader. Most of the people in it are summer associates. But you're right, Clara, Keith is in it. Maybe Mark felt sorry that he didn't get to do much in the way of activities, and invited him along."

Diana had a confused expression on her face. "I agree, that is Mark in the photo, and Keith, with his arm around Marnie and she's leaning her head against his shoulder. But there's something..."

Clara was holding the photograph to place it in the folder again, but Diana reached out her hand. "Can I take a picture of that? Or is it confidential for now?"

Clara handed it to Diana, who took a picture using her phone. While Clara was looking down to put the original photograph away, Hamish shot Diana a questioning look across the table, and she gave a discreet shake of her head. "Later" she mouthed silently.

"What's the next step?" Hamish asked Clara. "Do you want to stay and walk us through what will happen now?"

"I need to get back and continue the questioning. I expect Keith and Norm will each be charged. You're lawyers, you know the drill. Failure to report a death, failure to seek medical aid for an injured person, disturbing a potential crime scene, the works. If he's arrested, I expect he will be granted bail, if he can pay it. Obviously, it's not my call about his future at the firm, but..."

"He doesn't *have* a future." Diana spat out the words. "He's done at our firm, and he's done in Portland, if I have anything to do with it. Since he's English, can he be deported?"

Clara stood up. "Hang tight, Diana, one thing at a time." She turned to Hamish, who stood up also. "I assume you'll handle what needs to be done in terms of notifying clients he works with. I don't know what a patent agent does exactly. I'll leave all that with you."

She let out a long sigh before continuing. "I'll check with my superiors, but now that we have a confession and an explanation that fits all the evidence, it will probably be okay for your office to open again, let people get back to work. We've already sealed Keith's office, so leave that for us. An officer can let anyone in who needs a file or something."

Diana was still at the table. "Clara," she asked, "why did Keith wait so long to confess? If he was planning to confess, why not when it happened?"

She got up to be face to face with Clara, her eyes full of tears. "Why did *I* have to experience the trauma of finding Marnie, thinking I had killed her? You have to factor that into the charges, inflicting emotional distress. Seriously. It's been a nightmare for me and for Hamish. And the twins can tell something's up, with the neighbors having them over and taking them to school. Not to mention inconveniencing the entire office, and we've probably lost hundreds of billable hours. Add that to the damages!"

"I totally get your points, Diana. As to the timing, you'd better ask your husband." Diana fell silent, not knowing what to say to that.

Clara quickly walked to the front door, then she stopped. Hamish thought it was a bit of an act, to prevent any more questions from Diana. She reached into her briefcase again and retrieved a sealed white envelope. Hamish recognized the window-front style from the old days of billing clients, before his firm switched to electronic billing.

"It's from Norm," Clara said.

"Don't tell me, he's invoicing me for his presence when you first interviewed Diana?"

Clara shrugged her shoulders. "Beats me, he's claiming attorney client privilege for it. Who knows when he'll be back in his office."

Then she opened the door and marched down the path to a waiting police cruiser. Hamish stood in the foyer by the open door. He was tempted to toss the envelope on the desk in his office for later, but curiosity got the better of him. Surely Norm wouldn't have the nerve to bill him, after covering up a death at Hamish's own office building?

He tore open the envelope. It wasn't a bill, just a blank sheet of paper, apart from a single typed sentence which Hamish read to himself:

A criminal may confess to a lesser crime to avoid investigation of a greater crime.

Norm, he said to himself, what the hell are you playing at? But not wanting to upset Diana further, he stuffed the note and envelope in the pocket of his jacket, which was hanging on a hook by the front door.

Diana was seated again at the kitchen table, staring intently at her phone, with the photograph of a seemingly happy day outdoors.

"What is it?" he asked, standing behind her and placing his hands on her shoulders.

Diana pointed to Marnie's smiling face.

"I can't prove it right now so I didn't say anything in front of Clara, but I think this photograph has been altered. I'm sure Marnie was *not* on that hike. And if you look carefully, the lighting doesn't match with the other people."

Hamish sat down across from her. "Okay," he said, eyes wide in anticipation, "start from the beginning."

Chapter 28

Charlie was in his room at the hotel on Caraidsay Island, wishing he'd thought to bring hiking boots on the trip from Portland. And fighting off annoyance at Mark for not suggesting it. No, he told himself, as a first year lawyer, he had to do a better job of investigating situations ahead of time and not expect experienced lawyers to hold his hand.

But he was still mad at himself for missing a chance at spending an afternoon with Margaret, away from discussions about Marnie's death. He got up from the desk to look out of the window; he was thrilled to have a room directly over the dining room, with a view of the islands to the west and the intriguing tidal island just to the south.

His room had a set of binoculars on the window ledge, for unprepared guests like him who didn't bring their own, he figured, and he picked them up and had a closer look at the causeway across to the island. Margaret was right, he realized: his loafers would be no match for the seaweedy, uneven path.

He was familiar with Bar Island in Bar Harbor in his home state of Maine. That was a tidal island too, but even cars could cross at low tide. A person could cross it in loafers, he thought with a smile. He wondered now if the hotel had hiking boots he could borrow, maybe left behind by a guest... but before he could call reception, his phone beeped. He returned to the desk and sat down to read the message.

It was from Hamish: *Charlie please call me ASAP* it said, with Hamish's cell number. Feeling a twinge of honor at having the cell number now, Charlie tried it and Hamish answered right away. Charlie had rarely spoken to Hamish, and the man's position as managing director was intimidating for any first-year lawyer. He wondered why Hamish hadn't called Mark instead, or Margaret.

139

"Hello Mr. Murray," Charlie began nervously. "I received your text..."

"Charlie! I've been calling Mark and Margaret, but their phones have messages saying they're out of the service area. Is there a problem with the cell reception at your hotel?"

"No, Mr. Murray, I'm in the hotel and it's fine. Mark and Margaret are out. They walked over to the nearby tidal island. Is there something I can help with?"

He could hear Hamish exhaling, probably annoyed at only reaching the most junior lawyer on the case. He wasn't even sure if Hamish was calling about Marnie's death, or about the wind power project that had brought Charlie and Mark to this outpost in the first place.

Eventually Hamish replied. "This will sound like a strange request, Charlie, but I need to see the image that Mark uses for his laptop screen saver. At least, according to Diana, it's a photograph of a group posed near the Portland Head Light. Have you seen that picture?"

"Yes, Mr. Murray, it was after our call with you, and someone who works here said that..."

"Sorry to interrupt, Charlie. Do you know when Mark will be back?"

"Within the next two or three hours, I believe, Mr. Murray. The path gets covered over, so they'll need to walk back across while the tide is still low. Can it wait that long?"

He heard Hamish sigh loudly. "It really can't... listen, Charlie, I know this is going to sound intrusive, but can you get housekeeping or the manager to let you into Mark's room? I expect that if you just open his laptop and turn it on, the screensaver photograph should appear. You wouldn't need to know a password or anything."

"I *guess*," Charlie said warily. "What should I do if I can access it?"

"Take a photo of the photo, if you know what I mean. As good quality as you can, so we can see the faces clearly. It's an emergency here and I'm sure Mark will understand. I'll explain it to you both later, or when you get back."

140

After the call ended, Charlie went downstairs to the reception desk. Hamish's request made him uneasy, not just entering a guest's room when they were out, but looking at his laptop. At least the rooms didn't have large enough safes for laptops, but what if it was locked in a suitcase? Well, he'd find out soon enough.

And as soon as that was done, he'd call Hamish again and explain about the manager at the hotel thinking he knew Keith Jones, but by a different name. Or should he? No, he was the junior attorney, he reminded himself. Margaret and Mark had both heard the comment, and surely one of them would have told Hamish, if they thought it was important.

The manager listened to Charlie's request and seemed to feel equally uneasy, so they reached a compromise: the manager would go into Mark's room alone. If the laptop was in plain sight, he'd hand it out to Charlie for the sole purpose of photographing the screensaver picture, then return the laptop to where it had been. "I'll have to let Mark know when he gets back," the manager explained.

"Definitely," Charlie agreed. "It's a request from our boss in Maine. I can't help it if Mark is out of phone reach."

The manager looked at him in surprise. "What do you mean, out of reach? We have the best possible mobile reception here. The kind of guests we attract, they wouldn't put up with anything less."

"But Mark is over on the tidal island," Charlie reminded the manager. "Maybe the reception isn't as good there."

"Hmm. I'll have to work on improving it. We can't have guests wandering over there and not be able to contact us if they have an accident."

After a successful mission to Mark's room, Charlie returned to his own room and sent Hamish the photographs he'd taken: several views, including close-ups of faces, since Hamish seemed interested in who was in the picture. Charlie had been careful to take a couple of Keith, very clear ones, he thought.

141

Now his thoughts turned to Mark and Margaret. He went back to the reception desk where he'd seen a tide chart, with the daily "safe crossing" times highlighted. The manager was still at the desk.

"How strict are these crossing times?" Charlie asked. "I mean, is there much leeway?"

"A half hour, max. But don't worry, if your friends are running behind and the water starts to cover the path, there's a little rowboat that's attached to a rope on both sides of the channel. Worst case scenario, they can pull themselves across in that, if there's only a foot or two of water. But not more. I doubt the rope on either end would keep the boat safe from strong waves."

Charlie returned to his room, now starting to worry. What if one, or both of them, were injured? He used his binoculars to scan the island; there was no one in view, but the island featured a small hill, so anyone behind it would be out of sight. Should he ask the manager to call the coast guard?

Well, they still had an hour at least of safe crossing. He sat down again at his laptop and wondered what exactly was going on in Portland that necessitated the photograph. It *had* to be the man who the hotel manager had recognized. But why?

Charlie opened the law firm's website and scrolled through the photographs, starting with the partners, then the senior associates, the junior associates, and the of-counsel attorneys. No luck. The man identified as Keith Jones looked too old to be a summer associate.

He looked again at the options for searching people on the website. Then he remembered, Keith was the patent agent! Charlie clicked on the name, but there was only a photograph, no biography. *The mystery deepens*, he said to himself, smiling. He loved mysteries.

Chapter 29

Out on the tidal island, Mark and Margaret had walked for about twenty minutes, following a rough path at the edge of the island where the land sloped down to meet the rocky shoreline. Mark was disappointed that they had too little time for him to hike up the central hill on the island. He estimated it to be about four hundred feet, so not a long climb by his standards.

"Maybe tomorrow," Margaret had suggested, but knew it was unlikely: they'd either have some clarity about what to investigate for Hamish, or, if the case had been resolved, Mark and Charlie would be heading back to Maine. And she'd be on the afternoon ferry to Oban, then home to Finlay and Alistair. Perhaps, she hoped, Henri would have returned to France by then. Everyone back in their proper place.

She stopped to glance at her watch. "We should go back now." She pointed out to the sea. "The tide will be turning soon and we can't miss our safe crossing window to Caraidsay."

Mark agreed. From where they stood, the hill of the island completely blocked the view back to where the hotel sat, and the view of the causeway.

"You were going to tell me about your project, the wind power," Margaret reminded Mark as they reversed course on the path. "That is, if it's not confidential."

"I'm happy to tell you. Unfortunately, Charlie and I haven't accomplished much. All we can do is report back to Hamish that the project is at an impasse. The short version is, Caraidsay is owned by the residents, the community. They acquired it when the former owner couldn't afford to make the necessary improvements for, I guess you'd call modern life, I mean, dependable electrical power, internet access, cable, all the stuff we can't live without now. The community obtained various grants and loans, and with better infrastructure they began attracting visitors for the hiking, and the escape from city life. Visitors brought campervans or tents, or they stayed in B&B's and guest houses in the village near the ferry terminal."

"I remember seeing some of those," Margaret said. "It looks like there's a good selection of places to stay near the ferry."

"I've only seen the information on paper, but I agree. For many years there was a good balance. No one here made a lot of money, but they had a good living from the visitors. Craftspeople and artists too. You've seen the artwork in the hotel. It's really high quality, don't you think?"

"Yes, I'm tempted to buy one or two pieces but I'm resisting."

Mark continued his explanation about the project. "Up until now, all decisions were made by the community. It's been remarkably peaceful, in terms of no major disputes. But then the hotel where we're staying was built. Unlike the other places that have gone into business, which are supported by community loans and grants, the hotel was built by private money. The land itself is owned by the grandson of a farmer whose family farmed here for many generations, and ownership of that plot of land, forgive the pun, was kind of grandfathered in when the community took over the island. Unlike the other accommodations on the island, you can see that the hotel is very upscale. The land owner, the manager I mean, used his own and investor money, hoping to attract corporate retreat bookings, destination weddings, basically events that will generate a lot of income."

"But for him and his investors, right? Not necessarily shared by the village. Is that the problem?" Margaret asked. "At least, it seems you're building up to a problem."

"There is a problem, but not that. The community has a long-range plan to install wind turbines." He held up his hand to feel the breeze. "There's a good supply of wind out here, but to take advantage of it, the turbines need to be west-facing, otherwise the hill on the island will decrease the effect."

Margaret laughed. "I see where you're going. It's a Nimby situation, is that it?"

Mark laughed too. "Very perceptive. Yes, a *not in my back yard* problem. But here it's not so much Nimby. The hotel looks out to where the turbines would be, so it has to do with the view."

"Now I can understand the dilemma. I wouldn't stay in that hotel again if even one wind turbine was installed in my view, let alone a row of them." She shook her head. "I shouldn't feel that way. People all over the world live near places where power is generated, but there it is. Is the owner of the land blocking the wind power development?"

"He can't literally block it because he doesn't own the strip of land closer to the shore where the turbines would be installed. But he does own the land where construction would take place during installation, and where the power cables would run underneath. In effect, he can make it impractical if he denies access."

Margaret thought for a few moments. "It's hard to see a way around that. So you have to bring bad news to Hamish. Is it one of his corporate clients who are investing in the turbine construction?"

"Yes, but you know how those clients are. Companies owned by other companies, to the point where you really don't know who's responsible."

They walked in silence for a few minutes. Margaret was enjoying the view out to the water, and wondered if the hotel could be relocated to the tidal island. If it was orientated to face southwest, it would still have good views. The bedrooms and dining room wouldn't have to look out on the wind turbines. Perhaps a bridge could be built over the causeway... "Wait a minute!" she cried.

"Are you okay?" Mark stopped and watched as she turned in a full circle, evaluating what she was seeing.

"I was playing a mind game," she explained, "thinking the hotel could be rebuilt over here, and the turbines could go in as planned. But Mark, could the *turbines* be installed here on the tidal island instead? If they were at shore level below where we are now, they shouldn't be visible from the hotel, right? Although I guess it would depend on how tall they are. Some turbines in Britain are huge."

"Let's sit down for a minute." Mark indicated a dry flat rock near the path. Excited now, he took a small sketchpad from his pack, and Margaret was intrigued to see sketches of birds, buildings, and landscapes, as Mark flipped the pages over.

"I didn't know you could draw like that. Will you show me those later?"

"Sure, but they're just fun, for me to remember my trip. Hang on a minute while I think about this..."

Margaret watched while Mark sketched an outline of the shoreline in front of them, then he turned and sketched the hill behind them. "I wonder exactly how high it is?" he asked himself; he took out his phone to access a map online, but there was no signal. "Darn it, I'll have to look that up when we get back. But Margaret, your idea may be a valid solution. As far as we've seen, this island is unoccupied. Well, now, but obviously it was occupied decades ago, judging from the remains of the stone cottages."

"Yes, those would have been crofts. Probably with thatched roofs. It was a hard-working life, keeping sheep and a few cattle. And with no medical services nearby if there was an emergency. Do you know who owns the land now?"

She was surprised that Mark had a ready answer. "The community owns it, so they wouldn't have to get anyone's permission for the wind project."

Mark put away his sketchbook, then leapt to his feet, his face breaking into a huge smile. He reached out both arms as if to hug Margaret, then pulled them back and looked down.

"I was going to say I could kiss you, I'm so excited about your idea, but I don't want to be misinterpreted."

Margaret was reminded of their uneasy interaction earlier that afternoon. "I'll settle for a hug, as long as you don't think I'm sending a signal."

They decided in the end on a collegial handshake, then shouldered their packs and continued along the path, more briskly.

Chapter 30

Soon Caraidsay Island and the causeway came into view, to the accompaniment of a sustained series of alerts from both their phones.

"Should we stop and check messages now?" Mark asked Margaret.

"No, let's get safely to the other side. In fact, is that someone waving at us?"

From his seemingly bottomless pack, Mark took out binoculars and looked through them. He lowered them again.

"It's Charlie. The idiot walked down the steps onto the shore, but he's wearing boots. Maybe the hotel loaned him a pair."

"Does he look like he's in trouble?"

"Well, he is waving frantically. There must be news, judging from all the messages we have waiting."

Despite their hurry to get across and check their messages, Mark and Margaret were careful on the rocky, slippery causeway.

"Thank goodness!" Charlie cried when they were within hearing distance. "I was about to ask the hotel to send out a search party."

"I'm sorry," said Margaret. "I had an idea while we were there and Mark had to made some notes. Anyway, what's the news? We had no cell reception until a few minutes ago but we didn't stop to check yet."

Together they picked their way over the rocks and up the steps. When they were on flat ground in front of the dining room, Charlie excitedly gave them the update.

"Hamish texted that someone confessed! And before you ask, I don't know if he means to murder, or to causing an accident that killed Marnie, but his official message is that we can 'stand down' if that makes sense."

Mark and Margaret looked at each other. "I suppose Hamish means we don't need to investigate what Henri told us, I mean, Marnie's suspicions about the patent file and the email from Britain," Margaret suggested.

Mark nodded his head in agreement. "We can talk about it later, but first, Charlie, I need to tell you Margaret's idea. Or no, she can tell you."

Margaret felt a wave of gratitude: this was Mark's project for Hamish, and he could easily have claimed the credit for suggesting the alternate turbine location. She would have never known, since she wasn't officially on the team.

"Tell him, Margaret," Mark urged. She really wanted to go to her room, change clothes, and call Alistair, but this project was a priority for her two companions.

She gestured for Charlie to face the tidal island, and she pointed. "I had an idea that the hotel could relocate to that island and free up the land here for the wind turbines. Then I thought, why not reverse the scenario and build the turbines on the tidal island? With that hill in the middle, they shouldn't be visible from the hotel, unless the plan is to have really huge ones."

Mark asked Charlie, "Great idea, don't you think?"

"Great idea," Charlie agreed. Inside though, he felt deflated. If only he'd brought hiking boots, he could have been there too. Maybe *he'd* have thought of putting the turbines on the tidal island... Hamish surely would have been pleased.

But he kept it inside as he congratulated Margaret on the idea.

"Obviously it's not a done deal," Mark reminded him, "but at least we can go back to Hamish with positive news."

With plans to meet in two hours for dinner, the last at the hotel, they expected, they entered the building. Mark and Margaret headed up to their rooms, while Charlie sat on a bench in the reception area to pull the borrowed Wellington boots off and return them. Then he planned to call Mark and explain that Hamish had asked for a picture of Mark's laptop screensaver. He wasn't looking forward to the call, to disclosing that the manager had gone into Mark's room to get the laptop.

The bench was directly across from the reception desk. The manager's back was turned and he hadn't noticed Charlie sit down. Charlie heard "Portland" and sat motionless, waiting to see where the conversation was going. Maybe the manager was telling someone about having guests from a Portland law office.

"Yes," the manager was saying to the unknown party at the other end of the call, "Thompson Granger is in custody, something to do with the death of a person he worked with at the law firm. I'm sure his father will be on hand, so we'll have to reschedule..."

Charlie didn't want the manager to know he'd overheard, so he silently picked up the boots and crept away, his socks making no sound. He placed the boots on the floor by the outside door, as if he'd just arrived, and crept up the stairs to his room.

So the manager had been right: Keith Jones, the patent agent at the firm, was really Thompson Granger, or vice versa. Hamish had to be told, but Charlie's calls to Margaret and Mark, to ask one of them to convey the information, both went to voice mail.

Maybe, Charlie realized, this was another chance to prove himself. He thought about texting Hamish, but Hamish might wonder why Charlie, the junior of the three lawyers, was contacting him again, when they had spoken so recently. Better to be confident: he dialed Hamish's cell phone number and was pleased to be connected right away.

He quickly explained, too quickly, about the names; Hamish told him to slow down and explain in detail, which Charlie did, remembering the manager's conversation as best he could.

"Thank you Charlie, this could be a breakthrough. You're, let's see, you're beginning your first year with us, is that correct?"

"Yes, Mr. Murray, but I worked at your firm during law school, in the summer I mean."

"Last summer?"

"All three summers, actually, Mr. Murray."

"Well, Charlie, all I can say is, I'm sorry we haven't had a chance to work together before. Listen, my wife Diana and I host a holiday dinner in December with five or six associates. Consider yourself invited, but don't tell anyone, promise? The choice of associates is supposed to be objective, but really, it's up to me."

Charlie gasped in excitement. "Mr. Murray, thank you! I don't know what to say! I promise not to tell anyone."

"Good, and Charlie, please call me Hamish from now on. Come and see me when you get back to Portland. I'll find some interesting work for you. Oh, and I told Mark I asked you to photograph his screensaver. He totally understands, so I hope there's no tension there over that."

They ended the call. Now, instead of regretting that he hadn't brought hiking boots, Charlie was relieved, thrilled, in fact: if not for him overhearing the manager while returning the boots, would anyone even know about the suspicious identity of the man under arrest in Portland? After dancing around the room in his socks for a few moments, he took a can of beer from the minibar to celebrate.

Chapter 31

In her own room, Margaret was sipping a glass of wine from the minibar. She'd cleaned up from her island hike, but she really wished she could have a long soak in the whirlpool bath. After that, though, the energy to dress again and meet the others for dinner would have evaporated with the steam. Her phone showed a couple of missed calls, one from Charlie and one from Alistair.

Charlie could wait, since she'd be seeing him soon anyway, so she called Alistair.

"Thank God, Margaret, where have you been? Never mind. Listen to me carefully. Hamish has learned that the man under arrest in connection with Marnie's death has an alias, and is known to the manager of your hotel. Or maybe the Keith Jones name is an alias. Anyway, we can deal with that later. The more urgent issue is getting you off the island. There's a weather pattern moving in late tonight and dense fog is forecast for the west of Scotland, including the area where you are. It may last a couple of days. Certainly there will be no flights for Mark and Charlie to leave on, and the ferry might not even run."

He continued before Margaret had a chance to process what he was saying. "There's a company in Oban that does boat charters and they've finished the tours for the evening. Adam has arranged for the boat to pick the three of you up at the ferry pier on the island in two hours and take you to Oban. There, three rooms are booked in a B&B, walking distance from the pier. I'll text you that address."

Margaret shook her head, glad that Alistair couldn't see her annoyance. "I haven't looked at a weather report tonight, so I guess you know what's best. Should I tell the guys?"

"No, Hamish is calling them directly. He also said you should ask Charlie later about the news in the case. Charlie has the details."

With the abrupt departure, Margaret focused on logistics.

"Wait, how do we get from the hotel here to the ferry terminal? It's about five miles, and we can't walk with our luggage. I think the taxi has to be booked a day in advance."

"Adam is handling that too. He contacted the taxi service where you are and they'll pick you up in, oh, I guess ninety minutes from now. That should be time to pack and check out, right?"

"Yeah," she said, sighing, "just lucky I didn't decide to take a bath and wash my hair before dinner."

Alistair laughed. "Plenty of time for that when you get home. I'll pick you up tomorrow in Oban. We can talk later and arrange the time."

Margaret sighed again. She really hated last-minute changes in plans.

After they ended the call, she realized she'd see Alistair the next day, sooner than if she'd taken the ferry home, then two long train rides. Silver lining, she decided. She drank more wine, then pulled her rolling travel bag from the closet and started packing.

She was almost finished when Mark called. "Hamish told me Alistair would call you about the change in plans," he said.

"Yes, and I just realized, it means missing dinner. We can get something over in Oban, although it will be late."

"I've taken care of that. The kitchen staff are putting together what they call a hamper. I guess that's another British term I need to learn."

Margaret laughed. "If it's a hamper, it means the food should be a few levels higher than a typical take-out. Thanks for doing that. Listen, I need to get back to my packing. Do you, or Charlie, have any extra room? I picked up so many cowries that I can't fit them all in."

153

Now Mark laughed. "Sure, Margaret, bring them by when you're ready to leave and I can put them in a side pocket in my bag."

"Um, it's a bit more than that... like the size of a shoe box."

"No problem, Charlie said he brought an extra small bag for souvenirs, not that we'll have much time for shopping, so give him a call."

Margaret had hoped the full extent of her groatie buckie collecting could have been kept from the others, but with the rushed departure, there was no time to ask the hotel for a carry bag.

Chapter 32

While Margaret, Mark, and Charlie were frantically packing before heading downstairs for the ride to the ferry terminal, then back to mainland Scotland, Hamish was driving to the outskirts of Portland, Maine. He had a lunch meeting scheduled with the president of the firm's largest biotech client; it had the generic-sounding name of Portland Pharma, Inc.

The president was Louise Gorton. When Hamish had first met her, he'd addressed her formally as Dr. Gorton, but she insisted on first name use, for herself anyway. Within the law firm patent group Louise was privately nicknamed "Auntie Angie," but Hamish was clueless as to the reason for that. And he could hardly ask her.

Before the meeting, Hamish had reviewed the firm's history with the company. They'd been a client for over ten years, always paid on time, never disputed the sometimes large bills for their complicated patent applications. But that morning, Hamish had received an alarming email from Louise. She'd instructed him to suspend their patent work, effective immediately, and incur no costs without checking with her first. He'd called her right away and scheduled the meeting.

He hated to think that this development was tied in with Marnie's death and the fact that Marnie had been clutching one of this client's files at her death. According to Keith Jones, in custody for covering up the death, the file had been randomly selected to stage what was supposed to look like an accident. But Hamish wasn't so sure.

And on top of it all, the bizarre note from No-jail Norm that the detective Clara had handed to Hamish: *A criminal may confess to a lesser crime to avoid investigation of a greater crime.* He tried to clear his head as the entrance to the client's campus came into view. Louise liked to call it a campus, giving the activities the cloak of academia, at least by name.

He knew from previous meetings he'd attended that her office was in the main central building, so he parked in the visitor parking area and she met him in the front lobby. In her late forties, athletic, she was dressed like someone more used to being in the boardroom than a messy laboratory, although Hamish knew she had a PhD and had spent years at the bench.

She wore a simple black knee-length dress, a black and white tweedy short jacket, and black heels. Her hair, always looking newly cut, he'd noticed, was light brown and very short. Not someone who wanted to waste time with a hair-dryer, he imagined.

Soon they were settled across from each other in a conference room that could seat twelve; a collection of files, patents, he assumed, were arrayed on the table. He only handled financial matters for the client, nothing technical, so he hoped Louise wouldn't expect him to be up to speed on the patent side of things. With coffee served and lunch to be brought in later, she began her explanation for the morning's email.

"Hamish, how much do you know about the science end of what we do? Not that I expect you to understand it, but it will be helpful for what I need to discuss with you."

He sighed deeply and shook his head. "I'm embarrassed to say, Louise, but you might as well assume I know nothing. I barely scraped through high school biology."

She smiled. "No problem, I'll make it simple. I'm used to doing that for our investors. You'd be shocked at how many of them come here knowing virtually nothing, just that we have a portfolio of issued patents in the area of cancer treatment."

Now she stood up and walked to one end of the room, where a whiteboard was set up. She picked up a marker, then glanced at the windows. They gave a view out to the lawn and paths. She turned all the Venetian blinds, blocking any views from outside, and then switched on the room lights.

"Sorry, Hamish, but what I'm going to show you is supposed to be a company secret. I say 'supposed to be' for a reason I will get to."

Referring to a piece of paper she held in one hand, with the other she carefully drew a complex chemical structure using a black marker. To Hamish it looked more like an artistic honeycomb, with seemingly random letters—C's, O's, H's, N's, S's—connected by straight lines, or in some cases by dotted lines of graduated length that together resembled a triangle.

Stepping to the other side of the board, Louise drew the identical structure, at least to Hamish's eyes. She then picked up a different marker and circled, in red, the same group of letters and lines on each structure. The circled areas were near the center.

Replacing the markers, Louise returned to the table.

"Up until now," she continued, "most of our patent work has involved new cancer treatments. They're in various stages of pre-clinical work, but none are ready for the market."

"Really?" Hamish looked at her in surprise. "We've been handling your patent work for ten years now. None of those products are in the clinic yet?"

"It can take many, many years, Hamish, for a new drug to get to the point where we apply for FDA approval, and then another long wait while they consider the data, and sometimes require more tests to be done. Anyway, I didn't ask you here to talk about our existing patents. They all deal with treating cancer after it's at a stage where it can be diagnosed."

She pointed at the board. "This is our new baby. Our *precious* new baby. It stops cancer long before any diagnostic test could detect it." She stopped and thought for a moment.

157

"Picture a seed in the ground," she said to Hamish. "We all know that seeds need water to germinate. Imagine the seed having the power to send out a chemical message, drawing water toward itself from a nearby river. Creating tiny water channels in the ground. That's kind of what a cancer cell does at the very beginning. It sends a chemical message saying, 'I need a blood supply so I can grow into a tumor.' That message is received by the blood vessels in your body, and they respond by doing something called angiogenesis. It means new growth of a blood vessel."

She waited while Hamish took notes of what she was saying, including the spelling of the angio word, then he looked up and nodded for her to continue.

"For decades, there have been attempts to develop drugs that will block this angiogenesis before a cancer cell becomes more than a microscopic ball of cells. There are promising candidates, but under the current paradigm of cancer therapy, a new treatment is often tested against existing treatments in terminally ill patients. By then, and if you'll excuse my analogy to the seed, by then the cancer is like a huge shrub, spreading in all directions and able to find its own water. It's too late, for many patients, to attack the cancer by blocking growth of new blood vessels."

Hamish was writing furiously, even sketching a shrub and a river as a reminder of her analogy.

"I have a feeling you're leading up to something exciting," he said to Louise. "A way around this dilemma?"

She refilled both their coffee mugs, took a few sips, then returned to the board. She pointed at the left-hand drawing.

"This molecule, which we engineered here after literally thousands and thousands of tests, blocks the new blood vessel growth. It works in the petri dish, it works in every lab animal we've tried, which is rarely the case with a new drug, and it is non-toxic in humans, at least over a course of five years."

It took a moment for the last point she made to sink in, then Hamish stared at her in shock. "But, but, I thought you had to get FDA approval to test in humans?"

"Yes, to test it as a cancer treatment, that's correct. This, Hamish, is not a cancer treatment. It's a cancer preventative. It stops the seed in the field from recruiting a water supply. The seed dies, the first few cancer cells die. No cancer growth."

He shook his head, still not understanding. "Who has been taking this chemical for, what, you said five years? Is it an injection, like once a year, or..."

"It's a capsule. Twice a day. The people taking it report zero side effects. They're all volunteers. Most of the workforce here are taking it, including the top scientists and the cleaning staff. And many of their family members. I was the first. I took it for a year, just me, to make sure before I let anyone else volunteer. I monitored everything I could think of in terms of my blood stats, liver function, kidney function, brain function, the works."

Hamish was shaking his head. He sipped his coffee, sensing that Louise had crossed a line. Was she committing a crime, supplying an untested medication to employees, using them as guinea pigs? She claimed they were all volunteers, but what if they were coerced: take these pills or lose your job? Had she become that single-minded, that determined?

"Okay, for now I'll buy your arguments," he said finally. "But can we get into why you've asked the firm to put your patent work on hold? Seems to me you have a major breakthrough, and if anything, you'll be filing *more* patent applications." He stopped and gasped. "Oh! Now I get it, you're sending this new work to another firm, one of the big name patent firms in New York or Boston?"

"No," Louise quickly assured him. "I'm Maine-born and I want my patent work in Maine, where we can get together like this without one of us spending valuable time traveling."

159

Hamish suddenly thought back to his own cancer scare, almost two years ago now. He'd been a recalcitrant smoker, ignoring his family's desperate pleas to stop. It had taken a bronchoscopy and a bungled warning from his doctor to get him to quit. Until the mistaken diagnosis was rectified, agonizing days later, Hamish had believed he had just months to live, dying from untreatable late stage lung cancer.

Was he hearing correctly from Louise, a *pill* could prevent that kind of cancer from growing in the first place? He was almost afraid to ask, but he did anyway. He drank some more coffee for a mental boost.

"Louise, you may not be able to answer this, but in addition to your pills having no negative side-effects, are they... do they..."

"Prevent cancer? I'm getting to that, Hamish, but the bottom line is, I think so. We have hundreds of people of all ages, I mean, adult ages, taking them. From a randomly distributed adult population of that size, in this geographic area, there are statistical tables predicting the rate of cancer over those five years."

She stopped and sipped her own coffee. Hamish wondered if this was going to be the downside of the treatment: maybe the effect on cancer development was there, but too low to be meaningful.

"Hamish, there are zero cases of cancer in any of the people taking this drug. The company has paid for early-stage screening for the most common cancers, and so far every test comes back negative." She lowered her voice and narrowed her eyes, leaning to him across the table. "It's *statistically significant*, Hamish. We have a drug that beats the odds for developing cancer."

She sat back with her coffee while Hamish thought about this some more. Was it really lifestyle having the effect? People working at this company would be more aware of cancer risks, compared to the general public, and might be following all the guidelines he heard about for exercise,

160

eating vegetables, avoiding smoking. Was the effect really due to a self-selected group?

As if reading his thoughts, Louise said, "I'll share the proof with you if you want, Hamish, but for now, I'd like to focus on something else before the lunch is delivered." She lowered her voice again, even though they were alone in the room. "Hamish, *someone* is stealing our formulas."

Chapter 33

With Margaret on her way from Caraidsay Island to the B&B in the coastal town of Oban in western Scotland, Alistair turned his thoughts to dinner. Margaret's ex-boyfriend Henri had, as threatened, arrived from France. In an endless series of unwelcome texts, Henri had kept Alistair informed of his progress, and had somehow managed to get a room in the hotel in Finlay, despite Helen's claim that it was full.

Alistair wondered why Henri had kept his plans to come over. With Keith in custody in Portland, was there anything left to investigate? But since there was a patent aspect to the bigger picture, perhaps that would be their focus: not *who* had the motive, but why. According to Hamish, Keith claimed it was a romantic encounter gone wrong, but the patent file in Marnie's hands at her death was telling a different story. And there was the cryptic note Hamish received from Norm: was Keith confessing to one crime to defer attention from an underlying crime involving trade secrets?

He put those thoughts aside and focused again on planning dinner. The hotel was known for its Indian food. Alistair often ordered take-out, especially when he was on his own. But with Henri at the hotel, not knowing anyone but Alistair, he decided to be a good host. He texted Henri an invitation to join him for dinner in the hotel restaurant. The evening was warm, so Alistair suggested a table outdoors.

He received an enthusiastic reply, accepting the invitation. A line of *merci*'s, knives, forks, dishes, and colorful smiley faces cluttered up the reply. Alistair stabbed at the phone to delete the annoying text. Why can't people—adults—just say what's needed, without the elaborate children's cartoon effect?

That done, he returned to the task that had occupied his day until the urgent conversations about Margaret and her colleagues having to leave the island right away. Alistair could understand: he sure wouldn't want to be stranded there, with no air or ferry service for the foreseeable future.

The floor area around the dining table was still strewn with boxes from the basement of the former wartime convalescent home in Kilvellie. However, Alistair was no closer to learning who, if anyone, had forced six young men to repeatedly loot and damage a glass factory during the nineteen forties. His current roadblock was a pile of letters written in French, and he wondered about asking Henri to translate them.

But Henri, like Margaret, was a busy attorney who charged by the hour. Alistair was doing the work as a favor to the police department in Kilvellie, and he didn't know Henri well enough to include him in that favor. But *someone* would have to be paid to translate.

As his last task before leaving for dinner, Alistair called his contact at the Kilvellie police station, Helen. She still lived in the residence attached to the station, so whatever number he called—office or cell—she usually answered.

"Hi Alistair, what's up?"

"It's the boxes again. I know, I keep having questions. I've found a batch of about twenty letters, personal I assume, written in French. Some date from the World War One years and a few are later, up to nineteen forty-three. Do you understand French?"

"Just enough to order a croissant at the airport, but that's about it. Do you think they could be important?"

"I've no idea until I know what at least one of them says. The reason I'm calling now is, I'm on my way to dinner with a lawyer who's visiting from France. I could ask him, but he might expect to get paid for the work. Do you have something in a discretionary fund to use, maybe just to get one translated?"

"Sure. Probably not at his regular billing rate, but enough for a couple of dinners out. Here, I mean, not some fancy place in Paris!"

"Okay, I'll ask him about it. And in case you're wondering who he is, he's Margaret's ex-boyfriend. I'll leave you with that thought and call you soon."

After they ended the call, Alistair flipped through the letters and selected one from the late nineteen-thirties. If the correspondence had any bearing at all on what had happened at the factory, that date was close to when it started. Grabbing his black fleece jacket, he headed out to the car.

He found a spot in the parking area in front of the hotel. Before he left his car, the phone rang; he thought it might be Margaret, so he checked it, but instead, the caller was Christy Green. Alistair hesitated before answering. He'd forgotten about her plans to stay at the cottage for a couple of nights; with Henri in town, maybe he could put her off.

"Hi Christy," he answered. "Are you calling about your visit?"

"Yes, I'm so excited! I have meetings set up with a couple of people tomorrow, to talk about renting a shop there. I know it's last minute, but can I come down tonight? If not, no problem, I'll just get up early tomorrow."

The spare room was empty and ready for her, so he agreed.

"I can help make up the bed, anything like that," she offered.

"It's all set for you, Christy. Only thing is, I'm just about to have dinner with someone at the hotel restaurant here in Finlay. It's on the way to my cottage, so can you stop here first? We're eating outside and you're welcome to join us for dessert or coffee. It's a casual dinner, just an old friend." Well, he thought to himself, an old friend of Margaret's anyway.

With that plan in place, he locked the car and walked toward the outdoor seating area. He realized, he was glad Christy might join them; it would be a relief from having to entertain Henri.

164

He expected to recognize Henri after seeing his face on screen, but he didn't have to look around. Katrina, who was serving tables, saw Alistair and hailed him over.

"Your cute French friend is already seated. I gave him the best table, with a view of the water." Alistair just shook his head. Cute French friend indeed. He'd better not mention that Margaret used to date Henri, or Katrina might make a smart remark about why was Margaret with Alistair instead. Although, he wouldn't have minded: he and Margaret knew Katrina well, and were used to teasing back and forth.

Henri got up when Alistair reached the table. The young man stood out from the other diners, mainly locals, Alistair realized. Instead of jeans and a fleece, he wore navy light wool pants, another bright silk shirt, and a cream linen blazer. (*Did he not realize he was traveling to cloudy, rainy Scotland?* Alistair wondered.) Stylish mirrored sunglasses were nestled in his thick blond hair and serving no purpose, especially as the late afternoon was overcast.

"*Bonjour Alistair,*" Henri cried, smiling and extending his hand. Alistair was terrified that Henri would want to air kiss on both cheeks, but luckily he sat down after a handshake.

After preliminary chit chat about Henri's trip, his ease in finding Finlay thanks to Alistair's directions, and his delight at finding such a modern hotel, they were quiet again as they studied the menu. Alistair already knew what he wanted, but Henri suggested ordering a mix of entrees to share.

"That way we can have more variety, *oui*?" he asked, and Alistair found himself agreeing. After they ordered, they spoke briefly about Margaret, Charlie, and Mark spending the night in Oban, then Alistair would pick Margaret up the following day.

He wondered if he should invite Henri along to see another part of Scotland, but decided to wait. Henri may have made plans of his own, at least until they heard more from Hamish. He was distracted by the arrival of an array of spicy dishes, and both men focused on eating for the next half hour.

165

Chapter 34

"Have you investigated the email that *pauvre* Marnie sent me?" Henri asked Alistair when they'd finished eating and the dishes had been cleared.

"Not me personally. Hamish gave permission to involve a Scottish private investigator I know, named Adam. He's checking around for information on the sender, Craig Sutherland, and the company name, Forsyth Laboratories. I hope to hear back from him tonight or tomorrow."

"*Ah, bon.* Until then, I do not have much to do. I can sightsee in your village, and maybe drive to St. Andrews, where I have never been before."

They both looked up when Katrina arrived with a tray. She placed cups of spicy chai tea on the table, and a plate of small round shortbread biscuits.

"Would you care for pudding, I mean, dessert?" she asked Alistair, then said the same thing, or perhaps something different, to Henri in French.

"*Non, merci,*" he replied. "Sorry, Alistair. I am in Scotland so I should speak Scottish. Ha, I mean, English. Confusing, *oui?*"

Alistair laughed along as he imagined Henri expected. "Nothing for me either, thank you Katrina."

Katrina left, and after a few sips of the tea, Alistair took the letter from his jacket pocket. But before he could show it to Henri, Katrina returned, this time with another guest in tow. Alistair stood up to greet Christy.

She was as well put-together as he remembered from seeing her in Kilvellie: straight blond hair held back with a blue headband, and matching blue sea glass earrings. She wore jeans, sandals, and a blue and white horizontal striped pullover.

Henri was also standing now, obviously eager to be introduced.

166

"Christy, please meet Henri, who's visiting from France. He used to work with Margaret. Henri, Christy Green is a sea glass jeweler in a town north of here."

When they were all seated, Christy ordered chai as well, and an Indian dessert Alistair hadn't tried yet. After a brief chat about Scotland, France, and the usual weather complaints, Alistair wanted to make a start on discussing the letter.

But first, he asked Christy if she minded listening in on a discussion that might be upsetting, possibly involving the attacks on her great-grandfather's glass factory. She told Alistair that it was fine, and she couldn't imagine learning anything worse than the history she was familiar with.

Feeling reassured, Alistair turned to Henri. "I am doing some research for a police officer in Christy's town, Kilvellie. We're trying to solve a mystery from the Second World War. It affected the town in a very bad way. I found some letters written in French. I already spoke to the police officer, and she said she would compensate you for your time, if you could translate one. I brought it with me. It would help us to know if the letters are relevant, and if they should all be translated."

Henri's face lit up. "*Ah oui*, I would be honored to help, and no compensation as you call it is needed. May I see the letter you brought?"

Alistair handed the envelope across the table to Henri, then sat back, planning to sip his tea and eat some biscuits while Henri read through it. But instead of taking the letter out, Henri studied the front of the envelope.

"*C'est dommage*," he said. "It is zee end of a sad series of letters, I believe. A woman is ending things with her *paramour* who lives overseas."

Alistair pointed to the envelope. "How, how can you know that, Henri? You haven't even looked at the letter."

Henri turned the envelope around for Alistair to see, then showed it to Christy. The only thing Alistair had noticed was that the letter-writer had been careless, sticking the postage

167

stamp on upside down, so that whatever British king's likeness it was—they all blurred in his mind—it looked like he'd lost his head. Knowing British history a little, maybe he had...

"Look at the stamp," Henri said.

"Well, it's upside down, obviously," Alistair noted.

"*Oui, c'est vrai.* And do you know what that means?

Alistair shrugged his shoulders. "The sender was careless, or had bad eyesight? Was it a political statement?"

Henri put the letter down on the table and took his tablet out of the black leather shoulder bag that was slung over the back of his chair. He did a quick search, then turned the tablet for Alistair to look at the screen: an image of an old postcard, with a series of postage stamps in all different positions. There was writing under each, but in French. What was it, he wondered, an old French children's guide to putting stamps on properly?

Henri turned the tablet back to look at it.

"This, monsieur, is a guide to the meaning of stamp placement. From World War Two, judging from the year of the stamp. This is a French guide, but they exist in other countries and languages, in Britain of course too."

He lifted the envelope up again and pointed to the stamp.

"The message, you see, is that the person who sent the letter, she is saying 'I have given my heart to another, write to me no more.' *Vous comprenez*? You understand?"

Alistair thought the Frenchman was having a good joke at Alistair's expense: he'd never heard of anything so ridiculous.

"Can you open the letter, Henri, and see if the contents correspond to the stamp placement?"

"*Oui*, of course, but I will bet you the cost of our supper tonight that I am correct! Maybe we add a bottle of *champagne* too?" He stood up to catch Katrina's eye and order the champagne.

Christy nodded with approval, so Alistair smiled and decided to play along, exclaiming, "You're on!" He'd been planning to pick up the tab for the whole dinner anyway, so it was no loss if Henri was correct. And he didn't expect that the hotel carried any champagne that was beyond his budget.

Henri took out the letter, which Alistair already knew was two small sheets of light blue paper, with writing on one side of each. The pages were numbered at the top, and there was an addressee at the beginning and a signature at the end, so he was confident at having the complete message.

It suddenly dawned on him that Henri could say whatever he wanted; Alistair had no way of verifying the translation without finding yet another French speaker, but that would have to wait. Still, he was enjoying his time with Henri, against all odds, and he'd learned something interesting about postage stamps. Not that he ever sent, or received, personal letters these days.

Their attention was diverted by the arrival of a bartender carrying a silver tray with a bottle of champagne and three tall glasses.

He made a scene of popping the cork, drawing more attention to their table, then poured a glass for Henri to taste. It was to Henri's satisfaction, so the bartender filled all three glasses, then placed the bottle in an ice bucket by the table.

Henri held up the letter. "Alistair, may I show the letter to Christy?"

Henri seemed to be so in control now, Alistair wondered why he was being asked. He graciously agreed, then sipped the admittedly excellent champagne while Henri and Christy literally put their heads together to read.

They reached the end of the letter, then turned both sheets over to make sure they hadn't missed anything.

Henri sighed and nodded his head. "*Je suis désolé*, Alistair, but you will be paying for supper."

He then proceeded to translate the letter aloud as he read through it. To Alistair, it was a sad series of apologies, of regrets, of "if things had been different," of "good luck with your new medical training." He'd been ready to conclude that

169

the letters didn't, after all, have anything to do with the glass factory destruction. Until the last paragraph.

"Here is the saddest part." Henri read from the letter. "It ends, 'I beg you, Jerome, don't do anything you'll regret. My husband is a good man. He's no longer a German soldier like you were taught to hate more than twenty years ago. If you hurt him, you hurt me, and if you love me as you say you do, or did, please honor those memories of long ago and stay away.' Then here is the signature. Caelia. Not love, it only says 'fondly.' Maybe love once, but, *c'est dommage*, no more."

Alistair let out a long exhale: could this be the key? But how and why did a batch of letters, written in French and sent to an address in France, end up in the cellar of a care home in northern Scotland?

Christy had been sitting silently for a while now. In a soft voice, she asked Henri for the letter again. She studied the signature at the end, then looked up at Alistair.

"Do you not realize who wrote this?"

He looked at her in confusion. "No, but I'm hoping that the other letters will help. The postmark on this one is St. Andrews. I'm not sure how to even pronounce the name, which I assume is French, Cayalla, is that how to pronounce it, Henri?"

Christy held the letter close to her heart for a moment, her eyes full of tears.

"No, Alistair, this letter is from *my* great-grandmother, Sheila. That spelling is an old form."

Alistair gasped. "I'm *so* sorry, Christy, rummaging in your family's past like this. If I had *any* idea..."

She smiled and handed the letter to him. "It's fine, really, but I would like to see the others. I'm supposed to be an expert on the written history of my family's glass factory, but this is the first I've ever heard about letters my great-grandmother wrote that long ago. Are they all in French?"

"Yes," Alistair confirmed.

Henri had been following the exchange and now he looked back and forth between Alistair and Christy, eyes wide with excitement.

"*Alors, mes amis*, let us go now, *oui*? The letters, they are at your cottage, Alistair?"

Alistair thought for a moment. Dinner at a restaurant with Henri was one thing, but did he really want Margaret's ex-boyfriend at the cottage? He weighed that against getting expert help with a stumbling block in his search through the file boxes.

"Yes," he agreed, "if you want to spend your evening doing that Henri, it would be a huge help. As long as Christy doesn't feel it's an intrusion, reading her great-grandmother's letters."

"Not at all," she assured him. "I didn't even know they existed, and I have no idea who she's writing to. But just based on this letter, we may learn more about that generation."

Alistair stood up and took out his wallet. "You were right, Henri. I'll go inside and pay for this. Thanks for your help."

Henri quickly rose from his chair. "*Attends*! Wait! I was only making a joke about you paying if I was correct about the letter. It will be added to my room bill, *n'est pas*?"

Alistair stood his ground. "Thank you, Henri, but you won fair and square."

When he returned from paying the bill, Henri and Christy were waiting by their cars, and Alistair had to think through the logistics; the dirt parking area in front of the cottage had just enough room for one car to turn, so he'd have to factor that in.

"Christy," he said, pointing north along the main street in the town, "can you drive along first? When the paved road ends, just keep going on the dirt road and park as close to the cottage as you can. It's the only building along the dirt section. I'll follow, then Henri's car last. Or maybe I should drive Henri and bring him back later?"

"*Non*, Alistair, I will bring my car, then you don't need to go out again, *oui*?"

With that settled, the three-car caravan made its way along the dirt road, and soon the odd group was gathered around Alistair's coffee table, tea made and the remaining nineteen letters arranged on the table.

"First thing," Henri insisted, "we organize by date, and we look at the sequence of stamp placement, as a hint of what each letter says."

Alistair watched in amusement as Henri and Christy got to work. While his guests were occupied, he called Adam to ask if there was any news about the Forsyth company names, and who Craig Sutherland was, but the call went straight to voice mail. Maybe Adam was at dinner; Alistair would try again later.

Chapter 35

Hamish and Louise continued their meeting at the company's campus outside Portland, Maine. With the two of them in the conference room, concealed behind the closed Venetian blinds, Louise had just confided in Hamish, dropped a bombshell really. Someone, she said, was stealing the company's secret formulas for cancer therapeutics.

Hamish kept silent as he listened. He was sorely tempted to tell her about the email from someone at his firm to a French attorney, which in turn had evidence that a company in Britain had possession of a secret, and new, chemical structure. But he wanted to hear her explanation first.

He prompted her when she fell silent, staring into her coffee mug. His own coffee had cooled, so he got up and refilled both mugs. That seemed to break the spell, and Louise looked up at him.

"As you know, because your firm prepares them, we use non-disclosure agreements before the initial meeting with a potential investor. And before you ask, the agreements have been working fine, no complaints there. Problem is, I had a meeting with one of our long-standing investors a few days ago. I expected he would make a substantial contribution toward our new drug, our anti-angiogenesis compound." She stopped and pointed at the board, the two art-like jumbles of letters and lines.

Hamish felt a light go on above him: "Auntie Angie" was the nickname of the woman across from him, among people in his patent group. Now he saw the connection, anti-angiogenesis. But that gave him a crucial piece of information: people in his patent group already knew about this promising new program for cancer prevention.

"I have not disclosed that formula to the investor, Hamish, or anything like it. I only told him we have a

173

chemical structure ready for submission to the FDA, along with five years of meticulous data."

"And is he planning to invest?" Hamish asked, hoping the answer would be *of course.*

Instead, Louise reached for one of the file folders. "Are you familiar with the process for getting a patent?" she asked Hamish.

"Again, I'm sorry, Louise. I just know that our lawyers work with you and the scientists to write patent applications, send them to the patent office, then I hear there's a lot of back and forth before the patent office grants you a patent. Oh, and at some stage, you file that same patent application overseas. I've seen those invoices. That's a huge investment."

"It is, Hamish, and so far we have our investors to thank for covering the costs, for those anyway." She gestured at the file folders.

Now she opened the folder she'd selected. "This is our most recent cancer therapeutic. It's not related to those structures on the board. This folder contains something called a provisional application. After it's filed, sent electronically to the patent office I mean, it simply sits there for up to a year. During that time the inventors can generate more data, or ideas, and then roll all that into a final application just before the one year anniversary. *That* application becomes, you might say, set in stone, and it is the version that we file in foreign countries, and that the patent examiners look at to determine if we have something worth granting a patent on."

She stopped to drink some coffee and allow Hamish to finish his notes. "Okay so far?" she asked him.

He smiled at her. "Okay on the statements you're making, but I expect you'll explain the relevance next?"

"Yes, the relevance. Under international law, a patent application has to be published eighteen months after you first file it. This one," she said, pointing to the folder between them, "was filed as a provisional six months ago. The only people who should have access to it, outside the patent office, are my patent group, the scientists who did the research, and a few lawyers and support staff at your firm."

Hamish sat very still: he could almost feel an accusation coming up. Louise sensed his change in expression.

"Please, Hamish, I don't suspect your firm of doing anything wrong, not for now. This is a fact-finding meeting."

She opened the folder. "When I met with the investor, he said he has concerns about whether this patent application will ever become a patent. If the patent office finds evidence that someone independently discovered your invention first, they may deny you a patent. It's more complex than that, but for our purposes it's all you need to know. The investor brought me this publication."

She handed Hamish what looked to him like a completely incomprehensible chemistry article. It was not in English.

"I can't even tell what language it is," he admitted. "You'll have to explain."

"It purports to be, and I say *purports* because my IT people are still investigating, an article from a foreign language cancer journal, that contains the exact chemical formulas in this application."

She patted the file folder.

"A *secret* application, not to be published until next year?" Hamish asked.

"Exactly. I have no idea how this information got out. But the consequences are potentially devastating for us, as a company. The investor who brought it to my attention said he will still invest. However, he wants a lot more private stock in exchange. We really need his money, but if the drug is a success and we go public, it means he will profit at the expense of the insider stockholders, the company employees and managers, who've done all the hard work."

"Oh, I think I get it," Hamish said. "He's using the publication as leverage, almost like blackmail?"

"Exactly. Plus, now we have a legal duty to tell the patent office about the publication, which I have to say, we did not find in the databases despite detailed searching. And not just by us, by your people too. It almost goes without saying, if someone has already published a promising drug, *we're* not going to play catch-up, knowing we have a competitor. And the patent office may say that because of the publication, we can't get a patent. If we don't get a patent, it's unlikely that a major pharmaceutical company would commit to taking the drug into pre-clinical trials. Without a patent, other companies could make and sell a competing product."

Hamish had heard from Alistair with an explanation of the Forsyth email address and the Craig Sutherland name. Based on this news, Hamish decided the time was right to tell Louise about Henri's involvement in the mysterious email from the UK with a chemical structure. Hearing Henri's name, Louise became animated.

"I was so sorry when he left your firm, Hamish! He was not trained in the science and chemistry, but he loved the administrative law side of things, I mean, in terms of the patent process. He was so good at gathering data on what strategies to use, the timing of filing certain documents. Anyway, we do miss him."

Now Hamish told her everything: Marnie contacting Henri with the email from the UK, asking her for clarification about a chemical structure, and about Forsyth being mentioned in the email, and someone called Craig Sutherland. He had brought the printed email with him, and he placed it in front of Louise. Now, to his horror, he could see why Marnie had contacted Henri: even to Hamish's untrained eye, he could see the resemblance between the chemical structure in the email, and Louise's drawings on the whiteboard. The precious cancer prevention chemical secret was out.

"Have you asked Marnie for more information about this, Hamish? I know her, she works on our cases. But I can't *believe* she'd disclose... I'm not, I'm not accusing your firm, but, but..."

Hamish held up his hand. "I can't ask her, Louise." He shook his head. "I hate to break it to you suddenly like this, but she's, she's dead. Marnie is the person who just died in our file room. It's been in the news, but her name's been withheld for now."

He watched as Louise's eyes began tearing up, and she quickly turned away. He didn't know if it was over Marnie, over loss of her five-year-long secret chemical, a chemical that might prevent cancer, or both.

"I'll be back," he said, and he slipped from the room to let her grieve and process the information. He pictured Margaret, Mark, and Charlie in far-away Scotland, and suddenly wished he was there too, instead of possibly facing a huge malpractice lawsuit against his firm for betraying a long-term client's confidence.

Chapter 36

In the cottage in Finlay, Alistair and his two guests, Christy and Henri, were seated on the sofa and a guest chair, with the results of the evening's work arranged on the coffee table. Alistair had offered each of them a small glass of whisky; Henri had to drive, so Alistair didn't want to overdo it even though the cottage was a short drive back to Henri's hotel.

"This is amazing!" Alistair pointed to the carefully arranged series of envelopes on the table. "I never imagined you could learn so much from an envelope, but you're right. There's the evolving relationship between Christy's great-grandmother Sheila and her one-time boyfriend Jerome, laid out for any mail carrier to see."

Christy smiled. "I hadn't thought of that aspect to it, Alistair. Back in the days when a mail carrier would personally hand letters to people at home, they could judge from the stamp position what kind of expression to use."

"Good point," Alistair said. He picked up one letter, with the stamp lying on its side affixed to the bottom left-hand corner. "This says, 'I wish for your friendship, but no more.' So the carrier wouldn't hand it over and say, 'You've received some good news.' At least, it doesn't seem like good news."

"Or this one." Christy lifted up another letter, from early in the friendship, or the relationship. "It says, 'I think of you,' according to the angled position of the stamp."

At the sound of sharp knocking on the kitchen door, they all looked up from the table. Alistair went to see who it was, although he couldn't imagine who'd be visiting this late in the evening. Maybe Adam?

He opened the door to see Helen, the police officer from Kilvellie, and her good friend Richard Wilson, retired from the position that Helen now occupied. "This is a surprise," Alistair said, "I mean, a nice one. Come in!"

178

"I don't want to keep you," Helen began, as they stood in the kitchen. "Judging from the cars outside, you must have more than Christy visiting."

"Yes, I'll introduce you."

Helen motioned to Richard. "You go on through. I'll talk to Alistair first."

When Helen and Alistair were alone, she revealed the reason for the visit. She and Richard had just finished a late dinner at the Indian restaurant in the hotel, but Helen had been distracted. Adam hadn't been in touch for over twenty-four hours, and both his cell phone and home phone went to voice mail.

"I'm hoping you've heard from him, Alistair. I tried calling you a few minutes ago from the restaurant, but..."

"Sorry, I've been on the phone with Margaret off and on all evening. Long story, but she and some colleagues are heading to Oban for the night. Did Adam tell you about the project he's helping us with?"

"No, what is it?"

Alistair pulled out chairs at the kitchen table, and he and Helen sat down. He explained about Marnie's death at the law firm, the recent email exchange between Marnie and the French attorney Henri, and the names in the email: Sutherland, Forsyth, and an email address that seemed to originate in Britain.

"There's one more piece," he said. "Hamish, the managing partner at the firm where Marnie worked, received a note, anonymously, at home. It just said, 'Forsyth Industries.' We don't know how it all ties together."

Helen thought for a minute.

"Forsyth... aye, that name rings a bell. When I still worked in Edinburgh, there were a couple of complaints about neighbors. Not residential, it's an industrial park at the edge of a housing development. I don't know what they do, but it seemed to involve limousines arriving and leaving at all hours of the night."

"Goodness, were there private parties going on, only the wealthy invited?"

Helen shook her head. "I strongly doubt it. It's a low-end industrial park. I can't imagine anyone choosing it as a party venue. But I'm wondering if Adam could have gone there himself. Maybe he's on surveillance with his phone off, or on silent?"

"I guess," Alistair said, "but I only asked if he could do some research online. Truly, Helen, *I* didn't ask him to go all the way to Edinburgh for this."

Helen drummed her fingers on the table, then looked up when Richard returned to the kitchen.

"Everything okay, lass?"

"Sit down." Helen gestured to the chair next to Alistair. "Neither of us have heard from Adam, and it's been over twenty-four hours. It's unlike him not to check in with me once or twice a day. And before you ask, Alistair, I did call his girlfriend Justine in St. Andrews, and he's not there. She hasn't heard from him in a couple of days, but she said she wasn't worried. He told her he'd be busy on some research."

Alistair stood. "I want to check that Forsyth place you said is in an industrial park. I'm getting a bad feeling about this." Then he sat down again. "Shoot, I have to leave early in the morning to drive up north and collect Margaret from Oban. Otherwise she'll spend all day on the trains."

Henri and Christy had joined the group, standing just inside the kitchen.

"*Moi*, I can collect Margaret," Henri offered. "I still have no instructions from Hamish about zee research."

Alistair tried to process it all. He was wary at the thought of Margaret alone with Henri, but he'd asked Adam to investigate Forsyth, so his loyalties were torn.

"Christy," he said, feeling guilty at this not very subtle maneuvering, "since we don't know what's going on, I'm not comfortable leaving you alone at the cottage tomorrow. Can you possibly postpone your appointment and go with Henri to pick Margaret up?"

180

He waited, hoping she'd agree: with her along on the trip, he wouldn't worry so much.

"I guess so," Christy replied after thinking for a moment. "I haven't been to the west of Scotland in years. I suppose I can reschedule what I have on tomorrow."

"Okay." Alistair stood up and faced Henri and Christy. "That would be a huge help, and I'll give you money for gas, I mean, petrol, and food. I'll let Margaret know and you can coordinate with her about when to meet. I assume she'll be waiting at her B&B and I'll give you that address."

Alistair went to the bedroom to change into his black jeans and dark clothing, along with a black baseball cap. When he emerged, Helen said, "I've contacted an officer I know in Edinburgh. A couple of officers in plain clothes will meet us. We don't want a visible police presence yet, in case someone panics and does something..." Her voice trailed off.

Alistair felt a wave of dread: what had he dragged his pal Adam into?

But first, the biggest challenge of the evening was ahead of them: with Christy's car parked in the turn-around area by the cottage, how to choreograph getting three other vehicles parked end to end—Henri's, Alistair's, and Helen's, which Richard would drive home in, to Kilvellie—positioned to travel along the one-lane dirt road back to Finlay.

Chapter 37

Hamish returned to the conference room at his client Louise's office building, after giving Louise a chance to recover from Hamish's news: Marnie was the attorney who had died at his firm.

He had just taken his seat across from Louise when there was a knock on the door. She jumped up, erased the chemical formulas from the whiteboard, then opened the door to her assistant, a young woman carrying a tray with sandwiches and cookies. After assuring the woman that they didn't need anything else, Louise carried the tray and placed it on the table.

"I don't really feel like lunch," she murmured, "but I need to eat something." She helped herself to a sandwich, made a cup of tea, then sat down to resume the conversation.

Hamish quickly ate a sandwich, then took out his phone to show Louise an image of the file folder that Marnie had been grasping when her body was found. Louise did a quick search on her laptop. She looked back at Hamish.

"That's the patent application for the chemical structures I just showed you. It was only filed two weeks ago! Why would she..." Louise shook her head. "Of course, the first patent application was filed with an error in our key compound." She pointed to the now-blank whiteboard. "I wish I hadn't erased the structures, but I didn't want it on the board when anyone else came in. Do you remember, I circled a small section of each of the two compounds?"

"Yes," Hamish confirmed, "but honestly, when you drew them, they looked identical to me."

"They were, except one was right-handed and the other left-handed."

Hamish had to stop himself from an involuntary laugh: chemicals with hands?

"It has to do with how the chemical attaches to the receptor in the body," she continued. "You're familiar with right-handed and left-handed scissors, right?"

"I guess, although I never really thought about it."

"To make the explanation simple, the chemical with a core section in one position can grasp the molecule it needs to, I mean, to prevent the blood vessel growth, but the other doesn't work. On paper, you are correct that they look almost the same, because they've been converted to a two-dimensional graphic. And that's what happened here. The patent application was filed with the wrong structure. I'm not blaming anyone at your firm, believe me. We as the scientists are responsible for checking all the technical aspects. But two days later, one of the scientists pointed out the error to me. We immediately contacted the head of your patent group, and a replacement application was filed. No harm done, really. It's not an uncommon thing to happen."

"But now there's the problem of the email Marnie got, right?"

"Exactly." Louise finished her sandwich, and after Hamish declined any more food, she shoved the tray to the end of the table and made more tea for both of them. Hamish had his phone turned off and was anxious to learn if there were any developments following the confession by Keith Jones and, ironically, No-jail Norm, but he'd have to be patient.

The email was still lying on the table, and Louise compared it to the patent application: to two applications, in fact, the correct one filed two days after the incorrect one.

"It's difficult to see," she said, pointing back and forth to the chemical structures, "but the email Marnie received, from someone in Britain, is asking her about the *incorrect* structure, and it mentions the patent application by the unique number that the patent office assigns. At some point in the two days before the corrected application was filed, someone, either here at the company or at your firm, must have sent this chemical structure, the wrong one, to Britain."

183

She fell silent as Hamish contemplated the implications.

"Do you, do you have anyone in mind?" he asked, almost not wanting to hear the answer: was it Marnie?

"No, and I really hate to suspect anyone who works for me here. Not yet anyway. I've got myself in a bind. I'm going to rely on many of the employees, the ones who've been taking this drug for five years I mean, to sign affidavits about that. I can't risk alienating them."

"How about an outside investigation?" Hamish suggested. "I use a really good PI, and maybe he could quietly look into it."

"That's a thought. But can we first review who worked on the application at your firm? It would be easier to eliminate a handful of people at your end, before I have to investigate who of the dozens of people here could have done it."

Hamish could check the law firm records online and see who had billed time for working on that specific patent application. However, other people could have been involved: a quick question in the coffee room, a phone call to clarify a scientific point. Not everyone who knew about the file would show up in the billing records. Normally he'd ask the head of the patent group, but for all he knew, she could be the one.

"Okay," he said to Louise. "I'm sorry to say that I don't know exactly how the patent group assigns work or puts together teams. Let's find the patent personnel on the firm website and go through them together. I can identify which of them have billed time for working on that application, but maybe you'll recognize someone else who met with your scientists or spoke to you, even it if was briefly. And I hate to admit it, the work is recent enough that some attorneys may not have recorded their time yet in the system. We have our share of procrastinators, as I'm sure most companies do. They do their work on time, but at the expense of actually *recording* their time."

He watched Louise smile and nod her head knowingly.

They spent a few minutes going one by one through the names and photographs of the attorneys in the patent group,

184

as well as their legal assistants. The final person was the patent agent Keith Jones; Hamish hadn't wanted to start with him, as he thought it would be like leading the witness.

Keith's photograph was still included in the patent group listing, although an "on leave" message had been added; presumably the head of personnel didn't want existing or potential clients trying to contact him.

When the photograph came up on screen, Hamish looked at Louise to see if she recognized Keith. She had a worried look on her face, and she pointed at the screen.

"That's, that's... you've got him mislabeled. That's Thompson Granger. English guy. He was with us for a few months but it didn't work out."

Hamish grabbed his phone and scrolled through to a note he'd made for himself after his call from Charlie. Charlie had overheard the manager's conversation at the hotel in Scotland, the relevant piece being that Thompson Granger was in custody in Portland in connection with a death at a law firm.

As far as Hamish remembered, the patent agent known as Keith Jones had worked for his firm for five years.

"When did you know him?" he asked Louise.

"Let's see," she said, thinking. "It was when only I was dosing myself with that new chemical during the one year I mentioned, to see if it had any negative effects. So he would have been here more than five years ago and less than six years ago. I'd need to consult the personnel records for the exact dates."

"What more can you tell me about him?"

"Well, he'd come over from England." She sighed. "I have to confess, we hired him really as a favor to one of our big investors. He told me his son wanted to get into patent law and was hoping to get a feel for it. The guy, Thompson, or Tom as we knew him, was nice enough, but I think he really wanted to be on the finance side. Investing, I mean. I suppose he needed some patent background for evaluating potential investments. Anyway, he didn't do much and the other

185

patent people here said they were spending too much time explaining things, so we had to let him go. I suggested that he apply to a law firm, a big one with more patent agents and a training program, I mean."

"I know nothing about the circumstances of his being hired by my firm," Hamish admitted. "I'll talk to our personnel manager. But I can assure you, we have no formal training program for patent agents, so he didn't take your advice."

He thought for a few moments, then decided that Louise needed to be told everything he knew.

"Louise, it really complicates things that he used to work with you, under a different name. Oh, I hate to think this, but I wonder if he even faked his employment application. He would have had access to your records, your letterhead, and he could have created a fake letter of recommendation under his alias. And since he probably went to university in Britain, if he even went to university, those records would be harder for our personnel people to confirm. I'm sorry to say it, but possibly, faked employment records from your company might have been all they looked at. You are such an important and well-regarded client."

He pointed to the laptop screen again.

"This guy, Keith, or Thompson, whatever his name is, he is in custody in connection with Marnie's death. But before jumping to any conclusions, he's made a confession that he and Marnie were in a relationship and, well, had an accident in the file room and she slipped and hit her head. She probably died instantly, or close to, according to the medical examiner. But instead of calling the police or an ambulance, Keith called a criminal attorney, let him into the file room in the early morning, and they staged it to look like Marnie had fallen and hit her head while she was alone in the file room."

"That's sickening!" Louise dabbed her eyes, fighting off renewed tears. "How could he be so cruel? Her poor family!"

"It is ghastly. I assume they'll be charged with a variety of things as a result. But the point I'm getting at is that Keith claims that he or the criminal attorney randomly chose a file to place in her arms. I can't believe it was random, Louise, because it's the file we've been discussing. The one with the first filing a couple of days before it was refiled to correct the mistake in the chemical structure."

Louise took her time processing what Hamish was saying.

"So what do you suspect, Hamish? After Marnie received that email, the one she contacted Henri about, she went to the file room to compare the chemical structure with what's in the incorrect patent application?"

Hamish nodded his head.

"After speaking to you today, Louise, that's my guess. She was involved in filing both applications, according to the billing records, so she was bound to know why a second one had to be filed in such a hurry. Then to get an email from someone overseas, who had possession of the incorrect chemical structure? It's the only thing that makes sense to me."

"Hamish," Louise said cautiously, "are you suggesting that Marnie was really *murdered*? By the patent agent? Jeez, I thought he was a bit dense, but capable of killing someone? And if so, do we have our leak? Did he reveal my anti-angiogenesis discovery to someone he knows in Britain? And maybe other discoveries?"

"I don't know, Louise," Hamish replied cautiously. "We need to bring the detective in on all this. What's your schedule this afternoon? Maybe she can come here and go over everything."

"I'll be available. This is my top priority. Yes, please call her."

Louise left the room for a break while Hamish called Clara's cell number, and he was glad when she answered.

"Listen, Clara," he began quickly. "I'm meeting with the client, the one whose file Marnie was holding when her body was found, and we have some information that could implicate Keith Jones in theft of intellectual property. You need to question him about it, and that's not his real name..."

"Hold on, Hamish," Clara interrupted. "I was about to call *you*. I just learned that Keith's out on bail. Between us, Hamish, I'm shocked."

Hamish felt like throwing the phone across the room, and he took a few breaths to calm down before he reacted.

"Are you *kidding* me? The guy was present at an unexplained death, he altered the scene, and I've just told you about other possible illegal activity. How is he out so soon? Or at all?"

He could visualize Clara shrugging her shoulders. "He lawyered up, Hamish. His family is wealthy and they've got lawyers on speed dial. Including Norm of course, although since he's implicated, he isn't representing Keith."

"Was *Norm* released too? He's even more guilty, far as I'm concerned, because he knows the law!"

Clara chuckled softly. "No-jail Norm, remember? If his clients don't do time, you can be sure he'd be out of the police station like we have a revolving door."

"You should have *trapped* him in it. Both of them."

"Keith is English, as you know, and he's relinquished his passport and alien registration card. He's under orders not to leave Portland, but if he did, he's still not leaving the US. Not legally anyway."

"But Clara, he has an alias! Maybe he has two passports."

"Sorry Hamish, that suggestion about his other name is reaching us too late. But I'll make sure everyone here knows the situation. There's so much new information coming in to keep up with."

The conference room door opened and Louise returned; Hamish motioned her in.

"I'm going to speak to the client some more," Hamish told Clara. "But I do want the two of you to meet as soon as possible and go over the evidence for theft of intellectual property, okay?"

With Clara's promise to stay in touch, Hamish ended the call.

He looked sadly at Louise, who had taken her seat again across from him.

"Bad news, Louise, they let Keith, or Thompson, out on bail."

"*What?* I thought Marnie just died! How could they investigate so quickly?"

"He 'lawyered up' according to the detective, Clara, and maybe it means the evidence for intentional death is weak, not a fifty-fifty situation like the medical examiner said. And we hadn't had a chance to tell the police about the patent file, since you just explained it to me now. But I'd like you and Clara to meet, then they can pull him in again for more questioning."

Hamish's phone beeped with a new text; Clara again, he expected, so he looked at it. Not Clara, his wife, Diana, and she'd included a photograph. The text said, *Another note at the front door.* The image was of a white piece of paper with the words: FAMILY HAS A PRIVATE JET.

Hamish leapt to his feet, pressing the phone to call Diana's number back.

"Sorry, Louise," he said as he grabbed his laptop and briefcase. "Emergency, I'll call you later."

In the hallway, he reached Diana. "Don't touch it!" he cried. "Call Clara and tell her to come over with an evidence bag. I'm on my way."

Chapter 38

Alone in her B&B room in Oban, it was late before Margaret finally laid her head on the pillow and tried to sleep. She was more tired than she could remember, and mentally worn out from conversation, from the constant company of Mark and Charlie.

The boat trip from the island to Oban had been smooth, but she'd had no opportunity to relax and enjoy the passing scenery. The two lawyers engaged her with questions about Scotland, the wildlife, her relationship with the royal family—endless, it had seemed. On arrival in Oban, they'd walked a few blocks to the B&B.

After checking in, Margaret wanted to retreat to her room, maybe have a pizza delivered, and simply do nothing. However, Mark noticed a seafood restaurant on the waterfront and suggested meeting for dinner. The "hamper" from the hotel had contained cheese, crackers, and fruit, not enough for a proper meal. "It's my last chance for fish and chips!" he added.

Margaret reluctantly agreed: Mark was right, he and Charlie were flying back soon, and this would be their last evening all together until they met up again in Portland. The dinner had been good, though, and at least it gave a break in the conversations. Then, what Mark said would be a "quick" stop at a pub that turned into a long visit, before they finally returned to the B&B.

Margaret had berated herself all evening: the two men were perfectly capable of eating dinner and having a pint without her, but she felt responsible for playing host and tour guide in her native Scotland. Well, she'd thought as she climbed the two flights of stairs to her sea view room, *I've done my bit*. The guys would be heading out in the morning for a train south to Glasgow, and she could have a lazy morning waiting for Alistair to drive cross-country from Finlay and pick her up.

She'd been settled on the bed, reading a book, a cup of chamomile tea to counteract the heavy meal and the half-pint of ale, when her phone rang. Mark, or Charlie? Flip a coin.

Instead, it was Alistair, and he sounded like he was in a hurry.

"Margaret, I'm truly sorry but I can't pick you up tomorrow..." his voice trailed off.

"That's fine, I told you it was a long trip and I can get the train." Should she spend yet another few hours with Charlie and Mark, riding south to Glasgow? If she didn't get the morning train with them, it would be an afternoon train, then she might have to spend a night in Glasgow... she tuned in again when Alistair raised his voice.

"No! Don't get a train. Henri will collect you. Henri and Christy, remember, the sea glass jeweler?"

"What? Are they going touring together?"

"No, Henri can explain it. Listen, it's probably nothing to worry about, but no one has heard from Adam in a while. I thought he was researching Forsyth online, but we suspect he's gone to Edinburgh. Helen's in touch with the local police station. The address for Forsyth has been the focus of complaints. If I knew more I'd tell you. Don't worry, police are meeting us there. I'll see you tomorrow."

Margaret was about to say any number of things, but he was gone. Really, she had to ride home with *Henri*? But with Christy along, maybe it wouldn't be so awkward. Anyway, she'd be too busy worrying about Alistair to pay much attention to either of them.

Now that her relaxation was derailed, she decided to check her email. Maybe there would be something reassuring from Adam. Instead, there was a series of emails from Hamish. He was even more convinced that Marnie's death was related to the file she was holding, and that Keith, alias

191

Thompson, was involved: the death wasn't accidental, Hamish suspected.

One email summarized his meeting with the president of the company that had filed the patent application, as well as many others in the area of cancer treatment. And, Hamish said, the president had shown him a foreign-language publication that, she claimed, disclosed a cancer therapeutic from a still-unpublished patent application.

Hamish attached a copy of the publication and asked Margaret to use her research skills to find out all she could about it, and about the authors and the journal that published it.

She decided to spend half an hour on that, maybe salvage a little of the day by doing something productive. Wishing it was earlier and she could get the paper printed, she instead copied down the relevant information. Not any of the chemistry: even in English, she'd be lost with it.

As part of her work for Hamish earlier in the summer, the big workplace injury case, she'd had to get a few foreign publications translated, so she knew how to do that.

She stared at the article, trying to identify the language: Swedish? Norwegian? But then it hit her: the publication was in *Gaelic*! She knew that a revival of the Gaelic language featured in contemporary singing and writing, and there was a television station that broadcast in Gaelic, but a scientific article?

Unfortunately, the translator program also found chemistry in Gaelic too much of a challenge, and was unable to help. Instead, Margaret focused on searching the authors' names, but she could find no university affiliations for them. That meant they probably worked for one or more private companies.

After several searches, she finally had a breakthrough: although she couldn't understand the context, at the very end of the paper, the name "Craig Sutherland" appeared. He was not listed on the first page in the author section, so maybe it was an acknowledgment? A consultant? A lab technician?

So here was one link with the email to Marnie. But how did Forsyth fit into it? She began looking through the paper on the screen until she felt eyestrain, but she could find no mention of "Forsyth."

At least she had two things to report back to Hamish right away. First, translating the paper would require two specialists: someone who could translate Gaelic, and someone who understood the science. Or maybe she could find a Gaelic-speaking chemist? Second, "Craig Sutherland" was a real person, apparently, who had made some contribution to a paper that might prevent Hamish's client from getting a valuable patent.

Having exhausted her intellectual capacity for the night, Margaret emailed a preliminary report to Hamish. She closed her laptop and went to bed, sending out heartfelt wishes that Alistair was safe, and Adam of course, and that Alistair would be waiting for her at the cottage the next day.

Chapter 39

The clock was striking midnight in Edinburgh. Alistair, Helen, and two police officers in plain clothes conferred on a quiet road by an industrial park outside Edinburgh, where Forsyth Industries was located. With Alistair driving, he and Helen had rushed to the location from Finlay, an hour away in Fife, after neither of them had any word from Helen's PI son Adam.

However, during the drive south, Alistair's phone had pinged with a series of texts, and he asked Helen to look at them in case they were from Adam.

They were, but nothing to indicate exactly where Adam was. Instead, there were images that Helen could make no sense of. She described them to Alistair as he hurried across the Queensferry Crossing Bridge over the Firth of Forth, the latest addition to the transportation connections between Fife to the north, and Edinburgh to the south.

"There's a picture of an office with the windows covered, then a close-up of the metal grate over one of the windows. Let's see," she said, swiping along, "the next one shows a professional-looking printer, I mean, much bigger than in my office anyway, and then a stack of what looks like bound articles, or journal papers or something." She was quiet for a moment. "Oh! This may be helpful. A couple of printed emails from Craig Sutherland, the guy you've mentioned before. They were sent to... oh, goodness, they were sent to that woman who died, Marnie? That was her name, right?"

Alistair tried to focus on driving, at the same time mentally processing what Helen was telling him. But before he could react, she let out a cry.

"Oh, no! This last picture. It's blurry and at an angle, but it caught the floor and someone's shoes, not Adam's, in mid-stride."

She looked at Alistair. "You'd better stop and look at this. I hate to say it, but maybe he was interrupted and just had time to send the last photo."

They'd crossed the bridge, so Alistair signaled to the left and stopped in the first emergency pull-out that he reached. Helen handed the phone to him and he looked carefully at Adam's last picture.

"Let's not jump to any conclusions," he said to Helen, more to calm her than anything. But he was very worried now. If Adam had simply spoken with the person who had walked in on his photo-taking session, surely he would have been back in touch with an explanation for his long silence.

Alistair started the car up again and continued heading toward the industrial park, now just ten minutes away according to his GPS. There was no further word from Adam.

Helen and Alistair soon met up with the two officers who had been there for an hour, ever since Helen's call, and they'd identified what they believed was Adam's van, based on Helen's description and the number plate.

"It's not inside the industrial park," one officer said. "He left it two blocks from here, by a residential area, so he must have walked in."

"*If* that's where he went," Helen countered. "But it's all we have to go on. And based on these pictures, taken within the last hour, he's not at someone's house having a nightcap."

They approached the industrial park entrance; although it was fenced, there was no security gate or evening guard, according to the police officers, so they could walk in unchallenged, and, they hoped, unobserved. At the entrance, Alistair asked, "Which is the building with Forsyth Industries?"

"That one." An officer pointed to a one-story building at the corner of the nearest complex. The exterior gave no hint as to its function, but the windows did have bars that corresponded to one of Adam's photographs.

195

"He must still be in there," Alistair said to the officers. "If you've been here for an hour, then you would have seen him leave and walk to his van, which hasn't been moved, right?"

"That's correct," one officer confirmed. "How about if my partner and I go to the main door and request entry? We can say we heard a report of a break-in."

Helen and Alistair discussed this for a moment. It seemed extreme to imagine that Adam's life was in danger, in this innocuous-looking setting, but they had to factor in Marnie's death and the release, hours ago, of the only suspect: Keith Jones, aka Thompson.

According to a series of messages from Hamish earlier that evening US time, Keith had been released on bail, passport confiscated, but then Hamish had received a mysterious note about access to a private jet. Access for Keith? It was difficult to draw any other conclusion. But who had left the note for Hamish?

Alistair decided the best approach was to expect the worst, that Adam had discovered something behind those barred windows, and was being kept from revealing to the outside world what he knew.

Suddenly, it all came together in his mind: a laboratory, that's what it must be. They were stealing secret chemical formulas, drug formulas, from Hamish's client in Portland, and maybe others, and replicating them in a laboratory behind those barred windows.

"There could be lower levels under these buildings, right?" he asked Helen, while at the same time he forwarded Adam's photographs to Hamish, with a bare bones explanation: *From Adam's surveillance at Forsyth Industries in Edinburgh.* He trusted Hamish to check the date and time stamps of the pictures and realize the photographs were current.

"Very possible," Helen replied. "What are you thinking?"

"To me, the evidence suggests that there's a chemical laboratory under the office space, or maybe next to the office space, and Forsyth is stealing and replicating potentially valuable drug formulas. If Adam is still in there, someone could be holding him in a basement level area. The police officers might be shown around the office and told that nothing was wrong."

Before they came up with a plan, the office door opened. Alistair motioned for the group to retreat behind the perimeter fencing where it was darker and they wouldn't be seen from the building. He had his binoculars out and watched the door through a gap in the fence.

"It's Adam," he whispered to Helen. But she already recognized her tall, wiry son, his silhouette distinct in a shaft of light from the open office door.

Adam was led out of the building, arms held by two much bulkier men who stood on either side. Instead of walking toward the entrance where Alistair and the others waited, as if Adam was simply being escorted from the premises, the group walked around the side of the building and disappeared from view.

Alistair had to physically hold Helen back from charging in after her son.

"They may have weapons," he insisted. Meanwhile, one of the officers was calling in reinforcements.

Alistair secured his binoculars across his shoulder, pulled his black wool cap further down his face, and slipped back into the industrial park, keeping to the inside of the fence.

"Be careful," Helen whispered, although Alistair was too far away to hear. She turned to the two officers. "In my day in Edinburgh, I'd be the one going in first. Oh, I hate getting old."

The two officers conferred quietly, then one said to Helen, "My partner will stay here with you in case they bring Adam this way. I'll tail Alistair so that we know where he is, for when the back-up arrives."

Which couldn't be too soon, Helen knew, her parental instincts to chase after her son battling her police training not to plunge in and make a potentially dangerous situation even worse.

Chapter 40

Hamish and Diana lingered over dessert in their dining room, while the twins enjoyed their allotted half hour of appropriate television before their bedtime bath and story. Hamish's phone alerted him to a new message and he reached for it.

Diana groaned. "It's well past working hours, dear. Can't you ignore it? I spent half the day baking your favorite dessert."

"I'm sorry, but until this whole situation is settled I'd better check. It could be from Louise or Clara."

He opened the message and tried to make sense of the photographs and cryptic note from Alistair. The message had been sent recently in Scotland. And the photos were from a *surveillance*? Hamish knew nothing about any surveillance activity.

He shook his head and stood up. "I need to look at this on my laptop. Alistair's sent some photographs that I can hardly see on my phone."

"I'll be here." Diana eyed the half-finished coconut cake slice on her plate. "Let me know if you want me to look at anything."

Hamish studied the photographs: a generic-looking office, but the few contents Alistair's colleague had managed to capture provided a direct link to Hamish's client's work. And to Marnie.

But then the final photograph, a second person caught mid-stride, the angle of the picture—whoever took the pictures seemed to have been interrupted—and the lack of any additional pictures suggested that the second person was not part of the surveillance team.

A call back to Alistair went to voice mail. If only it wasn't so late in Scotland... the heck with it, he decided, and he called Margaret's cell phone. Surely she would know what

Alistair was doing and where this surveillance was taking place.

"Margaret," he said when she answered, "I'm *really* sorry to wake..."

"It's fine Hamish. Are you calling about the email I sent you earlier, about the Gaelic publication?"

"No, I was planning to call you about that tomorrow. I'm calling to ask where Alistair is. I assume he told you?"

She'd woken with a start, disoriented as she looked around her unfamiliar B&B room. She tried to remember what Alistair had said earlier that evening.

"I believe he was going to Edinburgh. He's asked a colleague here, Adam, to research Forsyth Industries. He said he ran it by you, right?"

"Yes," Hamish confirmed, "but I've just received some photographs forwarded by Alistair. I assume they were taken by Adam, possibly from inside the Forsyth office, although I had no idea that anyone would investigate in person. The most telling one shows printouts of emails to Marnie."

"That's great! So it's all coming together?"

Hamish hesitated. "Not exactly. Alistair's had no word from Adam since the photos came in, and I'm concerned that Adam was interrupted."

"Alistair will get the police involved, I think that's what he said."

"Let's hope so. I'm sorry to worry you late at night. I really hoped you'd know exactly where Alistair is."

"Hamish, I'm still in Oban, on the west side of the country, and there's nothing I can do from here!"

Hamish hesitated, then decided to tell her what he'd shared with Alistair. "Keith Jones was released from custody earlier today. The Portland police think he won't leave the country since they have his papers, but someone gave me an anonymous tip that he has access to a private jet."

She raised her voice, wide awake now. "You mean, he could be in *Scotland* by now?"

"Possibly. I don't know how this whole private jet business works. Could he leave without his passport? Sorry, that's a rhetorical question, I don't expect you to know."

"Does Alistair know he's been released?"

"Yes, I texted him," Hamish replied.

"That's good. If he shows up at the Forsyth office, although I can't imagine why at this time of night, at least Alistair will be prepared."

"I hate all this not knowing what's going on, and now I've caused more worry for you," Hamish said. "I'd better let you get back to sleep."

With her worries increased ten-fold, Margaret said goodnight. Now Hamish regretted making the call: he'd learned nothing from Margaret, but he'd woken her up and given her reasons for concern. He returned to the dining room, deciding not to share the burden with Diana.

Smiling, he said, "Is there more cake in the kitchen?"

In Oban, Margaret was very disturbed by the call from Hamish. Why hadn't Alistair told her about Keith? Or, maybe he'd only learned about it after they last spoke.

She looked at her phone: one o'clock in the morning now. Alistair would have his phone on silent or turned off if he was somewhere he didn't want to be noticed. Surely he'd text her to let her know as soon as he was heading back home to Finlay.

She wished she wasn't stuck on the opposite side of the country, and she spent a few minutes looking at the routes Henri could follow to pick her up. The most direct route should take him about three hours, so if he left early, he could meet her by noon, and they could be back in Finlay by about three o'clock.

If Alistair got in touch in the morning, and he and Adam were safe, then she and Henri could have a leisurely trip back, do a little sightseeing. If she hadn't heard from Alistair by noon, then she'd ask Henri to get her home as quickly as possible; not that she could do anything, but she'd be too anxious to play tour guide.

She texted Henri to ask what time he and Christy planned to leave in the morning; if it woke him up, that was his problem for leaving the sound on, she decided. Truth was, she was a little annoyed, but not surprised, that he hadn't already arranged what time he'd be there.

There was nothing more she could do for the night, so she lay back in bed and tried to sleep. Was this the pattern her future would take, married to a private investigator? So far, in her months of being involved with Alistair, he'd done nothing that put him in danger, or caused him to be out all night, unreachable.

Perhaps she wasn't cut out to be the wife of a PI after all. She remembered her reaction to Mark's recent, belated, expression of interest. At that moment, the idea of being married to a fellow lawyer hadn't been appealing: the constant comparison of metrics at the law firm, and the competition for clients, for billable hours, for partnership.

At least, though, she wouldn't have to worry about his being out all night on surveillance, or tracking down a potential killer, like Keith Jones. She finally fell asleep, worn out with worry and indecision.

Chapter 41

At the industrial park outside Edinburgh, Helen had watched from the distance across the empty dark parking lot as her son was forcibly escorted from an office by two men. Alistair had headed off to follow them, keeping to the perimeter and the fence, and he in turn was being shadowed by one of the two police officers.

Helen glanced up and down the road outside the industrial park, praying that reinforcements would arrive soon; the officer with her had called it in ten minutes earlier. She held her phone up, looking at the screen constantly for any reassuring word from her son or from Alistair.

She and the officer both turned at the sound of a vehicle creeping along the road, headlights off.

"Is *this* the back-up?" Helen asked the officer.

"Doubt it, not with the lights off. Stay here. Might be another employee."

He stepped out to wave down the vehicle, a sedan car, as it turned into the entrance to the industrial park. The car slowed and the driver rolled down his window, releasing a cloud of trapped cigarette smoke.

"Can I help you, sir?" the officer asked, coughing and holding up his identification. "I'm a police officer."

"I'm hoping I can help *you*," the man replied. "Trouble at Forsyth, right?"

American accent? Helen joined the officer by the car.

"What's going on?" she asked the man.

"I don't know myself. What are you both doing?"

"It's my son, a PI," Helen began. "I'm also a police officer, and I don't know why, but my son was in that building." She pointed to the office where Adam had been. "We just watched him being taken away by two men. From here it looked like they had a strong hold on him."

"Is anyone else with you?" The man lit a cigarette while Helen was talking.

"Yes, another PI followed them around the back of the building, and the other police officer who was here followed *him*. We haven't heard anything for about fifteen minutes and we're waiting for additional officers to arrive. Who are *you*?"

"Name's Norm, ma'am. I'm on it."

And with a grin, he turned on the headlights, revved the engine, and sped off in the direction that Helen had indicated.

Helen looked at the officer who was staring blankly at the car, unsure what to make of it all. "Come on," she said. "That guy must know something. And your back-up should be here any minute."

Before the officer could stop her, she took off at a run across the parking lot. He hurried to keep up with her. When they reached the office building where Adam had been, they hugged the wall and crept around in the direction where Adam, his two captors, Alistair, the other police officer, and an American man driving fast, had all disappeared.

As they eased around the second corner of the building, Helen suddenly stopped: she'd been moving sideways, her back to the wall, and had hit an obstruction in the form of Alistair. The officer stepped around them and kept going.

"*What are you doing here?*" Alistair whispered to her.

"*You must have seen a car drive by here a moment ago,*" she whispered back. "*There's an American man in it, said his name is Norm.*"

Alistair asked Helen to describe the man; she hadn't had a good look at him in the dark, but it was enough.

"*No-jail Norm,*" Alistair muttered to himself. "What the…"

Headlights illuminated the area in front of them and they fell silent. "Come on," Alistair said, "back the way we came, behind the building."

"It's okay, your son's safe," an American voice bellowed, and Norm strode toward them.

Behind Norm came the plain clothes police officers, each holding the arm of one of Adam's former captors. The two men were protesting loudly, with shouts of "I wasnae gonna hurt 'im!" and "Och, we done nothin' wrong!"

Following the group came Adam, rubbing his forearms and shaking his head. Helen once again resisted the urge to run and hug him, and managed to keep a professional demeanor.

The area was suddenly bathed in the glare of three more sets of headlights, the promised reinforcements. Uniformed officers poured out of the vehicles. Helen recognized one as a senior officer and hurried over to speak to her.

"Good to see you, Helen," the officer said, extending her hand. "What's going on here? Is everyone safe?"

"You'll have to talk to him." Helen pointed at Norm.

"Good evening, officer," Norm said. "There are two people here to take into custody." The first two officers presented their charges, who had quieted down in the face of the larger police presence.

"I can come to the station and explain," Alistair began, "but short answer, these men were holding my colleague Adam. I watched them trying to shove Adam into the back of a truck, but I didn't want to confront them without more help. No idea if they were armed. Adam can give you the details."

The senior officer looked back and forth between Adam and Helen. "He's your son, right?"

Helen put up both hands. "Aye, he is, but you know as much as I do about what's happened tonight and why he's here. He'll have to explain it."

Adam's two captors were secured in police cars and driven off to the station. Norm faced the senior police officer; she listened while Norm explained.

"I'm an attorney, criminal law. I represent a family back in Portland, in Maine. I knew that the son, Thompson, was being released on bail after a suspicious death. The Portland police confiscated his passport and his green card and told him not to leave Portland, but I, well, I have my sources and I knew he'd come straight to Scotland and get rid of the evidence. I mean, the evidence relating to theft of trade secrets back in the States. Evidence that ties him to the death."

"But, but..." Alistair began. There had been no sign of Keith, alias Thompson, so far.

Norm interrupted. "How come *I'm* here also? I've been representing his family for many years. Marnie's death was the last straw, and I wanted to make sure that the evidence at the Forsyth offices..."

"*Yes*, but..." Alistair tried to break in again. He could see that the remaining officers were anxious to get going, taking Norm with them, and begin the long process of sorting things out at the station.

Norm lit another cigarette and grinned at Alistair. "How did I get here so quickly, is that it? Thompson's not the only one with access to a private jet. Just had to make room for big ole me among the contraband, heh heh!"

And with that he turned toward his car, trailing cigarette smoke.

"Officers," he said, turning back again, "do one of you need to come with me, or can I just follow you?" He reached into his pocket, extracted a set of keys, and handed them to Alistair. "With those two guys in police custody, no one is on duty. Please lock up the office to preserve the evidence. Secure the truck too."

After giving Adam, Helen, and Alistair instructions to appear at the local police station in the morning to give statements, the reinforcements departed, followed by Norm in his car. Helen stood motionless in the dark, staring at the retreating taillights.

"What the *heck* just happened?" she demanded. "Was he *serious* about hitching a ride with drug smugglers?"

"*That*," Alistair said, sighing, "was No-jail Norm Adler at his best. Odd that he's given me the office keys. This place is connected to his client, but maybe he's switching sides, so to speak. Details later, but first, Adam, are you all right? Do you need to go to the hospital?"

"Nae, I'm fine. I hope those thugs won't try and accuse me of breaking and entering. Truth is, the office door was unlocked when I arrived. The two guys were moving things from the office to the truck and they came back in and found me."

Helen finally gave in to her motherly worry and hugged Adam as if she'd never let go.

"Ouch, Mum! You're hurting my arms!"

Helen released her hold. "Don't ever do that to me again. You should have told me where you were going."

Adam shook his head. "Mum, this is what I've been doing for years. If I told you about every case I handle, you'd spend your life worrying."

"But Alistair said they were stuffing you into a truck when Norm arrived and stopped them!"

Adam just looked at her, a twinkle in his eye. "You know me, Mum, I had a cunning plan to escape. I'd have been fine."

Helen waited while Alistair sent quick texts to Hamish and Margaret, assuring them that Adam was fine, and that Norm had handed over the keys to the Forsyth office.

Alistair locked up the office. He found the truck keys still in the ignition, so he locked the truck as well, then he returned to Adam and Helen. "What now? It's three o'clock in the morning. Sleep or coffee?"

Helen suggested that they decamp to the closest place that offered both options: her apartment in Edinburgh. Leaving Adam's van to be picked up in the morning, they headed into town in Alistair's car.

Chapter 42

Margaret was woken yet again by her phone beeping on her bedside table, but this time she was glad: Alistair was safe, Adam was safe, and she could finally relax. She drifted back to sleep, thinking of the trip home to Finlay the next day. With her mind at ease, she could perhaps play tour guide to Henri and Christy.

The morning arrived too soon after her disturbed night, but she got up at eight o'clock, showered, washed and dried her hair, then packed. Mark had texted to say goodbye, as he and Charlie had an early start to reach the train station.

With no need to consolidate and organize her possessions for ease of ferry or train travel, she threw things randomly into bags. Soon she was downstairs in the breakfast room, a large mug of tea to help jump-start the day. She'd brought her laptop down with her and was hoping that the B&B office might print the article, in Gaelic, that Hamish had sent.

Finally, a text from Henri came in and she read it while she sipped her tea. He was leaving now, and hoped to be at the B&B between noon and one o'clock. He was alone, however. Alistair had texted Christy that Adam was safe, so she had decided not to accompany Henri. Margaret felt her shoulders slump: she'd been looking forward to a relaxed trip home, showing the sights to Henri *and* Christy, but she didn't relish three or four hours alone with Henri. Still, he was giving up a day to collect her, leaving Alistair free to finish whatever work he had been doing overnight, so she would have to put on a smile and make sure he had a rewarding afternoon.

She closed the email when she heard someone addressing her, but she had to ask them to repeat it. She thought she heard, "Matin va."

"Sorry, miss," said the young red-haired woman who'd come to take her order. The woman wore jeans, a white blouse, and a cheerful yellow apron tied around her waist. "I mean, good morning. I was speaking Gaelic to Mum over there and forgot to switch over."

Margaret looked up at her. "You, you can speak *Gaelic*?"

The woman seemed annoyed at Margaret's surprise, so Margaret quickly explained.

"I don't mean to doubt you, just the opposite. I have a short document in Gaelic that I need translated. I'm happy to pay, since I'd need to hire someone to help."

The woman waved her hand.

"Och, no payment needed. It would be nice to practice with Mum using something real, not just textbook exercises."

Margaret laughed. "Don't say that until I show you what it is!"

A few minutes later, with three printed copies of the journal article, Margaret sat with Rhona and Fionola, the mother and daughter translating team.

"Don't bother about the technical terms," Margaret said. "I'm just interested in what the conclusions are, like if they suggest using the chemicals for medical treatment or anything like that."

"How soon do you need it?" Rhona asked.

Yesterday Margaret said to herself, but she didn't want to pressure the two people who might solve Hamish's latest dilemma.

"However long you need," Margaret replied instead. "As you know, I'm checking out this morning and I have a ride back to Fife. We can keep in touch by email or text, whatever works for you."

Rhona and Fionola each flipped through the five printed pages.

"We could have a preliminary translation of the conclusions by noon," Fionola offered, "then if we can have more time, I'll work with Mum on the rest of it."

Margaret thanked them, and after Rhona insisted she go out and enjoy Oban until her ride arrived, she ate her breakfast, then left the two women to puzzle over the strange publication.

While Margaret was enjoying a final morning in Oban, Helen, Alistair, and Adam reported to the police station in Edinburgh where the two Forsyth employees were being held. Norm was already at the station, looking surprisingly well-rested after the late-night drama at Forsyth Industries.

Helen quickly learned that the explanations were going to take a long time, especially since the original crime occurred in Portland, five hours behind. As she had no professional involvement in a dispute that arose in Maine, she was excused. She would keep in touch with Alistair so that they could ride back to Finlay together, and with any luck they'd be in time for Margaret's arrival from Oban. From there, Adam could pick Helen up on his way north, if he wasn't detained too long in Edinburgh. And if that didn't work, Richard had said he would drive down from Kilvellie to collect her at Alistair's.

With an unexpected free morning in Edinburgh, she decided to call her friend Marcus, former director of the Museum of Antiquities in Edinburgh. As Helen had learned recently, the museum loaned several pieces of old glassware to Kilvellie's Regenbogen Glass Factory in the nineteen thirties. The glass had been presumed lost during the war, but Margaret found it carefully hidden in biscuit tins, surrounded by groatie buckies. Helen decided the time had come to tell Marcus the glass had survived, and ask for his advice on what to do with it.

However, after Helen's unpleasant interactions with the current museum management, she was reluctant to return the items to them. Instead, she wanted it to remain on loan to the glass factory, now being reborn as a glass museum.

Marcus answered his cell phone right away.

"Helen, what a coincidence! I was just going to stop by and visit you."

Helen felt disoriented: she'd said nothing to Marcus about coming to Edinburgh, so how could he visit her here?

"You mean, visit me at my flat…" she began.

"Nae lass," Marcus interrupted, "at the police station! I drove up to Kilvellie last night to see this new glass museum I've been hearing about, and I was going to surprise you this morning."

Helen sighed deeply. "Oh Marcus, I'm not there, I'm in Edinburgh! I hope to be back this afternoon, but probably late. How long will you be in town?"

"Och, I have no specific plans. I'm at a B&B and they aren't busy, so I'll stay again tonight and maybe we can have a catch-up later or tomorrow?"

They ended the call, with Helen promising to get in touch when she knew her schedule for the day. She continued walking, then turned when she heard Adam calling to her. She stopped and waited for him and Alistair to catch up.

"Do you need me to come back?" she asked.

"No, Mum, they can't do anything until they talk to that detective in Portland, the one who's investigating Marnie's death. It's not so urgent that they need to wake her up so they'll wait until she's in her office."

"Are they charging the two men who tried to put you in the truck last night?" Helen asked Adam.

"I don't know yet. Apparently the men are claiming that they were only following orders from the man who had been taken in for questioning about Marnie's death."

"And then *released*," Alistair pointed out. "According to Norm, his whereabouts are unknown, so the police here can't verify the Forsyth employees' claim that they were working for him." He shook his head. "It's a mess."

They all turned at the sound of footsteps running toward them: Norm.

"Whew, I'm glad I caught you." He stopped to catch his breath. "The top priority is finding Keith Jones, or Thompson

211

Granger, Tom, whatever he's calling himself now. From my brief discussion with the two jerks in jail, he called them yesterday to tell them to clear out the office immediately. He said he's in Scotland and would get back in touch, but they don't know where he called from."

"Maybe he's gone into hiding," Alistair said while Norm lit a cigarette. "With all the remote glens and islands in Scotland, he could be anywhere."

"Well, not *anywhere*, Alistair. It's not disclosing a client confidence to tell you folks that his father is an investor in a new hotel on an island off the west coast. Name's Carrot, Carrotsy Island, something like that."

Alistair stared at Norm. "Not *Caraidsay*, is it?"

"Yes, that's it!" Norm exhaled a stream of smoke. "Don't tell me you've heard of it? Far as I know, it's pretty darn remote. They use it for corporate retreats, high-end clients and all."

Alistair turned away from the smoke and faced Helen and Adam. "This is terrible. That hotel, it's where Margaret and the two other lawyers from her firm were staying, but..." He tried to calm down. "Wait, let me think. All three lawyers left the island last night and they stayed in a B&B in Oban, on the mainland. If Keith spent yesterday flying from the States, then there's no way they would have overlapped on the island. Unless the private jet took him straight there? Maybe...uh... maybe the predicted bad weather hasn't developed?"

"I don't know the answer to that. And even if they crossed paths in Oban," Norm said, "Tom will be keeping a low profile. He's hardly going to acknowledge them if he happened to see them on his way to the ferry, or seek them out to talk to them, right?"

Alistair shrugged his shoulders. "You know him better than we do, Norm. Is he a threat to Margaret, to the other lawyers from the firm? What if he thinks they would tell the police they'd seen him?"

From the look on Norm's face, Alistair realized it was a question that Norm wouldn't, or couldn't, answer. They were all in new territory as far as the fugitive patent agent was concerned.

Alistair excused himself, and stepping away from the group, he called Margaret's cell phone.

"Is Henri there yet?" he asked.

"Hi Alistair, no, he texted that he'll be here around noon or one, then we should be back in Finlay late afternoon. Where are you?"

He was silent for a moment, trying to decide if he should tell her that Keith was on the loose, with a slight chance of being in Oban en route to Caraidsay. *Nah* he decided, why make her worry. Keith was either on the island by now after hiring a private boat or arriving by plane, or he could be halfway there on the morning ferry. Margaret was at her B&B waiting for Henri, so the chances of an encounter seemed minimal to non-existent.

"Sorry, I was distracted. I'm still in Edinburgh with Helen and Adam, but I hope we'll be able to leave soon. I should be at the cottage when you get back."

Margaret hesitated, then said, "I'm not happy that Henri's driving up without Christy, but I'll just have to tolerate him for a few hours."

"What? Did I hear right, Christy didn't go with Henri after all?"

"It's *fine*," Margaret assured him. "We'll just be talking about the investigation. I have *no feelings* for him now, truly."

Alistair tried to stifle a groan. "Just, oh, just don't let him lure you in again. He is pretty charming, I'll give you that."

With promises to stay in touch, they ended the call, and Alistair returned to the others.

"Margaret's in Oban for a few more hours, then Henri will pick her up. I debated telling her to look out for Keith, but no sense in worrying her, right? Henri might panic and take her somewhere even more remote!"

Helen and Adam nodded their heads, although he could tell that they weren't sure he'd made the right choice. Was he too focused on a potential romantic challenge from Henri, and ignoring a genuine threat?

Chapter 43

After a stop to drop Adam off at his own vehicle, still parked near the Forsyth industrial park, Helen and Alistair headed north. They drove over the Queensferry Crossing Bridge, then took the most direct route through Fife, not stopping at Alistair and Margaret's cottage in Finlay. Since Margaret wouldn't be home for a few hours, he'd offered to take Helen to Kilvellie while Adam stayed behind to continue working with the police in Edinburgh.

As they approached the outskirts of Kilvellie, Helen called Marcus, the former museum director, and arranged to meet him at the police station in half an hour.

"You're welcome to stay and meet him too, Alistair," she said when she ended the call. "I'm sure he'd like to hear about you and Adam discovering where Justine escaped from the coal chute, and then finding all the glass that's going to be displayed in the museum."

Alistair thought for a moment. Margaret wouldn't be in Finlay before four o'clock, or later if she took Henri sightseeing on the way back. If Alistair went straight home, he would brood and imagine Margaret and Henri rekindling their romance, despite Margaret's protestations to the contrary.

"I'd like that, Helen, thank you. And maybe…"

"If you were going to say 'coffee' I am already thinking we should meet Marcus and head straight to the bakery for lunch. Then I can take Marcus to meet Malky and see the progress on the glass museum. Again, you're welcome to join us."

A few minutes later, Alistair parked the car outside the police station. As he got out of the car, he could see a thin elderly man carefully standing up from where he'd been sitting on the front steps of the station. The man looked like an academic, Alistair thought, with thick white hair, a tweed blazer layered over a collared shirt and a Fair Isle vest, and brown corduroy pants.

The man held out his hand to introduce himself to Alistair, then Alistair stood back while Helen and Marcus shared a warm hug.

"What are you doing sitting out here on the steps?" Helen asked.

"Och, the door was locked and I figured I got here too early."

Helen looked at him in confusion. "Locked? My sergeant, Desmond, should be on duty." She unlocked the door. "Maybe he's been called out on an emergency, although he should have let me know."

Inside, there was no sign of Desmond and no indication of where he'd gone, so she tried his cell phone. After a short call, she smiled and shook her head.

"I don't know what I'm going to do with that boy, I mean, that young man. He has a very loose definition of police business. He's up at the new glass museum, helping Malky! I told him to finish what he's doing and come back here so we can go and have some lunch."

"I was hoping to see the glass museum," Marcus said. "I drove up there this morning, but I didn't want to barge in. Everyone looks so busy."

"I can take you after lunch," Helen offered.

Over lunch and coffee at the bakery cafe, Helen told Marcus that the old glass pieces on loan to the Regenbogen Glass Factory pre-World War Two had in fact survived the war, intact, and were currently at the home of Alistair's fiancée Margaret.

Marcus listened intently, unable to express his surprise. "In biscuit tins? Hidden among groatie buckies? This is the most exciting thing I've heard in years!"

"But what should be done with the pieces?" Helen asked. "They still belong to your old museum in Edinburgh, the Museum of Antiquities. When I talked to the current

216

management, they didn't know about the loan, but they also said they expected prompt return of museum property."

Now Alistair spoke up. "I've been thinking about this ever since Margaret found the glass. I wonder if the new management at the antiquities museum, which I had never heard of, would allow Malky to display it at his museum, along with some promotional information about the antiquities museum? Maybe even offer a discounted admission to it, with purchase of admission to the glass museum?"

"I like that idea," Marcus said, "even though I don't like what's been done to my old museum. Helen, why don't you suggest that to Malky? I could act as intermediary, since I know the people in Edinburgh."

Helen agreed, and with the plan set, they finished lunch.

Helen drove Marcus and Alistair north through town and parked in the large parking area across the street from where the glass museum was being built. The exterior of the building was shingled to give a driftwood appearance. It was having finishing touches added, with most of the work focused on the interior.

Malky was outside the building and saw the group approach. He greeted Helen and Alistair, then listened as Helen introduced Marcus.

"Oh goodness," Malky said, "it's an honor to have a visit from a real museum curator! We can use any advice you want to give. Have ye time for a wee tour?"

Smiling, Marcus agreed, and the group followed Malky to the front desk—a plywood board over two sawhorses, at this stage—where they were all given yellow hard hats.

"Health and safety," Malky grumbled as he fastened the strap under his chin.

"Don't complain, Malky," said Helen. "You don't want to be shut down for safety violations or injuries before you even open."

The guests stood by the desk and listened while Malky asked them to imagine how it would look; so far, the interior featured a series of floor to ceiling wooden supports, with walls in progress.

Helen was struck by the change in Malky's appearance and demeanor, in just a few weeks. She remembered her first meeting with him, when he and a teenage boy had almost come to blows over a bucket of marbles. Standing in the police station that day, he had exuded disappointment, frustration, and a sense that his family's history literally weighed on his shoulders. He had a slightly hunched stance, which Helen later realized was from decades of walking the local beach, peering down to find sea glass.

The Malky who she encountered now, a shiny, youthful version of himself, seemed to have grown in physical stature as well as confidence. He wore beige canvas trousers, dusty at the knees, and a blue tartan work shirt. Despite being in his sixties, he still had thick brown hair. However, it could use a trim, Helen thought, as the repeated donning and removing of his hard hat was doing the style no favors.

"Visitors will be taken on a walk through history," Malky was continuing, motioning with his arms. "We'll start with my grandfather Heinrich marrying Sheila, with photographs of them and their bairns on the back walls of the display cases. In the cases we'll have examples of glass made at the factory during each decade."

He turned to Marcus. "Do you think that dividing it by decade makes sense? That would mean twelve cases, with space to add contemporary glass, not made by the factory, but examples of what is made today."

Marcus nodded his head. "Aye, that makes sense to me, to illustrate the evolution of the Regenbogen styles and workmanship."

"And the people involved," Malky added. "We have a lot of old black and white photographs of people, and scenes inside the factory. It will take a while to organize them and

218

identify the people, but my two eldest, Christy and Will, are busy with that."

Helen didn't say anything, but she wondered what Malky had in mind for the nineteen forties, when the factory was looted and damaged by six teenage boys. Knowing him, he would put a positive spin on it. Without the looting, after all, the employees wouldn't have been motivated to hide the wealth of glass vases and marbles that would be the core of the museum.

Malky stepped away from the group to talk to someone on the construction team, and Marcus took the opportunity to speak quietly to Helen.

"Does Malky know that the very old glass, from the Museum of Antiquities, has been found?" he asked.

"Aye, but I haven't spoken to him about what will happen to it."

"Might be good to have the conversation now," Marcus suggested. "I can visualize another display case that would start the whole timeline, but it would go back more than two thousand years."

"You mean, the glass on loan to the factory?"

"Aye, lass. I would like to see it featured here. The Museum of Antiquities doesn't specialize in glass. If the pieces are returned to them, they might put one on display, but I suspect the other pieces would go back to the storeroom, which is where they lived before the loan in the nineteen thirties."

"I like that idea," Helen said. "Can you start the conversation with Malky today? If he wants to have the pieces here, then since you are willing, I expect he'd appreciate you acting as the liaison with the antiquities people."

Malky rejoined the group, and as Helen knew he'd jump right in where he'd left off, she spoke up quickly.

"Malky, remember that Margaret has the glass from the Museum of Antiquities, that was in biscuit tins at Richard's old house?"

"Aye, Helen, and I'm assuming it will go back to that museum. I'd love to have it here, but Greta always says, 'dinnae get yer hopes up Malky' so I've kept quiet."

Marcus took that as his cue. "I don't work at that antiquities museum now, but from what I've heard, I doubt the new curator would display all the pieces. Maybe even none of them. It would be shame for them to go back into storage. So with your permission, I'd like to offer to discuss the situation with the current management. Maybe, if you put the pieces on display, you could make it clear that they are on loan from the Museum of Antiquities, and have brochures about it at the information desk?"

Malky laughed. "Och, dinnae mention brochures tae my kids. It's all bar codes and mobile phone scanners for them."

"I know what you mean," Marcus said. "Nowadays when I visit historic locations in Scotland, it's all scan this, scan that. Even *trees* have wee signs to scan. Anyway, however you plan to present information, if you can sort of co-promote the antiquities museum, I like to think they would be amenable to the continued loan."

"I just thought of something, Marcus," said Helen. "What about insurance? Malky's going to be displaying valuable twentieth century glass, but adding glass that's over two thousand years old, wouldn't that raise the insurance costs a lot?"

"Maybe the old glass can be placed in a more high-security display case," Alistair suggested. "As Helen knows, I'm in the security business, so I could look into that if it would help."

Malky gratefully agreed to the offer. He then picked up a box from the front desk and showed Marcus that it contained some aging photographs of local residents displaying pieces of Regenbogen glass. Christy had put out an appeal on social media, and Malky had done the same in the newspaper, asking people if they'd like to share images of their glass collections.

"We have a whole lot more photographs that were sent digitally," he said, "but Christy and Will are handling that."

Finally, he reached into a box that had been shoved under the desk. Helen just stared at the flat wooden object, like a game board, that Malky was now showing to Marcus.

"Couple of old timers, they stopped by and offered to donate, or loan, their own antique marble holders. See, the little round indentations, you can lay a marble in each one. Maybe in a pattern."

Marcus nodded his head. "I like that idea. These will do well in a central flat display case, so people can look at them from all sides."

"It really is turning into a community education project," Helen commented. "I for one had never heard of wooden marble display boards."

"Aye," Malky agreed as he replaced the board, "lots of folks here, they heard them stories from parents and grandparents, 'bout working in the factory or receiving glass as a special gift, so they're enjoying the idea of it coming back tae life this way. Their family mem'ries not being lost."

With nothing more to see in the future museum space, they took off their hard hats and went back outside.

"Thanks for showing me the space," Marcus said to Malky.

"If ye all have a wee bit more time, I'm sure Greta would love tae meet ye, Marcus. Let's go to the caff for a wee blether and have some pastries."

"Wait, Malky." Helen held back. "Greta must be busy getting the cafe set up. Are you sure she won't mind?"

"Och no," Malky declared, already heading along the front of the building to where the cafe entrance faced the main road.

Chapter 44

Inside the cafe, Malky, Alistair, Marcus, and Helen sat at one of the few tables that had been set up, while Greta insisted on serving tea and coffee, and an assortment of small cakes.

"I serve snacks to the construction workers," she explained. "I bake things at home, and we have the hot water and coffee equipment set up. We did that first."

Helen was tempted to invite Greta to take a break and sit with them, but presumably she heard plenty of conversations about the museum construction at home. After serving everyone and saying she had to get back to work, she disappeared behind a swinging door.

Next to the door, Helen noticed a cooler with brightly colored bottles, and she got up to take a closer look. Malky got up too when he saw what she was looking at. Grinning, he took a bottle from a shelf and guided Helen back to the table.

"Is that Japanese soda?" Helen asked. "Seems so incongruous with the traditional tea room décor that Greta's working on."

"Aye, you're right aboot that!" Malky said. He held the bottle up and turned it over a couple of times. The others could hear something rattling in it. Helen peered more closely.

"Is that a *marble* inside?"

Malky nodded his head.

"Right again, Helen. This is called Ramune. It's a kind of lemonade. The marble is nothing new. There's a type of bottle called a Codd-neck bottle, popular in Britain at one time. On some beaches, people find marbles from the old Codd-neck bottles. Who knows, in a few decades the kids will be pickin' up sea glass marbles from Ramune sodas!"

"I've heard of Codd-neck bottles," Marcus said. "The marble keeps the carbonated liquid from escaping, I believe. The pressure helps seal the bottle."

"Exactly," Malky agreed. "I only know about this here modern version because me daughter Justine works in a caff in St. Andrews. They have such an international customer base, they stock all sorts I've never heard of!"

After offering the bottle to his companions, who all declined to try the colorful drink, he chuckled to himself and returned it to the cooler.

Marcus took a long drink of coffee, then raised the issue of the old glass again. "Malky, I've been thinking more about the glass from the antiquities museum. I understand it was found recently, hidden in biscuit tins?"

"Aye," Malky confirmed. "In wee old boxes, surrounded by groatie buckies."

Marcus smiled. "It may sound comical, but how about displaying one biscuit tin with the groatie buckies inside, and maybe a corner of an original box poking out?"

Helen laughed. "I love the idea, Marcus, but when people see that, everyone and their granny will be searching through biscuit tins in the cupboards and attics!"

"And that would be a *good* thing in my opinion, Helen. Who knows what treasures are waiting for someone to do just that. My only concern about the old glass, and I should have mentioned it earlier..." Marcus stopped and shook his head. "Och, never mind, I don't want to raise an issue that may not exist."

"Go on," Malky urged him. "This is the time, since we're still plannin' the displays."

Marcus glanced at Helen, apologetically, then turned back to face Malky. "Helen is familiar with this, from her help at the museum in Edinburgh now and again. Once in a while, the museum would get a request, or a demand, from some foreign government, or even from a collector in this country, saying that one or another of the pieces on display actually belonged to them, and they wanted it back."

"Like the Elgin Marbles?" Alistair asked. "That's in the news now and again."

Before Marcus could respond, Malky cried, "Belgian marbles! Goodness, I thought the old marbles were mainly made in Germany! I'll have to ask Will to look into this, for the museum..."

Marcus waved his hand to interrupt Malky and spell the word. "E-L-G-I-N. Elgin Marbles. They were in Greece in the..."

Malky cried out again, "Oh, so some old marbles were made in *Greece*? You mean, ancient Greece or more modern?"

He had an expression of grave disappointment on his face, like he was missing out on a whole chapter in the history of marbles. Alistair did a quick search on his phone and held it up for Malky to see.

"*These* are the Elgin Marbles," he explained. "They're not marbles like you know, they're *carved* from marble, from stone. These marble statues and friezes were part of the Acropolis in Greece, and are now in the British Museum in London. Greece wants them back and it's a big controversy."

Malky burst out laughing and put his hand to his head.

"Och Alistair, you had me all worried. Okay, thanks for showin' me what we're really talkin' aboot. I sure have a lot to learn."

He stopped to drink some tea, then asked Marcus, "Ye think that if we display that very old glass, some from two thousand years ago, we'll have an Elgin Marble problem? The countries they're from will demand them back? I couldnae afford the legal fees! Maybe..."

"Don't get ahead of yourself," Marcus said. "I'll check the provenance with the museum in Edinburgh. I expect that the pieces were all either bought or donated through legitimate channels, but it would be good for you to have copies of the documentation if anyone asks. Leave it with me just now."

Helen looked at Marcus. "The pieces would only be on loan to Malky's museum, so he's not responsible for proving provenance, is he?"

"Och Helen," Malky broke in, "I would like to have the peace of mind. If Marcus here disnae mind lookin' into it, I sure would be grateful."

The group fell silent while they made a start on the cakes. After a few moments, Alistair spoke up. "If you decide to include a tin full of groatie buckies, to show how the old glass was hidden for all those decades, since the war, I mean, will you have an information sign to explain who hid the glass, and who discovered it?"

"I havenae thought aboot that yet, laddie," Malky replied. "Are ye thinking, we could say that Ronald Wilson, the guard I mean, took the glass home to save it from the looters, then it was forgotten about until a few weeks ago, when his son Richard gave Margaret the tins?"

Helen raised her hand. "Hold your horses, everyone. Richard is still very torn about his father's actions in the war years. I don't know if he'd be comfortable with the idea that his father sort of forgot about twenty pieces of old glass, that belonged to someone else. Maybe this is a situation where someone's wartime behavior might not withstand the scrutiny of later generations, who can't imagine what life was like then."

"Aye, Helen, ye have a point," Malky agreed. He looked over to the kitchen door, which was still closed, and Greta was nowhere in sight.

"Me own *wife* doesnae know this, and I will never tell her, but I have a secret aboot my grandmother, Sheila I mean."

"Are you talking about Sheila marrying a former German soldier?" Alistair asked. "I didn't think that was a secret."

"Nae laddie," Malky continued. He motioned for the others to lean in while he shared the story, even though they were the only customers in the cafe.

"Afore dear Sheila passed away, she was confined tae her bed. I heard this later from me own father. Sheila asked to see the minister, so he was summoned and he sat by her bed while the family left them together. The hoose back then, it had thin walls and space around the door, and my father overheard the beginnin' of what turned out to be her confession. He heard her tell the minister that she had killed a man during the war, in order to protect Heinrich, and she was askin' for the minister's forgiveness, afore she died, ye see."

"I'm so sorry to hear that, Malky," Helen said after a few respectful moments. "Did, did you, I mean, did any details ever come out?"

"Nae. Of course after she passed away, there was some discussion among the family aboot who it could have been, but accordin' to my father, they concluded that Sheila must have killed someone when she was nursing in France. Heinrich was a German soldier in a British field hospital. There must have been injured lads who resented it. Maybe one of them, or maybe an officer, tried to get Heinrich transferred out, or not cared for. From all I've heard, he was very ill, so any lapse in his care could have been fatal. Anyhoo, I decided to believe that she killed one man to save another. Like Helen said, them wartime decisions and acts, we cannae judge them from our safe existence now."

He shook his head sadly and finished his tea, then spoke up again. "I only told ye so that you'd know it's not only Richard's father who carried a huge burden from the war. But none of me children know of Sheila's confession, and not dear Greta, so ye'll all keep it to yerselves, please?"

He looked from face to face as the other three all nodded their agreement.

"Okay," Marcus said, leaning back in his chair, "you obviously have some decisions to make about how much, or how little, to reveal about the discovery of the loaned museum glass, so let's leave that for now. For the Regenbogen glass, Malky, do you have the displays all planned out at this stage?"

"We're just startin' on it. A carpenter pal is buildin' 'em for me. The first one is doon at the hoose. Do you, och, I shouldnae impose any more on yer time..."

"If you're offering to show it to me, Malky, I'd be delighted. I've been retired for a while now, and I do miss the planning stages of new exhibits."

Helen glanced at her watch. "Much as I'd like to go with you both, I should get back to the office. Alistair, what do you plan to do? I can drop you off at your car."

Alistair accepted the ride. After arranging to meet Marcus later for dinner, Helen accompanied Alistair back across the street to where her car was parked. Alistair checked his phone; it was two o'clock, and there was no word from Margaret. Henri should have picked her up an hour or two ago, but Alistair was reluctant to act the jealous fiancé. Margaret would get in touch in her own time. If for some reason the rendezvous had fallen apart, Henri would surely have let Alistair know by now.

"Nothing from Margaret?" Helen asked.

"I'm a bit surprised, but I suppose she and Henri are on the road and she's busy being tour guide. Do you have a few minutes to chat when we get back to your office? Seeing the interior of Malky's museum has given me an idea."

"I'm intrigued. Hold that thought and we'll discuss it over tea in my conference room."

Belatedly, Alistair wished he'd accepted the bottle of Japanese soda that Malky had offered. It would have been a nice break from the endless tea, with the bonus of a marble for Margaret.

Chapter 45

While Helen and Alistair were driving south through Kilvellie, Margaret was in the lobby of her B&B in Oban, frantically searching through her belongings. All thoughts of privacy were cast aside, along with her clothes, toiletries, bags of groatie buckies, shoes, and various papers and cards, all strewn over chairs and tables.

She stood back, hands on hips, and looked at Henri, who was sitting in the only free chair.

"It's definitely not here," she announced.

"And it's not in your room, *Cherie*. I and the staff looked everywhere there, under the furniture, in all the drawers. We would have looked in the safe deposit box if they'd had one."

"Oh. My. God!" Margaret cried, throwing her arms in the air. "*That's* where it is! I left it in the room safe at the hotel on the island! We were in such a rush to leave last night, before the bad weather came in." She stopped and pointed at the bags of groatie buckies. "I was so preoccupied with finding space for those, I completely forgot my routine of double-checking everything in the room."

"Could the hotel manager get it and mail it to you?" Henri asked, as Margaret began shoving her belongings back into bags.

She turned to glare at him. "Would *you* trust your passport to some stranger and to the mail service? I have to go back and get it now! If one of my parents has a medical emergency, I need to be able to fly home right away."

Henri nodded his head. He checked his phone for the ferry schedule, then turned it around to show her.

"There eez a ferry at three o'clock, and the weather looks fine for now. We stay overnight there and get the morning ferry back, *d'accord*?"

"You don't have to go with me," Margaret argued. "I've already wasted your day. I'll go on as a foot passenger and, I

228

don't know, maybe the hotel can send a taxi to meet me at that end. Then tomorrow Alistair can drive to Oban to meet me, or I can get a train back."

Henri stood and began re-closing her bags.

"*Non*, Margaret, I weel take you over on the ferry and drive you to the hotel. But you must call them and tell them what has happened. If they clear out the safe for the next guest..."

"I know! I won't relax until I have it in my hands!"

While she called the hotel on Caraidsay, Henri ran back and forth from the lobby to his car parked outside the B&B from when he'd arrived to pick Margaret up. After securing all her possessions in the trunk, they leapt into the front seats, and with Margaret calling out directions through the one-way streets of Oban, they headed for the ferry waiting area. The ferry crew had begun boarding cars, but thanks to the dire weather warnings, the ferry was not fully booked and Henri was able to drive right on.

Once the car was parked on the deck of the ferry, Margaret forced herself to calm down. Smiling, she turned to Henri.

"The hotel had cancellations due to the weather, so housekeeping hasn't even been into my room yet. They said I can stay in it tonight, and they have another room for you." She stopped to take a deep breath. "It's expensive, but I'll pay for your room, Henri. It's the least I can do."

They left the car and climbed the stairs to the restaurant deck. Sandwiches and coffee in hand, they went further up in the ferry and found seats with some shelter from the wind, then settled in for the afternoon's journey.

Now that she could think clearly, Margaret realized with a pang of conscience that she hadn't told Alistair what was happening. He'd be expecting her home any time now, yet here she was, sailing away in the opposite direction with her ex-boyfriend. And her phone had no signal. She drafted a text, hoping that it would go out if they entered a cell service area as they passed one of the islands along the way.

By four o'clock, Alistair was ready to head south to Finlay. He'd spent the past hour with Helen, discussing his ideas for an additional display case in the glass museum. The issue of the factory vandalism in the nineteen forties, and the night guard Ronald's role, was a sensitive subject, but Alistair felt strongly that Ronald had to be acknowledged in the full history of the factory.

While going through the boxes from Ronald's care home, he had found a number of photographs of Ronald as a security guard when the care home was a hotel. Ronald obviously had made a good impression on the visiting members of royalty and the show business celebrities, judging from the photographic evidence. These famous people seemed to enjoy having their photographs taken alongside uniformed Ronald, who smiled for the camera as he held a door open, or escorted a member of the royal family to a waiting limousine.

The photographs presented a very different image of the grouchy biased man who Alistair had heard about from the man's son and grandchildren. Surely this side of poor Ronald deserved to be known too?

Helen liked the idea, and as they finished their tea, they decided that Alistair should choose a selection of the pictures, then ask Malky for his thoughts.

Alistair was distracted when his phone pinged with a text message. "It's probably Margaret in the cottage, wondering where I am," he told Helen as he opened the message.

"What?" he cried, leaping to his feet. "I, I can't believe she'd do that to me!"

"Alistair, sit down and tell me. What's happened?"

He sat down and read the text to Helen, just a couple of sentences.

"It says, 'Alistair, I left something at hotel on island. Henri and I on ferry. Will call from island. Cell service bad on ferry. Margaret xx'. Oh no, I should have warned her about Keith after all! This is terrible!"

Helen thought for a moment while the news sank in. "Are there flights to the island from the mainland?" she asked.

"I think maybe from Glasgow and from Oban, but not every day. And there's no way I can get to an airport in time to fly today." He stood up again. "I'd better, um, I'd better drive out to Oban now, see if I can hire a private boat like Adam did, when he got them off the island last night. The weather wasn't as bad as predicted, and now, all that effort for nothing."

Helen's commanding voice broke into his thoughts. "Alistair! Sit down again and focus. One thing at a time. When is the first ferry back from the island tomorrow?"

He did as told, looking up the ferry schedule on his phone. "There isn't a morning ferry. First one is at noon. It's the return of the morning ferry from Oban."

"We have to assume that they'll get that noon ferry. There's no point in you making a heroic effort trying to get to the island tonight. She'll be tucked up in bed before you even get there. The best you can do is drive to Oban tonight, get the early ferry, and meet her when she gets on the noon ferry back. But think about it, what would be the point? She'll be with Henri, and you can speak to her later and tell her about Keith possibly being on the island. If she's in the hotel the whole time, with employees and other guests around, nothing's going to happen to her, really."

Alistair sighed deeply. "I should be most concerned about Keith, but I hate to admit it, I'm worried about her being with Henri! What if he, I don't know…"

"She's engaged to *you*," Helen reminded him. "She could be with Henri if she wants to, but she has chosen you. I don't know Margaret well, but I'd be shocked if she has a fling with Henri while she's planning to marry you."

"I want you to be right," Alistair grumbled, "but I've never known Margaret to be careless and leave something in a hotel room. And even if she did, why can't the hotel send it to her, like if she left some clothing or paperwork?"

231

"Based on my experience with forgetful tourists in Edinburgh," Helen said, "it's most likely to be something really important. Does she carry her passport with her? She wouldn't want that put in the mail. Or maybe she left her wallet. I'm sure she's only going back because it's something of value."

"Yeah, her groatie buckies."

At that, Helen laughed. "Look, Alistair, do you really want to drive to Oban tonight and get the morning ferry?"

She waited while he shook his head, then continued. "Good. Come to dinner with me and Marcus and take your mind off the situation. She's not alone, and you'll see her tomorrow. Okay? You can even bunk in the spare room in the residence, if you want to have some wine with dinner. Or whisky later."

He was silent as he considered Helen's offer. He had overnight things in the car, and he really didn't relish driving back to Finlay, brooding all night. And brood he would.

"Yes, thank you Helen. You're right as usual, a good dinner followed by whisky is the best solution yet."

But before fully committing, he called Christy, as he felt bad leaving her alone at the cottage for a second night. He reached her and discovered she was at the Templeton Hotel restaurant. It was between meals, but Dougie the chef was trying new appetizers and she was happily joining in. Feeling reassured, he said he'd see her in the morning, then left Helen to close up the office for the night.

Chapter 46

Early that evening, a weary Henri steered his car down the ramp from the ferry, with Margaret in the passenger seat, watching her phone for a sign of cell reception. She had been relieved to see that her text had gone through to Alistair at some point, so at least he wouldn't be worrying that she'd been in a car accident on the way back to Finlay from Oban.

Finally, as Henri drove away from the terminal and joined the main road south to the hotel, service resumed and she called Alistair.

She had to wait a moment after he answered. "Sorry," he said. "I was in a restaurant but now I can talk."

"Are you at the Templeton?" she asked.

"No, long story, I'm in Kilvellie with Helen and someone from Edinburgh. But listen carefully, that guy Keith, well Thompson Granger, the patent agent from your firm? He may be on the island. On Caraidsay..."

"What?" Margaret interrupted. "What's he doing here?"

"Hiding, most likely. His father invested in that hotel where you were staying. Just, I don't know, if you see him, don't approach him, and make sure you are with other people all the time. Well, I don't mean overnight, but when you're outside your room. Or maybe you should stay at a B&B near the ferry?"

"No, I think I'll feel safer in a modern hotel with good security. Anyway, the police in Portland released him, so maybe he had nothing to do with... with poor Marnie. I still start to cry when I think of her, lying in that file room..."

She felt Henri reach and hold her arm for a moment of comfort.

"I know, Margaret," Alistair said. "I checked the ferry schedule and I assume you'll be on the noon ferry, getting into Oban around three or four o'clock tomorrow?"

"Yes," she confirmed. "Then we'll head straight back to Finlay. In time for Indian food!"

Alistair could hear Henri laughing softly in the background. He tried to keep his voice calm, not at all happy with the image of them in a car together. In a hotel together. In a hotel *room* together. No, Margaret wouldn't do that, Helen had to be right.

"Wait, before you hang up," Alistair said quickly, "what did you leave behind? In all the time I've known you, you are always so organized with your packing and keeping track of things."

She laughed. "It's the darn groatie buckies!"

He raised his voice. "Margaret! You went back to the island and you're risking seeing Keith for *groatie buckies*?"

"No! Those, they could have mailed to me. Let me finish. Remember, we all left the hotel that night in a huge rush. I was so focused on packing the groatie buckies that I forgot to check the safe in my room. I left my passport in it. At least, I sure hope I did."

"Let me know right away, okay?" Alistair insisted. "I'd appreciate knowing you have that off your mind at least."

With promises to stay in touch, they ended the call.

"Everything okay?" Henri asked, glancing over at Margaret.

"Yes, thank you. Here is my evening plan, in order of priority. First, check into my room and find my passport. Then, dinner with you in the dining room, with a bottle of French wine, your choice. And finally..."

She knew she was teasing him, but she couldn't help it.

"*Oui*?" he prompted. "Finally?"

"*Finally*, a long soak in my Jacuzzi tub! Then blissful sleep."

To Margaret's huge relief, her passport was exactly where she'd left it, in the small safe in the closet of her hotel room. With that done, she could finally relax for the evening. She really just wanted to order dinner in her room and then have a long soak, but she owed it to Henri to be sociable over dinner. At least, she thought he'd want that. It occurred to her, maybe *he* would like to eat alone in his room, but since he had agreed to meeting in the dining room at eight o'clock, that is what she did.

On arrival at the hotel, she'd been told that she and Henri were the only guests that night. She wondered if rumors of Keith/Thompson being on the island were misplaced. He could be at a B&B closer to the ferry, she thought, but if your father is an investor in a luxury hotel, surely that's where you'd stay, and he probably wouldn't be classified as a guest. She'd just have to be alert for his possible presence.

Despite that worry, she was able to enjoy a long relaxed dinner with Henri, and actually listen to his stories and jokes in a way she hadn't appreciated when they were dating. They sat at a window table facing the tidal island where Margaret had collected so many shells and trash just days before. Now she thought back to her last visit to the island, with Mark, and her comment about possibly locating the wind turbines there, out of view of the hotel.

That thought took her further back, to her initial annoyance that Hamish had not involved Margaret in this project, and instead had sent Charlie, a junior associate, from Portland. Maybe, she realized, this unexpected return to the island could work to her advantage. There would be time in the morning to dash over to the tidal island, take photographs of possible wind turbine locations, and present them to Mark, for Hamish.

Yes, with a low tide in the morning, that's what she'd do. Henri would be welcome to go along, although he'd set off that morning for a day trip. Judging from his footwear, he was not prepared to negotiate a slippery path over the causeway to the other island. Anyway, she'd been over there alone enough times, she'd be fine.

Chapter 47

In Portland, Hamish and Diana were clearing up from dinner. As usual, the twins were watching their allotted half hour of children's programming before their baths.

"What's the latest from the detective, Clara?" Diana asked Hamish. "I was getting used to her coming over for brownies and coffee."

"I spoke to Alistair briefly, earlier today. The Portland police are furious that Keith broke bail and they want him found. His Scottish accomplices are in custody and they named him as being, I suppose, the mastermind, but it's a dilemma. Since the police here don't have clear evidence that he murdered Marnie, or committed a serious offense, it's hard to ask another country's police force to use resources looking for him."

"But you and I know he lied about having a relationship with Marnie, right? Remember, the photograph that he presented to the police, showing him and Marnie together on a hike, and he'd really photoshopped it from the image Mark uses as his screensaver. That photo is also on the firm website's summer associate page, so anyone can access it."

Hamish nodded. "Yes, but it's pretty tenuous proof. Someone could argue that Mark photoshopped Marnie *out* of the picture. Then we get into proving that Marnie wasn't on the hike that day. Anyway, according to Alistair, Norm thinks that Keith may have gone over to that island, Caraidsay, where his dad invested in a hotel. But with our three people gone from the island now, I'm not concerned about them encountering Keith and him doing something stupid if he feels cornered."

"So does that mean I get Mark back?" Diana asked, smiling.

"Yes, he should be in the office in a couple of days. He said he has an interesting proposal based on something Margaret suggested."

"Huh? You mean, in relation to your work there? It figures. Margaret was already in Scotland, so you should have sent her to do your research, not fly Mark and Charlie all the way over there!"

Hamish nodded his head. "You may have a point..."

He was distracted by his cell phone ringing.

"Better not be work," he mumbled as he answered the call.

"Oh, Margaret, we were just talking about you!" Smiling, Hamish listened for a few moments, then wished her a good night and ended the call.

"Wow, she's up late," he said to Diana. "Anyway, that foreign language article that I told you about, that an investor showed to the head of the biotech company, Louise? Margaret discovered that it's written in Gaelic and she found someone to translate the conclusion section of it. She's still working on the full article. She emailed me the translation so I'd better go and read it."

After several minutes in his office, during which Diana made a pot of decaf coffee and arranged yet another batch of brownies on a plate, Hamish returned to the kitchen. He brought two documents which he placed side by side on the table before sitting down and accepting a mug of coffee from Diana.

"Progress?" she asked, sitting next to him and looking at the documents.

"I hope so." He pointed to the top page of one document. "According to Margaret, this is the English translation of the conclusion of the Gaelic publication. Margaret's also read the patent application, and allowing for some slight variation in the translation, it appears that the publication is based on the patent application."

"Like plagiarism?"

237

"I don't know yet. If the Forsyth Industries people in Edinburgh are working with Louise's company, perhaps without her knowledge, the research paper may be a legitimate outgrowth of the patent application, if it was published after the application was filed. The problem is, the publication date appears to be a month *before* the patent application was filed. Something is not right here."

Diana shook her head. "You've already lost me."

"Don't feel bad. I'm only repeating what Margaret said in her email. I think the next step is to take this to Louise and ask her if anyone in her company could have gone against her instructions, or behind her back, and sent the patent application to Scotland before it was filed here. If she's confident in the loyalty and honesty of her employees, then the problem must be in the law firm, I'm ashamed to say."

"Probably the patent agent Keith, right? So did poor Marnie die because she accused him of disclosing client secrets?"

Hamish placed the documents in a single pile and pushed them to the side of the table.

"Only one person knows the answer to that, Diana, and by all accounts, he's currently beyond reach of the Portland police."

Diana sat silently for a few minutes, sipping her coffee while Hamish checked his phone for recent emails.

When she spoke again, it was nothing Hamish expected to hear.

"Darling," she said, looking him in the eyes, "you should go over to Scotland. If this new anti-cancer drug is as promising as Louise told you, then you owe it to her to put right what has gone so badly wrong. You've got Alistair over there, and from the bits and pieces I've heard from you and Margaret talking, he has a Scottish PI colleague, and he's become friends with a police officer in Kilvellie. Assuming Keith is holed up on that island, they could go out there and keep track of his movements, then when you arrive, you can all confront him as a group. Bring the police."

Hamish slowly nodded his head. "You must be reading my mind. I'm very concerned about Margaret and Henri continuing to investigate the possible link to Forsyth, especially after the two guys there tried to bundle Adam into a van." He stopped to sip his coffee. "So," he continued, "I have your blessing to go over to Scotland right away? Again?"

"Yes, but this time you won't need to be there alone," Diana announced. "If you stay for more than a few days, the twins and I will come over. Who knows how long this will take? They can do their schoolwork remotely. Yes, I've been thinking about this and already checked with the school. Your ex-wife will look after the teenagers. What do you say?"

"I like how you're thinking," Hamish replied, smiling. "We both need a break from the firm, you especially."

With the germ of a plan in place, they spent the evening working on the logistics. For the first time in days, Hamish felt like the future was looking up. Was it anticipation of a return to Scotland? Thoughts of his teenage daughters spending a gap year in Scotland before starting college began swimming in his brain, but he pushed those aside. First things first, where would he, Diana, and the twins stay, and how soon could they leave Portland?

Chapter 48

Alistair was used to late-night texts and emails from Hamish, who was five hours behind in Portland. The text that had just come in, however, surprised and shocked him. It began by saying that Hamish was flying to Scotland the next day, with the goal of finding and confronting the fugitive patent agent Keith Jones. And Hamish wanted to enlist the help of both Adam and Alistair, plus he had a pre-approved budget from the law firm to pay for their time and travel expenses.

Since it was not late in Portland, Alistair decided to call Hamish instead of exchanging a long series of texts. He was staying in what was now his usual B&B in Kilvellie, after spending a pleasant evening with Helen and her museum curator friend Marcus. Most of the discussion had centered on Marcus's visit to Malky's house to see a mock-up glass exhibit case and offer his advice. According to Marcus, he allowed himself to be so infected by Malky's enthusiasm that he was now a volunteer expert curator in advance of the museum opening. With a possible extension after that.

"It's all fine," Marcus had assured Helen. "I don't feel he's taking advantage. I offered, and I miss using my decades of experience for something relevant. Plus," he'd said, lowering his voice, "enthusiasm can't make up for a good grasp of how to set up a display case and how to organize traffic flow around it, to maximize viewing."

Helen and Alistair had just smiled; they both knew that Malky would plunge in to designing his museum displays without doing the plodding work of research first. Marcus planned to take Malky on a whirlwind tour of galleries and museums in Edinburgh and Dundee, with the goal of having Malky experience for himself what worked and what didn't.

With the glass museum design in safe hands, Alistair focused on this sudden change in plans: the arrival of

Hamish, followed soon by Diana and the twins, if Alistair understood the text correctly.

He poured himself a small glass of whisky and, snug in the B&B's luxury guest bathrobe, he lay back on the bed and called Hamish.

"Please Hamish, begin at the beginning," Alistair said, then sipped his whisky and let Hamish talk. The background took a good five minutes, before Hamish summed up his interpretation.

"After reading what Margaret sent, and after talking to Louise, the director of the biotech company, I am pretty confident that Keith Jones, the patent agent, is behind the leak of the patent application and the incorrect chemical structure in the email to Marnie. For the anti-cancer drug, I mean. There is no legitimate way that the information in the patent application would have reached what's probably a bogus company in Scotland. Separately, there's a fake scientific publication written in Gaelic of all things."

Alistair felt himself nodding his head.

"Hamish, most of my very limited patent knowledge comes from recent conversations with Henri, but I also have some experience since I'm an inventor on that patent from the research in the Himalayas. I remember the lawyer drummed it into us that *nothing* could be revealed to anyone outside the laboratory, at least until the patent application was filed. So the existence of a Gaelic language research article, which purports to have been published a month before a patent application was filed, is not normal in my experience."

"Good," Hamish said. "We're in agreement about the background. Now to the practicalities. We have no proof that Keith Jones was responsible for what we might as well call a leak. But given what you learned from Norm, Keith was a party to whatever was going on at the Forsyth office in the industrial park in Edinburgh. It may be where this Gaelic publication, and others, were fabricated. A whole separate question is whether he attacked Marnie because she found this out, or if, as he claims, she fell during a romantic interlude…”

Alistair interrupted. “A romantic interlude gone wrong, *very* wrong.”

“No question about that. The bottom line is, we need to find Keith, and since the only lead we have is Caraidsay Island, I would like you and Adam to get over there right away. Learn about the various routes on and off the island, and question the hotel employees in case they’ve seen him. Depending on what you learn, I’ll either fly to the island from Glasgow, as soon as I get to Scotland, or we’ll rendezvous somewhere else. How does that sound?”

Alistair thought for a few moments. “In principle it sounds fine, but the wild card is whether Keith Jones is a dangerous man. I’m no pathologist, but in all my years of studying industrial accidents, I’ve never seen an injury like Marnie’s. I just keep thinking it was a deliberate attack, to kill her so cleanly.”

“I hear you, Alistair. I also know that you won’t put yourself or Adam at risk. Don’t confront Keith, just keep tabs on him if you see him. He doesn’t know who you are, right?”

“Not that I’m aware of, Hamish, but I’ve been visiting your law firm for years. He could have seen me in a hallway or the cafeteria, and if he notices me on the same Scottish island as him, he’s bound to make the connection and think I’m there to find him.”

“Well, use your initiative, Alistair. Pretend it’s deep undercover work. Wear a red wig and a kilt, something to help you blend in.”

“I think I can blend in without looking like an American trying to be a Scot!” Alistair countered.

After making final arrangements for contacting each other once Hamish landed in Glasgow, they said goodnight. Alistair sent a text to Adam, knowing full well that Adam would hear the alert, no matter the time, and would call him right away. With a small top-up of whisky, he lay back on the bed again.

As Alistair waited for Adam's call, he searched online for the most efficient way to get to Caraidsay. He was currently on the northeast coast of Scotland, and Caraidsay lay far from the west coast, a long ferry ride away. The least efficient route would involve public transportation: buses, trains, and ferry. The most efficient would be to drive through the night to Oban and take the early ferry, thereby having a car on arrival in Caraidsay. If Adam agreed, they could share the driving. It meant that, after all, he would arrive on the ferry that Margaret was scheduled to leave on, the following day.

That raised a new dilemma: should he ask Margaret to stay on the island with him while he searched for Keith? And possibly put her in harm's way? The alternative was to insist that she take the ferry back with Henri as planned and head to the cottage in Finlay. With Henri. Somehow, that scenario gave him no comfort either.

And yet another thought: what if Keith was on the ferry with Alistair and Adam, or waiting to return on the same ferry as Margaret? Alistair quickly looked up the ferry information; he felt reassured when he learned how large the ferries were. If at any time he caught sight of Keith, it should be easy to follow him at a distance without being detected.

Whatever happened, he truly hoped that Adam was free to take the assignment. And even more, that Adam's mother would let him go, since he'd just been rescued from Forsyth Industries' clutches in Edinburgh.

He was tempted to take another sip of whisky, but with the possibility of a nighttime drive in the next few hours, he reluctantly pushed the glass away.

Chapter 49

In her hotel room in Caraidsay, Margaret awoke the next morning feeling determined to make the best of the day. She and Henri would have to leave the hotel by eleven o'clock to arrive at the ferry terminal to board the noon ferry to Oban. That meant being back from the tidal island by about ten-thirty, in time to grab her belongings from her room—especially her passport, she reminded herself.

At dinner the previous evening, she hadn't told Henri of her plans to visit the tidal island and photograph possible locations for the wind turbines. The less time he had to consider and prepare to go with her, the better.

As she finished her mug of tea at breakfast, she slathered some raspberry jam on a piece of cold toast, and added another piece on top. She wrapped it in a paper napkin.

Standing up, she announced, "That's me off. I'll see you in the lobby at ten forty-five."

Henri leapt to his feet. "What do you mean? Are you leaving the hotel?"

"Yes, I have to dash over to that tidal island." She pointed out the window. "I'm just going to walk on the path until the hotel is out of sight, then I'll take some photographs for Mark and Hamish to use. I won't get lost!"

Henri gently placed his hand on her arm. "*Attends, Cherie*, wait! What if you fall or get hurt?"

She considered how to reply. She had her phone, but there would be no signal once she left the causeway.

"How about this," she offered, "if I'm not back here by ten-thirty, then the hotel should send someone. The phone service out there isn't reliable. But really, I'll be *fine*, Henri. I've been over several times before. I'm careful, I won't fall."

"Maybe I should go with you..." he began, but his voice trailed off when he looked down at his almost-new leather shoes, with, as Margaret had noticed, no grip at all on the soles.

She considered telling him that Charlie had managed to borrow some Wellington boots, but decided not to. The less time alone with Henri, the less Alistair would have to complain about. She wouldn't tell Alistair about a trip to the tidal island with Henri, but she couldn't trust Henri to keep it to himself.

"No, Henri, come back to the dining room around ten and you can have coffee and watch for me coming around the corner over there and crossing the causeway. And if, God forbid, I am hurt, there's a little rowboat attached to rope at both sides of the causeway, so you and people from the hotel can transport me back."

She laughed, but Henri didn't. "*Non*, Margaret, that is not funny. Just be very careful, *oui*? Your Alistair will never forgive me if you are hurt, and I am no match for his strength!"

Henri watched from the dining room window as Margaret, in her hiking boots, khaki hiking pants, white cotton turtleneck and blue windbreaker, and carrying a small backpack, picked her way across the now-exposed causeway to the tidal island. He glanced at his shoes again, wishing he'd thought to bring something suitable, but when he'd set off the previous morning, it was simply a drive back and forth between towns. No rough terrain to walk on.

The hotel provided binoculars at each table for viewing wildlife, and Henri watched through these until Margaret disappeared from view around a headland beyond the end of the causeway. Out of curiosity he tried calling her cell phone, but it yielded a message that the party was out of reception area. She'd been right.

With nothing to do until she expected to be rounding the headland on her way back, Henri went to his room and settled in to catch up with email.

One had come in from Hamish early that morning Portland time, presumably an update on the case, but the contents alarmed Henri.

Hi Henri and Margaret,

I assume you are both back in Finlay by now. We're still trying to find Keith, the patent agent. I don't know if you've spoken to Alistair in the past few hours, but we have information that Keith might head for Caraidsay to hide out at the hotel there. I'm flying to Scotland later today. Alistair and his friend Adam told me they planned to drive to Oban and catch an early ferry to Caraidsay. Their instructions are to keep a low profile but ask around about Keith. If they find him on the island, Adam's mother, a police officer, is on standby to get local help. We simply don't know if Keith is dangerous, especially if he's feeling trapped, so we aren't going to take any chances. I'm relieved that Margaret, as well as Mark and Charlie, were long gone from Caraidsay before we learned any of this.

Will be in touch when I get to Scotland.

Cheers, Hamish.

Henri stared at the email for several moments, trying to decide what to do. He and Margaret had seen no sign of Keith anywhere, and no evidence of food trays being taken up to a guest room, either at dinner the night before, or during breakfast. Hamish must be mistaken, Henri decided, and forced himself to stay calm.

He tried to reach Alistair, but the call went straight to voicemail; either Alistair was on the phone, or maybe the reception on the ferry wasn't good. He stood motionless, torn between sitting in the dining room and watching for Margaret, or staying in his room until ten o'clock.

If Keith was at the hotel, it probably made sense to stay put, Henri thought. The two men had worked together in Portland, and Keith was sure to recognize Henri; Keith might panic and do something irrational. As if what the man had been doing lately wasn't already irrational.

On the tidal island, Margaret was enjoying the fresh air and peace and quiet. She'd surprised herself by also enjoying Henri's company, but her mind needed a break from talking to him. Just one more day, she figured: a short drive to the ferry terminal, the noon ferry to Oban, then straight back to Finlay. And Alistair.

Now that she was out of sight of the hotel on the main island, she took photographs of her surroundings. She knew nothing about wind turbine planning and installation, but she could at least provide Hamish with an idea of what she and Mark had experienced: building the turbines on this, the far side of the tidal island, might solve the dispute over placing them within view of the hotel's guests.

With her phone, she took photographs in all directions, giving a good impression of the geography, the physical features, the shoreline, and the central hill. If she'd had time, she would have climbed the hill to get additional views, but it was nine-thirty, her self-imposed turnaround moment.

She secured her phone in her pack. She was tempted to have a few bites of her toast and jam sandwich, but decided to wait until she was within sight of the causeway. That way, if Henry was in the dining room early to watch for her, she could ease his worry.

Her walk had been accompanied by the calls of several bird species—gulls of all kinds, oystercatchers, Arctic terns—but over them she heard a sound she couldn't identify. It sounded like bleating, like a sheep in distress, but as far as she knew, the sheep had long since been cleared from the island. She slowly turned in place, trying to identify the source, and then she saw the roofless ruin of a small cottage, or croft, further along the path, away from her route back.

She decided she had to investigate. Maybe a sheep had strayed across the causeway. An injured animal shouldn't be left to suffer, and if she could report the problem, the hotel could call for a vet, or perhaps a local farmer could help. She hurried along the path to where the noise grew louder, and she stopped just outside the opening where the door would have been. Steeling herself for the sight of an injured, terrified sheep, she gasped when she saw the source of the sound.

"Help me, somebody," came the pleading voice of a man lying against the interior stone wall, surrounded by filthy, ancient straw, his blood-soaked parka covering his right leg, which was lying at an awkward angle. Despite his years in America, his English accent was strong and gave his words an extra gravitas.

Margaret took a few steps back to orient herself. *Keith?* But was this a ruse, pretending an injury before he leapt up and held her hostage, or worse? Or was he really injured?

Hoping he wouldn't realize her phone had no service, she retrieved it from her pack and held it in front of her, recording as she approached him.

"I've called nine nine nine," she said confidently. "Someone should be here soon, with the tide still low. What happened to you?"

Her worry about it being an act was resolved when Keith pulled the parka aside to reveal barbed wire twisted around his bare leg, puncturing his calf in numerous places. He was wearing knee-length khaki shorts and light blue Topsiders, although they looked much worse for wear.

Fighting nausea, Margaret crouched down to look.

"Keith, I, I don't have any medical training and this is way beyond any first aid I know. What happened to you?"

"What are *you* doing here Margaret? Oh, please, I'm in such pain!" He pointed to her pack. "Do you have anything in there? Aspirin?"

"No aspirin, with all the bleeding, but I have some emergency codeine. It's not as strong as prescription but maybe it will help."

The relief on his face told her all she needed to know, and she quickly pulled her small emergency pouch from the pack.

248

In it was a vial of pills; she tipped a few codeine tablets into her hand, planning to give Keith one or maybe two, but he was ahead of her. He clawed at her hand, managed to get several pills, and swallowed them quickly, gulping from a water bottle at his side.

Margaret looked at the label: one every six hours was the recommended dose. *What had she done?*

All she could think of was to give him some food, to try and slow down the release into his bloodstream. She took out the jam sandwich and handed it to him.

"It's not much, but I assume you haven't eaten for a while."

Shakily, she walked back out from the chilling scene while Keith gobbled down the sandwich and drank some more water. Now what? Leave him alone and go to the causeway to call for help? Stay and comfort him, knowing that Henri would soon raise the alarm and send out a search party? That seemed the best option. She had to try and keep him awake.

"I'm assuming you can't walk," she said, returning to Keith's side and taking off her own jacket to make a pillow for him. She eased him flat on the ground.

"No." His voice was shaky and weak. "I'm sure my tibia's broken, the pain is worst below my knee anyway."

She stood up again.

"You remember Henri, the French lawyer? He's here with me and he's going to be watching for me to get back. I'm going to walk quickly along the path until I'm in sight of the hotel, then I'll, I don't know, I'll wave my arms madly and hope he realizes I need help."

"No!" Keith cried out, struggling to sit up, then giving up and yelling in pain as he eased himself back down.

"Margaret, they think I murdered Marnie. I didn't! I'm probably going to die from septicemia, lying in this old straw and muck, open wounds everywhere. I need to tell someone what happened before it's too late."

249

"You're not dying," Margaret tried to reassure him, but as she said it, she realized she really didn't know. His wounds from the barbed wire were grotesque, and he was clearly running a fever. A glance at her watch—ten o'clock. Help would be on the way in half an hour. If she walked back to where she could be seen from the hotel, that would take ten or fifteen minutes, so at most, she would gain fifteen minutes before Keith could be helped.

She imagined herself in his place, accused of something, wanting to unburden himself in the face of possible death.

"I'll stay. We wouldn't really speed things up by me trying to get their attention at this point."

She rummaged in her pack again for more food and found a chocolate bar, which she broke into pieces. Keith raised his head to accept a piece, but then slumped back and let it melt in his mouth. Obviously the codeine was kicking in, Margaret thought.

"Do you want to tell me what happened, Keith?" she asked gently, hoping to keep him from passing out. Putting images of Marnie's body aside, she took one of Keith's hands in hers and held it tightly, which prompted him to burst into tears.

"It was horrible!" he sobbed. "The way her head... oh Margaret, if I could turn the clock back..."

"Unfortunately, none of us can," she said, keeping her voice soft. "We can only reveal the truth, so that people who cared for Marnie aren't left imagining the worst."

"What," he cried weakly, "like I killed her deliberately? Of *course* I didn't. I ran away because I panicked, because I took bad advice from my father's lawyer. Norm."

"Take it a step at a time," Margaret encouraged him. She squeezed his hand for reassurance, although it felt like it was on fire. With her other hand she poured some water from her own bottle onto the small travel towel she had in her pack, and used it to cool his forehead.

"Marnie suspect... she suspected I'd sent confidential data to Scotland. It's all my father's doing. I should never have listened to him."

When Margaret began to ask him a question, he said, "No, please, let me ex... explain. Oh, I'm feeling woozy from the pills. I, uh, I, I followed Marnie down to the file room. She had taken a file from the shelf and was walking toward the file room door. I stopped her. She tried to... she pushed past me and I lost my bal..."

He sobbed loudly for a moment. "Oh, the memory of it... I could feel myself falling backwards, so I reached over Marnie's shoulder to steady myself by grabbing a shelf, but it came away in my hand. My weight pulled me backwards, and I didn't let go of the shelf quickly enough. It slammed into Marnie's neck, from the back. Oh God, Margaret, her poor neck. Her head, it just, it just rolled to the side, like a broken doll. I knew she was dead. It happened in a moment, Margaret, a tiny horrible moment."

His whole body relaxed, as if he'd been physically holding in the truth.

Margaret couldn't help but remember back to law school, the concept of a dying confession, when someone tells the truth, believing themselves to be near death. And she still had her phone on record...

Keith's eyes were closed now. She was tempted to leave and get help, but if he woke and found her gone, would he think she'd abandoned him to his fate, to an agonizing death alone? No, as ghastly as his actions had been, in his current state he deserved some compassion.

In his telling of the story, the blame lay with the person or persons unknown who left a shelf unsecured. *Res ipsa loquitor* she thought to herself, *the thing speaks for itself.* The legal concept was drummed into first year law students, but until now, Margaret hadn't encountered a possible real life version of it.

Still holding Keith's burning hand, she leaned back against the cold wall of the croft to wait for help, trying to forget the image of his mangled leg beneath his blood-soaked coat. How on earth had he done that? But answers would have to wait. If he woke up after taking too much codeine. If he lived.

Chapter 50

At eleven o'clock that morning, Alistair stood in bright sunshine by the railing in the front of the ferry from Oban, watching the island of Caraidsay come into view. He was mentally thanking the ferry company for having the foresight to provide decent showers on board.

Any other time, he would have taken advantage of his location to search the nearby shoreline for wildlife, an otter even, or for an eagle soaring high above. But after glancing at the low heathery hills and the grouping of houses and B&B's that made up the village beyond the ferry terminal, he focused his binoculars to scan the line of cars waiting to drive onto the ferry for the noon departure. So far, there was no sign of Henri's car, but Alistair wasn't surprised, as he knew that the deadline for vehicle check-in wasn't until eleven-thirty.

Leaving Alistair to exit the ferry on foot, Adam had gone to the car deck to be ready to drive off the ferry and meet Alistair in the parking area; they figured that gave them the best chance of one of them getting a glimpse of Keith, whether arriving on the island or leaving.

The early morning drive had gone smoothly, with the two men taking turns, and they'd slept for a couple of hours in Adam's van, the vehicle he used for surveillance work, before lining up for the ferry in Oban. They'd been glad to find a hot breakfast service on the ferry, and had enjoyed a full meal with plenty of coffee. After that they'd separately strolled around the public areas of the ferry, but saw no sign of the runaway patent agent.

The Caraidsay ferry terminal was small, with no overhead walkway for arriving passengers, so at the announcement that walk-on passengers could now leave, Alistair made his way down two flights of stairs to the car ramp, then proceeded to the nearby parking lot. Once the foot passengers were all disembarked, the cars rolled off one by one.

With Adam's van parked nearby, Alistair and Adam took positions close to the cars waiting to leave; this also gave them a view of the foot passengers lining up for the ferry. If Keith was among either group, surely they would spot him.

After twenty minutes, the announcement came for foot passengers to board. After the thirty or so passengers, mainly hikers it looked like, had boarded, cars and campervans drove one by one across the ramp and onto the ferry. There was still no sign of Henri's car, and Adam could tell that Alistair was agitated.

"Dinnae worry," Adam said. "Maybe they have engine trouble or a flat tire. Could be anything."

"Wouldn't she have called?" Alistair asked.

"Why? You didn't tell her you were coming on this ferry, did you?"

"No, you're right. But since she didn't know, what if she and her ex-boyfriend have decided to stay over here another day or two? I *knew* I shouldn't have let Henri pick her up from Oban!"

With the final vehicle boarded, the ferry ramp was raised and Adam and Alistair watched as the ropes were untied. Soon the ferry was on its way, back to Oban. Without Henri and Margaret.

Alistair tried Margaret's phone, then Henri's, but both went unanswered.

"I *knew* it!" Alistair cried again from the passenger seat as he and Adam headed for the hotel. He felt like he was in a bad romance film, playing the jilted fiancé storming in to pull his future wife from the arms of her former boyfriend. *Get a grip* he admonished himself silently. There was bound to be a rational explanation. Soon they would see the car broken down at the side of the road, outside cell service, and Henri would be trying to flag someone down to help.

But that scenario did not materialize, and now Adam and Alistair were standing at the reception desk of the hotel,

Alistair convinced that Margaret and Henri were in a room upstairs. Henri's car was parked outside, the hood cold to the touch, so they hadn't even tried to go to the ferry.

"Calm yerself, Alistair," Adam urged, not for the first time.

Alistair sighed deeply. "What other explanation can there be?" He turned at the sound of loud clunking as someone came running down the stairs from the bedrooms.

"Alistair!" cried a man's voice. A French man's voice. "*Mon dieu*, thank goodness you are here. We need to rescue Margaret!"

"What's happened to her?" Alistair demanded, facing Henri. "Tell me, where is she?"

Henri nervously took a few steps away. "All we know eez, she went to the leetle island out there, hours ago. She said she would be back by ten-thirty, but *non*, she does not come back!"

"You let her go *alone*?" Alistair stepped forward to confront Henri. "I thought Hamish emailed you that Keith might be here. How could you let her go? She was supposed to stay in her room or be in a public area of the hotel!"

"*Oui, je comprends*. But Margaret, she is very insistent, *n'est pas*? I only got the email after she left. She wanted to take photographs to give to Hamish, for his client project. That is all she tells me. I couldn't go right away because of my shoes, but now I finally have some to borrow, so I am going over."

He pointed down, and Alistair could see that Henri was wearing a pair of well-worn hiking boots, quite a contrast to the expensive loafers he usually wore. The three men hurried to the dining room window and looked toward the tidal island.

"We're too late," Adam said, swearing to himself. He pointed. "The tide chart at the front desk says safe crossing ended half an hour ago, and you can see, the causeway will be covered any minute."

255

"We can still go across in shallow water, *non*?" Henri asked, poised to get going.

"No!" came a man's voice from behind them. "Sorry, I'm the manager. I just got to the hotel a few minutes ago and learned about Margaret. I gave Henri those boots to wear but even if they protect his feet, the causeway is slick with seaweed and if he falls, the current could drag him away."

Alistair turned to face the manager. "How can we get out there before the next low tide?"

"There's a wee boat down on the shore. But if you go over in it, you'll have to stay on the other side for a few hours. It's risky to use the boat when the tide is high."

Alistair and Adam ran to Adam's van and changed into hiking boots, at the same time grabbing various pieces of emergency equipment: a first aid kit, a length of rope, and a splint in case of a broken arm or leg. They also grabbed their flasks. Inside, Adam took the flasks to the kitchen and asked for them to be filled with coffee.

"And a spare one for Henri, if you have it?" he added.

"Of course," the manager replied. He was busy loading bottles of water, sandwiches, and biscuits into a pack.

"This should keep you going until the next low tide. Luckily there's no rain forecast until tomorrow. You chaps can get to the beach by the stairs at the edge of the grass. I'll be right there."

When Adam joined Alistair at the door, he realized Henri was missing.

"Loo?" Adam asked.

"No, he went ahead to the beach. We'll meet him there."

But as Adam and Alistair negotiated the slippery steps down to the beach, they were alarmed to see Henri starting across the causeway in ankle-high water.

"Henri!" Alistair yelled. "Why didn't you wait for us by the boat?"

"Eet eez my fault!" Henri cried back, over his shoulder. "I must help her!" And he plunged on ahead, one foot in front of the other with seemingly no care for the rising water level.

"Damn it, we'll have to rescue him too at this rate!" Alistair raged. He and Adam made their way across the seaweed-covered rocks on the shore and reached the rowboat. After securing the emergency equipment, Adam sat inside and Alistair maneuvered the old wooden vessel into the shallow water. Where it immediately began sinking.

"NO!" Alistair cried. "Adam, get out before you get soaked."

Adam retrieved the equipment, tossed it beyond Alistair onto dry rocks, and got back out of the boat. Now both their feet were soaked up to their ankles. They looked to where Henri had just reached the far side of the causeway.

He stopped and yelled to them, "Aren't you coming?"

"Boat's leaking!" Alistair yelled back. "We'll follow you!"

It was not to be. In the short time wasted with the decrepit boat, the water on the causeway had risen to over a foot high and climbing, as waves approached from both sides. Crossing now would be an invitation to drowning.

Henri threw up his arms in despair, then yelled, "I weel find her," before proceeding up the path, following where he'd watched her walk that morning.

The manager caught up with them. He was carrying the pack of food and water, and quickly realized what was happening.

"I am *so* sorry. No one's needed the boat for weeks. Maybe months. I know, I know, I should check it regularly, but..."

Alistair just shook his head in dismay. "Is there another boat?"

"There are two high-speed boats that take people on excursions to other islands, but I was just at the harbor and they're both out for the day. They go out two or three hours from here, so it will be at least that long before we could get help, even if I could convince one to end their excursion early. I mean... sorry, but we have no evidence that anyone is in danger. Margaret went over there on her own several times recently. She's probably collecting shells and lost track of

257

time…" His voice trailed off and he fell silent in the face of Alistair's glare.

"She promised Henri she'd be back by ten-thirty, to catch the ferry! Margaret is very time-conscious. She absolutely *has not* lost track while she's collecting shells!"

"Okay, okay," the manager said. "I'll go to the hotel and call around, see if I can find a boat to take you out there. Do you want to come back up with me or wait here? Maybe she's not even in the direction Henri's walking."

Adam and Alistair conferred for a moment, a whispered conversation about Keith.

"I'll stay here," Alistair said to the manager. "Adam can go with you and explain the situation. It's, ah, it's not just a question of whether Margaret fell. We're worried about her safety for another reason."

"You mean Thompson Granger. Well, Keith Jones. It's okay, his father's lawyer Norman called me this morning looking for him. I told Norman in all honesty I have not seen the guy, so I think that's one thing you don't need to worry about. I'd heard he was in custody for something in Portland, but he was released, so I figured maybe there had been a mistake. Can't see him doing anything illegal. He's shy, a bit of a recluse when he stays here."

Alistair scrutinized the manager's face, looking for any sign that he was not telling the truth, but the statement seemed, to Alistair anyway, to be genuine. He just hoped his judgment wasn't misplaced. With nothing to do but wait—for a boat, for Margaret, for inspiration—he and Adam found some dry rocks to sit on and drink their coffee. The manager went up to the hotel to start the search for a seaworthy boat.

Adam muttered something to himself and let out a groan.

"What was that?" Alistair asked.

More loudly, Adam declared, "How often is happiness destroyed by preparation, foolish preparation!"

Alistair stared at him like he was losing the plot. "Are you complaining about me bringing a pack of emergency equipment, because if you are…"

258

"Sorry, pal, no, I'm quoting Jane Austen. Something about seizing pleasure and not spending too much time preparing. And in this case I have to say she's right. Henri did no preparation, he just seized…" Adam stopped, realizing what he was implying.

"Well, he may have seized the *moment*," Alistair said, "but he's not prepared for anything he might find over there, if Margaret is injured. So I stand by my approach."

He sighed and got his binoculars out, ready for a long wait.

Chapter 51

Unused to heavy, wet hiking boots, Henry's feet were in agony after he'd climbed the sloping path to the headland, where the path rounded a corner and was lost from sight behind the central hill. Still there was no sign of Margaret. He wished he had binoculars with him, and felt regret at charging over the causeway with no food, water, or even a first aid kit. But his decision seemed to be correct, after seeing Adam and Alistair struggling with the leaking boat.

He stopped for a short rest and a good look around, back the way he came, in case Margaret had approached from another direction, then continued along the path. He was looking down often, alert for any sign of her having passed that way. Although, he knew, she was compulsive about not leaving trash or anything behind, making tracking her a challenge.

When he'd fully rounded the point, with the hill directly between him and the hotel on Caraidsay, he stopped again and looked in all directions, as well as down to the shore below. He dreaded seeing her there, as it could mean she'd slipped over the edge. Finally, his search was rewarded: a crumbling stone cottage lay a short walk ahead.

Maybe she'd twisted her ankle and taken refuge there? At this point it was his only hope. Picking up speed as the trail began to head downhill again, he called her name as loudly as he could. At last, to his enormous relief, he saw her step out from the protective walls of the cottage. She seemed to be walking normally, so a broken leg or sprained ankle couldn't be the explanation for her failure to return on time.

In fact, she was so well that she took off at a run to meet him and threw herself, crying, into his outstretched arms.

"*Ma Cherie*, what has happened to you?" he asked gently once she'd pulled away. She was still crying, but gesturing back toward the cottage.

260

"I think, I think he's dying and it's my fault," she was spluttering through tears.

She was making no sense at all to Henri. Who or what was dying? An animal?

But he had his answer soon enough when Margaret led him into the shade of the old stone walls: lying completely still was a man he knew well, his head resting on Margaret's parka, and his legs covered by a red, no, a *bloody* jacket.

"*Mon dieu!* Did, did he *attack* you, Margaret?"

"No! I found him like this." Margaret carefully lifted the jacket from Keith's legs, and Henri gasped.

"*Quelle horror*, barbed wire! And so much blood. Was he conscious when you found him?"

Margaret covered the leg again and motioned for Henri to sit nearby, so that she could sit also. She held Keith's hand but he no longer responded to her touch. And his skin had cooled.

"He was able to talk when I got here. I was turning back like I promised, then I heard a noise and I thought it was an animal, like a sheep in pain, and I couldn't leave not knowing. He was in such agony, I took my emergency bottle of codeine out. Henri, I was only going to give him one, maybe two, but he grabbed them and swallowed several! He talked for a while and then went very quiet."

Henri crept closer and felt Keith's neck and wrist.

"He is still alive, Margaret, and I don't see how a leetle extra codeine would keel him. He's gone into shock, *non?*"

"He had a fever earlier. I don't know how long he's been like this."

Margaret wiped her tears and took a few sips of water.

"You don't have a pack," she said to Henri when she was able to focus. "I thought you or someone would get here more quickly. That's why I didn't come back along the path and try to get your attention earlier. I didn't want Keith to wake up and think I'd left him to die."

"For what he did to Marnie, you mean?" Henri asked.

"No! Just, I didn't want him to be alone. Not in the state he's in."

"I am so sorry *ma Cherie.*" Henri pointed to his boots. "The manager was not there at ten-thirty, and it took me ages to find a pair of boots to wear across the causeway. Then Alistair and Adam arrived and..."

"*What?* Why are they here? And where are they? Didn't they come over to the island to help you search?"

Henri grew worried about Margaret's panicked state, and he placed his arm around her shoulders.

"Of course they tried to come and help. I crossed the causeway on foot, but there was already some inches of water. The other two, they tried to come over in a leetle boat, along with equipment and food, but zee boat, it had a leak. By then, the causeway, it was too deep to walk over. I do not know what they are doing. Looking for another boat I assume."

Margaret just shook her head. Three men desperate to find her, and the one who gets through isn't someone who could actually handle a medical emergency, it's Henri. With no food or water and not even a Band-Aid.

She shrugged her shoulders and shook her head to rid herself of the ungenerous thought: he had, after all, risked his own safety by plunging across the causeway. If he'd followed Alistair's lead, she'd still be here alone with a dying man, and no idea if help was on the way.

"At least we have some chocolate," she said to Henri, dispelling the tense moment.

"You have it, *Cherie. Moi*, I am too worried to eat. I need to let the other two know I've found you safe. Will you stay here while I go back along the path and wave to them? They have binoculars so they'll be watching. Or I can stay with Keith while you walk along?"

Margaret thought for a moment. Even if she or Henri let the others know she was safe, it didn't mean they could get to her any sooner. For now, Keith had to be their priority, although there was little they could do except try to keep him comfortable.

"Thanks, but let's both stay here," Margaret said. "I don't have the energy to walk far, and I don't want to be alone with him any longer in case he…" She stopped. "Anyway, what if *you* fall on your way back, then we'll be in even worse trouble."

Henri stood up. "*Bien*. But let us at least be more comfortable, *oui*? The stone wall, it is cold in the shade. Not good to lean on it." He held out his hand to help Margaret up, but she was reluctant to let go of Keith's hand.

"Margaret, he is not aware of you just now. Come along, you need to warm up in the sun."

Sighing in agreement, Margaret carefully slipped her hand from Keith's; Henri was right, Keith seemed completely unaware of her. They moved just outside the front entrance of the cottage and sat together against the sun-warmed outer wall.

"Better, *n'est pas*?"

"Much better." Margaret let Henri place his arm around her shoulders, and she leaned her head against his chest. Before long, she allowed the stress of the past few hours to fall away and she dozed in the warm breeze coming across the heather. She had the vague thought that maybe they should light a fire and generate smoke to indicate their location, but she had no matches or a lighter, so that thought drifted away too.

Chapter 52

The tide had risen enough that it was no longer safe for Adam and Alistair to wait on the shore by the causeway. Reluctantly, they gathered the emergency equipment and the food pack, and carefully climbed the slick staircase back to the grassy area in front of the hotel.

"I'll keep watch," Adam offered. "Go find the manager, see if he's made any progress with a boat."

Alistair obeyed without a reply. Adam was getting worried about his pal. Alistair had been, in Adam's mind, over-reacting to Margaret and Henri being together on Caraidsay. Now he was really getting irrational, saying that Henri had planned to go over to be with Margaret, and maybe he had sabotaged the rowboat.

Adam could see that Henri was attractive, and he was, after all, Margaret's ex-boyfriend. But if she'd decided to leave Alistair for Henri, fleeing to an uninhabited island only accessible a few hours a day was hardly the way to do it. Still, Adam knew there was no end to how irrational jealousy could make a person feel. He just had to keep Alistair from acting on his irrational thoughts.

Inside the hotel, Alistair could hear the manager on the telephone, so he decided to try and reach Hamish before his flight to Glasgow.

Hamish answered right away. "You called just in time," he told Alistair. "Diana's about to drop me off at Logan Airport. We drove down to Boston. Any news? Any Keith sightings?"

"No, Hamish, and the hotel manager insists that Keith has not been here. Keith's father, or maybe Norm, called the hotel looking for him apparently, so I guess they don't know his whereabouts either."

"Since Keith's not there, are you going back to Oban?"

"Margaret and Henri were supposed to be on the noon ferry, but things have gotten very weird, Hamish. Let me ask you, do you think Margaret still has feelings for Henri?"

Hamish laughed, then apologized. "No, it's way in the past. She's engaged to you! Why? What's going on?"

Alistair explained that Margaret had walked over to the tidal island, then was not back at the agreed time. Henri had made a mad dash across the causeway, leaving Adam and Alistair to use the rowboat, which in turn had a leak. He refrained from mentioning his suspicion that Henri had done that; even he knew how silly it sounded.

"When was all this?" Hamish asked.

"Margaret walked over to the island around eight-thirty this morning, according to Henri. She was supposed to be back by ten-thirty. Henri got over there about quarter to one, I think. Now it's three o'clock."

"What's probably happened," Hamish said, "is that Margaret has fallen, maybe she can't walk. Henri found her and is staying with her until more help arrives. That makes the most sense, right?"

"I guess," Alistair agreed. He looked up to see the manager motioning to him, making a big thumbs up gesture.

"I gotta go," he said to Hamish. "We may have a boat. Have a good flight!" He ended the call, leaving Hamish more confused than at the beginning of the call.

The manager had found someone with a Zodiac waiting for engine repair, but it could be rowed. The owner was driving the Zodiac to the hotel on the back of a truck, and from there they would drive together to a location to put the Zodiac into the water.

"Before you go to all the effort of rowing the boat, the boat owner said he'll also bring his drone. He can do a quick reccy over the whole tidal island and find them that way. Then you'll know the direction to take the boat."

"Great plan," Alistair agreed, although secretly dreading the worst.

Half an hour later, the worst seemed to be happening: the drone had sent back images of Henri and Margaret together, with Henri's arm around Margaret. Alistair was beyond consoling by now.

He ran outside to tell Adam the bad news, and then they gathered their packs for the slow boat trip over to the island.

"Good thing the tide's rising," the manager said, trying to calm Alistair down. "Makes it easier than trying to drag the thing over the shore."

An hour later, arms exhausted from rowing, Alistair handed the oars back to Adam so that he could take a turn looking up at the island. Battling the strong waves of the incoming tide, they'd followed the coastline of the island to the rough location identified by the drone, and were now as far as they could get from the causeway side.

Alistair groaned. "I see them. Yep, I was right. She *has* chosen him over me. Let's turn around. I can't bear it."

"Alistair, man, get a grip!" Adam secured the oars and looked at what Alistair had seen. Well, the drone's image had been right about one thing, Margaret and Henri were sitting awfully close together; in fact, too close, with Henri's arm around her shoulders, and she appeared to be sleeping, leaning against him. Henri's eyes were also closed.

"She must be hurt, and Henri doesn't want to leave her," Adam insisted.

"Right, that's exactly what Hamish said, but she sure doesn't look hurt to me!"

"Alistair, whatever's going on, we have to investigate and bring them back. Pull yourself together and help me get this thing to shore."

It took several more minutes of rowing, and another round of soaked footwear, but they eventually secured the Zodiac above the high tide line. The land sloped gradually up to where Margaret and Henri were sitting, leaning against a rough stone wall. Adam rushed ahead, hoping to get an explanation that would pacify his irate friend.

266

"Margaret, *Cherie*, wake up, help is here!"

Henri gently nudged Margaret's head up from his chest and took his arm away from her shoulders, then helped her to stand up. Facing them were two men, one with arms crossed over his chest and still wearing his backpack, looking like he was about to explode. The other, a tall red-headed man, Adam, Margaret realized, dropped a pack and a large duffel bag on the ground while he tried to catch his breath.

"Thank God you're both here!" Margaret cried. "You're not going to believe..."

Alistair lowered his arms and took a step toward Henri.

"I *trusted* you, Henri, and this is how you behave? She's my fiancée!"

"Alistair! Stop it!" Margaret took his hand and dragged him into the cottage enclosure.

"*This* is why we're both here. I found Keith. He's badly injured. I'm a wreck, and Henri was consoling me. There is nothing between us!"

Alistair tried to switch gears. So, Henri and Margaret were *not* out here to be together, away from prying eyes? He crouched next to the injured man and felt his forehead, then checked for a pulse. "He's alive. Where's all this blood from? Margaret, he didn't try to hurt..."

"No! I found him like this. He's got barbed wire all tangled on his leg and he's lost a lot of blood. I may have overdosed him on painkillers, I think that's why he's unresponsive."

Adam at least had had the presence of mind to bring the first aid supplies and the food pack from the Zodiac. After he also took a quick look at Keith, he led Margaret back to the sun and sat her down, then he handed the food pack to Henri.

"There's sandwiches and flasks of coffee. Both of you, relax and get your strength back. Alistair and I will assess Keith's status. I don't see how we can get him to the Zodiac, not without hurting him more. We'll need to wait for low tide and get a proper team out here to bring him back by the path." He looked up. "Hmm, maybe a helicopter could land nearby."

He stopped and scratched his head. "What the heck is the idiot doing out here in the first place?"

"No idea," Alistair said. He placed a hand on Adam's shoulder. "*I'm* the idiot. Sorry Adam. Behaving like a jealous teenager."

Adam grinned. "It's okay. Why don't you just marry the lassie and stop worrying! Now, let's see how we can help this poor creature."

They both turned to see Margaret standing in the doorway. She approached Alistair and said quietly, "He confessed. I have it recorded on my phone."

"He confessed to *murder*?" Alistair whispered.

"No, he explained how it happened. How the shelf hit Marnie's neck. *Someone* is responsible, but if he's telling the truth, he didn't set out to harm her. But all that can wait. Getting him to hospital is the priority."

Alistair held Margaret for a minute, then looked her in the eyes. "If he lives, it will be because you forgot your passport, you came back to Caraidsay, and then set off on one of your missions. He's a very lucky man, thanks to you."

She glanced down, feeling another wave of nausea at the thought of his mangled leg under the blood-soaked jacket. The image of the filthy straw rubbing against the infected wounds in his legs…

She shivered and turned away. "You know what, I think you're right. He probably wouldn't last another day or two alone."

Alistair guided her back outside. "Go sit in the sun with Henri and try to eat something. You've done all you can."

With flashlights illuminating the gloomy scene, Alistair and Adam made a more thorough check of Keith's status. His right leg was definitely fractured, but with the barbed wire around it, getting a splint on seemed impossible. Alistair considered using his wire cutters, but was afraid of making the injury even worse. He'd have to leave it for the experts.

Together, he and Adam eased a Mylar emergency blanket under Keith and wrapped it over him.

"Let's make sure he can be moved when help gets here," Alistair said. "I'm worried that the barbed wire might be attached to something under the straw."

With Adam holding the flashlight, Alistair donned thick gloves and carefully followed one end of the barbed wire, then the other. Both were free.

"He probably fell on an incline and rolled, and some old barbed wire got twisted around his leg. I mean, look at his shoes! He's not even wearing proper footgear for hiking. It must have taken all his strength to haul himself in here for shelter," Alistair concluded.

As the flashlight moved away across the straw, Alistair saw a glint of bright metal.

"Adam, focus it here, I think there's something, maybe fell out of his pocket."

He pushed straw out of the way to reveal a set of keys. And not old keys, new ones. He held them in the beam of the flashlight and described them to Adam.

"There are four keys, and the key fob is, um, I thought at first it might be a flash drive, but it's too light. Wait, it reminds me of the buoys that hang off the sides of yachts in the harbor."

Adam held out his hand and took the keys from Alistair.

"These could be boat keys! A client of mine gives key fobs like these out with his logo on them. He sells boat parts."

"This might explain how Keith got out here and why he's wearing those shoes. We didn't see a boat on shore between here and the other island, so maybe it's..."

Adam stood up and finished the thought. "It could be hauled up further along. If we can find it, maybe one of us can get back to the main island in minutes and get help." Grabbing his binoculars, he hurried from the cottage.

269

"Be right back!" he called to Henri and Margaret as he passed and took off along the path, further away from their return route.

Margaret got up and went in to ask Alistair what was going on.

"There were some keys lying in the straw," he explained. "They have a floating key fob, so Adam thinks there might be a motorboat down below. He's gone to look."

She smiled. "That would be great." But then she turned serious again. "There's no way we can get Keith to a boat, right? I guess the best we can do is go and summon help. And, I hate to add to your worries, but I don't think Henri can walk back. He borrowed some hiking boots the manager found in a storage closet, but they're too small. I couldn't bear to look at how he's damaged his toes on his fast walk up here. And getting his feet soaked too."

Alistair pointed to his own pack.

"Henri's feet look about my size, so open my pack and get my old sneakers out. He can wear those to get down the hill to the Zodiac, then he won't have to walk all the way back. And take some Band-Aids and blister bandages from the first aid kit. They won't do poor Keith much good."

Margaret kissed his cheek. "You are a very generous and forgiving man, Alistair Wright!"

Adam returned soon with what he hoped was good news.

"There's a boat, a tiny two-seater speedboat tied up at a dock. About as far along the other way as the Zodiac is from here. Assuming the key fits and the engine starts, one of us should head back and summon help. Do you want to?"

"No, Henri should go," Alistair said quickly. "From what Margaret's told me, he used to work on cruise ships, so he must have more experience with boats than the rest of us. If there's room, he should take Margaret back too. Tell him to tuck her up in bed with a hot chocolate."

Adam shook his head in amusement. "You are a changed man, sir!"

"It gets worse. He's wearing my sneakers. Margaret said the boots he found are too small and he's gone and mangled his toes."

Now Adam laughed out loud. "He's filling your shoes, eh? Better watch out!"

The sudden noise made Keith stir. He cried out in agony and opened his eyes wide for a moment, looking all around in terror. Alistair told Adam to explain the plan to Margaret and Henri while he tended to his patient. "Get the codeine pills from Margaret before she leaves!" he called to Adam's retreating back.

He placed his hand gently on Keith's shoulder, swaddled in the silver blanket. "You're going to be fine, just hang on a little longer."

"Please, sir, don't leave me alone again," Keith begged before closing his eyes and letting his head fall back onto Margaret's jacket.

Chapter 53

The following two days were a whirlwind of activity in several parts of Scotland and in Portland, Maine. After Henri and Margaret had sped back to the main island of Caraidsay in Keith's motorboat, Margaret ran up to the hotel, with Henri hobbling behind in Alistair's sneakers. The manager leapt into action and summoned emergency services. Two hours later, a stabilized Keith was in a helicopter en route to a Glasgow hospital.

Adam had accompanied him, to be on hand to explain the circumstances to the emergency team, and also to coordinate with Norm and Keith's family. Margaret, Henri, and Alistair stayed on at the hotel on Caraidsay as guests of the management, in thanks for saving the son of their major investor.

Next, Hamish had flown to Caraidsay from Glasgow, to speak to them in person and also to visit, for himself, the site of the proposed wind energy project. He was staying in touch with Adam and with Clara, the detective in Portland. From what Adam said, it could be weeks before Keith would be well enough to travel to Portland and assist in the investigation into his role in Marnie's death. Or perhaps it could be done earlier by video; no decision had been made, pending the outcome of surgery and the intravenous antibiotic treatment.

Unknown at this time was whether, as a British citizen, Keith would refuse to return to the US voluntarily, but that was all in the future. Clara had taken legal advice about Margaret's recording of Keith's confession, as he had arguably confessed in belief of impending death. After listening to the recording, which Margaret played for her during a video call, Clara sent a forensic team back to the file room.

It was still sealed off with only limited access for urgent file retrieval, but now the forensic team could focus on

Keith's new version and look for evidence to support his claim that the death was entirely accidental, thanks to an unsecured shelf.

It was eight o'clock in the evening in Scotland, and Margaret, Hamish, Alistair, and Henri had finished their main course at a table for four in the Caraidsay hotel dining room. At Margaret's request, they had a table at the back of the dining room, away from the view of the tidal island she'd enjoyed so much until the day she found Keith.

While they waited for dessert and coffee, Henri excused himself to check on texts and messages. With some of his immigration work based in the US, he would be working well into the evening.

Hamish looked back and forth at Margaret and Alistair, who were sitting on either side of him.

"So, you two, what's next?"

Alistair and Margaret shared a look, before Margaret responded.

"I assume we'll go back to Finlay on the noon ferry tomorrow, then pack up the cottage and head back to Portland. I'm so grateful that the partners let me work in Scotland all summer."

Alistair was nodding his head, but Hamish could tell that the prospect of returning to Portland wasn't filling the man with joy.

"What if I said you don't need to come back, not for work, anyway?" he asked Margaret, then immediately regretted his choice of words. Margaret had struggled hard to build up her self-confidence, but his question sounded like a lead-up to "you're fired," although not in those words.

"Sorry!" he added quickly. "I mean, what if you could keep working for the firm but stay in Scotland?"

Margaret felt her eyes widen involuntarily at the prospect. But what about Alistair? Before she had a chance to start worrying again, he joined the conversation.

273

"Hamish, as long as Margaret will have me, I want to be where she is. I haven't told her yet, but I took on a research project for the Kilvellie police officer, Helen, I mean, Adam's mother. It will probably last another week at least, then maybe some follow-up work. My only time constraint is that I can't stay here much longer without applying for a visa extension, and that day is on the horizon. I can leave and come back in, but I haven't checked the time limits on that."

Hamish looked up to see Henri returning.

"Good," Hamish said as Henri sat down. "Alistair, you can ask our immigration attorney friend here for help with that."

"What deed I miss?" Henri asked, looking at the faces of his three companions.

"I may want help with staying longer in Scotland," Alistair replied. "I'll let Hamish explain, but he's just said that Margaret can keep working from here and not go back to Portland yet."

Henri smiled. "*Mon ami*, the answer is simple, *oui*? You are already engaged, so what are you two waiting for?"

"Good point!" said Hamish. "You've been engaged for a while, according to Margaret's parents, so were you waiting until you're back in Portland to have the ceremony?"

"Actually," Margaret explained, "we've talked about getting married in the church in Finlay. The minister has become a good friend. But we'd need time for people to arrange travel from the US, if any want to make the trip, that is."

"You could get married right away in a civil ceremony," Henri suggested, "and save the party for later in the year, or in the spring? That would at least take care of Alistair's immigration problems."

Margaret was watching Alistair's expression: she knew he disliked other people making decisions for him, discussing his personal life openly, but he was hiding it well. For her, the big question was, what work would Alistair do?

He couldn't survive, financially or professionally, by helping Helen with projects now and again.

Hamish had another announcement, taking everyone by surprise.

"You three are the first to hear this, so keep it to yourselves, but I've had preliminary discussions with a law firm in Edinburgh. Since I'm handling more and more international work, as is Diana, we're hoping to establish a cooperative arrangement that would lead to setting up a branch of the Portland office over here."

He put up his hand to hold off any questions.

"Before you ask, I plan to spend several months here to start with and I'll bring over a couple of associates if I can get any volunteers. Margaret, I'm sure I don't need to say it, but you would be a founding associate, if there is such a thing."

He turned to Henri.

"We could really use your expertise for Louise's company. Keith did serious damage that needs to be undone. She told me she misses your help with the patent laws and regulations. No need to decide now, but if you could see having a kind of hybrid immigration and patent practice, you would be welcome too. And since you're just a short flight away, you could be based in France or Scotland, whatever you prefer."

Conversation stopped while coffee and tea were served, and a platter of small desserts was arranged on the table. Hamish asked for champagne as well, and they shared a toast to the success of Hamish's new Edinburgh office.

"I *love* how it sounds, don't you?" he asked, eyes bright as he looked around the table. "But I'm feeling the jet lag now, so I'll take dessert and coffee up to my room and leave you three young people to enjoy the rest of the evening."

"Goodness!" was all Margaret could say after he left.

"I agree," Henri said. "I feel like our lives have just taken a major detour, or maybe now we are on the path we should be, *non*?"

"So much to think about," Alistair added. "But if we're going to have the wedding in Finlay, we'll need room for guests. The first thing I have to do is finish that project for Helen and clear the cottage of all the boxes of papers and photographs."

"Ah, *non, monsieur*, that is not necessary."

"What do you mean?" Alistair looked at Henri in confusion.

"We have not had a chance to discuss what happened after you went to Edinburgh to rescue *monsieur* Adam. Christy and I, we stay up very late and we solve the puzzle!"

Now Margaret was glancing back and forth between the two men. "What project? What puzzle? Why haven't I heard about any of this?"

Alistair stood up and stretched his back. "If you both want to stay up longer, I suggest we move to the chairs by the fireplace in the lounge, and I'll start the story at the beginning. Henri can finish it, since he obviously knows more than I do."

He told the waiter about their planned change in location, and soon the threesome were comfortably arrayed in overstuffed high-back chairs in the lounge, a fire burning in the fireplace.

"Actually, I'm going to let Henri start," Alistair said. "It all begins with… the shifting position of postage stamps!"

Chapter 54

Margaret knew that Henri enjoyed spinning out his stories, so she grabbed a tartan mohair blanket from a nearby sofa and draped it over her lap and legs. She was still adjusting to the thought of being married to Alistair within weeks: was that really possible? And to the concept of keeping her job but being based in Scotland. She felt she could wake from the dream any minute.

Henri's voice reminded her that, no, it was not a dream, it was reality, and she tried to put thoughts of the future aside for now. Before he spoke, he handed her his cell phone, and she looked at the confusing image on the screen: it looked like a child's collage, with postage stamps stuck to envelopes any which way.

"Makes no sense to me." She handed the phone back to Henri. She was curious about why he hadn't shown the image to Alistair as well, but most likely, Alistair had seen it when he and Henri were together in Finlay.

"Margaret," Alistair asked, turning to look at her, "have you heard of using stamp placement to indicate emotions, like a preview of what the letter inside is going to say?"

"Not that I can remember. My father collects stamps, but not so much nowadays with many of them being self-adhesive, like stickers. Before those stamps came into widespread use, Dad would insist on having the envelopes from any mail we got, especially from overseas. He'd soak the corner with the stamp, then dry it and catalogue it for his collection."

"Ah *oui, c'est dommage*," Henri said. "By soaking the stamps off, he lost any indication of the meaning of the placement. *Alors*, let me start my story. I met Alistair at the hotel cafe in Finlay when I arrived there, and he asked if I would translate a letter that was written in French."

277

"A letter to you, Alistair?" Margaret asked, then smiled. "Sorry, I am going to drink my coffee and eat pastries and let Henri talk!"

Henri answered. *"Non,* a letter from a mystery woman. But before I open zee envelope, I show Alistair the placement of the stamp. It was one of your kings, a George, I believe."

"From the nineteen thirties," Alistair confirmed.

"Oui, c'est vrai. The stamp was pasted on upside down. Zee king, his head pointed to the bottom of the envelope. Very sad. The end of the affair, *oui*?"

Margaret laughed. "Or, the sender wasn't paying attention when he or she stuck the stamp on. Happens to everyone, right?"

Henri held up his phone to remind her of the picture on the screen. "Maybe once, yes, it is a mistake. But then I read that letter, and sadly, I was correct. The sender, a woman, was ending a relationship with a man in France."

Before Margaret could object again, Alistair said, "Let Henri tell the story. You'll see that he was right in his interpretation of the stamp placement."

Margaret shook her head. "Okay, I will keep quiet. But I could keep more quiet if I had a hot chocolate instead of this coffee. They make really good..."

Alistair was on his feet. "Whatever my future wife wishes!"

He was back moments later after speaking to the waiter who had served them dinner. "I ordered some for all of us. Sitting around the fire and listening to a tragic story of lost romance, yeah, hot chocolate seems more comforting."

Henri sat patiently while the hot chocolate was served. He took a few sips then resumed.

"By now, Christy from the sea glass shop had arrived, so Alistair kindly invited us to his cottage. I mean, to *your* cottage, Margaret. There we looked at many letters and as you will see when you are back home, the placement of stamps predicted the content of the letters. It began as a love affair between a nurse in France in nineteen fifteen, and her *amour*, a French officer. But he went missing and was presumed dead in battle."

Henri stopped to drink more hot chocolate. Margaret kept quiet, letting him proceed without interruption.

"*Alors*, you may wonder why we have a letter dated so long after the officer went missing. Well, he was not dead. But in nineteen twenty one, his *amour*, zee nurse, she had married a German soldier and they lived in Scotland. They founded a..."

"A glass factory!" Margaret cried. "Right? This is all sounding familiar."

"*Oui*! The nurse, she was Sheila, but we didn't know until Christy said that the signature in the letters, Caelia, was the old spelling of her great grandmama's name. And the husband, he was Heinrich, or Henry, like *moi*!"

"I know the story up to this point," Alistair said, "but I don't know what you and Christy found after that. I can't wait to hear."

Henri glanced at his phone for the time. "Eet is getting late, but I will finish quickly, *oui*?"

Margaret and Alistair answered "*Oui* please!" in unison, and Henri laughed.

"I will have you both speaking in French soon. But to finish, the man who Sheila was writing to, a doctor, his name was Jerome. When the convalescent home for soldiers was set up in Kilvellie in the late nineteen thirties, Jerome was assigned there due to his medical expertise from the First World War. He knew that his former love, Sheila, she was married to the owner of the glass factory, the German. Judging from Sheila's replies, Jerome must have written to her and threatened that if she didn't leave Heinrich and come back to him, Jerome would take his revenge out on the factory.

"*Naturelment*, poor Sheila, she would not leave Heinrich and their four children, so she begged Jerome not to hurt Heinrich. Soon after, Heinrich went into internment. Maybe Jerome, maybe he informed on Heinrich and insisted on it, we do not know from the letters. But as soon as Heinrich was away, Jerome, he bully some young men at the hospital to make the damage to the factory."

Alistair leaned forward and looked at Henri. "Is this all documented in writing?"

"*Oui*, Alistair. We find documentation in your boxes at the cottage. Christy and I, we have placed the important documents in a separate box, so you can look at them yourself."

"Are *they* in French? I mean, if Jerome wrote them?"

"Ah, of course they are in French, Alistair, but I translate for you. I have made notes of the translations."

Alistair leaned back again, an astonished look on his face.

"Henri, I left the cottage with Helen at around eleven o'clock that evening, and you drove to Oban the next morning. You and Christy must have been up all night looking in the boxes!"

"Ah, *non*, not all night. We find a folder with Jerome's name, with his personal papers. He kept a journal, you see. He wrote his plans. He wrote the names of the young men he was forcing to hurt the factory. It is all there, *monsieur*."

Alistair looked back and forth at Margaret and Henri.

"I can't believe the man would leave behind something so incriminating. Did he, did he die suddenly?"

"*Enfin*, we do not know. The last journal entry we find, it says, in French, that Sheila had sent a note that she was going to visit him late that evening. He wrote nothing in his journal after that."

"When... when was that entry written, do you remember?" Alistair asked. He had a sickening feeling now.

"*Oui*, it was in July of nineteen forty-four. The exact date I do not remember, we looked at so many entries, but you can see when you go home tomorrow."

Alistair got up slowly and excused himself. He crossed the lobby and went outside through the door to the dining room. The night was cool and the stars were bright. He didn't dare walk far, as he knew the ground fell away suddenly, down to the rocky shore below. Not as long a fall as at Kilvellie's cliffs, but potentially fatal anyway.

July nineteen forty-four, that was when the six vandals, the young men so badly treated by Jerome, had faked their own deaths to be free of his clutches. Alistair knew exactly what date that was, from the police record: the long-hidden police record. Was that also the last night of Jerome's journal?

His thoughts were interrupted by the sound of the door opening again, and he turned to see Margaret approaching. He walked quickly to meet her.

"It's cold, let's go back in. I'm ready to put Kilvellie out of my thoughts forever and focus on the future. What about you?"

"After Henri's story tonight, I can't agree more."

They returned to the lounge. After a few more minutes with Henri to plan the schedule for the next morning, they headed upstairs. Alistair was already visualizing getting back to the cottage, tossing every last piece of paper from the care home cellar, every last photograph, into the boxes and taking them back to Helen. So much for his romantic thoughts of writing a book and finding closure for the boys and their families. The story might be just too dark to ever see the light of day.

Chapter 55

Henri stayed by the fire, feeling comfortable and not in any hurry to go up to his room alone. At dinner, he'd let the others assume he was replying to work-related texts and emails, but in fact he was keeping in touch with Christy. He'd been disappointed that she declined his invitation to drive to Oban and pick up Margaret, but as things turned out, he was relieved that she stayed in Finlay. Her priority was to investigate whether she could help set up a sea glass store, not to go traipsing across Scotland with a man she'd just met. And then, get delayed by Margaret's missing passport and all the consequences of that.

However, in their series of texts, they had made it quite clear to each other that they'd like to stay in touch. Christy said she'd expected to see him when he arrived home with Margaret the same day he left, but after he'd been delayed on Caraidsay, she'd reluctantly returned to her home and work in Kilvellie. Maybe Henri could visit her there, her text tonight asked, before he went back to France?

Now he was wondering how to reply. Hamish's surprising offer of a job with the future Scottish branch of Martin & Sawyer was tempting, but Henri had to make sure he accepted for the right reasons, not because of a potential love interest. Or because of his past love interest, Margaret.

He decided not to say anything to Christy, but he wasn't needed back in France yet. He finally texted her that he would like to visit her in Kilvellie in the next few days, and left it in her hands to issue a more specific invitation, if she really wanted to see him again.

He looked over at the sound of his name.

"Henri, you're still up!" It was Hamish approaching from the staircase. He fell into a chair close to the fire. "I need a wee dram, a spot of whisky to help me sleep. Is the bar still serving, do you know?"

"*Oui,* and may I join in you in your *wee dram?*"

"Of course, I'd enjoy the company. I'm tired, but I'm still partly on Portland time."

Instead of the waiter from earlier, the manager was now on duty and he asked if he could get Hamish anything.

"Just a small whisky, if it's not too late. And the same for Henri here, please."

The manager pointed to the bar, where rows of bottles were arrayed in front of a wide mirror. "We have the full range, Mr. Murray. Highland, Island, blended, single malt, single cask... and American if you prefer!"

Hamish laughed. "Sacrilege, drinking American whisky over here. No, I'll have a single malt Islay, please. Bowmore, if you have it?"

The manager nodded and turned to Henri. "For you, sir?"

"*La même chose,* sorry, same as Hamish, please."

The manager went to the bar; he poured the whisky into two glasses and brought the glasses on a silver tray, along with a jug of fresh water.

"I'll be closing the bar in a few minutes. Would either of you like a soft drink for later? You have the minibars in the rooms, but maybe something different?"

Both men declined, and Hamish focused on tipping just enough drops of water into his own whisky, and the same for Henri. The manager lingered, then sat on the arm of a nearby chair.

"I'm glad you're here. It will save me sending texts tonight. As I understand, all four of you are booked on the noon ferry to Oban tomorrow, is that correct?"

"Yes," Hamish replied. "Why? Is there a problem with the weather?"

"No, mechanical problems. It's not uncommon out here. I just learned that the ferry schedule has changed for tomorrow because they have to shuffle ferries around on routes. The ferry company should be notifying the person who made the booking. One ferry broke down, not from this route, but they need the Caraidsay ferryboat to take its place.

283

Bottom line, a different ferry is sailing over tonight and will be leaving here at nine-thirty tomorrow instead of noon."

He stopped while Henri sent texts to Margaret and Alistair to alert them to be ready earlier in the morning, then continued.

"Separate issue, there's a group of naturalists arriving in the morning, on a private charter from Oban. The boat's dropping them off and returning empty to Oban. I believe you have two vehicles, so two drivers will have to go by ferry. If one or two of you would like to ride back to Oban on the charter boat, I'm sure the crew would point out the sights on the way. You might spot some dolphins and seals and other wildlife."

"Um, would it cost a lot, being a private charter?" Hamish asked.

"No, they wouldn't charge you. Anyway, talk to Margaret and Alistair if you want. The boat will be here at about nine in the morning, so if you can let me know by eight-thirty, I can make sure they don't leave without anyone who wants a ride. The company's called Coast Adventures, if you want to look them up and see what kind of boat you'd be on."

He left to finish clearing up, and Henri and Hamish sipped their whisky quietly for a few moments.

"What do you think about his suggestion?" Hamish asked.

"I drove Margaret here, and I weel have to drive the car to the ferry and back to Finlay. But you should go, Hamish. It sounds like a rare opportunity. These private charters, they are more than I could spend."

"I like the idea of giving Margaret and Alistair some time to catch up on the ferry together, before the inevitable video calls with the Portland police and trying to sort out what Forsyth Industries was really up to. I wonder... if you drive your car to the ferry terminal, Margaret could drive it onto the ferry, then you'd be across to Oban in time to take over as soon as she drives off the ferry. Alistair will be driving Adam's van, I assume."

"Hmm," Henri began, "but I am afraid for the insurance. Margaret is not on my rental car policy, and if she is stopped by the police..."

There was a burst of gentle laughter from the bar.

"Sorry," the manager said, "I didn't mean to eavesdrop, but there is no police presence on the island. You don't have to worry about a traffic stop or anyone checking insurance. Margaret could drive your car all the way from the hotel to the ferry without being stopped."

Hamish finished his whisky. "That settles it, Henri. If Margaret and Alistair are in agreement, then I suggest you and I take up the kind offer of a ride back in the private boat and let them take the ferry together. We will meet at breakfast and see what they say, okay?"

"*Très bien*, Hamish, that is a good plan. And although I am trying to *put on a brave face* as you say, my feet are still quite painful and it will be nice not to drive tomorrow morning." Henri finished his whisky as well, and with a goodnight to the manager, they headed upstairs for the night.

In his own room, Hamish changed and got into bed, then looked up the charter boat website. Fast boats, it looked like; bright orange, open in the back, with seating for perhaps eight people. Highly experienced captain and crew, according to the information section. Crossing time to Oban, about ninety minutes, although longer if they stopped for wildlife.

Next, Hamish looked up the ferry information. Four hours from Caraidsay to Oban, no stops for wildlife, although the captain would announce if he spotted anything for the passengers to see.

Hamish closed the websites and placed his tablet on the bedside table. Four hours and no wildlife, versus ninety minutes or so, with wildlife. He'd take the charter boat, whether or not any of the others did. Not for the wildlife, though. It was his guilty secret, a tendency to seasickness. But no one had to know, especially not seafaring Henri.

He set his alarm for seven o'clock and soon fell asleep, lulled by the relief that he'd only be away from dry land for two hours tops. He was tempted to fly back to Glasgow from the island and get a train to Edinburgh, but there was much to discuss with the team and that had to take priority.

Chapter 56

After an early breakfast the following morning, Alistair and Margaret met Henri and Hamish at the reception desk. The plans were set: Margaret and Alistair would travel by ferry with the two vehicles, and Hamish and Henri would leave on the charter boat, arriving in Oban before the ferry docked.

When they rendezvoused at the Oban ferry terminal, they would switch around. Henri would drive Margaret back to Finlay in his car, while Alistair drove Hamish to Edinburgh. Alistair would meet Adam there; Adam planned to take the train from Glasgow to Edinburgh, now that he'd done all he could to help with the Keith situation, as he was calling it.

Just after nine o'clock, Henri and Hamish were escorted along a dock near the ferry terminal, where their ride, a bright orange open-back boat just as Hamish had seen on the website, awaited. After they were seated and had listened to the emergency instructions, including the location of the life vests, the captain and his one crew member left them to enjoy the trip. Any wildlife would be brought to their attention, then it would be up to Hamish and Henri to decide whether to slow and detour for a closer look, or keep going. *Keep going* Hamish replied, but left it unspoken for now.

"I'm glad we have a chance to talk again," Hamish said to Henri once the trip was underway. "I am serious about offering you a job with the firm, with you based in Europe. You wouldn't be expected to spend time in the Portland office."

Henri smiled and his eyes twinkled. "Hamish, I am looking forward very much to being part of the team again. And to working with Louise and her company. It won't be the same without Marnie, but we will do all we can to honor her memory, *oui?*"

"Of course. My only concern is... oh, it's not my place to ask, but I do need to know. Will there be any tension with Margaret, since you and she..."

Henri held up a hand. "*Non,* there will be no tension, no worries. Margaret *et moi,* eez all in the past."

"That's good to hear, Henri. I confess, I had wondered, when you came to Scotland following the video call we had, right after poor Marnie died."

Henri smiled sadly. "I confess *aussi,* I did wonder if perhaps Margaret and I, but, *alors,* now I have met my competition, I mean, Alistair, I no longer stand a chance!"

"I can't say I agree with you on that, Henri, but it is a generous sentiment. So, is there someone else...oh, here I go, doing what I tell Diana not to do, meddle in peoples' personal lives."

"*Oui,* there is a chance of someone else, but we have just met. She is Christy, the sea glass jeweler. I met her in Finlay, when she was visiting the same evening I arrived. She and I spent the evening working on Alistair's big project."

"Ah yes, his project for the Kilvellie police department. He hasn't told me anything about it."

"Eet is quite interesting, if you would like to hear what we found?"

Hamish knew a distraction would be good as the boat sped across the open water, far from any islands. "I'm very interested, so yes, please tell me."

"Ironically," Henri began, "it has helped me realize I would be foolish to reveal to Margaret that I still care for her. I mean, while she is with Alistair. The project we were doing, it involves correspondence between a young woman and her *amour.* She was a Scottish nurse in France during World War One..."

Hamish interrupted. "The project involves *that* war? How did Alistair get into such ancient history?"

"*Non,* Hamish, it eez a mistake to call it ancient history. This nurse, she was called Sheila. In France, she and this French captain were very serious, and then near the end of

288

the war, he disappeared. She believed he was killed in action. She continued working as a nurse, and a badly injured German soldier was brought to her ward by mistake. Still, she helped care for him and surprisingly, despite being on opposite sides, they fell in love."

"And all this time, there was no news of her French boyfriend?"

"*Non*, it seems she believed he was dead. So the war, it ends, and Sheila goes back to her family farm in Scotland. Her German *amour*, he goes back to Germany for two years, then he comes to Scotland to find her and they marry. They have four children, and the German, his name is Henry, *comme moi*, he builds a glass factory, like his family before him in Germany."

"Oh, this sounds familiar," Hamish said. "Margaret's told me about the glass factory, and how that town has great sea glass on the beach."

"*Oui*, I am getting to that. So sometime in the late nineteen thirties, Sheila's old boyfriend who she thought was dead, is really alive, and he gets assigned as a medical officer in the town of the glass factory. Sheila is there, married to an enemy soldier, and I do believe it affected his mind badly. We only have Sheila's letters to him, but he must have been threatening her family, if she didn't return to him."

Henri stopped to sip some coffee that the crew member had made for his two passengers.

"That must have been awful for Sheila," Hamish prompted him, eager to hear the whole story before the boat reached Oban. "What did her husband, Henry, what did he do?"

"*C'est dommage*, he could do nothing. *Rien.* You see, he was taken away for internment soon after that. He spent four years in custody as an enemy alien."

"Wow! Even with a Scottish family to care for and a successful business, he was still considered the enemy? That's so wrong."

"*Oui*, and more irony, the former French boyfriend, he was the real enemy. He forced some young men to loot and damage the glass factory, for most of the war. Maybe he threatened to have them sent to fight, *je ne sais pas*. But they must have believed him, and they damaged the factory and the glass several times in those years."

"Guillemots! A big raft of guillemots portside!" The call came from the crew member, leaping out from the wheelhouse with binoculars in hand.

Hamish took a quick look through the binoculars, saw enough to report later than he'd seen twenty floating black birds with white patches on their wings, then handed the binoculars to Henri.

"Ah, *non merci*. Looking through them, it makes me, ah, queasy they say."

Hamish laughed. "Henri, I thought you worked on cruise ships for a couple of years?"

"*Oui*, but as a guest activities manager. I never got over feeling seasick when I was outside, looking through binoculars. It made me too disoriented."

The crew member took the binoculars back. "I sympathize. We get more than a few wildlife enthusiasts on our tours, but then I learn they've never been in a speedboat with the engine off, sitting in choppy waves, watching for a whale…"

Hamish held up his hand. "Now that I know the water bothers Henri, I admit I'm the same. So, maybe best if you don't finish that description!"

The crew member returned to the wheelhouse, and Hamish smiled when he heard laughter coming from the captain. At least the men were getting some amusement from their non-paying passengers.

"Where were we?" Henri asked Hamish.

"You mean, before the Gilly-birds… oh, you were talking about the damage at the glass factory."

"*Oui*, in the letters from Sheila, she is begging the French captain to stop the looting. Then, *alors*, no more letters. But we find, me and Christy, a journal that the captain kept. At that point it was perhaps two o'clock in the morning, and Alistair, he has been gone a while, to Edinburgh with the policewoman. Christy, she goes to bed, so I read the journal. Zee last entry, eet is in July nineteen forty-four, and it says that Sheila is going to visit him that evening. *Eh voila*, no record of zee captain after that, I mean, not in his journal, and no more letters or notes from Sheila."

Hamish thought for a moment. "It must mean she persuaded him to leave town, right? Or he realized he had no hope with her, and he stopped keeping a journal?"

"*Non*, I think she keeled him. That night. She was a nurse, she would know how to give him something to mimic a heart attack, *non*? Do you not agree, Hamish?"

"Honestly, Henri, I have no idea. This whole story is so tragic. Anyway, those people are long gone, so does it really matter?"

"It matters, *oui*, because Christy, she is Sheila's great-granddaughter. She must never know her great grandmama might have been a *keeler*, even if she was protecting her family."

"What did you do with the journal?" Hamish asked, disturbed at the modern repercussions of formerly buried secrets of the past.

"I placed it in a drawer for Alistair to look at when he returns to the cottage. I have told him what it says, and he is thinking about it. He said he had to check the date."

"Castles? Do you want to see a castle?" It was the crew member again, minus binoculars.

"If it doesn't involve binoculars, castles I can do!" Looking around, Hamish realized that the boat was approaching what must be Oban, their destination. The crew member sat on a bench and pointed toward the shore.

"That stone building you can see up on the point, it's Dunollie Castle. The castle itself is a ruin, but you can visit the nearby house and museum. There's a cafe too. The castle is walking distance from Oban, if you're going to be staying a while."

"Not today, I have to get to Edinburgh, but another time."

The crew member pointed out more sights as the boat slowed and entered the sheltered harbor area. Further ahead, Hamish could see a large ferry docked at the terminal.

"Is that the ferry from Caraidsay, so soon?" he asked.

"Nae, that'll be the ferry to Mull, the closest large island. About an hour away. People do day trips out there and catch a bus to the Iona ferry, which is a quick crossing from Mull."

"Wow, Iona! It's on my list of places that Samuel Johnson visited," said Hamish. "Thanks, now I have a better idea of how to get there."

He looked at Henri. "Margaret gave me a book at our Christmas dinner two years ago, about Dr. Johnson's visit to Scotland. I'm using it as a guidebook for my future travels."

"*Oui*, I remember eet well. A gift from her grandpapa to her. Very precious. She is a generous person."

"Very true, Henri..." Hamish stopped when the crew member spoke again. He'd turned to face away from the ferry and was pointing across the water.

"If you're interested in Johnson and Boswell's trip to the Hebrides, you should visit Tobermory, over on Mull. It's the big island over there. Far as I know, the building that was the inn where they stayed is still in existence from when they visited in seventeen seventy-three. Part of it's a shop, but last time I was there, the other part hasn't been changed much since Johnson's visit."

Hamish was standing now, steadying himself against a railing and trying not to look at the water. He grinned at the crew member. "I'm tempted to ask you to turn the boat around, but it will have to wait for another time. Thank you so much for the information!"

The crew member excused himself when the boat pulled close to a dock in the center of town, then he jumped ashore and secured the ropes before helping Hamish and Henri. Hamish insisted on passing some cash to both the crew member and the captain, then he and Henri set off slowly along the waterfront, heading for the ferry terminal.

"Thanks for making the trip go quickly," Hamish said.

"And you too, Hamish. So now you see why I will not attempt another relationship with Margaret, *oui*? We must let old relationships stay where they are, in the past. That is the lesson of Sheila and her French captain."

Especially if it involved murder of that captain, Hamish said to himself, but didn't pursue the topic with Henry. Instead, he pointed to a coffee shop next to the ferry terminal ticket office; they each got coffee and a scone to go, then sat on a bench in the sun and waited for the Caraidsay ferry, bearing Margaret and Alistair.

Chapter 57

After a scenic drive across Scotland in Adam's van, Alistair and Hamish arrived in Edinburgh. Alistair stopped the van outside the front door of Hamish's hotel at the West End, the Caledonian.

"Good choice," he said as he helped Hamish get his bags from the back of the van. "The Caley is Margaret's favorite, but only for an occasional night. Too expensive for my budget."

"Mine too. I can justify a couple of days on law firm expenses, but I'll find a more reasonable place for me and Diana and the twins."

Hamish looked up at the imposing front of the hotel. "I studied the website before I booked a room. I want to look at the stained glass city emblems. The one of Oban will have more meaning for me, after visiting it."

He turned back to face Alistair. "Now I have the challenge of renting long-term accommodations, assuming the Edinburgh branch of the firm becomes a reality."

Alistair hesitated, then decided to make a suggestion.

"Hamish, you haven't met Helen yet, the police officer I work with in Kilvellie. She had a career in Edinburgh before moving north, and she still owns a flat, an apartment I mean, in central Edinburgh. It's in what they call the New Town, just a few blocks from here. Anyway, I stayed there the night we rescued Adam. It's large enough for the four of you, and your teenage daughters could sleep on air mattresses for short visits."

"That sounds ideal, Alistair. Can you check with Helen and ask if it's something she'd consider? Then I can get in touch to discuss the details."

A kilted doorman hurried over to help Hamish. After handshakes and warm farewells, Alistair drove off to his next challenge: finding somewhere to park the van near

Haymarket Station so that he could meet Adam off the Glasgow train. Haymarket, a few blocks from the West End, was a convenient train stop in the west side of Edinburgh, easier to access than the main station, Waverley, in the heart of town.

As he drove away, Alistair remembered learning that the Caledonian Hotel had once been part of a train station; *too bad that's not the case now*, he said to himself.

He was waiting at a red light when Adam texted: *I'm outside the station, drive along the main road and I'll watch for you.*

With a thumbs up emoji in reply—Alistair normally hated emojis, but they were convenient when texting from a vehicle—he proceeded along to Haymarket and soon saw his tall red-headed pal waving furiously from the tram platform outside the station. Alistair slowed to a stop while Adam leapt into the passenger seat and stuffed his pack at his feet.

"Quick!" he said. "The traffic wardens are strict around here."

Alistair had expected Adam to take over driving, but instead, they kept going until they found a parking area outside a cafe. With fresh coffee and sandwiches, they exchanged seats before continuing, and soon the bright white outline of the Queensferry Crossing Bridge came into view in the distance.

"How's Keith?" Alistair asked, when Adam had drunk half of his coffee and said he was feeling more alert.

"The poor wee man isnae goin' anywhere soon. He's still on intravenous antibiotics, and his leg will need extensive plastic surgery if he's ever to wear shorts again, without people askin' awkward questions. Barbed wire leaves pretty distinctive wound marks, I could see from his leg when we first found him."

"And has he said any more about Marnie, about what happened in the file room?"

"Nae, the doctors say it's too soon to make him face police questioning, either in person or by a video link with Portland.

295

But based on his confession to Margaret, I know that yer detective over there, Clara, is takin' that scenario seriously and they're examining the condition of shelving in the file room, to see if it backs up his story."

Alistair sighed. "I hope it does. I would rather imagine that Marnie died from a tragic accident, and not because someone wanted to deliberately kill her. It won't make the loss any easier for her parents, but at least they won't have to spend months, or years, watching someone being tried for murder of their daughter."

Adam turned to glance at Alistair. "But *someone* is to blame, right? Someone began dismantling that shelving unit, then either got lazy, or it was the end of the workday, and they left it looking secure when in fact it wasn't."

"I know," Alistair agreed, "but we can't solve that yet. For now I have some other developments to tell you about."

Adam looked at the dashboard clock, they'd crossed the bridge and were heading through Fife.

"I assume we're going to Finlay, to drop you off?"

"Yes, please, and you're welcome to stay... oh, I spoke too soon. I forgot Henri may be there. I don't know if Margaret will have offered him the guest room upstairs, or if he'll manage to get a hotel room somewhere."

Adam let out a howl. "Henri and Margaret are together yet again? You are handling it well!"

"This is one of the announcements I have. Margaret and I are getting married soon."

Adam reached one arm to pat Alistair hard on the shoulder.

"Yes! Thank goodness Alistair, it's been a while coming."

"Well, it's become urgent because of another piece of news. Hamish has decided to open a branch of his law firm in Edinburgh, and invited Margaret to stay on in Scotland and keep her job, but work from here."

"Oh, I see the dilemma. Your visa's going to run out, and..."

"Exactly. Henri is looking into the details. Did you know he's an immigration lawyer? Anyway, it will be within the next several weeks. And probably in Finlay, so that we can get married in Calum's church. He's been suggesting it for weeks now."

"All I can say, Alistair, is congratulations! And, um, will ye be needin' a best man, or will ye bring one of yer mates over from America?"

"You beat me to it Adam, I hadn't even thought as far as that, but since you offered, I will gladly accept. I reserve the right to review your best man speech in advance!"

They had half an hour to go before Finlay. Alistair drank more of his coffee, then said, "I hate to break the happy mood, but I'm struggling with yet more information about Kilvellie and the glass factory, in the nineteen forties."

Adam glanced over in disbelief. "*Really*, Alistair? I thought everything was done and dusted."

"It was, except for your mother and I deciding to try and find the person or persons who had forced the six young men to do the damage at the glass factory. I will share all the details another time, and you're welcome to come over one day and look at what Henri and Christy and I found. But the bottom line is, there was a French medical officer named Jerome stationed in the Manor House when it was a convalescent hospital just before and during the Second World War. Turns out, he and Sheila the nurse had been together in France during the First World War. Long story short: she thought he had died, she met and married Heinrich, and they had children and built the glass factory. So when this French officer gets to Kilvellie and sees a former enemy soldier with a successful business, *and* with the woman he loved, he went a bit nuts."

"How do you know this?"

"It's all in writing, believe it or not. We have Sheila's letters back to him, begging him to forget about her and to stop threatening her family and her husband, and we have a journal he kept. Well, I say 'we' but I mean, Henri has

297

skimmed it, and it stops abruptly. The same day that Jerome wrote that Sheila was going to visit him that evening. I can't wait to get back to the cottage and look at the journal myself."

"Alistair, *why*? You have spent a huge amount of time on this whole glass factory tragedy. And for little or no pay, right?"

"Yes, but I just want to tie up this loose end of what happened to the French officer…"

Adam broke in. "You keep sayin' that! I don't mean to be critical, but this is about the sixth loose end you say you have to finish up. We had Justine's disappearance, which was good to investigate, don't get me wrong. Then the glass hidden underground, and you had to investigate why it was hidden, which led to learning about the factory being trashed during the war." He stopped to catch breath. "*That* led to investigating why Ronald the guard didn't do a better job, then who might have killed him… well, as your American TV show says, *yadda yadda yadda*."

Alistair laughed. "I know, but I promise you, the final *yadda* is going to be what happened to Sheila's French captain. I want to see if there's any record of whether he died that night."

"You mean, you think *Sheila* killed him?"

"Maybe, or Sheila and Heinrich. He was out of internment by then. Maybe she told him about her past."

"And *when* did this guy die, if he died?"

Alistair hesitated. "July nineteen forty-four."

It took a moment for this to sink in. "Oh, dear," Adam muttered, turning serious. "The same month…"

"Yes, the same month that the six young men faked their deaths to get away from Jerome. At least, at the time, Heinrich and Ronald thought they'd drowned."

Their conversation had taken them to within a couple of miles of Finlay, and Adam pulled the car into the parking lot for a popular farm shop and cafe.

"Oh good, they're still open. I want to pick up some things to take home. I also want to finish this conversation before I drop you off. All right, I've changed my mind. This last *yadda* could be important. I need to rewind. Did you say you *know* what date it was in July, I mean, the date of his last journal entry?"

"Not yet, but if it's the same date that the young men disappeared, then..."

"Cause and effect." Adam finished the thought. "So there's a chance that Sheila, or maybe Sheila and Heinrich, killed Jerome for revenge after they thought the six young men, the factory vandals, had drowned."

"I'm not quite there yet, but for my own peace of mind, I need to know."

Adam opened the van door, then turned back to look at Alistair. "I want to know too. I dinnae have to get home to Inverness right away. If Henri isnae staying in the guest room, how about if I stay over, we go through whatever papers and journals you have, and we bring this long saga to a close?"

Alistair smiled in relief. "*Thank you*, Adam. That's what I hoped you'd say. And you know what, Henri can sleep on the couch if the hotel is full. It's all getting a bit..."

"A bit *French*," said Adam, and they both laughed, thinking of a scene in yet another of Helen's favorite films.

Chapter 58

There was no sign of Henri's rental car when Adam and Alistair made their way along the two-mile rutted dirt path to the cottage in Finlay. Just one car was outside the house, the used Saab convertible that Alistair and Margaret had purchased.

"Good, no Henri." Alistair immediately apologized. "I can't fault the guy, he's contributed so much to the Kilvellie issues as well as looking after Margaret when she found Keith, but still…"

"Still, ye dinnae need an ex-boyfriend hanging about, especially as Margaret has been away for what, two weeks? Three?"

"Three, counting the extra time in Caraidsay."

But inside the cottage, they didn't find Margaret alone: she was with Calum, Finlay's minister. She'd gone to the front door on hearing the car arrive, and greeted Adam and Alistair with big embraces.

"Tea?" she offered, and made a fresh pot while Adam and Alistair joined Calum at the kitchen table.

"Sorry to interrupt what I understand is a bit of a reunion, after some wild adventures in the Hebrides," Calum said.

"It's fine, I'm happy to see you," Alistair assured him. "Has Margaret told you our news?"

"Which news? It's a wee bit difficult to know where to start! So I'm to have the honor of marrying you, sooner than I expected, and then you're both staying on, since Margaret's job is moving over to Scotland?"

"Kind of," Alistair confirmed. "Her boss Hamish plans to open a small branch office in Edinburgh, and Margaret can work from there. Or maybe keep working remotely from here. But whatever we do, Calum, I'm *thrilled* that we aren't leaving Finlay."

Margaret placed the teapot on the table, and then a large dish of shortbread and biscuits. She sat down and poured tea into four mugs.

"*Thrilled?*" she asked Alistair. "I thought you were fine going back to Portland, if that's what we decided."

"I didn't want to influence your decision," he admitted, "but yes, I am thrilled. There's so much to do and see here. All those tidal islands to explore..."

"Oh, I'm done with islands for now, having to check the tide times, and getting my boots soaked," Margaret said, shaking her head. "Give me solid bedrock of Edinburgh Castle for a while."

Calum helped himself to a piece of shortbread, then asked Margaret if she wanted to resume their discussion, or wait for another time.

"Let's keep going," she replied. "Alistair, we're talking about logistics, like how many people the church will hold, so you and I can decide who to invite. Not that I expect many people would come over from Maine and Boston. But actually, between us we know so many people in Scotland now, we could probably fill the church without any transatlantic guests."

"Your parents will attend, obviously," said Alistair, "and I'll invite mine, although since their divorce I haven't been as close to them as you are with yours."

Adam interrupted and asked Alistair if the offer to stay in the guest room was still open.

Alistair looked at Margaret, eyebrows raised. "Is that okay? I assume Henri's back at the hotel, or did he head home?"

"Neither. He's driven north to Kilvellie, to see Christy!"

Adam groaned in mock dismay. "Don't tell me, I may wind up with *him* as a brother-in-law? Sorry Calum, inside story. I'm dating Christy's younger sister Justine, and I guess, I haven't told you Alistair, but we are getting quite serious."

Calum smiled and rubbed his hands together in glee.

"Another wedding, eh? I'd better check my calendar again!"

"No hurry!" Adam said, then headed to the living room, with Alistair following.

"You know your way around," Alistair told him. "Let me know if you need anything to get settled."

"*Just one thing*," Adam whispered, so that Calum and Margaret wouldn't hear. They moved further away from the kitchen. "Can I look at the journal, the one Sheila's French captain kept? If I can pinpoint the date and compare it with when the six young men disappeared, that might clear things up. I can also have a look online for military records, maybe learn a cause of death."

"*If* he died that day," Alistair clarified.

"Aye, if he died the same day that Sheila was scheduled to visit. My money is on *yes*."

Alistair went into the bedroom and found the journal where Henri had left it, in a drawer. He handed it to Adam.

"This is going to be the end of it, right? Then I have to find some real work if I'm to become an official resident of Scotland. Maybe you can throw a few cases my way, things you're too busy for."

"Oh, I'm a step ahead of that, Alistair. I think we should open an agency, partners in private investigation. But for now, let's find out what happened in July nineteen forty-four and finally close *that* case."

Leaving Adam to get on with his evening, Alistair returned to the kitchen and refreshed his mug of tea.

"Okay, I'm ready to focus. First, what's the date you two have chosen?"

"Alistair!" Margaret chastised him. "You have a say in it also! And based on Calum's schedule, we have several options before your visa runs out."

He leaned back in his chair and sipped the hot tea, letting the animated discussion between Margaret and Calum swirl around him, possible dates rising like calendar days on a cloud, then being substituted with others. In six weeks tops, he'd be a married man. It was taking a while to sink in, but he realized he felt no resistance building. After his false hope with previous relationships, maybe this really was his path, at last.

Chapter 59

Later that evening, after Margaret was asleep behind the closed door to the main floor bedroom, Adam and Alistair sat at the desk in Adam's room upstairs and looked at the journal together. The final date entry was, as Alistair had feared, the day that the six factory vandals, who'd done the captain's bidding for over three years, were recorded as dead from drowning.

Adam had taken the research several steps forward and found an obituary for the captain. The sudden death that night was attributed to pulmonary failure, his lungs already seriously damaged from gas exposure in the First World War.

"Seems reasonable," Alistair said on first reading what Adam had found.

"Aye, it does, but there are a number of drugs that could cause the lungs to fail suddenly, and as a nurse, Sheila would have been familiar with them. Or if his lungs were badly compromised already, alcohol or opiates could cause it. She might have staged the scene to make it look like he'd been drinking whisky alone. In the context of a military convalescent home, where the patients and some of the staff were not well, I doubt that foul play would be the first thing on anyone's mind."

Alistair looked up at Adam.

"Is this the end? Have we covered all the bases?"

"Aye, I'm ready to close the book as it were. The question that will haunt me is the timing. If the six young men faked their deaths to get away from the captain, and he died anyway, then in retrospect, they didn't need to disappear, did they?"

"I don't know, Adam. Henry was back from internment, and knew they'd been the factory vandals, almost putting him out of business. Would he have pushed for their prosecution? We'll never know that."

"So we're back to poor Ronald Wilson, the factory guard, suffering the long-term psychological damage and never being told that the lads hadn't in fact died on his watch. That still rankles. Both his son and grandson, and Malky's family, only see the bad in him. In their eyes he was a failure, to this day."

"Maybe..." Alistair began.

"What? Do you have an idea?"

"Yes, but it would have to be Malky's decision. And his family. And Ronald's son Richard as well. Hold on, let me get something from downstairs."

Alistair returned a few minutes later with a stack of color photographs, some small, some portrait size. He spread them out on the desk.

Adam whistled. "Wow, ol' Ronald sure moved in fancy company."

The photographs documented Ronald's years as a security guard and doorman at the Manor House Hotel, between its role as a convalescent home in the nineteen forties and its conversion decades later to a luxurious care home. Alistair and Adam recognized some of the actors and royalty who'd allowed themselves to be photographed with Ronald; he in turn beamed at the camera, looking proud in his gold-trimmed uniform.

"I think it would be a fitting tribute to Ronald if these were matted and framed, then displayed in Malky's glass museum."

"I agree," Adam said. "Let the poor man have some dignity and fame in death, if not in life."

Alistair carefully collected the photographs and placed them in a folder. He picked up the captain's journal.

"Shredder?"

"Aye. Now that the journal's seen the light of day, it's too explosive to keep around and risk any of Sheila's descendants seeing it. She lives on in their minds as the beautiful young nurse who married a handsome enemy soldier, symbolizing an effort at peace after a horrific war. This ugly side of her life, being harassed for years by a cruel man who should have been sympathetic, after being in the war himself, leading to her possibly having a role in his death... well, it serves no purpose to have her family discover it. That's my opinion."

And so, for the second time, Alistair was a party to concealing wartime history. The first time, he, Helen, and Adam had agreed together to secure Ronald's diaries that documented the factory damage, and named the perpetrators. Perpetrators who'd been forced to carry out the damage, as recorded in the captain's diary. Ronald's family need never know.

This diary recorded the thoughts of a cruel man, twisted by his former love marrying an enemy soldier. A soldier who might have been responsible, symbolically anyway, for the captain's poor health.

"Another line drawn," Adam declared when the shredder finished its work and fell silent.

"Not a moment too soon," Alistair agreed, and the two men said goodnight.

The next morning, they set off in two vehicles for a trip to Kilvellie to bring the photographs to Malky and check progress on the glass museum. And, of course, for Alistair and Margaret to let their friends know to expect wedding invitations. Alistair and Margaret rode in their Saab, and Adam drove his van, planning to continue north to Inverness afterwards.

They met up in the parking lot across the street from the glass museum site. After a stop for coffee, tea, and pastry at the clifftop cafe, they crossed the street and were greeted by Malky. He wore paint-stained coveralls and smiled like he was in heaven.

"If you dinnae mind wearing hard hats, you're welcome to visit!" he said, inviting them in.

The interior was having finishing touches applied: a few walls needing paint, and baseboards on the finished walls. Installation of wall-mounted and free-standing display cabinets was the main activity now, and Malky proudly walked around and pointed out where different items of glass, and old glass-making tools, would be displayed.

"It's all credit tae Helen's pal Marcus," Malky explained. "He took me tae see other museums, and now I have a much better idea of what to do here."

With the tour complete, they returned to the front desk, now an actual wooden reception desk instead of a board over two sawhorses. With hard hats removed, they all headed out the front door. Alistair opened the folder he had brought from the car.

"Malky, you'd need to check with Ronald's son Richard about this, but I found these photographs of Ronald with some film stars and members of the royal family, when he worked at the Manor House Hotel. I don't know if you plan to mention anything about the war years, but..."

"Aye! This is grand!" Malky accepted the folder from Alistair. "Ronald, yes, he will be credited with hiding so much of the glass in the coal chute. These photographs, they provide a super addition to his later life. But yes, I will check with his son, of course, dinnae you worry aboot that."

Margaret had been listening quietly, and when the two men finished discussing the photographs, she asked Malky if Greta was around.

"Aye, lass." With the folder under his arm, he guided Margaret along the front of the building toward where the sea-facing cafe was being installed.

"I'll text you when I'm done," she called back to Alistair, who wondered what she was doing. She'd become more secretive, now that the wedding was actually happening.

He looked at Adam. "Guess I'm free for a while. Are you planning to visit your mother before you head north?"

"Aye, let's go down there. I expect she'll have the kettle on."

"Maybe you can help us solve a wee disagreement," Malky said to Margaret as they walked. "Greta wants to offer punch cards, ye ken, wee cards that folks get stamped or punched each time they buy a drink, and they get the tenth one free."

"I like that idea, Malky. I have several from different coffee shops, and when I see them in my wallet, it's kind of a reminder to stop in one of them. So it works as advertising also."

"Och lass! You read me mind! But the kids, they do everything on their phones. They said wee cards are old-fashioned, and people should be able to track their drink purchases on an app. I tell ye, it's all Greek to me and Greta! What do you suggest?"

Margaret thought for a moment. She'd heard stories of how frugal Malky was, and Greta wearing clothes made from vintage thrift-shop fabrics. Maybe that's why Malky was resistant to buying the necessary equipment.

"To track your customers' drink purchases, you'd need some kind of device, right? But punch cards would be inexpensive in comparison. You could even print them at home, like business cards. Actually, here's another thought. Why not do both? The museum is a bridge linking the past and future. Offer old-fashioned punch cards, but also a reader for people's phones. Maybe you could get a local tech company, or a company from Dundee or Edinburgh, to sponsor it in exchange for their name being featured?"

Malky almost jumped with joy. They'd just reached the cafe door. Greta unlocked it from the inside and Malky held it open for Margaret.

"Greta, I've brought ye a wee lass with the solution to the punch cards! Give her a good selection of pastries afore she goes, eh?"

And he was off, leaving Margaret to explain to Greta what Malky was "on about" as Greta called it.

Chapter 60

Greta locked the door again, then ushered Margaret into the cafe adjoining the museum. Eventually there would be a door between the two spaces, but for now, access was only via the street entrance, a glass door. The kitchen and dining areas were still under construction, but there were tables and chairs set up for workers to take their breaks. The counter held an array of individual pastries that Greta said she'd baked at home for them.

"Tea?" she asked Margaret, standing behind the counter and holding up a vintage Chintz teapot. "And what would you like to eat?"

Margaret smiled, thinking of the contrast between the dusty, overall-clad construction crew, and the dainty, floral cups and saucers. She focused on the pastries, but felt it impossible to choose.

"You select for me, Greta, as long as it's chocolate!"

Soon the two women were settled across from each other at a window table, tea and cakes at the ready. They were distracted by a determined-looking customer lingering at the door; she seemed confused by the "Closed" sign, when she could see people having tea inside.

Greta stood up and excused herself. "Sorry, Margaret, I'll explain that the cafe isn't open yet."

Margaret watched while Greta opened the door and greeted the prospective customer. In contrast to Greta's make-do-and-mend look, the woman looked to Margaret like she might be involved in the arts. She wore a knee-length dress in shades of apricot, with a long black silky jacket and black low-heeled boots. In one hand she carried a black canvas portfolio case. She had a ready smile that lit up her face, and wore her brown hair parted to the side and tucked behind her ears.

Perhaps cheered by the customer's enthusiasm, Greta evidently had taken pity on her, not only inviting her in for a cup of tea, but pulling a chair out so she could join their table. Margaret felt a wave of annoyance; she was here to consult with Greta on the most important baking project of her life, and didn't want to share the moment with a stranger.

Her annoyance was fleeting, however, once she realized that she knew who the new guest was: Caroline Watson, a wildlife artist whose work Margaret had admired at a recent exhibition at a gallery in Edinburgh.

"Are you in Kilvellie for business?" Margaret asked Caroline, while Greta poured tea and placed a selection of her best pastries on a serving plate.

"Yes," Caroline replied, her accent marking her as a fellow Scot. "I'm visiting galleries and shops beyond the Edinburgh area. Some of them have ordered my cards and prints."

"Do you have samples with you?" Greta asked. "I'm sorry not to be familiar with your work, but I rarely leave the town. Malky and I, we've been so busy with the museum."

Caroline opened her portfolio and removed a packet of greeting cards, which she handed to Greta.

"These are *lovely*," Greta said, taking time to admire the images of seabirds. "I don't know all the names, but I recognize the oystercatcher with the orange beak, and the little plovers. We see these birds on the beach here."

Caroline took the cards back, thanking Greta for her interest. "I'm hoping to have time to visit the beach. My husband's there, walking our dog. If I see some birds, I'll take photographs for future designs. I had a good look around the shops here and I didn't see much artwork of local wildlife."

Margaret laughed. "I'm not surprised. You may or may not know, but this town is all about sea glass. Greta here will tell you the history, if you have a few hours that is! But before we get to that, you mentioned your dog. Is that the dog in the art at the gallery? Those poses were amazing. You really captured, I guess I'd call it the joy of being a dog. A Border Collie, I think?"

"Yes, thank you!" Caroline said. "And one advantage is I can sketch him in real life, not from photographs like I do with many of the birds."

While Caroline was talking, Greta got up to go to the counter and returned with a Mason jar full of marbles. Most were clear, with a few multicolored ones mixed in. Caroline and Margaret turned their attention to Greta.

"Margaret's correct, most visitors are here for the beachcombing," Greta said. "Several people in town make a living selling glass, or jewelry made from glass. And sea glass marbles like these of course."

"Greta's son and daughter are glass artisans and sellers," Margaret added. "You should visit their studios if you have time, in the cooperative studio building."

"I will," Caroline replied. "So far I was focusing on shops that sell cards and artwork."

She picked up the jar and looked carefully at the marbles inside, before replacing it on the table. She had a surprised look on her face.

"Greta, you said these are *sea glass* marbles? All of them?"

Greta looked nervous, and she reverted to her native German for a moment. "*Ja*, I mean, yes, at least that's what Malky says. My husband, I mean. He's been beachcombing his whole life. His grandfather founded the glass factory, the source of so much of the beach glass here."

Now Margaret picked up the jar and examined the contents. "The clear ones look very uniform to me. If they'd been rolling around in the pebbles and surf for years, I'd think they would be more varied."

Caroline smiled and took a small tablet from her purse. "I agree. I don't want to take issue with someone as expert as your husband, Greta, but if you don't mind, I'd like to show you a short video from my art school days, when I learned about printing methods."

She set her tablet up on the table so that they could all watch. The video began by showing the inside of what looked like a factory or workshop, then the camera focused in on a huge flat metal table, the size of a large bed, which in turn was supported by a mechanism underneath. The table was surrounded by edges a few inches high.

A technician pulled a lever and the entire table began to tilt slightly and agitate rapidly in all directions. What looked like liquid glass oozed from one corner, but as it slowly spread out across the table, Margaret and Greta could see it take on the distinct appearance of hundreds, thousands, of frosty colorless marbles. Eventually the marbles covered the whole table surface, at which point the table was leveled and continued to shake.

Greta picked up the jar again. "They look the same as your video."

She gasped and stood up abruptly. "I must call Malky and have him watch this! He's using these in the marble exhibit in the museum and he's mislabeling them."

While Greta called Malky and asked him to meet her in the cafe, Caroline paused the video and set it up to play from the beginning. Moments later, Malky came bursting through the doorway, his hair going in all directions, his hard hat in one hand.

After quick introductions, Caroline and Margaret listened while Greta explained to Malky why she'd called him.

She held up the jar. "These clear marbles, *nicht* beach marbles! Caroline says they are used in artwork, in litho, lithog, oh, Caroline can give you the details. But Malky, you mustn't label them as beach marbles!"

Shaking his head in confusion, Malky placed his hard hat on the window sill, then sat next to Caroline to watch the video. Greta poured a cup of tea for him, but he was too engrossed to notice.

In the final moments of the video, the table was tilted once again, allowing the marbles to gather and pool in a trough at the end. Soon the table came to rest.

"Och now, what have we just watched?" Malky asked Caroline, full of curiosity.

"The marbles, or glass beads, are used to give the lithographic plates a grain so that they can be re-used in the printing process," Caroline began, pointing at the screen. "The machine is basically a large metal tray with the marbles introduced in it. An electric motor drives the movement, shaking the tray round and round. But after repeated use, eventually the marbles get too worn to be effective."

She looked up and pointed out the window, towards the cliff. "Who knows, maybe some were discarded into the sea and ended up on beaches like this one."

"So in a way, they can still be considered sea glass?" Margaret asked, hoping to restore some validity to Greta's and Malky's belief that the jar held sea glass marbles.

Caroline wavered, looking back and forth from Malky to Greta. "I don't like to disagree with your initial assumption, but the ones in this jar, they look identical to marbles that we would discard at the school. I don't see any evidence that they've been rolling around in the North Sea."

"*Genuine surf-tumbled* is the technical term for selling sea glass on the internet," Margaret said, smiling. "At least, that's what I've learned from my visits here."

"Well, I doubt these marbles have ever seen salt water, not for any length of time anyway," Caroline said. "It's an easy mistake. They have a frosty appearance like old sea glass, and if someone hadn't heard of the use in lithography, it is a logical assumption."

Instead of being upset, Malky sighed with relief.

"Och, lass, you've saved me a heap of embarrassment!" he exclaimed. He asked Greta for a plastic bowl, and he carefully tipped the contents of the jar into it. Now Margaret could see that the weathered, colored marbles were in fact genuine Regenbogen marbles, almost a century old.

Using his thumb and forefinger of each hand, Malky held up a lithography marble and a vintage marble, side by side.

"These look the same size and are the same weight," he pointed out, "but the manufacture is very different. Mass-produced marbles begin with a large vat of melted glass, some maybe recycled. Small globs of the liquid glass drop ontae a machine with rows and rows of turning rods with wee compartments, and them rods and compartments shape the glob until it's a perfect sphere. After cooling, these industrial marbles go through a sortin' process so the final batch is uniform."

He placed that marble in the bowl and stopped to take a drink of tea.

"Now this multicolored marble, it took a lotta skill and many hours ta make by hand. The glass artist built it up layer by layer, addin' them different colors, and the glass rod that will become marbles is put in and out of the kiln several times. In the old days, like my grandad's day, they used marble scissors to separate each marble from the finished rod. Them old marble scissors are still packed away, Caroline, but I can demonstrate the process next time ye visit!"

"Where did *these* lithography marbles come from, do you know?" Margaret asked Malky, pointing to the bowl.

He turned to her and nodded his head. "Aye Margaret, them marbles were a wee gift for the museum from an artist William knows. Somewhere along the road the explanation was left out, and by the time they were delivered tae the museum, the jar was unlabeled. I added them multicolored ones just to make the jar stand oot. Greta here said she'd display it on the counter in the caff to trigger conversation, but this isnae what we expected!"

"I hope it isn't disappointing for you, to learn what they really are," Caroline said, earnestly looking back and forth at Malky and Greta again.

"Nae, lass," Malky assured her. "I want things to be accurate in the museum. I'll still display them, but with a proper description."

He selected five brightly colored marbles from the bowl, asked Greta for a paper cup to put them in, and handed the cup to Caroline.

"It's our wee thank you for yer help, lassie," he said, when she hesitated.

Further discussion was halted when a construction worker entered the cafe, calling for Malky to come back to the museum right away. After quick goodbyes, Malky slurped down his tea, grabbed his hard hat, and followed the worker at a run.

Greta sighed. "*Ja*, another typical day around here. Now, tea refills for you two?"

Caroline thanked her but said she had to get going.

"The museum will have a gift shop," Greta said as Caroline stood and gathered her belongings. "We'd be honored to sell your cards and anything else you have. If you give me your address, I'll send you an invitation to the museum opening."

After Caroline and Greta exchanged contact information, Margaret stood up also and accompanied Caroline out to the street.

"It's been lovely to meet you, Caroline. Speaking of invitations, I'm getting married soon and I'm overwhelmed with the planning. Would you be interested in designing the invitations, maybe a bird theme based on the seabirds near my Fife cottage?"

Caroline smiled and thought for a moment. "I'd love to do that. I have a little time before I start preparing cards for Christmas. How about puffins? They mate for life."

Margaret tried not to look shocked: somehow puffins didn't quite fit what she had in mind.

Caroline laughed. "Just kidding! Anyway, puffins nest on the Isle of May, not on the Fife shoreline. I'll send you some

315

ideas that don't involve birds that people think are funny. Swans might be a good start."

Margaret thanked her and accepted a business card, itself a work of art with a miniature image of one of Caroline's diving gannet cards. Then Margaret pointed to the paper cup that Caroline was holding.

"Caroline, do you realize what Malky's given you?" she asked.

"Some old marbles that they aren't using in the museum, I assume?"

"Not just old, they could be a *hundred* years old, or more," Margaret explained. "I believe these are handmade vintage marbles that were tossed over the cliff near the glass factory during World War Two, and they've been collected on the beach here, many decades later, as weathered sea glass marbles. Take good care of them. You may have at least a thousand pounds worth of glass in that little cup."

Caroline almost dropped the cup in shock.

She gasped. "Oh, I can't accept this! All I did was barge in and identify the lithography marbles. What was Malky thinking?"

"He wants you to have them. Believe me, he is a generous man. I'd love to see you again and tell you the background. It's a very long saga."

"That would be great. And you can meet our dog Gordon, since you're familiar with his portraits."

Margaret was tempted to accompany Caroline to the beach and see Gordon in real life, racing along the sand, but instead she glanced at her watch: she still hadn't achieved her mission with Greta. With thanks and a reluctant goodbye to Caroline, she hurried back in to speak to Greta before the cafe really closed for the day.

Chapter 61

As Adam had predicted, Helen was indeed making tea when he and Alistair arrived at the police station.

"Hello son!" she cried when Adam joined her in the small kitchen at the back of the station.

"You're happy to see me, Mum?" Adam knew she was still annoyed at him for not telling anyone he'd gone to the Forsyth Industries office, and as a result, he'd almost been kidnapped by two men who'd been helping the patent agent Keith.

"Of course." She handed him the tea tray. "Let's sit in the conference room. And you can get me up to date on what's happening in Portland, Alistair."

Once they all had their tea, Alistair told Helen that the Portland detective and her team were conducting more forensic work in the file room. They were looking for evidence, or lack thereof, that would support or refute Keith's claim about the shelf he grabbed coming away in his hand, then hitting Marnie hard in the neck.

"At least," Alistair concluded, "that's as far as I got talking to Hamish while I drove to Edinburgh yesterday."

Helen looked at him in surprise. "I hope you didn't have a long mobile phone conversation while you were driving!"

"Sorry, there's so much to catch up on. No, I drove *him* to Edinburgh. From Oban. He's hoping to set up a branch of his law firm over here, in Scotland I mean. His wife Diana will arrive at some point with their young twins. They must be eight, I think."

"That will be nice for Margaret, right? I mean, if she's going to work in the Scotland branch. But what about *you* Alistair? You haven't had much of a career for months, just helping this crabby old policewoman, sorry, police officer, with a series of strange investigations."

317

Adam replied for Alistair. "We're just starting to talk about it, Mum, but this could be the answer to your worries about me. I'd like to team up with Alistair, form a partnership for private investigation. Cover for each other, what have you."

Helen looked back and forth at the two men. "Sounds great, but my next question is, Alistair, as an American on a short-term visa, are you permitted to work here?"

He grinned. "I sure hope so. After I'm..." He paused for effect. "Married!"

Helen shook her head. "Goodness, this deserves something more than tea, but it's too early in the day for champagne or whisky." She held up her tea mug. "We'll just have to pretend. A toast to Alistair and... Margaret, I assume?"

"Of course Margaret! Although, I had a few sticky moments recently when I thought she'd run off with her French ex-boyfriend, but Adam drummed some sense into me."

After they'd all refreshed their tea mugs, Alistair switched the conversation to the topic he wanted to discuss with Helen.

"If it works out for Hamish and his family to move to Edinburgh for a while, they'll need somewhere to live. I wonder, what about renting..."

"My flat there? Aye, if there's the two of them and two young children, there should be plenty of room. And as you saw the other night, it's all set up to move in anytime. They can rearrange furniture and things to suit."

"But Mum," Adam said, "not that it isn't a good idea, but what will you do when you visit Edinburgh?"

She smiled. "Och, the Caley'll do me fine, son. I can afford it for a night here or there. Or I could probably stay at Marcus's flat..."

Adam held up his hands in a "time out" gesture. "Wait, Mum, are you and Marcus..."

"No! He's spending most of his time here, helping Malky, and he said I could stay in his flat in Edinburgh if I decided to sell mine. So, no, son, I am not involved with Marcus."

"Since we're onto discussing relationships," Alistair said, "Helen, how are things with Richard? I expect there's been so much to process, with his father dying suddenly."

"I know." Helen sighed. "The more he learns about his poor dad's background, the worse he feels. And now he's really upset that people in town, their descendants I mean, suspect the six factory vandals didn't drown, as Ronald thought. And yet they never gave him the comfort of knowing that his actions hadn't led to their deaths. His revealing their identities to Heinrich, I mean."

She sipped some tea. "And worst of all, Richard's contribution to Ronald's death."

Alistair involuntarily glanced sideways at Adam. Had Helen told Adam about Richard's grandson damaging the walking stick, possibly causing the elderly Ronald to fall over the cliff?

"Mum told me, although it took a few days to get the full story," Adam explained. "That's a horrible burden for Richard to carry, knowing he gave his grandson the saw."

"Aye, son. I think he may go back to Spain sooner than he planned. He talks about me visiting him there, maybe eventually retiring there, but..."

"I can't see you over there, Mum, and not just because I'd miss you. Anyway, you're going to work for a few more years, right?"

"As long as the town will put up with me." She pointed out of the open conference room doorway, toward her sergeant Desmond's empty desk. "And I really need to get that kid trained up. Richard said that he wouldn't hold it against me if I asked to have Desmond transferred. He thinks it's a professional conflict, me dating him while his son is my sergeant. I've considered it, but the kid grew up here, his mates and his sister are here. I know he's slow catching on, but heck, after all the people I trained in Edinburgh, if I'm not up to training one more youngster, then I might as well retire to Spain now."

The conversation was interrupted by Helen's phone beeping from her pocket. She took it out and looked at the screen, then, smiling to herself, declined the call.

"I can talk to him later," she muttered as she put the phone away.

"Richard?" Adam asked.

"Nae, it was Calum..."

"*My* Calum?" Alistair interrupted. "Our village minister? I didn't know you were keeping in touch."

Helen smiled again and let out an embarrassed giggle. "Aye, we are. After he told that story about the origin of Kilvellie's name, he continued sending me more place name stories, so I'd have plenty to talk to tourists about. I *kind* of think there might be more to it, but if there is, he's sure taking his time." She paused. "A girl needs a bit more than anecdotes, right?"

"Weddings are good opportunities to make a move. Our wedding, I mean," Alistair said. "Ask him to dance, that should cure him of the anecdotes."

"Hmm, I like the idea. I expect Richard will be back in Spain, so I'll be going on my own."

"Alistair," Adam asked, "where's the reception going to be? Somewhere large, if ye plan on having dancing?"

"Good question, Adam. Margaret and I are working on that. As you know, we want to get married in Calum's church in Finlay. The only place that has a reception room is the hotel, where we get Indian food. But their facilities won't hold many people."

Helen went to her desk to fetch her tablet, and when she returned to the table, she opened the website for the nearby Manor House care home. She turned the screen for Alistair to see.

"They make their main floor facilities available for parties and weddings. I bet you anything, they'd let you use the space at no charge, after all your work organizing the boxes of documents and photos from their cellar. That raises another issue..."

She paused while she put the tablet away, then looked at Alistair again. "Did you find anything useful yet in the boxes, I mean, about who ordered the damage at the factory, if that's what happened?"

Alistair and Adam looked at each other, Adam giving what he thought was a subtle headshake, but Helen caught it.

"*What?* You did find something?"

"We found those letters," Alistair reminded her. "The letters in French, that Henri translated? Turns out that they were written by Christy's great-grandmother Sheila. During the First World War, Sheila and a French medical officer called Jerome were in a relationship in France, where she was working. He disappeared and she thought he'd died, then she met Heinrich. Henry. Fast forward to the late nineteen thirties, and Jerome gets assigned to the Manor House convalescent home. Based on the replies to his letters, Sheila was increasingly angry at his attempts to rekindle the romance, and his threats to her family. Did I say? He'd been writing to her, trying to win her back."

"And he *happened* to get sent from France to northeast Scotland, to Kilvellie?" Helen frowned. "Sounds to *me* like he must have engineered that assignment to be close to her."

"I should have thought of that!" Alistair cried. "I assumed he'd been sent here because he had some medical specialty, but of course, he must have tracked her down in the hopes that his physical presence might help persuade her."

"But it obviously didn't, right?" Helen concluded.

"Nae," Adam said, "the letters, they just end, and the trail went cold. We cannae make a link between him and the boys, the factory vandals." He made a show of looking at the time on his phone, and he stood up.

"Och, I'd better be going if I want to get to Inverness in time for dinner. Thanks for the tea, Mum."

He was gone before Alistair and Helen could even say goodbye.

Alistair made to get up, but Helen told him to wait.

"That's not all, is there? I know you too well, Alistair. Can I assume there's been some shredding activity?"

He nodded his head, shoulders slumping.

"Helen, *promise* you won't tell Adam that I've shared this? He obviously thinks the story will upset you."

"Of course, but if involves people in the town, I feel I have a right to know."

"It can never be verified, so you have to reach your own conclusion. The captain kept a journal, very unwisely I must say. He wrote what he'd been making those young men do, breaking glass and looting the factory. Then in his last entry, he wrote that Sheila was going to visit him that evening."

Alistair stopped and looked carefully at Helen before continuing.

"*That* was the evening of the day the six boys disappeared over the cliff. Well, it's what Heinrich thought happened. So then his wife is scheduled to visit the captain, who is never seen again. No, I lie. His *body* was seen that night, or the next morning, dead from respiratory failure. The obituary attributed it to long-term damage from being gassed in the First World War, but…"

"You think Sheila was responsible?" Helen asked quietly.

"If she was, it just adds to the complete tragedy of that day. And that night. If she, or she and Heinrich, killed the captain in revenge for the poor six boys supposedly drowning, but they didn't really drown, then that's just more sickening damage from the deceit. The faked deaths. Anyway, since Adam and I connected the dots in that particular way from reading his journal, we decided to shred it. Can you imagine if the sainted Sheila's grandchildren, great-grandchildren as well, read it and wondered?"

Helen sipped her tea while she thought back to their impromptu gathering in Greta's new cafe, when Malky told Helen, Alistair, and Marcus about Sheila's confession on her deathbed: she had killed a man during the war, to protect her husband.

"This is tragic," Helen said. "From what Malky shared that day, I assumed that Sheila had killed someone in a true wartime context, maybe in the battlefield hospital, and that she was protecting a wounded soldier, her future husband. Her confession seems to apply equally to killing a man during the *Second* World War, not the First, but still to protect Heinrich."

Alistair hesitated. "Helen, would Malky want to know what we think really happened?"

"You mean, that his beloved grandmother, a woman with four children, left the house one evening, either alone or with her husband, and killed Jerome, *not* in a true wartime situation."

"You're right, Helen. I think he has a hard enough time suspecting she killed someone in the First World War, over in France, but if..." He looked up and glanced around before continuing. "I mean, if she killed someone just a few blocks from here? No, I really don't think he should be told."

"My conclusion too. So maybe it's finally over, Alistair, getting to the truth of what happened. Anyway, that journal might never have seen the light of day. The boxes could have been sent straight to the trash if I, well, *we*, hadn't got involved with them. So the journal has just been destroyed sooner rather than later, that's how I see it."

Alistair hesitated. "You aren't, you aren't mad at me?"

"Nae, I'm sorry that I inflicted that project on you. Now you have the burden of knowing about Sheila. We were so focused on the men, I mean, Heinrich and Ronald."

They both looked into the office at the sound of the front door being flung open, triggering frantic ringing of the bell that hung near the top. Thinking there was an emergency, Helen got up and was confronted by Richard, a furious look on his reddened face.

"That Malky, damn him, you won't *believe* what he's planning to do!"

Alistair stood up, said a quick hello to Richard, mumbled something to Helen about going to find Margaret, and fled the station as quickly as Richard had arrived. He had a horrible feeling that he was responsible for this latest episode of animosity between the two families.

Chapter 62

Alistair didn't have to look far: ahead of him on the main road, he could see Margaret sitting on a bench outside the bakery cafe, head down as she checked her phone.

"Margaret!" he called, and she stood up and walked quickly along the sidewalk to meet him.

"I'm famished," she said. "I was about to call you!"

"I'm ready for lunch too." He took her arm and they entered the cafe, choosing a table by the window. They each ordered a large bowl of leek and potato soup with homemade bread, and Alistair ordered a strong coffee. Margaret surprised him by ordering a glass of white wine.

"I need it," she explained after the server left with their order. "It's been a stressful couple of hours."

"Stressful how? I thought you were having a social visit with Greta."

"I'll tell you when I've had some wine. What about you? And where's Adam?"

"We met Helen at the station, got her up to date on the Keith situation. And good news, she is willing to rent her Edinburgh apartment to Hamish and Diana. I'll leave them to sort out the details."

"I'm glad. I've never seen her place, but from Adam's description, it sure sounds elegant."

"It is. But after Adam left to go back to Inverness, something disturbing happened. Richard came charging in and he's furious with Malky. I have a sinking feeling..."

"That you have something to do with it," Margaret continued for him. "Yes, that's why I need the wine. Something awkward happened at the glass museum."

They fell quiet and looked out at the main street, watching the passing shoppers and tourists. Alistair wished he could reverse time and not have placed the photographs of Ronald in Malky's hands. What was he thinking, making himself the savior of Ronald's reputation? Bringing him back to life as a friend of the rich and famous, trying to substitute that image for the curmudgeonly, mean-spirited man as he was known to his son and grandson?

It was Kilvellie's fault, he knew. The place had got under his skin, invaded his thoughts, substituted emotion for his otherwise good judgment. This, he told himself, would be his final visit to Kilvellie. And he really meant it.

He pulled his mind back to the present: Margaret was taking generous sips from her wine, and his mug of hot coffee was sending up a welcome aroma.

"Sorry, I was a million miles away. Is your wine good?"

"Any wine would be good at this point. Let me tell you what happened. After you and Adam left, Malky called Richard and said he had something to show him at the glass museum. I heard some of this after it happened. I was having tea with Greta in the new cafe at the time. Richard arrived about ten minutes later, goes in and puts on the hard hat, then wanders around looking for Malky. Poor Malky, he thought he'd give Richard a lovely surprise, but it had the complete opposite effect. Malky had arranged some color photos of Ronald with members of royalty, and a few famous movie personalities, along a table in one of the empty parts of the museum. He tells Richard that the wall display will be a tribute to Richard's father, for his work as a factory guard and for helping to save so much glass from destruction."

Alistair put down his coffee mug and held both hands against his face before shaking his head sadly.

"I can guess what happened. Richard went ballistic?"

"Worse, he started grabbing the photos and tearing them in two! By then Greta and I had arrived as we'd heard there was a commotion. It's about the saddest scene I have ever witnessed. Richard was crying by then. Saying the man in the *photographs* should have been his father, not the mean b-word who would come home from work every night year after year and holler at his wife and family."

326

"Margaret, that probably *was* the real man. I think the happy images in the photographs were as fake as some of the jewels those people are wearing. If a member of the royal family asks to have a photograph taken with a doorman, guard, whatever, who may have done them favors during their stay, he's hardly going to grimace at the camera, is he?"

"No, you're right. But Richard says he has never seen any of the pictures. That means his dad never came home at night and said, 'look at this lovely picture of me and a princess' or whoever. He must have taken no pride in his work."

Alistair sipped his coffee, then nodded in agreement. "Maybe by then he felt his family didn't care about what he did for work. Perhaps he'd already alienated them too much, being grouchy."

They both looked up to see the server arrive with bowls of soup and a basket of bread, thick-crusted and with a small dish of olive oil for dipping. If Alistair had been on his own he would have asked for butter, but since he was marrying Margaret, he decided to go along with her preference.

"Enough of Ronald and Richard," he declared. "Let's enjoy lunch."

"Agreed. And then I have lots to tell you about the wedding plans!"

Wedding plans. In all the drama of the day, Alistair had—sort of—forgotten he was getting married. Panic hadn't set in yet, but he was starting to worry that it would. He never forgot the shameful relief he felt when he boarded that plane in the Himalayas, leaving Paula behind. They'd been happy, settled in their cottage, surrounded by natural beauty... but it had been her world, her work that kept them there.

Now he worried that he'd repeated history, fallen for a woman far from home, cozy in a cottage, surrounded by natural beauty... was this it? Was this to be his future? But he had to stifle any doubts and live with his commitment. Anyway, with Hamish setting up a branch of the law firm in Scotland, and Alistair's possible partnership with Adam,

327

perhaps his life as he defined himself—above all, a private investigator—would get back on track soon.

Margaret was still talking away, so he tuned in again. "What do you think about that idea for our wedding cake? And the artist I met, and the wedding invitations?" She was smiling in anticipation, shining eyes open wide. Had she really changed so suddenly from a shy, serious lawyer to a bubbly bride-to-be?

He smiled. "All sounds great, darling!"

But he had no clue about what he'd just agreed to. Oh well, on their wedding day, he would pretend not to be as surprised by the cake as the guests were.

Chapter 63

While Alistair and Margaret ate lunch, Helen made fresh tea and sat in the conference room to listen to Richard. He had forced himself to calm down, and apologized for barging in.

"I wish I hadn't come back to Kilvellie," he moaned. "Look at all that's happened. And now, I see a side of my father that I never knew. A happy side. A man proud of his job. Why, Helen, why did I never get to see that?"

"It's impossible to know, Richard. He must have been so damaged by his glass factory work during the war, and his sense of failure for not protecting the factory, then thinking he saw the six drowned lads. The lads he was supposed to be supervising. It wouldn't be normal for someone to just move on from that. Can't you be glad for him that he finally achieved some professional success, at least in the eyes of the people he helped at the Manor House Hotel?"

"Aye, lass, you're right as usual. I can't begrudge him that. Oh God, I feel *terrible* now, lashing out at Malky the way I did. That poor fellow, he's been so happy with the progress of the museum. He thought he was doing something nice today to honor my family, and I go and tear up some of the pictures."

Helen put her hand on his arm. "Maybe they can be restored. And there are others, right? That's what Alistair..."

She stopped suddenly, regretting her rash comment.

Richard became agitated again.

"*Alistair?* What the hell does he have to do with all this?"

"I'm sorry, Richard, he's been organizing boxes of old photos and documents from the care home. The original point of the project was to learn more about those six lads who we thought drowned, well, five of them, since we know one was Kathryn's brother, that woman in the care home whose room was next door to Ronald's. Alistair came across

329

the photographs of your father, and he just jumped to thinking Malky might use them in the museum. Alistair was *only* motivated by honoring your father, you understand that, don't you?"

He sighed and drank some tea. "Oh, I s'pose. But them photos, they're *family* pictures. He and Malky, they have no right to..."

"You said you've never seen the photos, Richard, but how were Malky and Alistair to know that? Please don't blame them. They're just doing what I wish had been done decades ago, showing your dad in a better light than you came to know him. Restore his dignity, if you will."

He sat quietly, processing what she was saying, and another thought came to her mind.

"If you've never seen the photos, then I'm guessing that Desmond hasn't either. He's one generation removed and perhaps he could embrace the idea that his granddad had been a success at the hotel. Think about it, people seeing the photos and then telling him how proud he must be. People unfamiliar with Ronald's history before working at the hotel. That could become a new version of Desmond's granddad, one he could be proud of. It would help his self-assurance in his job and personal life, don't you agree?"

Richard took Helen's hand in his and looked her in the eyes. His voice softened.

"Move to Spain with me lass, please? I feel like you're the only person who can keep me sane, keep me from being consumed by what this town has done to my father. And now the burden of my own grandson causing Dad's death... how can I stay here with all that around me?"

Helen squeezed his hand, then let it go.

"I can't come with you Richard, not just now. I love my work, and I love seeing my son. Look, this is going to sound hurtful, but just listen. Your father was never close to you, he kept so much inside. But Richard, you have a son who loves and admires you, and now you're about to flee back to Spain and avoid dealing with the truth of your own family's history. You're the only parent, or grandparent, that the lad has now. Won't you stay around a while, for him at least?"

"You missed your calling, Helen. Shoulda been a shrink instead of a copper. But you are right, absolutely. I still have to flee back to Spain as you say and let my mind process all that's happened recently, but I will buy Desmond a ticket for a visit. Very soon."

Helen smiled. "*If* he asks nicely, his boss may give him the time off. I'd say three weeks sounds about right, eh?"

With a lingering, warm hug, Richard took his leave. He promised to be back sometime, he just didn't know when.

Helen didn't have time to dwell on what was the end of a promising relationship, though, as her phone began ringing. When she saw who it was, she answered. She spoke quickly, hoping to head off an anecdote before it even started.

"Hullo Calum, I was just thinking about you. I kind of fancy some Indian food. What do you think about meeting at the Indian restaurant by you soon?"

She listened to his reply.

"Aye," she said, grinning. "See ye tomorrow night!"

Chapter 64

It was a hectic few weeks for Margaret and Alistair, but at last, the wedding was just one day away. Alistair was getting used to the prospect of being a married man. For a role model, he had decided on Hamish, Margaret's boss. Alistair knew him professionally, but as they spent time together in Edinburgh, the personal side of the man came to the fore.

The Edinburgh visits were for Alistair to get fitted for his wedding outfit: full Highland dress, courtesy of Hamish. In a tailor's shop on the Royal Mile, Hamish and Alistair had chatted while measurements and fittings were taken for the large number of pieces required, from the kilt and jacket, to the shirt and sporran, and even the length of the socks.

After having no success in finding a Wright clan with an associated tartan, Hamish and Alistair had selected a tartan called the Earl of St. Andrews. The blue background with black and white lines suited Alistair's coloring, as most of his clothing was in that color scheme. And Alistair loved visiting St. Andrews, so he felt the association was appropriate.

At the final fitting, after which Alistair would take the outfit with him, the salesman had warned, "Have a care when ye travel, laddie. Thon *sgian dubh* will cause a bother with security!"

By that stage, Alistair had been so worn out trying to follow the accent, he just thanked the man. Presumably, the unfamiliar phrase meant a piece of metal, of which there were several in and on the outfit. Not that Alistair ever expected to approach airport security in this get-up.

In fact, he didn't expect to be approaching airport security anytime soon, whatever the outfit. Henri had been busy working on obtaining residency and a work permit for Alistair. It must be a complex process, Alistair realized, based on his frequent video calls with Henri and the complaints about British law versus Scottish law.

"*Moi*, I thought it was one country, Great Britain, *non?* Ah well, I'll get back to work," was the oft-repeated refrain.

Driving north to Finlay, Alistair thought about how well Hamish juggled his busy job, his responsibilities for mentoring young lawyers, his twins with Diana, and his teenage daughters from his previous marriage. That ended in divorce, but from what Hamish had said, the divorce had not been acrimonious, and the formerly married couple continued to cooperate in raising their teenagers.

It was such a contrast to Alistair's parents and their divorce. Each had become distant toward Alistair, and now, with his wedding a day away, he'd finally received replies to his invitations. "Sorry, Alistair, but let's have a video call soon. Best of luck." He received warmer messages from friends he hadn't seen in years. From rarely-seen colleagues even.

But why was he thinking of divorce, with his wedding day approaching? He put those thoughts from his mind and focused on the drive home.

Margaret had moved into the Templeton Grand Hotel for a couple of nights, where her parents and most of the wedding party were staying. That morning, she and her mother Jilly were busy with their own final fitting for her wedding dress. It had been designed and sewn by Margaret's first and best friend in Finlay, Katrina.

The fabric was off-white silk: Katrina said it suited Margaret's red-headed coloring better than pure white. Not a giant meringue, it was instead an A-line shape, ankle-length, slightly longer in the back. The sleeves were long, and the bodice was topped with a collar that was embroidered in a Pictish scroll design, serving more like a decorative choker. Margaret planned to wear some Pictish jewelry from her house—replicas, she'd tell people, although she and Alistair knew the truth. With the jewelry in mind, Katrina had designed a dress that would show off the necklace and the bracelets.

As a finishing touch to the Scottish theme, purple heather was embroidered around the hem, as if Margaret was walking across the moor.

She wouldn't wear a veil, but her thick red hair, now grown below her shoulders, would be loose and held back with a wide tartan headband, the lines sewn over with silver thread. Hamish had told Katrina the name of the tartan of Alistair's kilt, which Margaret would not see until the wedding, so the couple would be happily surprised at the coordinated outfits. That was the plan, anyway.

Katrina declared that she was satisfied, at last, with how the dress fit. After carefully hanging it up and replacing the zip-closure cover, she said goodbye, leaving Margaret comfortable again in sweats, and Jilly still in her bathrobe.

"I really should go and dress," Jilly said, not for the first time. She poured herself another cup of tea from the room-service tray. "It's just so wonderful, being here with my daughter and preparing for her wedding."

"I can't believe it either." Margaret helped herself to a refill of tea and a bite of scone. "I just hope..."

"As long as it feels right to *you*," Jilly assured her.

"Oh, I guess. When I first accepted Alistair's proposal, I had second thoughts almost immediately. I never told you, but he and I had an afternoon apart. I suspected that he was only marrying me for security once he learned I had a good salary and the cottage here. He misinterpreted something I said and he stormed out, suitcase and all. We're really only together again because one of our friends here stopped him from driving off, and told him to give me a second chance. Since then we've been fine."

She sipped her tea, then added, "Well, fine until Henri showed up, and Alistair acted really jealous. It seemed kind of irrational to me, but I've given him the benefit of the doubt."

"*Dear* Henri," Jilly said, her tone wistful.

334

"There's no dear about it!" Margaret countered. "He dumped me to go back to France. He didn't even invite me to go with him, or keep the relationship going long-distance."

"Yes, but Margaret, you were *so* happy with him, have you forgotten that? Oh, I can still remember the magical night of Hamish and Diana's Christmas party. You know the phrase about sweeping someone off their feet, and I really thought Henri had done that with you."

Margaret began tearing up. "Mom, why are you doing this? I'm marrying Alistair, and you're going all nostalgic over a guy who broke my heart."

She stood up and paced over to the window, then turned around. "You don't like Alistair, Mom, that's what's going on!"

"No! I, I can't say I like him or not like him, but how can you expect me to? I just met him in person yesterday! With Henri, I saw you together in Portland and Boston several times and I felt really drawn to him from the first time we met."

Jilly was silent as she sipped her tea, then said, "And Margaret, why aren't his parents coming to his wedding? He's their only child, right? Can't they put their feelings aside, even though they're divorced, and attend such a happy occasion?"

Margaret had wondered about that also, but felt she had to defend Alistair.

"It's a long way to come over from the west coast, you know that. Flying from Boston is much easier. Who knows, maybe they don't own passports. Not everyone is a world traveler like you and Dad."

"I agree with all that, dear, but Alistair just seems... what's the word... *unconnected* to anything. Are you sure he hasn't latched on to you because he's, I don't know, lonely?"

Margaret gasped. "Mom, do you know how *mean* that sounds? How is it you think Henri could love me and you can't imagine someone like Alistair loving me?"

Now she burst into tears, and her mother got up to hold her.

"Darling Margaret, I'm behaving very badly. Maybe the wedding is reminding me of thoughtless things people said when I got married, and I'm just repeating them. Forgive me?"

Margaret gently pulled away and dried her eyes.

"I will. Let's forget we had this conversation. I have a lot to do before we go to lunch, so why don't you take your tea and scones to your room and have a leisurely morning. You must be feeling tired from getting up early."

"I am dear, thank you. I doubt your father's even awake yet!"

Alone in her room, Margaret felty oddly unsettled, but attributed it to her mother's obvious preference for Henri. She could understand it, in a way. Leaving aside how Henri had broken off their romance to return to France, he was still a loveable guy, and no one could argue with his attractiveness and attentiveness. Steeling herself, she grabbed her bathrobe and headed for the shower.

Today, her last day of being single, she would focus on enjoying the time with her parents and her Scottish cousin Jeannie. And Hamish. They were taking her to a new restaurant at a nearby distillery, not for the whisky, but because the food was being widely praised. Then later was her hen night—Katrina and Jeannie had organized it together, but hadn't given Margaret any hint of where they would go.

Alistair would be out with the guys, although Margaret hoped they wouldn't be on a pub crawl, with Alistair barely able to stand the next day. No, that wasn't his style, she felt she knew him that well, even if her mother viewed him as remote, distant.

The hot water and steam of the shower soon relieved her mood. She pictured what to wear to lunch. Her fashion advisor, Katrina, had insisted that Margaret buy some wedding event-appropriate clothes for the days leading up to her wedding, and for departing for her honeymoon.

"There will be lots of friends and family members taking photos," Katrina pointed out. "You can't appear in all of them looking like you just came in from a beach walk!"

An hour later, wearing a new knee-length natural silk dress with matching jacket, shoulder purse, and heels, Margaret locked her hotel room door and headed down the stairs to the lobby. She had a sudden flash of memory, back to Hamish's Christmas party, which her mother had annoyingly mentioned. Then, she'd worn a dress more suited to a teenager, and high-heeled sandals, as she descended the stairs at Hamish's house.

Just as now, she'd heard Henri's enchanting voice drifting up. She stopped partway down the stairs. *Henri?* She was supposed to be meeting her parents and Hamish in the lobby, but as she reached the bottom step, there he was, dressed to kill as usual. Her heart did an involuntary flip-flop. He stepped forward and took her hand to guide her to the rest of the waiting group.

With a nervous glance at Hamish, Margaret's father Oliver watched to see how this would play out, but *he* wasn't going to get involved. Jilly looked at Margaret, her eyes pleading. "*Poor* Henri was alone here, waiting for the hotel restaurant to open, and we couldn't let him eat by himself, could we?"

"*Cherie*, I hope you do not mind." Henri smiled at Margaret. She had her eyes narrowed, shooting mental daggers at her mother.

Of *course* she minded, but she felt she had no choice. She'd have to make sure not to sit next to him at lunch, or her resistance might just start weakening.

That resistance was tested almost at once. With Hamish leading the way and Margaret's parents following, they proceeded out to Hamish's rental car, a Range Rover large enough for his family plus luggage. Margaret could sense Henri behind her, and to her dismay he reverted to the familiar ways from their relationship, placing his warm hand against her back to guide her forward. Jeannie was driving

337

her own car, and Margaret wished she'd had the foresight to say she'd ride with Jeannie.

Suddenly, time slipped and she felt the cocoon of familiarity asserting itself as she sat too close to Henri in the back seat, with Jilly on Henri's other side and Oliver in the front with Hamish. Another jolt of memory from earlier that summer, when she'd had an eerie, sickening sense that Alistair was a complete stranger to her. Was her mother right, that Alistair was just in it for the security, to avoid being lonely?

Maybe this little bubble was where she belonged after all: with Henri, with her parents' approval of the handsome Frenchman, and with her boss Hamish, who'd nurtured her career and helped her personally for almost two years now.

Should she really embark on a life far from all that safety, that sense of home? She shivered for a moment, imagining the years, the decades rolling out, alone with Alistair in that cottage two miles away, growing distant from all the people she held dear. Would he be off on work assignments all the time, leaving her on her own with children, worrying at night for his safety, and her mother three thousand miles away?

She shook her head to try and dispel the sense that she was making an existential mistake by getting married the next day. Oh well, she thought to herself, we *are* going to a distillery for lunch. Two hours to get through with Henri, three tops. She'd just start her hen night early. Very early.

Chapter 65

In the restaurant, Margaret maneuvered herself between Jilly and Hamish, with Henri on Jilly's other side at the table. As it was circular, she could avoid looking directly at Henri.

When they had placed their orders, Margaret getting a glass of red wine to accompany the appetizers, Henri asked Hamish if there was any news from Portland about the investigation into Marnie's death. *Petite Marnie*, Henri kept calling her.

"I'm glad you asked, Henri, because I was going to give you an update anyway. Clara, the detective, said that considering the condition of the file room, with some shelving in the process of being dismantled, Keith's story is believable. There's an outside company doing the work, not our own employees. They have a contract to dismantle the unused shelves and take them away, but whoever's doing the work has been lackadaisical about it."

"Lackadaisical meaning negligent? Legally negligent?" Margaret asked.

"That's the real question, whether the shelving company knew they were creating an unsafe environment."

"It obviously was unsafe," Margaret argued. "Isn't Marnie's fatal injury enough evidence?"

"To us, it seems that way," Hamish replied, "but consider the use for which a filing shelf is intended, which is to place things on and take them off. It's not intended to be a guard rail, or a handle to grab when you lose your balance. If shelves are held to that standard, I'll have to get the maintenance people to go around and secure every single one in the office. I know in my office, some shelving is just balanced on those little pegs inside the unit. A shelf like that wouldn't survive being used to stop someone from falling."

"Sounds like a legal mess," Oliver said. "Does that mean Marnie's poor family will have no recourse, no lawsuit?"

339

"They can *file* a lawsuit," Hamish explained, "and an aggressive lawyer would name several defendants: the law firm of course, the building management, the file room clerks, the company removing the shelving, and they'd probably think up a few more."

"So you're looking at a huge budget, to bring a suit like that to a resolution."

"Correct, Oliver. But Marnie's parents came to Portland and they had a long conversation with Norm..."

"*No-jail Norm*?" Margaret broke in. "But, but, he was at the scene of her death, right?"

"Yes, although that's being kept quiet. He didn't cause her death, and her parents have been told nothing about the ghastly decision by Norm and Keith to stage it as if she fell off the shelving when she was trying to reach for a file."

"This is despicable!" Oliver cried, putting down his wine glass and pointing at Margaret. "My God, if it was *our* daughter who'd died, I'd be out for blood!"

"My blood included, I'm guessing," Hamish added. "And you'd be completely correct. But Norm helped them to see how a lawsuit would play out. Margaret, this will seem familiar from our case with the chemically-injured plaintiffs."

"I get what you mean. The 'blame the victim' scenario," Margaret confirmed.

"Yes, if a civil suit by Marnie's parents went to trial, I can just imagine the kind of defense that would be raised," Hamish continued. "Defense attorneys would assert that Marnie was not in the file room on law firm business, no partner had given her an assignment to go there, she was having a clandestine meeting with Keith... need I go on? And they'd dig into her personal history, see if she'd had suspicious meetings with other employees, even students while at law school."

"They'd basically trash her reputation, Dad," Margaret summarized, "and that would be unbearable for her parents to hear, wouldn't it?"

"So there will be *no* liability for her death, no compensation?" Oliver persisted, still outraged at what Hamish and Margaret were telling him.

"I'm getting there, Oliver," Hamish assured him. "Keith has accepted full responsibility, but the death was ruled accidental. They're working on a deal for him to do community service in Portland, in lieu of jail time for not reporting her death immediately, and for interfering with the scene of her death. As for compensation, the building management and the firm are going to establish a scholarship in her name at her law school. Norm said he'll make an anonymous contribution to that. We'll also arrange a celebration of her life soon, at the firm. Along with a suitable visual memorial, like her photograph on the wall and a description of what she meant to the law firm in her brief time with us."

"I guess that all sounds appropriate," said Jilly. "Let the memories of poor Marnie be good ones, and not conjure up fake stories to smear the poor girl's memory."

"And Keith, or Thompson to use his real name, will still be facing a possible trial," Hamish pointed out. "It will take a while to unravel his role in stealing intellectual property, but that's in the client's hands, to bring a suit or not."

By now, one bottle of wine had been consumed and a second opened, with Hamish and Jeannie limiting themselves to one glass each since they were driving. And they were only on appetizers so far. Margaret decided she'd better refuse a refill of wine, but then Henri tested that resolve.

He turned to face Margaret's mother, after topping up her wine glass. "Jilly, I am so very sad about *petite Marnie*, but I am also relieved our *cher* Margaret was not in the file room that night, *oui? I* would not have let Marnie go there."

Jilly raised her glass in a toast to Marnie's memory. "Yes, Henri dear, I don't know how I could manage if I had to go through what Marnie's parents must be experiencing. Too

341

bad Marnie didn't have someone like *you* looking out for her. She never should have been out at work that late, in an empty building, and in a file room no less."

Margaret just shook her head. "Mom, why *shouldn't* Marnie have been there? She had just as much right to work whatever hours she chose, and in any room of the firm she chose. Are you saying women, even women *attorneys*, need to be protected from working under the same conditions as the men?"

Wow, Hamish thought to himself. This was more assertiveness than he'd ever seen in Margaret, and he was quick to defend her position.

"Margaret's right, Jilly. I hate that it was my wife Diana who found poor Marnie's body, but I never for a moment considered telling Diana not to go into the office so early that day, or not to go to the file room alone to look for a file she needed."

"And I suppose there is what you call a silver lining," Henri continued. "You and Diana are taking a long break here, in Scotland, to help her recover, *oui*? And because of that, we can all be united again working at your firm. *Moi*, and *cher* Margaret!"

He raised his glass; Margaret took that as her cue to excuse herself to go to the restroom. But she walked straight past the restroom door and out to the parking area in front of the restaurant. She took her phone from her purse and called Alistair.

"Where are you?" she demanded, with no preliminaries.

"Uh, I'm at the cottage, packing for our honeymoon. What's up? Aren't you at lunch with Jeannie and your parents?"

"I am, and with Hamish, but then Mom went and invited Henri! He's driving me crazy! Alistair, can you rescue me? I'll give some reason, like we need to meet with Calum, whatever. *Please*?"

"Of course, darling. You're at that new distillery just south of St. Andrews, right?"

342

"Yes. I'll wait for you outside. I'll get some food to go, and eat in the car. I need to sop up the wine. I'm so stressed. I've had too much."

"You *must* be stressed. Too much wine at lunch? Okay, see you soon."

Margaret spent a couple of minutes composing a believable excuse, something about receiving a text from Alistair and a last-minute glitch with the church—they could hardly argue with that. Jeannie offered to leave with her, but Margaret insisted that she stay and catch up with her aunt and uncle.

Alistair arrived fifteen minutes later, and Margaret felt herself relax right away as they headed back to Finlay. She had a fleeting thought that she was more at home in their comfortable old Saab than she ever would be in a Range Rover like Hamish had rented, and that Henri had praised during the drive to lunch. She munched a cheese sandwich while complaining about Henri between bites.

"Why isn't he back in France by now?"

"Don't be hard on him, Margaret. He's being a huge help to me with the immigration process. Have you looked at the websites? It's a convoluted nightmare to figure out what I need to do."

"Okay, I know he's a good lawyer and he's helping you. It's just that Mom, she's still besotted with him. Drives me up a wall."

Alistair glanced at her. "Well, he is so *charming*, that's what everyone says. I'm sorry I can't be like that for your parents."

"Oh, they're fine. Mom just has this romantic memory of when I first dated Henri, and now she's stuck there. Okay, no more about him, apart from immigration work. Wait, is he going on your stag night?"

Alistair groaned. "Yup. I really don't like these rituals, but I guess all the guys expect to be included. I promise *I* won't be overdoing the wine!"

"Me neither, not tonight. I don't know what Katrina has planned, but it's sparkling water for me, no alcohol until our champagne toast at the reception tomorrow."

She was quiet as Alistair drove the last couple of miles back to Finlay. As protected as she'd felt earlier, surrounded by the familiarity of Henri, of her parents, of her mentor Hamish, the lunch had burst that sensation. She imagined being married to Henri, and after his sexist comment, that *he* wouldn't have *let* Marnie go to the office late at night, even to access an important file, she knew it wouldn't work.

Alistair was protective, but in a way that suited her independence. If she wanted to fall into a forgotten dungeon in Orkney, or cross a slippery causeway in search of shells on a remote Hebridean island, that was her prerogative, in his mind as well as hers, and they'd just have to face the consequences. Together.

Chapter 66

At two o'clock the following day, the sun was shining down on the village of Finlay. However, no one was outside to enjoy it, and the shops were all closed. All the local residents, Margaret's family, and friends from near and far, were packed into Calum's church in the center of town.

With Margaret's Pictish silver jewelry shimmering in the light from the stained glass windows, she and Alistair stood facing each other in their coordinated-tartan outfits, ready for Calum to conduct the wedding ceremony. Margaret glanced out at the congregation now and again, spotting so many familiar faces. It was as if her past and present were gathered in celebration, sweeping her forward to her future with Alistair.

She felt honored to see a number of new friends there: police officer Helen, out of uniform for a change; Malky, Greta, and their three children; and in place of honor near the front, artist Caroline and her husband. The wedding invitations designed and printed by Caroline featured not puffins, but two swans, one facing right and one facing left, with their graceful heads and necks forming a heart in the center. Judging from the enthusiastic comments from recipients, the design was perfect.

She looked further back over the crowd and realized, not *all* of her past was there. Among the sea of faces, there was no Henri. His sun-bleached hair normally stood out, but he was not in the church. She had yet to hear how the stag night went. Maybe Henri overdid it and was sleeping off a hangover?

She focused again on the man in front of her. He looked surprisingly at home in full Highland dress. Smiling, she turned to face Calum as he began the ritual of the wedding vows.

There was the sudden noise of a door banging shut, and people turned to look toward the back of the church. Standing in the aisle, hair mussed as if he'd been running, was Henri. He held his tablet up.

"*Attends*! Wait, *mes amis*, you must stop zee marriage!"

"What the *hell*?" Alistair mumbled, then quickly apologized to Calum.

"It's fine, Alistair, I think your sentiment is correct. What the hell?"

Adam, as best man, was standing by in his own full Highland dress, poised to see what Henri was up to. But Henri just stood there in the aisle, his tablet held high and threatening to reveal some terrible secret.

"I'll escort him out," Adam whispered. "Calum, carry on without me."

Calum looked back and forth at Margaret and Alistair.

"*Is* there some reason the wedding can't take place today?"

They both shook their heads.

"Please, Calum, continue," Margaret begged. "That's my ex-boyfriend, but I never thought he'd disrupt our wedding. Alistair, is he still drunk from your stag night?"

"He wasn't there," Alistair admitted. "He texted about some last-minute work."

They watched in dismay as Adam returned up the aisle, shaking his head and carrying Henri's tablet. He took Alistair by the elbow, motioned for Calum to follow, and the three men sought privacy in Calum's office. Henri had already retreated through the main door of the church.

Margaret burst into tears and fell into the pew next to her mother. She pulled off her tartan headband and flung it away; it bounced and rolled a couple of times, finally disappearing behind the pulpit.

Behind the closed door to Calum's office, the three men looked at the image on Henri's tablet. Most of it was not in English, but Alistair recognized the likely source: the

Himalayan country where he'd been with Paula, several years back now. The yaks and mountains and prayer flags gave it away.

"What *is* this?" he asked Adam. "Why did Henri bring it to the wedding?"

Adam hesitated before replying in a soft voice, "Alistair, according to Henri, this wee document says yer already married."

"Is that true?" Calum cried. "We need to sort this out!"

"That's ridiculous!" Alistair spluttered. "Sure, I dated Paula over there for a while, but I never proposed to her! There's *no way* we're married."

"Henri said he's had this translated," Adam countered. "It says you *are* married to Paula."

"Not true! I think Henri faked whatever this is, this certificate. He's trying to break me and Margaret up."

Calum cleared his throat. "Be that as it may, I'm sorry but we can't proceed with the wedding until this is resolved. Alistair, where is this Paula now? Maybe I can talk to her?"

"She's still living in the Himalayas. She and I are inventors on a patent and we talk by Skype occasionally. Let's see, it's not too late to call. Knowing her, she's probably still at the lab."

He patted his jacket pockets. "Oh, Adam, I gave you my phone. There was no room for it in my sporran."

Adam stifled a laugh and handed the phone to Alistair. The three men crowded close and watched the screen while they waited for Paula to answer.

Suddenly, there she was. Feeding a toddler in a high chair?

"Hi Paula, I'm really sorry to disturb your evening," Alistair began, "but believe it or not, I'm in the middle of getting married, and someone's objected because they say I'm already married to you."

Paula burst out laughing, and Alistair noticed how much her skin had weathered from the sun at the high altitude. It had aged her. He almost asked her why she wasn't using sunscreen, but he caught himself... she was no longer his responsibility.

"You're *kidding*," she said, then turned serious. "It's not really funny, but it is kind of. I mean, we were never even engaged. And I'd better not be married to you, because I've been married for three years now, to Pasang. Remember Pasang?"

Someone emerged from the background, a dark-haired man in what Alistair remembered as the local native costume, a robe of handwoven fabric. Pasang was the scientist Paula worked closely with at the traditional medicine hospital. So she'd married him.... Good match, he thought.

After waving hello to Alistair, Pasang took over feeding the toddler so that Paula was free to talk.

"Alistair, why do you think we're married?" she asked.

"I hope you can see this." Alistair held up Henri's tablet so that Paula could look at the document.

She laughed again. "Oh, for heaven's sakes, Alistair, that's the rental agreement for the cottage we stayed in. Don't you remember signing it?"

Alistair lowered the tablet and looked at the document more carefully.

"Honestly, Paula, I have no recollection of ever seeing this. I vaguely remember a lease, but just the signature page. Since I couldn't read the text, I relied on what I was told it said."

"Who else is there with you?" Paula asked. "I can see a couple of people hovering. Is your almost-wife there?"

"No, she's outside, probably getting ready to run off with someone else. I have my best man Adam here, and the minister, Calum. We're in Scotland."

"*Really*? I thought you were living in Portland. Anyway, the cottage was only supposed to be rented to single people or married couples. Since you and I weren't married, but we were a couple, they made an exception, and the language says we were married. Just to satisfy the religious authorities at the hospital."

"Hullo Paula, this is Calum speaking, the minister. Nice to meet ye, although odd circumstances. So to be clear, this *isn't* a government document? Alistair can still get married today?"

"Of course he can! I just wonder what's taken him so long. Alistair, you have some catching up. Pasang and I already have one child and another on the way."

Alistair wasn't going to get drawn into a conversation about future children, so he thanked Paula and they ended the call.

He looked at Calum and Adam, a furious expression on his face. "Bring me that traitorous Frenchman," he demanded. "And one of you hold me back, or he'll feel the pointy end of my *sgian dubh.*"

Calum grinned, his eyes crinkling in delight. He glanced down at the black and silver hilt of the dagger secured in Alistair's sock. "Aye laddie, you're going to fit in here just fine!" He and Alistair sat down to wait while Adam left by the outside door to Calum's office, to find Henri.

A long ten minutes later, Henri was standing before the still-seated, kilt-wearing Alistair, apologizing like a servant called before the clan chief.

"You must understand, Alistair, I only look out for your immigration status, *oui*? That document I found, eet looks so official. I thought, maybe the immigration people here will say you became married to a girl in a foreign country once before, to stay in that country. And now you do that again with Margaret. It could put your immigration status in jeopardy. You might get sent back to America, and that would be bad, *non*?"

"I hate to admit it but Henri may be right," Adam said. "How was he to know it was a rental agreement? He told me he only had the part with your names translated, and it clearly states you are married to Paula."

349

"I don't care about the immigration issue," Alistair argued. "I did, but it's more important to me to marry Margaret *today*, and if we have to live apart while I deal with this mess, so be it." He stood up and turned to Calum.

"Can we *please* go back to the church and finish the ceremony?"

Before Calum could answer, Adam looked at Alistair sheepishly. "It won't be so easy, pal. When I was looking for Henri, I discovered that Katrina took all the guests down to the hotel for drinks and tea while you sorted this out. Margaret's with her mother there also, although, I don't know, maybe they've given up..." He had one hand behind his back, and now he produced Margaret's headband, which Katrina had retrieved on her way out.

Grabbing the headband from Adam, Calum declared, "No time to waste, that's where we'll go!" He ran into the church, gathered his Bible and a few other papers, and led the men at a brisk march to the hotel. Henri was not with them; he'd taken his tablet back and slunk away.

The guests were milling around outside the hotel, some with drinks in their hands, others gathered over afternoon tea at the outdoor tables. Calum went inside to find Katrina, who helped him drag out a tall table from the bar. Calum set himself up as if it was a lectern, while Katrina returned to the hotel to fetch Margaret.

Half an hour later, Margaret and Alistair walked along the main street hand in hand as a married couple, followed by all the guests. The wedding ceremony might have been untraditional, taking place spontaneously in an outdoor cafe, with the wedding march played by a bagpiper instead of an organist, but she still wanted traditional photographs of the wedding party and of the happy couple on the steps of the Finlay church, just like her parents had as newlyweds.

Chapter 67

In the weeks leading up to the wedding, Margaret and Alistair had considered their options for where to hold the reception afterwards, somewhere suitable for dancing. The Manor House care home in Kilvellie had been tempting, but Margaret was adamant about Calum conducting the ceremony, and having wedding photos outside his church in Finlay.

Calum suggested a compromise: hold the wedding ceremony in Kilvellie's charming seaside chapel, with a photography session in Finlay first. But Alistair was equally adamant about not using the chapel. It held too many bad memories for him, reminders of the staged deaths of the six boys whose memorial brass plaque had now been removed.

The idea was raised of chartering buses to bring the guests from Finlay to Kilvellie after the ceremony, but then there was the problem of getting everyone home afterwards. Residents of Finlay might want to leave at different times, but wouldn't have driven their own cars so that they could enjoy the champagne and wine.

Guests staying at the Templeton Grand Hotel in Finlay could equally get stranded in Kilvellie. They even discussed the reverse: find hotel rooms for all the guests in Kilvellie, then bus them to Finlay for the ceremony and back again.

In the end, they decided the simple solution was the best. The Templeton Grand Hotel did not have the large rooms and grandeur of the Manor House, but it was convenient, it was recently remodeled and updated, it was by the sea, and best of all, the food was superb.

The people Alistair and Margaret knew who worked there, including Chef Dougie and housekeeping manager Katrina, assured them that the hotel would meet their needs. The only wild card was, of course, the weather, as dinner would be served outside, allowing the dining room to be cleared of chairs and tables for the music and dancing afterwards. For once, the weather more than cooperated.

Late that evening, before the guests began drifting off to their homes and hotel rooms, Margaret and Alistair sat together and watched as couples enjoyed last dances. They'd been amused that Helen, the police officer from Kilvellie, had danced every dance with Calum, including the intricate Scottish country dancing that left Alistair tripping over his own feet and grabbing the wrong partners.

"So is Richard out of the picture for good?" Margaret asked.

"Far as I know, he's back in Spain indefinitely. Helen is encouraging him to invite his son to visit, so that the estrangement Richard had with his father isn't carried into the next generation."

Alistair took a few moments to think about Richard: of all the revelations about Kilvellie's past that Alistair had been involved with, Richard seemed to have lost the most. Well, he realized, second to Richard's father Ronald who had the ultimate loss, his life.

Richard had the burden of knowing that the toy saw he'd bought his grandson had likely damaged Ronald's cane, possibly leading to his death by falling over the cliff. He also had to live with knowing that his father led almost a double life: the smiling, proud doorman and guard at the Manor House Hotel, and the grouchy, bitter father and grandfather at home.

Richard also lived with knowing that his father hadn't, after all, witnessed six young men drown in nineteen forty-four, but certain people in Kilvellie kept the truth from Ronald until his tragic death.

And to top it off, Richard seemed to have lost his new love, Helen, who was cozying up to the local minister. Yes, Alistair decided, he could understand Richard preferring Spain, even though it meant being separated from his own children.

But Richard had left behind the gift of life, although he couldn't know it. If he hadn't told Margaret about his secret groatie buckie collecting place on Caraidsay's tidal island, and if Margaret hadn't traveled there, forgotten her passport, and gone back, it was likely that Keith, aka Thompson Granger, would have died alone in that broken-down cottage, just beyond sight of his father's fancy hotel.

Richard should get recognition for his role in that outcome, Alistair decided. Maybe he and Margaret could visit him in Spain, as it didn't look like Helen would be doing that anytime soon. No, why put off sharing the news? He had Richard's contact information, so in the next few days he would let him know that his generosity to Margaret had probably saved a man's life...

His thoughts were interrupted by his Continental nemesis materializing in front of him. Henri had disappeared for a couple of hours and hadn't attended the ceremony at the hotel, but here he was, with Christy behind him.

"Is it all right weez you both if I stay and dance with Christy? She didn't bring a date, and, ah, we have been getting along quite well."

"Of course," Margaret answered for both of them, feeling generous toward the whole world. "Go and enjoy yourselves."

Once Henri and Christy had moved away out of hearing, Margaret looked at Alistair. "You still haven't told me why Henri burst into our wedding and what you and Adam and Calum talked about in Calum's office. I almost asked Mom and Dad to take me back to Portland. It was Mom who persuaded me to give you a chance, she said it had been some language-related misunderstanding on Henri's part."

"Really?" Alistair smiled with relief at Jilly's apparent change in allegiance. "That was good of her, especially as I thought she preferred Henri to me!"

Margaret laughed. "Not after his dramatic entrance today at the church. That was in such bad taste, I doubt she'll forgive him. Embarrassing us like that in front of all the guests."

"I know, darling, and frankly, I'm still trying to figure out his motive. He said that as part of his careful work on my immigration application, he discovered a document that might make the immigration authorities suspicious."

"What, like a criminal record or something?"

"No, something personal." He hesitated. "I'm sorry to mention her today of all days, but it has to do with Paula. When we were in the Himalayas, we rented that cottage I told you about. I remember being asked to sign a lease, but it wasn't in English so I just signed. Turns out I was also attesting that Paula and I were married. The cottage was only supposed to be for single people or married couples, to prevent groups of students living there. But I knew nothing of this at the time, honest!"

"So Henri tried to break up the wedding because he thought you were still married to Paula? He was trying to protect me from you? What a *weasel!*"

Alistair shook his head. "That's only one interpretation. *He* claims he was trying to make sure my immigration application raised no red flags. He said that it was a red flag if I'd become married to successive women in different foreign countries, like I was using them to stay on."

Their conversation was interrupted by the DJ, a friend of Dougie's, announcing the last waltz of the evening.

Alistair stood and offered Margaret his hand. "Last dance? Then we should make our departure before everyone leaves. You have to throw a bouquet or something?"

"Yes, and I know just who my target recipient is."

She refused to tell him, so as they made their way around the floor, he glanced at the various couples, wondering who would be next to walk down the aisle. Adam and Justine? They'd been dating for months now and seemed close, but if they got married soon, would Adam start focusing on having a family, and decide not to have a PI partnership with Alistair after all? Maybe they would settle in Inverness, a long day's journey from Finlay.

Katrina and Dougie, they would be a good fit as a future married couple: both worked at the hotel in Finlay, loved their jobs, and had been school sweethearts. For them, it was just a matter of time. Maybe Katrina didn't need a bouquet to move the process along, but she seemed the obvious choice thanks to all her help with the wedding.

In fact, she'd done more than any other person to make the day a success, from designing and sewing Margaret's gown, to co-hosting an elegant sit-down dinner in St. Andrews instead of a boozy bar-crawl of a hen night, something Margaret had dreaded. Then, she'd salvaged an awkward development during the wedding, by catering to the confused guests and taking their minds off Henri's intrusion.

Maybe cousin Jeannie was the target? Alistair had met Jeannie earlier in the year, and had barged in on Margaret and Jeannie's trip to Orkney. Jeannie hadn't brought a date to the wedding, so perhaps she wouldn't be planning her own wedding anytime soon.

Caroline and her husband swept past, enjoying the dancing and very happily married as far as Alistair could tell from his brief conversations with Caroline when she visited the cottage while she was creating the invitations. Caroline had brought Gordon the Border Collie to the cottage, and Alistair remembered thinking he would like to acquire a dog to run on the beach outside the cottage. He shook his head, his mind was wandering. Anyway, that couple did not need the bouquet.

Now Henri and Christy crossed Alistair's line of sight. That was a complicated situation. Alistair would love to see Henri safely married, preferably safely married and living in France. But if Christy was serious about setting up a sea glass jewelry shop in Finlay, and if Henri did take a job with Hamish's Edinburgh branch of the firm... their relationship was only weeks old, but still, Alistair almost shivered at the prospect of Henri moving to Finlay and being a constant presence in their lives.

355

Not that Alistair believed a wedding bouquet had power over peoples' destiny, but he realized that, selfishly, he hoped Margaret would aim it at Katrina.

Later, with the last dance finished, Alistair and Margaret stood by a waiting limousine, their packed bags in the trunk. Also in the trunk was Margaret's large haul of groatie buckies. She'd present these to the prince in Orkney, to be tallied up for the beach-cleaning competition.

Inside the limo was a wicker hamper, "sustenance for the road" as Chef Dougie had promised. In it he had placed half of the top, smallest layer of the elegant wedding cake concocted by Greta.

The four layers provided cake to suit most tastes: traditional fruitcake, sponge cake, dark chocolate, and white chocolate. The dark chocolate was the top layer. The layers were covered in smooth creamy icing, and decorated with tiny chocolate shells and marzipan shells.

When Dougie told Alistair that, traditionally, the top layer should be saved for the christening of the first child, Alistair had just laughed.

"You really expect our Margaret to keep a chocolate cake in the freezer, uneaten for goodness knows how long? No, serve half to the guests, and we'll take the rest of it on our honeymoon. The baby can just get its own cake!"

Now, grasping her bouquet, Margaret eyed the gathered guests, looking for someone specific. With her target located at the outer edge of the crowd, she turned her back and aimed, using both arms to fling the bouquet up and over her head in what she hoped was the right trajectory.

She turned around quickly to see an embarrassed-looking Helen clutching it.

"Och, I didnae mean to catch it," Helen protested. "It was just defensive reflex when it came straight at me. Margaret, surely it's meant for one of the younger lassies."

"Accept it graciously, my dear," Calum said, putting his arm around her shoulders. "The best life is one full of good surprises."

With shouts of "Good luck!" and "See you soon!" accompanying them, Alistair and Margaret climbed into the back of the limousine. Leaving their friends and Margaret's parents behind, they set off for the future: the Caledonian Hotel in Edinburgh for a couple of days, then, in their car, which Adam had arranged to be driven to the Caledonian, they would head north to Orkney, maybe Shetland and the Fair Isle. They had all of Scotland ahead of them, and all the time in the world.

Printed in Great Britain
by Amazon

33736421R00209